DIFFERENT WOMEN DANCING

Jonathan Gash

CHIVERS PRESS
BATH

First published 1997
by
Macmillan
This Large Print edition published by
Chivers Press
by arrangement with
Macmillan
1998

ISBN 0 7540 2102 5

British Library Cataloguing in Publication Data available

Printed and bound in Great Britain by
REDWOOD BOOKS, Trowbridge, Wiltshire

Susan, with thanks

CHAPTER ONE

Goer—*a male hired by a female, implicitly for sexual purposes.*

Bonn liked to stand at the corner before his next woman.

He loved the decayed city square. Girl stringers touting at the station, bike couriers arguing over piston performance, pickpockets comparing skills, a lone temazepam flogger hoping to sell his yellow jellies before Martina's standers caught him. The traffic was a snarled-up maelstrom, some lunatic taxi creating mayhem. Sheer beauty, Bonn's world.

The next woman was new. He had no need to check the crowded bus station. Rack would be there, giving out some barmy theory to whoever, but ready. Clockwork.

The traffic surged a yard or two. Horns blared, drivers shouting real anger.

Bonn shook his head. That taxi, daft as a brush, cutting in front of a great old maroon Humber. Somebody would get killed.

* * *

Dr Clare Burtonall was in a temper. She hauled her heavy maroon Humber Supersnipe aside, giving a stupid cab room to misbehave, and stabbed her foot at the brake.

'Oaf,' she muttered. 'You'll kill somebody.'

She had been displeased right from early morning. Had she realised that Dr Shacklady was going to be off duty, she never would have done the

1

locum job. Not that she hated Dr Therle Bettany, whose endless saccharine-sweet charm swept all before her, but enough was enough. Clare felt conned. The locum bank had specified 'Locum to replace Dr T. Bettany . . .' And who should greet her, as she'd pulled in to the Farnworth general practice's forecourt, but the charming Therle Bettany herself, saying charmingly, 'Oh, Bert's *so* grateful you could locum for him!' Inevitably, Dr Therle Bettany had brought in, with her own lily-white hands, a charming cup of coffee. Cow.

Clare gritted her teeth, knowing her anger was unfair. If Therle spent a little less effort on being so bloody charming, she'd get more done. But Therle Bettany's charm was purchased at the expense of others. Inevitably, Clare had to cope with an extra five patients, all from Therle's list, while the wretched woman spent hours sighing on the phone to friends about her 'positively *staggering* workload. Bert's away again.'

'Next time, lady,' Clare seethed, as the lights changed and the cars inched forward, 'you do your own *charming* bloody locum. At least Bert pulls his weight for the patients.'

Five—repeat, *five*—times this morning, Therle had 'just liked to mention that in Aberdeen we *always* . . .' Or 'in Aberdeen, we *never* saw a thyroid scan as anything other than a . . .' Clare had never been to Aberdeen, now hated the place.

That impossible taxi. Pedestrians crowded the pavement. The London Road station concourse was disgorging more passengers. Splendid, Clare thought, abandoning bitterness for resignation, I'm here for the duration. She turned on the radio.

Drivers were leaning out, calling irritated what-

2

the-hells as the taxi stopped to let its passenger alight. In stalled traffic, yards short of the traffic lights, would you believe. Clare was tired, and paid little attention.

She would be needed soon.

*   *   *

'Better get out here, sir,' Oz said over his shoulder. 'Looks like we'll be here all day.'

'You think so?'

'You'll make it before the lights change, but watch it.'

The man paid casually, like he knew that money made the world tick. So different, Oz thought, from new-money folk. Their stingy disdain kept the city down.

'Tall building, near the shopping mall, okay?'

The man alighted. The door clunked shut. Oz breathed a sigh of relief. The passenger was out there, vulnerable, with his briefcase. His pockets were sewn, as all new off-the-pegs. A meticulous man. Oz had done his time at Seven Dials among London's best subtle mongers.

'Come on, Salvo, Christ's sake,' he muttered.

Salvo, the burke, ought to be among the waiting pedestrians. That was the plan. Sometimes, Oz thought Salvo was out of his pond.

He saw him at last, the lazy sod, chatting up some bird. A goon tried to flag Oz's taxi down on the amber. His former passenger dithered between vehicles, should he go for it or backtrack.

Salvo knew his job. The scene was kaleidoscopic, a pattern of bits, the Warrington exit signed for the coast, the white van in front of Oz's taxi dowsing its

3

tail lights.

The lights greened. Oz's nightmare at this millisec was a stalled engine. Salvo came from nowhere, clumsily nudging a little old dear carrying shopping. The marked man hesitated, tried for the pavement as the traffic moved.

Oz gunned his engine, shoving at the startled fare and his briefcase. The cab's nose lifted him and his astonished face hard against the rear of the van. The image froze in Oz's mind, Salvo yelling and hauling the old lady to the kerb, pedestrians gaping, the man abruptly aware, trying to look round, maybe demand what the fuck, then realising the horror, staring at Oz as he slid smudging dark-red blood down the van's white doors.

Predictable sounds began, screams and shouts, Salvo's crazed roar. Oz heard his own yell, double-stamped the accelerator so the cab almost stalled before kangaroo-leaping onto the body on the ground.

Salvo was nowhere. Oz opened his door, shouting For-Chrissakes and OhmyGod. It wasn't a bad act, though not new. Salvo always pulled his leg about it, mimicking Oz's stock phrases in falsetto to annoy.

Oz bawled that he hadn't stood a chance, that man just rushed forward, dramatic shit he should have got an Oscar for.

'Get an ambulance!' he was going. 'The police! Quick!'

'It's the man who pushed me,' the old lady said, unforgiving, an instant star witness, brilliant.

Some moron grasped Oz's lapels, shouting right into his face, 'Reverse off him, you fucking idiot,' over and over, as if Oz was deaf. There was always

4

one hero, a barmy fucking breed of their own.

'Call an ambulance!' Oz yelled. 'Anybody!'

He wondered if he could sob convincingly, except he'd tried it that time he did the Liverpool girl in the St Helens canal and tears failed, so he decided to keep up his babble for ambulance, police, simple hysterics always the safest.

The hero in disgust shoved Oz aside and restarted the stalled engine, reversing the taxi off the crushed man with a sickening crump.

'I can't look!' Oz whimpered, hands covering his face but taking a quick shufti. The destruction wasn't clean. This was major blood on his front bumper, the wheels all gristle and bone flecks. It would be a bastard to clean, two fucking days at least.

'It's the man who shoved past me,' the righteous crone was giving it as Oz was spectacularly sick over his own rear mudguard, no acting needed. 'Poor man,' the old lady said. 'He's the cabbie.'

'Help him. Please,' Oz blurted between retches.

'No helping him, mate,' from the hero.

'There's too much of it these days,' the old bat said. 'Hurry, hurry, hurry.' She had them all nodding, a consensus Oz would have paid bag money for.

'You the driver?' some plod asked, materialising at last.

'I think he's the fare I just dropped. Insisted on getting out in the traffic.'

'He tripped,' Oz's favourite witness announced, proud of her senile prominence.

'I swear to God I never saw him,' Oz said, trying to look grey, retching busily, bored stupid, angry about the mess on his mudguard. He hated solvent

5

cleaners.

There would be no comeback, maybe an inch in the local rag. It would be forever accidents, the need of a bypass, the council idle, the usual crap they could print weeks before anything happened, lazy sods. Acting away, Oz almost yawned.

*   *   *

Clare saw the man go down, the taxi's horrid leap, heard the din. Quickly she got out, grabbed her emergency bag, and pushed through. A young man was kneeling by the injured figure, touching its face though it was covered in russet blood. He muttered quietly.

'Please let me pass. I'm a doctor.'

The news was taken up. Folk spread arms to allow her through. A sweating man climbed out of the taxi, telling the young helper it was no good.

'No helping him, mate.'

Clare arrived just as the policeman banished the young man. 'Shift, you. Sod off. Leave it to the doctor.'

The taxi driver was making a show of feeling sick. An old woman was reciting her favourite litany, people never taking their time so now look. Clare made a cursory examination. The crushed man almost bisected. The young kneeling man had risen, and seemed to melt into the crowd.

Something was not quite right. She wanted to ask who'd seen it happen, but everyone was talking. She shook her head at the policeman. He was painstakingly taking notes.

Oz felt aggrieved. That bitch of a doctor didn't take the slightest notice of him, when he was all but

6

fucking dying from shock, real hysterics, Christ's sake. Still, it was a clean job in one sense. His taxi was crapped up, but you couldn't have everything. He'd dun the wallet for extra. Money was always paid on the nail.

'See, constable,' he started up, 'I wanted to drop him at the kerb . . .'

The briefcase was gone. In its place, a new one of the same colour and type. He hoped Salvo, fucking mental age of eight, had had the sense to take the price ticket off before pulling the swap.

CHAPTER TWO

Stander—*one who protects a goer during the hiring period.*

Rack fell in with Bonn as he crossed to the Vivante Hotel. 'See that, Bonn?'

'The accident?'

Rack barked a laugh. 'You talk like everything's got no answer, Bonn.'

'You talk like anything has.'

Rack fell about. Women got on well with Bonn, though nobody on Martina's syndicate ever knew what Bonn was talking about. Rack called half-insulting greetings to Grellie's line girls. Until dusk they had nothing to do but chat up the motorbike messengers who were waiting to zoom up the Affetside moorland road.

'I didn't see it.' Rack sounded aggrieved, still calling out cheery jibes to Grellie, who was eyeing Bonn as usual. 'Know why he got topped?' Rack

7

demanded, walking backwards to challenge Bonn better.

Bonn could have done with a few minutes' quiet. If it was simply seeing one woman, it would be easy. But a stranger, every time? You needed a moment's solitude, to gather yourself.

Rack bounced along, black widow's peak shorn close, pudgy, short, black leather jacket, thick corrugated-sole boots a questionable tan, offering non-stop theories. All his notions invented for the instant, then forgotten.

Bonn gave up. 'Why, then?'

'He was thinking about holidays.' Rack yelled something in numbers to a girl, listened to numbers called back, turned to walk normally. 'Was he smashed up? They're saying a taxi and a van.'

'I didn't see much, Rack.'

Rack gave him a look. He had seen Bonn come from the crowd, slide into the gents' by the newsagent's. Bonn had bloodied hands. But saying nothing was Bonn's way, and you didn't ask.

'Leave now, Rack. What's the room number?'

'Four-oh-seven, Bonn. You got nine minutes.'

Bonn went to the lifts without a word, pressed the button. Rack had never let Bonn down. Best stander in the business.

Two shoppers drifted chatting from the hotel's foyer. The lift came. Bonn stepped in, glad to be alone. From now until the woman left the hotel, Rack would be invisible, but close by.

Room 407. He was there when the woman arrived.

*   *   *

She was younger than others Bonn had seen lately. He smiled, moved towards her as she entered, took her coat, did the essential ordinary reassuring gestures.

Mousey, plain, nervous almost to the point of panic, she was steeling herself. She stood as if waiting to be asked at a dance. Mid-twenties, maybe? It was easier when there was more of an age gap. Like actors; age up is easy, down near to impossible.

'Phew.' Bonn smiled to mock his relief. 'Can I offer you a drink, something hot, coffee, tea?'

She said no thank you, formal, smoothing her dress. He took her hand and drew her in, taking charge.

'I'm glad you came, Devina.'

'Yes.' She said it shrilly, as if expecting derision at her false name.

He gave her a quick embrace, immediately releasing her. Her hair was newly washed, her twin set brand-new. She was spotless, must have planned this for weeks.

'And I'm really pleased you chose me, Devina.'

Words were hazardous. She was not merely treating herself, as some women did, using him as self-rewarding present. He sensed that this Devina was desperate to learn, perhaps fighting some complex, maybe paper over some emotional disaster.

'Oh, I didn't . . .' She coloured, broke off.

Bonn went gently over her anxiety. 'Then it was just my good luck.'

The balance, he knew, was between words and silence. Smiling, he led her into the bedroom, the curtains giving just enough daylight. Progress would be inchwise, deliberate enough not to offend yet steady enough to reassure. Pace was everything with women. Hesitation might give her screaming hysterics. Go too fast, she could just as easily assume she was being ravished against her will.

'I've never done this before.' She pulled back, wanting to explain.

Bonn remained with her. 'Whatever you wish, Devina, and however you wish it.'

He shrugged, to disarm. Her silence was all to the good. Let her solve her own doubts, while he created none.

'I'm here for you, Devina, to do what you want. Is that all right?'

She stood, desperate to speak but panicked by lack of words. Bonn went to the window, adjusted the curtains, and stepped away as if gauging his efforts. 'Can I tell you what I would do?'

Devina's mouth pursed. She gave a stiff nod, her gaze fixed on the carpet. Bonn started speaking, giving way, recognising her fear.

'Security, and all the reassurance a lady deserves. They are my responsibility, Devina. The risk of interruption, somebody tracing you? No. With me, you're perfectly secure. Those terrible consequences you've heard about? Also no, Devina. There can be none. The lady must be protected at all times.' He let his slow words linger. 'I want you to know that. Stay only if you believe. It's a belief in your right to life, as much as in anything.'

She finally spoke. 'I've always felt that.'

'It's all up to the lady.' He smiled. 'If the lady was hesitant, perhaps starting to wonder what she was doing'—he went on over her sudden look—'then I would take her handbag, like this, gently, to show

10

her that she was completely in control.'

She saw her handbag go onto the occasional table.

'Everything is just to please her.'

'I . . .'

He gave her the chance to speak, then stepped in. 'Because where's the harm?'

'It's only that I'm not sure . . .'

'Then I would lead her.' Bonn moved her, holding the fingertips of one hand. 'Only so we might sit down if we wanted to, nothing ominous.'

He stood still, not too fast.

'Maybe then I would ask if she wanted the curtains drawn, something like that, wanted to talk. It's anything for the lady. Our meeting is for you, Devina.'

'For me,' she said dully.

'Of course. I am yours, the rooms, hotel services, my time. You alone. Nobody else.'

Devina's gaze was almost childlike in its wonder.

'Like,' he went on, sitting on the edge of the bed, taking her down with him, 'what if the lady wanted the bedroom dark? Or brightly lit? Or flowers, something she'd always imagined? My only question is, why not simply please her? There's no harm in it.'

Devina shook her head, an inch each way. He looked at her fingers. She tried to draw them away, but he smiled and kept gentle hold.

'Lovely hands, Devina.'

'They're not,' she said. 'They're pudgy. My nails are terrible. They used to mock them at school.'

Bonn wouldn't have it, but didn't make an issue. 'You talk yourself down, Devina. Nice name, nice hands. That's why I say, if the lady has definite ideas, then they become my duty. Ideas about what she wanted, maybe to chat, be made love to, just about anything. She doesn't have to *do* whatever. She might like to say it right out. Or just be here.'

'I'm . . . I'm . . .'

Like that, Bonn finished mutely for her.

'Then I'd wait in case she decided,' quietly confiding now. 'Maybe talk about her life, something going wrong, her hopes, dreams out there. I have to respect that, Devina, because in here she's utterly secure. Here, the lady is queen.'

'Secure.' She spoke in a whisper, glancing round.

'A lady deserves listening to. It's not too much to ask, is it?' He answered himself just as quietly, 'It's only fair. Some people have marvellous lives, nothing ever wrong, people admiring them. Others . . .' He shrugged. 'Well, not everybody has that kind of life. They deserve something better.'

'It's just that lately . . .' she started bravely, then petered out.

'Soon, I would rub her shoulder, not hard. She would hardly know.' He touched a light hand to her shoulder to explain where. 'After a while, no hurry, I'd help her off with her cardigan, if she wanted.'

He'd turned up the heating moments before Devina had arrived.

'I'd try to fold her cardigan just right, though I'm hopeless at that. Place it on the chair, hope I'd not creased it.'

Devina followed it with her eyes, started to say, 'Oh, no. It's fine,' before her voice faded.

'Then I would admire her form. You can't help it. A man can't avoid wonderment. It's only natural. It's simply her. She might think nothing of herself, yet her presence still overwhelms him. A woman

12

does. It's night following day.'

His eyes took in her features, her eyes, cheeks, her mouth, the contour of her face, openly marvelling. Her eyes watched.

'Then I would let my finger touch her cheek, just once, and move away after an instant, but showing how she'd impressed me.'

She showed no alarm at what was happening. He passed his hand, slightly firmer, over her cheeks, down to her neck.

She said huskily, 'I haven't got a nice figure.'

'Devina, every woman has her own beauty. It starts within. A man sees the truth in a woman's form. Don't you see? She's the emblem of loveliness.'

'Every woman?' She was honestly asking.

'Of course. I believe it from the bottom of my heart.'

His palm cupped her breast briefly, and moved away.

'Then I might take her breast, not making a movement that might disturb its magic. Pass my fingertips to touch the inner thigh, hardly at all, careful not to break the spell that her loveliness casts.'

'I was never . . .'

'I would shush her,' Bonn whispered, closing her eyes with his fingers, 'when she believed in her woman's power over me. I would stroke her, not roughly. It would be absurd to disturb so much attraction.'

'I'm not . . .'

His finger pressed on her lips. 'I would place a finger there, as a child quietens a loved one, then gently pass a finger along her lips . . .'

13

His mouth descended to hers, quickly moved away, came to her cheek.

'The vital thing is for her to know how compelling she is, know her allure.'

Her eyes opened, filled with mistrust. 'People said I—'

He shook his head, and spoke with quiet fervour.

'People aren't here, Devina. *You* reign here. I want to see how much she means, so desirable, so fetching. To prove how irresistible she is, by drawing my hand down her lovely form, moving to her.'

He half closed his eyes in wonder.

'There can be nothing else, Devina. Thrilled by beauty, admiration that she engenders.'

'Bonn,' she said eventually, breathless, then asked, 'Bonn?'

'The sense of her woman's beauty envelops me. She would see that she fills my soul. It simply *is*. And where is the harm, when a woman is suddenly so precious to a man she is all he can know?'

'Bonn. I never meant to go through—'

'Her presence replaces the whole universe. The world vanishes away. I would take her down, softly reach for her sacred perfection . . .'

*   *   *

'You went over time,' Rack told Bonn in annoyance. 'What was it, a benefit match?'

'It needed time.' Bonn was never impatient.

'Martina keeps on at me.' Rack always caught it, like Bonn was sacrosanct. 'Paid by the fucking minute. Piece work.'

'It needed time.' Nor exasperated. 'Please mind

14

your talk, Rack.'

Disbelieving, Rack shook his head. 'You're hired to shag some tart stupid, and I've to watch *my* talk?' They crossed into traffic noise.

Bonn slowed and halted, gazed steadily at Rack until Rack felt uncomfortable. 'That's it exactly, Rack.'

'Sorry, sorry. Martina wants you, urgent.'

Rack never knew what the hell Bonn was on about. They resumed their walk to the Shot Pot. Bonn was the only person on earth could make Rack go red, except Mama, but she was as evil as Bonn was . . . Rack's thought-words ran out. Maybe there was no opposite for his troublesome Catholic once-Italian mother. Seconds later his embarrassment had run its natural course.

'Hey, Bonn,' he said. 'Know how women learn to shag? It's a joke, from Jogger Hemming.'

'Please pay in the money for me, Rack.'

'She paid in *money*?' Rack was aghast.

'Yes. To Jay this time.'

'The silly bint never heard of credit cards? Martina oughter set a rule. Money's going. Y'know why, Bonn?' Rack was relieved. Bonn always forgave in two-three beats.

'No,' Bonn said resignedly. 'And get Grellie, please.'

Rack was delighted. He'd failed to pull Grellie himself, so reasoned that Bonn should dick Grellie, home use. Going without a bird crippled a bloke. Bonn slipped Rack Devina's money.

'Only for a chat, Rack. See you at the Granadee.'

'Shag Grellie, Bonn,' Rack said seriously. 'She'd do you proud. Know what happens when a bloke goes without a bird? His skin turns colour. Know

15

why?'

'Go now, Rack.'

Bonn turned through the bus-station gardens. Five minutes of Rack's wild talk, he was exhausted. Grellie was watching him from her position by the football stadium's shuttle bus. He quickened his pace. Martina was dynamite on punctuality.

CHAPTER THREE

Upper—*a female who hires a male for one episode of sex.*

Clare drove south ahead of the city rush, holding the Humber aloof from the traffic's jousting, the duck-and-drive churning races with the huge slab-sided pantechnicons with their menacing rainspitting wheels. Today's lesson was, you didn't need to rush down a motorway to kill.

The accident had begun innocuously enough, from what little she remembered. That poor businessman—had she seen him alight?—crushed in an instant between the taxi and the van. Police had taken statements, made arrangements for her to clean up in a nearby hotel, though her hands still felt tacky and blood-soiled on the steering wheel. The victim hadn't stood a chance. Firmer images eluded her.

A Ford crowded her. She sighed, gave way. A young male driver roared past, rejoicing. She felt in a fret, something nagging and she didn't know what. Young males died in and killed with cars, a steady statistic. Which made her recall the kneeling figure

16

TO RENEW ONLINE GO TO www.hants.gov.uk/library:
or telephone Hantsdirect on 0300 555 1387:
* * * * * * * * *

ITEMS CURRENTLY ON LOAN TO:

Name : Foster, Giovanna Elenor
ID   : XXXXX22071
Date : 22/04/2016   Time: 13:41

TITLE/ITEM   DUE DATE

Different women dancing   20 May 2016
C013226637.

Please retain this receipt and return
  items before the due date.

* * * * * * * * * * * * * * * *

THANK YOU FOR USING YOUR LOCAL LIBRARY

so peremptorily dismissed by that policeman's 'Shift, you. Sod off,' when everybody else was allowed to remain, talk silliness, give witness. Except that one. Why?

The traffic loosened, flowing steadier. She kept pace, signs white on green instead of the motorway blue.

Her image clarified as she drove. The young man, kneeling, had looked up. Pale, slim but not too slim, brown hair a thatch over blue eyes, his clothes nondescript but not quite, hands bloody. Was he talking, possibly giving reassurance, the meaningless ritual of the would-be helper? Not handsome, not ugly, though why should she even classify so? Wasn't it sexist or something, these days?

Another thing. He had gone without demur. He had expected dismissal. She ought to have asked was the youth a pickpocket, ghoulishly robbing a victim. She abandoned the problem.

Clifford would be home by now, tapping finance details into his latest computer. Keeping abreast of technology, in he would come, with, 'Clare! Come and see! I got a twenty-nine-per-cent reduction!' Then would follow an incomprehensible hour while he extolled silicon-microchip gigabytes. Medicine used the blessed things, of course, but why extol their inert innards?

She tried to drift left for the A6, a racecourse. She blessed her episcopal trundling saloon car, of which Clifford was so proud. Its maintenance cost a fortune, but he justified it. Teenage joyriders would never steal a tardy, elderly motor. Traceable, its maroon colour unmistakable.

And other motorists did make allowances. She

17

abused her status, of course. A woman driver could always gain concessions, making irate men grin their what's-the-use by flinging her hair about in exasperation. Her car phone rang. She pulled into a layby. The locum bank. It was the same girl who'd conned her about charming Dr Therle Bettany's locum earlier.

'Are you available to do a locum at Breightmet, Dr Burtonall?'

'I'm sorry, but I can't manage.'

Clare's anger evaporated. She clicked off, judged the traffic for re-entry. Let them whistle, find some other doctor. She'd done two days out of the last four. Enough. Her always-on, never-off, period at Farne was over. She was married now, 'got a life', in the phrase currently making the rounds.

Fifteen minutes, she was home.

The Ashdun Road house was not quite grand. Six windows, two bayed, set off the front door, some stonework about but no ugly soffits to the windows, thank heavens. No awnings or external blinds—she'd hated those at Farne's scrimpy little surgery.

Clifford's newish saloon car was parked. The house had been Clifford's when they married two years before, she the interloping wife. His mother was still sceptical.

She drove the Humber in, garaged it with a cosy sense of relief. No more today, that accident the last straw, poor man. She gathered her case and handbag to take in. Her useless attendance at the scene meant paperwork, reports, giving professional witness at the coroner's inquest.

'Hello, Mrs Kinsale.'

'Hello, doctor. Mr Burtonall is already home.'

The housekeeper was capable, smiley, always in

18

the pinafore. It looked a grannie's hand-me-down, blue-black with dimming orange flowers. She too had come with the marriage. Clifford's family menial, who would wear the same apron all her life, proving stolidity, here long before Clare upset the routine. You needn't count the silver teaspoons after Mrs Kinsale had done her day. Always that distancing 'doctor', for Clare.

'Thank you, Mrs Kinsale. Could we have tea now, please? I'm gasping.'

'You must be! Mr Burtonall has one of his engines going.'

Clare inspected the mail on the hall stand. Two letters, one from the Chief Medical Officer in outer space. Probably about the side effects of hypotensive drugs, the consistency needed to define abreactions. She felt a disgraceful twinge of relief, at being a locum doctor of no fixed medical abode. Administration was still there, but responsibility was lighter.

Clare had space now. No clothes in the hall except sudden weather-changers, raincoats, plastickery, umbrellas. Really heavy wear, like hoods, wellingtons, was kept by the side door for garden forays. This had been her first edict, and Clifford, with a reluctant Mrs Kinsale, had obliged. A home's orthodoxy made easy.

She showered and felt better. Separate changing rooms were a feature of this house—were they a constant of Edwardian design? They made love, no longer with the same pallyness of newlyweds, but with satisfaction. So far they hadn't had any of those sniping rows that passed for marital exchanges. God, how some couples ever even got together!

Before the dressing-table mirror, Clare inspected

19

today's damage, and set to work with moisturiser. Surgeries were all so dreadfully overheated.

She remembered a middle-aged couple at a Walkden day surgery. Each demanded her support against the other. She had listened, appalled, an impotent referee, as they'd decried, accused, harangued. When she'd finally got rid of them, the unconcerned receptionist blithely told her that the couple always did that, came to brawl before an impartial listener, and invariably left blaming whatever doctor they'd seen. 'They'll be back in a fortnight,' Clare had learned, 'just the same.'

People mystified Clare. She remembered that police constable's curt dismissal of the kneeling youth, who'd only been trying to help—hadn't he? Maybe everyone had some little mad core that kept them going in a malevolent world.

Mrs Kinsale called that tea was ready. What was Clifford's miniature lunacy? He had none, except perhaps his obsession with finance. She examined her reflection. She looked tired. Accidents were an ordeal. Skimping, she managed to be downstairs before Mrs Kinsale called a second time.

'Clare.'

Clifford came to her smiling, kissed her in greeting. On the rear lawn a morello-cherry tree had sadly gone wrong at the roots. He'd had a high old time making bonfires, for days coming in stinking of smoke. He was so natural. In fact, it was his easy manner that had appealed at first, that and his tousled handsomeness. They had met at a medical fund-raiser—bitter white wine and inedible biscuits—at which she'd been astonished to learn that this boyish looker was the principal benefactor. He had visited the paediatric unit where Clare was a locum the week after. Matters then took their course, with Clifford's humour eliminating every doubt and obstacle.

Everything about the house was familiar to him. This chair his sister Josephine tried to set on fire aged six; over there he'd failed to espalier plum trees sent by cousins in Hertfordshire. Clare was still learning. Did an incoming wife make changes to have less to catch up on?

'Planning the garden, darling?'

'Just thinking what a shame February is.'

'February? But Easter's come and gone.'

'February lingers, like a bad taste.'

Clifford had lived in Italy two or three years before she had met him. He mentioned Florence, Rome, Venice, but only as a duty, get the reminiscence over with. Her attempt to decide a Tuscany holiday had failed abysmally, though the Norwegian cruise a year after their Gibraltar honeymoon, with a Greek afterthought, had been successful. Clifford was pleasing company. They were both professional people who matched well, thank you. She could talk to him.

She told Clifford about the accident, not giving details that might disturb. Mrs Kinsale brought in the tea tray, started clinking saucers. There was a ration of biscuits, a practice Clare detested. The woman would never bring in the biscuit barrel, but laid out two Peak Freans apiece—no more, never less. Endlessly told about this, Mrs Kinsale only laughed, 'Oh, I'll forget my head next!' and did the same tomorrow. Clare hadn't decided if it was mere forgetfulness.

'What happened in February?' Clare asked.

Clifford went to the window, a small surprise.

'Those visitors. Endless. First Josephine and hers, then those others. Don't you remember? The Year of the Rat, we had the Month of the Visitor.'

'So we did.' Clare poured. Stingy Mrs Kinsale had doled out miniature creams. It *was* a campaign. 'Some road contract?'

He sat opposite, took the tea. 'I felt like a chef whose food went wrong.'

Clare sipped, decided that it was time the whole suite was re-covered. It would be costly, but the only problem would be finding a good upholsterer.

'Nothing sporting, then?'

It was a jibe, and he smiled, remembering her gratification that he was a wholesome bachelor, not a divorce, when they'd met. His interests were swimming, and watching sport. He went to the races, though he'd abandoned York after a calamitous hotel booking. He gardened, more to fume about old Stan than take an active part.

'I don't like you lingering in February, Clifford. You should be here.'

'I am, I am.' He talked with less than his usual enthusiasm about the day. She knew so few of his staff, but their professions ran on separate lines.

February? Vaguely, she recalled his secluded hour-long calls. He hadn't slept for several nights. Clifford always had simultaneous contracts on the go. She'd once studied under a chief—the consultant doctor heading a 'firm' of junior doctors—who drifted round his wards with seeming indifference. Later, he would accurately summarise every patient's condition, treatment, laboratory investigations, in brilliant detail. But he had to stick to the order in which he had examined the cases. Deflect him, and he lost it. It was a fluke of mind.

22

As a crystal handles light, so some minds treat facts. Clifford's mercantile mind must be like that.

She felt disturbed this evening, something wrong that she couldn't fathom. Perhaps she ought not to have mentioned the accident. Medical events did make him squeamish. Not that she gave names or locations. Reticence came with the diplomas, the endless medical training.

'Is it the central development?'

He started on about it without preamble, proving to Clare's relief it was that all along.

'The notion's fine,' he said. 'A central lake, connections with the ship canal, bridges, shopping malls, big medicine—sorry about the pun. The fringes of a thing are always the worst.'

She knew he loved abstracts of an enterprise, hated the essentials.

'They can be settled, though, can't they?'

His problems were all one pattern, she now knew. First, he excitedly showed her plans, maps, charts of some project. Then came doubt, and finally this phase of self-analysis, even gloom, and not a sod turned or a brick yet laid. The city's central redevelopment was unavoidably political.

'Will it matter if you don't get the consultancy?'

'Oh, we'll get it, no doubt of that.' He seemed surprised by her question. 'It's just the bits that go along with it.'

They separated with banter. It was warming, despite Clifford's worry. Clare went to see Mrs Kinsale off, and returned upstairs. Once, she had conducted a series of intelligence tests on a little boy. Simple multiple choice, tick one of the three answers. The boy was ten years old. His teachers knew he was bright, yet he failed every time. Sure

23

enough, he got every one of Clare's questions wrong. Zero. Nil. Even a gorilla would get at least one-third correct, simple random chance. The little boy was deliberately failing so he could stay with his family. They'd intended to send him to boarding school.

'The problem was,' she remembered telling Clifford the punch-line, 'once they realised, they sent him off to boarding school anyway. I almost cried.'

'Why were you so upset?'

'Well, it just shows,' Clare had explained lamely. 'I blew the gaff. I felt a traitor.' Too much honesty could damage families, marriage, even a conversation.

She changed into gardening clothes. A tweed skirt, a thick cardigan from her Farne Island days that she was too sentimental to throw out.

The garden was becoming a shared interest. Those disastrous herbaceous borders. Lady's-mantle was a godsend. Daphne, candytuft, scabious (perhaps a dark-crimson variety), penstemons— she'd had a rather sour relationship with those, so they were non-starters—and the usual Solomon's seal. She had decided this year to go for pinks and reds, really make a show. Safe plants—wallflowers, pansies—were utter cowardice. Happy, she decided to abandon cowardice in everything, including the slight matter of Clifford's parents and his sister Josephine.

Her own parents were great ones for duty and 'keeping going'. Duties, though, were controlled by others. That was the *rub*. Clifford's parents were safely—or not so safely—in Altrincham, in visitor range, and held strong views on reproduction.

24

Meaning it was time she started a family. Clifford's mother emitted this, as Farne's lighthouse had beamed its signal.

What were Clifford's views, though? From her window she saw him by the hedge. Worthy professional or not, a new wife was always under test. Within days friends called, sweetly implying the wrong distribution of her furniture, nowhere to put a cup down. It was the wife's job to dispose, and get the blame for housekeeping faults. At the time she'd been working a seventy-hour week. Soon, Evadne and Arthur, Clifford's parents ('Now, we positively do not mind. Use first names, my dear!'), would come asking again about offspring with that urbane enmity of in-laws.

'What about schools?' Clare asked no one.

A stupid thing to blurt out. Before schooling you had to produce a child.

She thought she heard a noise downstairs and paused to listen. Nothing.

Words were silly games, and her a career woman. Those tiresome antenatal classes, being weighed, urine for albumen, and the rest, erythrocyte sedimental rates every two seconds, the whole Rhesus business—though wisely she'd been born O Rhesus positive, no problems there until proved otherwise.

Another noise?

'Clifford?' she called.

No answer. A card falling off a shelf, or perhaps the wind. Except there were no cards on the mantelpiece. Clifford was still out there in the garden, doing something with a hoe.

The sound had come from inside. Had Mrs Kinsale come back for something?

25

'Mrs Kinsale?' Clare listened.

The evening was drawing in, not yet the vigorous eventide of summer. She only minded autumn's remorseless heel-dragging into cold winter.

'Darling?' A footfall. Downstairs, definitely downstairs.

She rose, went to the window, wanting signs of normality. Clifford was still at it. Four people waited by the bus stop opposite. The distant church with the blackish tower where she went to evensong of a Sunday. She watched. Nobody on the gravel drive.

Clifford wasn't much of a gardener in truth, a snip-and-tuck clipper. He turned to inspect some japonica leaves, his campaign against parasites—

And something downstairs went over with a small thud. They had no cat.

Mrs Kinsale had clearly returned. Clare slowly went down the stairs, giving whoever it was time to escape. She called out Clifford's name, the doubter's is-that-you. The hall was empty.

On the hall stand was a briefcase. It had not been there when she'd gone upstairs. It was scratched, as if it had been dragged, whitish scags along the dark-brown leather. Clifford was in the garden. Therefore?

'Hello?' she called out. Absurd to feel her heart banging so, with people at the bus stop, occasional cars, her husband so near.

The kitchen door led out into the small herb garden. A field was visible over her feeble soft fruit canes, nothing doing this time of year. That door now stood ajar. A man's head showed briefly at the field's edge, ducked out of sight. A motorbike sounded, dopplered away to nothing.

'Who is there, please?' she called, querulous and frightened.

She walked quickly out of the front door and round into the garden. There was no gate, just an ornamental trellis that must go when she finally got up enough courage to confront Evadne. Old Stan would also have to be argued down and his sabotage quelled.

'Clifford?'

Her husband straightened, holding some spray gadget. 'Catastrophe here, darling,' he said. 'Bloody greenfly shouldn't be out so early.'

'Were you in the house just now?' He couldn't possibly have been.

He questioned her with a brief look, dismissed the problem. 'What do you reckon? I didn't think they went for quinces, greenfly. The old gardener used Jeyes Fluid, tablespoon to a quart of water. Swore by the stuff.'

'I thought I heard somebody. You weren't expecting a courier or anything? There's a briefcase on the hall stand. I didn't hear anybody ring.'

'Briefcase?' It brought him up short.

'I heard somebody come in. At least I thought I did.'

'Perhaps Newton stopped by.'

'Wouldn't he have rung the bell or something?'

Clifford smiled, shrugged. 'Maybe he sent a courier, those motorbike lads who pretend they're in the Tourist Trophy.'

'I suppose that was it.' No relief came.

'Did you leave it where it was, darling?' He was a little too casual.

'The briefcase? Yes.'

'Let's go in.' He took her arm. 'It's getting chilly.'

27

It wasn't as cold as all that, but Clare went along. The briefcase was still there, its new pale marks suggestive of having skittered on some rough surface.

'Better take a look, I suppose,' Clifford said lightly, 'see what rubbish Newton's letting me in for.'

Clare, restless, felt compelled to suggest something different.

'I wondered if we could walk to the old church after supper,' she offered, out of the blue. 'Mr Torrance practises organ pieces until nineish.'

To her disappointment Clifford declined. 'I ought to give this a glance, seeing Newton went to all the bother of sending it over.'

Moments ago in the garden a total surprise, yet now he knew all about this special delivery from Newton. And didn't they come in bags? They always had before, as did her own medical manuscripts. This damaged briefcase was uncovered.

'I'll not go on my own,' she decided. 'It's rather a walk from Old Seldon across the fields.'

She was preparing supper when she realised her self-trickery. The dead man had somehow seemed familiar, crushed as he was. Not merely the situation—accident, frantic observers, police, the gore, her despairing resignation that she could do nothing.

It was him, the fatality. She should remember him. In life, he'd been sweating and uncomfortable. But when and where? February came to mind, a printed word on some invitation, ornate engraving on a cream-coloured card.

Supper would have to be simpler than she had planned, commonplace, nothing more than a background to a pretended conversation. That would give her time to think, make some good guesses about the killed man.

Tomorrow, first thing, she would buy newspapers. At the hospital, she would call on the pathologist before he got round to the autopsy.

CHAPTER FOUR

Key—*a goer who controls a group of goers, usually not more than three in number.*

The snooker hall was a hundred yards down a side street off Victoria Square, its tables islets of green-shaded lights in a sequence of cones. To Bonn, snooker players were somnolents moving with the reverence of devoted acolytes. No nights, no days, mere zones of timelessness. Osmund was playing patience.

'Red six, black seven, Osmund,' Bonn said.

'I see it.' The old man never cheated, maddening everyone.

A row broke out, coloured Moss Side lads riled at someone playing for baulk. Canno howled in a phoney Kingston, Jamaica, tone Bonn liked, 'We gotta *flower*, man, yo playin' lak ee bamba claat.'

Someone took a swing. Two ponchos—the only swingers allowed and thrilled to prove it—moved in. They had pride, reputations to keep. Bonn wanted to reach Martina, but watched the riot quelled.

'Know what's done for yon game, Bonn?' Osmund asked. 'Telly.'

29

Osmund believed in Bonn, right from the day he'd walked in out of the rain and stood waiting for someone to ask what. Osmund kept playing, black ten on a red jack, in his glass booth. Bonn thought the snooker hall quite beautiful, an enchantment that painters should be painting instead of three-minute blotch-and-liners. He never said this.

Bonn was in awe of brawls. Tooth, the player who wasn't fighting, leant on his cue. His opponent was folded over holding his belly. The ponchos wandered, affably cuffing resisters insensible, moving with grand pride, hulks held in suits by stretched stitches. Two minutes, Bonn'd see Martina.

Osmund was old. Bald, skeletal, waistcoated, watch chain, sleeves cufflinked, black shoes highly polished of a morning. He'd worked at a loom back when the mills had thrived, hived, and finally dived in cotton.

'Look how they dress theirselves,' he said. 'Ponces.' And was immediately contrite. 'Sorry, Bonn. Snooker on telly, though, what d'you see? Fine damask, bishop sleeves, Jap silk, hair like tarts.'

The racket was over, the ponchos shyly lumbering off, conversations starting, what was the score, my turn on the yellow wernit, moaning about Oldham tonight.

'Martina sent for me, Osmund.'

The old man couldn't stop a grumble. 'Davis—greatest ever—bought the world cup with his own money, won it himself year after year. People forget that, Bonn.'

People don't even know it, Bonn thought sadly. The players resumed. He watched Fortress,

30

erstwhile aggressor miraculously recovered to jauntiness, line up on the black, trying to screw into baulk for an easy red. Fortress missed by a mile. Osmund chuckled.

'See, Bonn? Useless. Aye, Martina's already seen Rack.'

Martina astonished Bonn. Osmund pressed something. The door, overtly a coat rack holding the same clothes month and month about, slid back. Clever, except it opened with a screeching melody, the noisiest secret door on earth. Bonn often thought to say something. Osmund once allowed Bonn to press the button, but the clothes rack hadn't budged. Maybe lean over it worked okay, sit upright it didn't, something like that?

Bonn stepped inside the little space. He read the grubby Safety First notice on the wall as the door squealed shut. *In the event of fire . . .* Count five, then the side opened, right-angle turn into the world's smallest corridor. A door swung.

'Is this really necessary? Black Hand Gang of the Lower Fourth?'

'It's as I like it, Bonn.'

Martina was beautiful, and lame. He tried not to be put out by her spectacular smile. She sat at a desk, clearly from a Macclesfield government-surplus auction, four quid top weight and your own transport.

Worse, the room was on the kilter, every plane skewed. Existentialist? Not an honest rectangle there. On her desk a small tin filing cabinet, a phone, a picture of her dad, Posser. Bonn liked Posser.

'When will you get a proper office?'

'Mind your own business.' Martina smiled, worth

31

waiting for, dimples, lovely colour. Anyone else, Bonn would have wondered what she was doing in the business. He didn't even know where she went for meals.

Her silence became a prompt. 'The councillor's wife from the Wirral?'

'Yes. The complaint.'

'I've explained.' Martina was always fair, and trusted Bonn's account.

'Now, she wants to book you again. How do you feel?'

'Feelings don't come into it, Martina.' Her dad, Posser, established the rules when he'd started the syndicate yonks since. Now Bonn said it as doggerel.

Martina wafted his words away with a shake of her glinting hair. 'Take your time with her.'

'Very well.'

Martina didn't pause. Any of her other goers would have said yes or okay, right, sure. She looked up from her one sheet of paper, forever blank. Martina made no notes, her sharpened pencil, he'd swear, unused since he'd joined. There was nowhere to sit, never anything in the wastepaper basket, Martina's empire a sham from which she might do a moonlight flit leaving no trace.

'How long have you been with us, Bonn?'

She knew, but he answered. It was her game. 'Three months.'

No way she could forget that interview at the Rum Romeo in Tibb Street, him lost and sweating, Martina unsmiling, Posser asking questions to gauge Bonn's possible usefulness to Pleases Agency, Inc, Martina's syndicate.

'Have you thought up anything new?' she asked.

'The logo? No. It's daft making it an acronym.

Why not leave it?'

The best so far was Personal Leisure Enhancement And Satisfying Ease Service. Grellie said it was silly, Pleases Agency, Inc, being enough for anyone with half a brain.

'It isn't as if we'll neon it on the Bolton-to-Macclesfield, is it?'

She smiled, and he saw it had been her lead-in to his summons.

'I'm moving you, Bonn.'

He was unperturbed. It wouldn't be Sheffield, Birmingham. It'd have to be local. She read him.

'Not as in distance, Bonn. Promotion. You've made key from midnight.' He shifted one foot to the other in question, and she answered, 'Complete today's goes. You've done that Devina?'

'I have one more client.'

'Your pay doubles. You can stay a regular goer, or go piecemeal.'

In the trade's terminology, one session with a client lady was a go, Bonn was a goer. A key was the head of a 'firm' of three goers. It meant money, influence, power on the street. He drew breath, but she was quicker.

'You also get a weekly one-bonus dollop direct from syndicate funds, weekly averaged. Draw from the Rum Romeo's till.'

Best be frank. He had doubts about Martina's casino. He got ready. 'I don't like that, Martina.'

'Don't like what? Key, money, the bonus grossed out?'

He said bluntly, 'Leaving with a wadge is trouble.'

Martina was annoyed at this quibble. 'No cheques, no parcels you didn't come in with, Bonn?'

'That's elementary,' he said politely, 'but word

33

spreads.'

'You're worried how I'm to pay you, right? You win it in the casino. Choose your game. Roulette, cards, horses, cricket.' She spoke the last dryly. Astonishing that cricket, new to the Romeo casino, had outstripped every non-table take. It was weird. Bonn sensed that Martina knew something was wrong.

'Every week, like Friday's payday?'

She let her pleasure show, Bonn still an innocent. She adjusted herself on her chair. Did her crippled leg get sore, he wondered, in this dead-and-alive hole? He never knew how long she stayed here. Five minutes? Half a day?

'It has drawbacks, Bonn, but I never use a cran.'

A cran would be unwise—a lockup garage, hole in some wall, the payee snooping up for his illicit dosh. The whole city would know, slope along for a laugh to see the lurk's face when he discovered it nicked.

'An intermediary?' he suggested, saw her face darken.

'Who? Osmund's out. I won't have Rack doing that sort of thing—he's too valuable. Grellie's got her work cut out running the street girls.'

'One of the crowd?' The syndicate owned the three Babylon game parlours, a score of low-graders with five section bosses in each.

Martina was unsure, as convincing a negative as he would ever get. 'They're reliable. Is default likely?'

'Not from thievery. Forgetting's different, especially after some dicey match.' He chanced his arm. 'You?'

She eyed him in astonishment. 'Are you serious?'

34

'Why not?'

'That will do, Bonn.' His mother used to say that after he cheeked her, next time a clobbering. 'Not me, nor Posser.'

He gave in. 'Then it's the Romeo till girl, but erratic.'

'I agree. The sums are not inconsiderable, after all. Weekly?'

'At good intervals,' he said. 'Ring the changes. Use bikers, switch dates.'

'This must come out as my suggestion, Bonn,' she warned.

Martina's syndicate had several firms, with four goers in each, Bonn's now the ninth. They both waited, one question to be settled, in his court.

'You choose three for your firm, Bonn.'

'I won't have Penner or Frankie or Blakeston.'

She was surprised. 'Not Penner? I'd pencilled him in.' But not on her blank sheet, he observed laconically. 'He's as good as . . . most.'

As good as you, Bonn, she'd almost said. Bonn let nothing show. There was rivalry in the goer game. He'd once seen Penner drunk, yapping his head off in the Bottom Quarter. Bonn would have enough problems without Penner's big mouth, drunk or sober.

'Not Penner, please.'

She was taken aback, but it didn't slow her. 'Galahad and Lancelot?'

'Is it take or leave?' He didn't exactly jump at the names.

'Galahad's beautiful!' she exclaimed. 'Every woman's dream.'

'Of a goer, aye.' Bonn didn't make too much of opposing Galahad. It would call his promotion into

35

question. Galahad was a body builder, Lancelot your effete ballroom dancer. Both had a following, no problem, but he was uneasy.

'Recruit as you like, but no rival outfits.'

Everything was settled. She nodded dismissal. He wondered when, if, Martina herself ever . . .

'You've got tomorrow, until four o'clock, Bonn.'

'Very well.' Her business after all, in more ways than tax returns knew.

He left the snooker hall, on the way out telling Osmund he wanted Rack soonest. He hadn't gone a furlong before Rack fell in beside him, grinning.

'Key man, eh, Bonn?' He did a spin. 'Doing auditions? Who?'

'Please stop, Rack.' Rack instantly mimed an exaggeratedly staid walk, hands behind his back like a queen's consort. 'Galahad, Lancelot, we suss out first. Walk properly, please.'

Rack obeyed. Anyone but Bonn would have said cut it out or jack that in. From Bonn you got walk properly please.

'Galahad's pumping iron. Lancelot's having dancing shoes fitted.'

Bonn paused at the newsvendor's. Police kept warning Fat George about his billboards' obstructing the pavement. Bonn bought a paper. Rack was incredulous.

'You *paid*,' he accused. 'The fucking *Evening News*.'

'Mmmh.' Bonn read, slowing, Rack steering him among the pedestrians.

'You listening? Martina *owns* Fat George, you *pay* him for a paper?'

'That accident, Rack. He died.' Bonn gave Rack the paper. He only glanced at the victim's photo.

36

They walked on. 'Have you seen him before?'

'No.' Rack dug Bonn's arm. 'Thought you wanted to see Grellie?'

'Thank you. But I must get my firm. Do please apologise to Grellie.' He smiled. 'Better do as Martina says.'

It was the nearest Bonn had ever come to a joke, Martina's word being harder than law.

'Galahad'll be at the Troc tomorrow.'

One day, Bonn vowed, he would ask Rack how he knew everything.

*   *   *

The news had a curiously dulling effect. Bonn went for a coffee in the Butty Bar. It was only a wedge of converted warehouse in Victoria Square, an afterthought, some preoccupied Victorian merchant absently squaring one last circle. It faced the bus station, which was why Bonn liked it.

A few people nodded to him as he entered. Crump the racing tipster gave him half a smile. Packster, leader of a courier squadron, didn't look across, but his black leather swaggered as he passed Bonn. The counter girls whispered. Word was about. They must share Rack's osmosis trick for news.

'You're a celebrity, Bonn.' Zen slid into the seat opposite, accepted the coffee one of the girls hurried over unasked. 'Word spreads like a moor fire.'

Zen had been a second-hand car salesman, but built up such a lucrative sideline among women customers that it had come to the attention of Posser. Within two weeks the young entrepreneur was a goer. One year to the day, Zen made key, with a firm of four goers, and never looked back.

A pleasant round-faced bloke with brilliant teeth, Zen, the ideal goer, had to slog to keep his pludges under control. Bonn got the dazzling grin.

'Thank you. It was unexpected.'

Zen leant forward. 'A tip, Bonn. Get Evelyn to do your savings. She's got National Savings off pat, index-linked, flat-raters. And unit trusts. Every month she gives you a printout. Multo money from now on.'

'Thank you, Zen.'

'Another tip. Don't choose your goers for flash. Them kinky buggers down Blenheim Street are more trouble than what they're worth. They look good, but you're into serious psychotherapy.'

'I'll bear it in mind.'

Zen had more to say. 'There's talk of two goers getting involved. Irons, subbos.' Meaning guns and drugs. 'You'll hear all sorts, Bonn. But none of them's my goers. If I hear any mother about your goers, I'll tell you within minutes, okay?'

Bonn nodded thanks. It was a kind offer, to pass on solid news.

'It's good of you, Zen.'

The other sipped his coffee, grimaced, made a Latin gesture of helpless appeal. A counter girl immediately flew across with a fresh cup.

'Don't underestimate my selfishness, Bonn.' Zen opened his palms, his old selling manner. 'See that lass, swapped my coffee? She did it fast, sure, but she smiled at you. It's the difference, Derby winner and any other thoroughbred.' He grinned, shrugged away the admission. 'I've common sense, youth, I like the birds, do a decent turn for Martina's

38

syndicate. And I'm not daft. Best living I'll ever have.' He laughed, shaking his head in disbelief. 'You're supposed to say "But . . .?" with a knowing air, Bonn.'

'Am I?' Bonn considered this, complied. 'Very well. But . . .?'

'I don't *believe* you, Bonn. It's like you're just out of the egg. Other times you're . . .' He gave up before Bonn's curious stare, allowed three school lads to move past on their way to the caff's game machines.

'I hope I don't give offence, Zen.'

'You fucking wear me out, y'know?' Zen eyed the ceiling in mute appeal, resumed. 'What I'm saying is, there's only one of us who's within a light-year of getting further. And that's you. See the lads knocking about the square? They'd give anything to become a goer, money, all the crumpet they could want.'

'I do know we are privileged, Zen.'

'There isn't a goer in the kingdom wouldn't give his teeth for promotion to key.' Zen leant back. 'But you're the only one who'll make the syndicate.'

'This is kind of you, Zen. But you are addressing one who doesn't exactly know what the syndicate is. Or who.'

The other became serious. 'Remember your first day as a goer? There was me with Grellie, waiting to say hello at the Shot Pot?'

'Yes.' Bonn smiled. He felt shy, remembering.

'Three months back. Grellie'd never met you. Know what? I've never told you this before. She groaned out loud. I asked what's up. She didn't say a word.' Zen candidly inspected Bonn. 'You're not handsome, average mark.'

39

'But . . .?'

Zen grinned at his hands. 'Tooshay, Bonn. It's there, like you'd been here before, done it all. Know what Grellie told me later?' Zen tapped the table gently. 'She said, "It's like I already know him." It's the bit a woman can't buy, Bonn.'

Bonn waited. 'I don't understand, Zen.'

'Nor do I,' Zen said, wry. 'But hang on to it, Bonn.'

Bonn was lost. 'Thank you for your advice, Zen. I shall see Evelyn.'

'Good luck choosing your goers.' Zen stood a moment, went for it. 'Is it true Martina's marked two of your cards?'

'Yes.' Zen must already know, Galahad and Lancelot.

'Didn't you squawk?' Zen was curious, wanting detail. 'I've never known it before. But not straight off.'

'To protest is not my privilege, Zen. Thank you for stopping by.'

Zen laughed, and went shaking his head, giving a wave, the girls smiling at him. Bonn suspected that Zen found his manner quaint. He thought *But . . .?* again and went to change. He had another go soon, his very first after being made key. He felt unable to meet the girls' eyes as he went among the tables, just called a quiet 'Thank you.' They stared after him, then bent to whisper.

*   *   *

Parents, Rack knew from a lifetime's experience of one, were a pain. Papa had taken off the instant Rack showed.

40

The one was Mama.

You wouldn't look twice at her in Old Seldon market, her black shoes, her cane straw hat's Ping-Pong hat pins, just write her off as some old git. But you noticed her eyes, and thought, Whoops, better not get in the way of *that* when it's moving. Close to, Mama was straight out of some old black-and-white movie of Marshall Tito with maybe Trevor Howard, a British major, looking down on an unsuspecting enemy column. Rack saw Mama as a partisan, the one that took your breath away. Compelling attention because she *knows* the .303 Lee Enfield bolt-action, carries it like a piccolo. He'd seen other folk take one look at Mama and go, Oops, don't jump *her* place in the queue.

Mama was Rack's Italian cross. He'd never been further than Southend. She had a personal line to Almighty God for the sole purpose of giving Rack earache, and had ears like a frigging bat.

He arrived at the old folks' flats where Mama lived. She was sitting stony-faced in her rocker, an Oriental potentate awaiting terms from redcoats while her tribes massed in the hills. Rack said hello. She punished him with silence.

Rack told her how holy he'd been this week.

'. . . sent money to the Saint Don Bosco, Mama. You know, Pendleton?'

'Uncle Gianni,' she said.

Rack halted. Who the fuck? Mama's words were shellfire. You had to guess the direction.

'Oh, Uncle Gianni!' Why didn't he have a load of sisters, help him survive Mama? 'I can't keep track.'

He'd conned her that he was a computer wizard at ICI, Runcorn. She blamed him for not being married. She could insult a daughter-in-law, for

41

breeding children to row with him about.

'What does he want?'

'Come from Calabria to say hello.'

Mama proved how the Inquisition pulled it off. Deadening repetitions, then the switch. You agree to anything so they'll shut the fuck up. Rack never asked much of Il Signore up there on his almighty cloud, except maybe pull the frigging plug out of this Calabria and let these uncles glug into the ocean.

'Your toys too important to help Uncle Gianni, spit in his face?'

Christ, was this a yes or no? Rack'd tried to teach her to talk proper when he was five. Another winner. This Goldoni must be yet another scrounger from Back 'Ome. Like the others, he'd be smart-suited, handmade shoes, wanting free lodging, somehow too poor to buy bog paper.

He plunged into gloom. He promised, and Mama intoned reproaches. Martina would never give him time off. Even if she did, it would drive Bonn into one of his forgiving silences. Which would nark old Osmund, who never wanted Bonn riled. Which would infuriate Martina, because she was secretly crazy for Bonn. Which would ruffle the lads, because Bonn was made key now and they wanted to be among Bonn's new goers, because Bonn had that magic pull that guaranteed superlative life here on earth and, who knew, maybe life ever after. Which would piss off Posser, Martina's poorly dad, who hadn't to be narked at any price. Which would send Grellie spare, because she'd split for Bonn, and the girl street stringers'd go berserk, because God in His infinite wisdom sent the girls nuclear when the smooth-running prostitution at the railway station got ballsed up. And it would all be

42

Rack's fault for not finding this Uncle Gianni a free living.

He started damage limitation.

'Holly Mass, Mama.' He smiled. Her lips stayed welded. He'd heard that Italian daughters were shit hot at quelling maternal friendly fire. 'I'll take him to church this Sunday.' He let that sink in. 'Unless he goes with friends?' Fat chance. The chiselling bastard would want a free car. Mama stared. 'He want a car, Mama? On the firm?'

A nod. Mama knew about milking organisations. Her wayward son was learning responsibility.

'Good boy. Your belov' papa . . .'

She started to weep. Rack never had a beloved papa. He'd ask Grellie, maybe Jenny, if mama tyranny was everywhere, sonhood a perennial crucifix. He really wanted to ask Bonn, but you didn't ask things. Questions wounded him, and not even Martina did that.

'And a free flat, Mama.' He was desperate to hit the vicious street, where it was safe. He left in abject misery.

CHAPTER FIVE

Firm—*a group of goers controlled by one.*

Bradshawgate was no longer a city gate. Now it was a mere triangular recess where children played tap footer with a frayed ball. Unemployed men hung about. On clement days elderly women went through to the supermarts. Here Posser observed the city, strolling his four laps.

43

Northern unemployed men lean on walls, Posser noted, and drink bottles of sour clag. They were doubly deprived, by wage and booze—the latter the cheapest source of calories. He'd had his spell of both. Now it was the vitamin E, obeying the doctor's stern admonition, and sickening cod-liver-oil capsules. And the precious TNT, little white jobs, for the chest pain.

He liked Bradshawgate. He'd been born here, only because nobody would look at a house numbered 13. He squinted, breathless on a bench facing his old home. A lawyer's office now, for God's sake, knocked into one with Mrs Mason's, the Townsons', the whole run of 15, 17, 19, and 21. Travel agents gaudied up the corner. A council hut stood where Maggie's shop used to be, for council workmen to smoke fags and play pontoon. They didn't bring their lunch baggins. Now they had a pub session. Traffic roared round the main square.

'Dad?'

Martina came and sat by. Posser had moved away to Rivington moors, raised her single-handed in a cottage overlooking Bowton. Eventually, affluence struck, a bolt from the blue. He'd moved back to Bradshawgate, appalled by the changes but determined. Him and the city, with their wonky hearts and all.

'Hello, love. You did it? Promoted Bonn?'

'Yes. He was taken aback.' She paused. 'I can't ever tell with Bonn.' She laughed openly at a little lad cheating, moving the ball slickly with his hand as he dribbled past. 'I wish I knew him, Dad.'

'We don't need to. We only need to guess right.'

She changed her approach. 'Promotion gives all that power.'

44

'Some are naturals, love. Worth their weight in gold.' Posser smiled on his beautiful but lame daughter, not liking her resentment. 'Women sense trust. They respond to him.'

With frank curiosity she inspected her father as he spoke on.

'When old Mrs Ainsworth died, I saw myself for what I was, a kept man, a *cicisbeo*, nothing more than a *damigello*, a "walker" in London cant. A Jemmy Jessamy. Ridiculed, a pub joke. You were still at school. It must have been hard on you, love.'

'You had a proper job! Mrs Ainsworth's estates, Dad!'

He patted her hand. 'Aye, the stables, rent-free cottage. And, when she'd passed away, her land and investments, God rest her loving soul.'

Martina watched him. He had never before admitted his feelings for the old lady. For her father to have such emotions seemed improper.

'Her family contested, frauded most of it!' Martina grew heated.

Posser wheezed, having a hard time breathing out. In was easy.

'This country has no law against general fraud, love, only specific. Settling for twenty-six per cent was wise, or we'd still be in court, lawyers worrying me into my grave, you unprovided for. No, love. Pragmatism's the game.'

More than pragmatism, though. Mildred Ainsworth had once lent Posser—lent as in *lent* him—for a single night to a sick friend. He'd consoled the lady, then returned bitter with accusations. It was the closest he'd come to leaving her. But Mildred's gratitude had been so touching, filled with compassion. The other lady had died not

45

long after. It had taught him something new about humanity.

'Dad?' she asked, as if she'd just that minute arrived.

He leant forward, hands pressing down on the bench helping to lift his chest. 'I'm wondering about selling, love.'

She was startled. 'Selling *out*? Have we had an offer?'

'Not yet. I'm trying to out-guess time.' He grinned ruefully. 'We've only muscle enough for local purposes. The city centre is being redeveloped—marinas, leisure complexes, theme parks, God knows what. They'd bring regiments to force the sale.'

'Can't we go on just as we are?' She seemed frightened.

'Not if heavy money moves in, love, no.' Posser tapped his chest for emphasis. 'Our syndicate's just you and me, when all's said and done. I know we talk as if there's a giant power in control. But our syndicate's an ailing bloke with his daughter, and a few willing scrappers.'

'We've expertise, Dad!' Martina was offended; her cheeks were red.

'Which they might want to use for a while.'

'And then we do what?'

He looked at her sadly. The afternoon light was starting to fade. Lights were on in the insurance offices.

'Me? Doesn't matter, love. You? Become respectable. Go where you wish, move in different circles.'

She tried to concentrate. Coming to meet him, she'd been so pleased. Now look. 'I'm scared when

46

you talk like this, Dad.'

'I'm trying to plan ahead, that's all.' He looked askance. 'I started with two goers, set up the snooker-hall office. Bought freehold when I could, leased short when I couldn't. Took on Osmund.'

She had heard the story a hundred times. 'The five tough lads, arrangements with three hotels.'

Posser chuckled. 'I must say I guessed well. A standing start, but not as ramshackle as it might have been. And you did brilliantly, love.'

'Then what's new, Dad?'

'The city, love. Its decay is over. This is as bad as it'll get. She'll redevelop. Whoever's in the way'll get blammed. It'll be real hoods, money men, who'll make an offer.' He pulled a face. 'Oh, it'll be genteel enough—to start with. As long as we accept and leave.'

'We can refuse, and make a fight of it.'

'They'd laugh. Then get angry, and simply take everything. We're obsolete. Like the old films they made yonder.'

'The Granadee Studios?' Martina could just see where the huge fluorescent sign blinked night and day. She bridled. 'They use our services, Dad. Three uppers, regulars, not counting occasionals.'

Uppers being lady clients, Posser was not impressed. Martina smiled.

He caught her look. She'd been defiant and brave even when small. He'd been scarred by poverty, she never. Immunity from hunger allowed luxuries like freedom.

'I'd die before I'd be poor again, love. Nowadays, poverty's only putting your hand out for the dole, three pints a night instead of eight, smoking twenty, not thirty a day.' He took her hand. 'Face it. We're

47

miniatures, collectable like some ornament.'

'You'll accept when the offer comes,' she said quietly, trying not to hurt.

'We'll have no choice. A foreigner's coming from the Continent.'

'Very well, Dad.'

Posser smiled. He spotted her new catchphrase. An indicator of a possible boyfriend? Very well, indeed.

'How's Angler doing?'

'Leading the pack. I'm pleased with him.'

But no change of breath, no sudden quickening, so it wasn't Angler. He said, idly, 'Wigan through and through him. He used to do pub imitations of Angelo Dundee, y'know, boxing promoter who cheated Henry Cooper.'

'Rack says he's fine.'

'Then they must be doing right.' Posser's hopes, he realised with a canny inward look, were on Bonn. It was time he brought them together to find their valency. Christ's sake, the village matchmaker at his age.

'We need another blower, Dad.'

That took him by surprise. 'Five, on one switchboard? That's a hell of a lot.'

She counted on her fingers, like homework from the convent school. 'Miss Janet does days, Miss Rose tea to midnight. Miss Merry and Miss Hope alternate days. I spell them, front at the snooker hall. It's too thin, Dad.'

He'd chosen them for their honesty, and their mellifluous voices could reassure at a hanging. They were tact personified, could reassure any lady client who was losing courage. Their judgment—when to call in Martina, somebody trying it on—was cast

48

iron. They were paid a fantastic salary, with perks unknown to tax gatherers. Posser's latest perk was overseas holidays, two fortnights in one year. They lived rent-free, with investments. Now one more?

'The question is who to hire, love.'

Their one failure was a treacherous girl who had tried to set up her own service. Posser had sent Akker. She now languished in gaol on a three-year sentence for arson of a derelict mail-order warehouse in Stockport. Posser had been pleasantly surprised—Akker's perjuring witnesses had been so cheap. He'd kept Akker on ever since that success.

'When do you see Dr Winnwick?'

'Nine tomorrow.' Together they rose and walked haltingly from Bradshawgate towards Victoria Square. 'Let me know who Bonn chooses, eh?'

'I will. Sometimes I wonder if he's very bright.'

He knew better than argue. There was encouraging asperity in her voice.

Martina said without heat, taking his arm, 'He can't converse, as if he's some idiot boy scout.'

'Doubt he was ever in those, love.'

'How do you know?' Martina was too sharp.

'A guess. See you in an hour?'

'Right, Dad.' She stood at the kerb. 'I'll wait until you're across the road.'

Christ, Posser thought, here's my dotage, but he took it gamely and waved back when he'd survived the traffic. He saw her limp off and thought, Martina needs something more than an ailing dad, that's for sure.

*   *   *

'Never known a noisier nick,' Hassall complained,

49

reading the list. Sergeant Younger had known him years. 'Nor a gungier noticeboard.'

'Always the case, Mr Hassall. Every spare bit of paper, up it goes.'

'Who's next?' Hassall never expected the best. 'Don't give me some freak who's playing for the police college at Hendon.'

'Tim Windsor. Accident fatal.'

Windsor came up. 'There's a ton of witnesses.'

'Here,' Hassall asked Younger. 'Why say everything backwards?'

'Excise ledger system,' Windsor cut in. 'Nouns go first, qualifiers next. Like: cup, coffee, officers, for the use of.'

'Bright bugger,' Hassall said. 'Old, this accident fatal?'

'Middle-aged businessman.'

'Wasn't pushed, was he? Get the camera tape.'

'The camera at that corner of Victoria Square's been vandalised,' Windsor said, blinking his sandy eyes. To Hassall they looked scabby, the trouble with pale redheads.

Hassall said heavily, 'It's odd squared.' Hassall asked after the taxi driver. 'Let's have him looked at.'

CHAPTER SIX

Punter—*gambler, a prostitute's client, a customer.*

Clare was up early. She had slept badly, wanted nothing to do with anything. She'd made breakfast with disguised amiability, talked to Clifford about

50

the garden, those tall white romneya flowers attractive enough but don't they travel so, that inconsequential patter that means so much in marriage. She left the things for Mrs Kinsale, and against her intentions faxed the locum-doctor bank. She felt restive.

By the time Clifford was ready for off, the locum bank had answered, allocating her to Farnworth General. Not her first choice—what would have been, today?—but frankly she felt out of kilter, her vague unease recurring. Clifford had collared last night's *Evening News*, and it hadn't been evident since. Things seemed odd. She wondered if Clifford was as unperturbed as he seemed. It was lucky that she loved him.

On the way in she stopped at a convenient layby and bought the morning papers. The man's photo was speckled and grainy, the accident baldly reported. Leonard Mostern was his name, identified from credit cards and driver's licence. She remembered meeting him at one of Clifford's firm's events. Pinning down dates was always hard, but it was around last bloody February, that month so much on Clifford's mind last night.

Faithfulness was a marital problem, that and deceit. She ought to simply ring Clifford and say outright, 'That accident was Leonard Mostern. We met at that do, didn't we? Poor man. And to think that I attended his accident, how terrible ...' And so on. Bring it into the open.

She knew she wouldn't do any such thing. This morning was certainly not the time, she with her hospital locum to get through, Clifford with his—presumably his—briefcase filled with financial documents. An odd compulsion was on her to get away, ignore Farnworth General, drive up to the moors and sit watching the shifting colours on the fells in emblematic escape. But she folded the newspapers, put them carefully into her bag, and drove to work.

*   *   *

The hospital had seen better days. Clare had been in worse, but why did they always smell of cabbage and ether? She entered the main corridor, conscious that today she had chosen the wrong shoes, too noisy on the imitation-tile flooring. Once, in this same hospital, a patient's little girl had told Clare, 'These are my hammer shoes!' The defiant six-year-old had clacked her heels about the consulting room until Clare, striving to hear the mother's systolic murmur through the stethoscope, had got Sister Ellison to stir herself and distract the child.

So today here she was, walking with undue diffidence into the Admin offices to scan the allotment board. Here too she'd drawn the short straw. Locum-tenens doctors were cannon fodder, invariably Admin's easy way out. Therefore they had to suffer. Inevitably, the nursing staff would be irritated at having their precious routines upset. Clare had even met with frank abuse from nurses whose sacrosanct rituals were to be observed at all costs.

'You're in neoplastic counselling, Dr Burtonall,' the overweight secretary informed her airily. 'Starting ten minutes ago.'

Clare swallowed at the unfair criticism. She turned to look. Why did secretaries adopt that nasal

52

whine? Did they speak so with their husbands, on holiday with friends, or was it taught in secretarial school?

'Who of the regular staff is off duty, please?' she asked. 'And which clinic?'

'Dr Daubney's down with flu. His wife phoned yesterday.'

'I think you have grounds for complaint, then, Mrs Wensford,' Clare said, frowning. 'It is your Admin's own rule that locum-tenens doctors like myself must be fully informed of clinic, identity of physician for whom they are to deputise, time of start, patient numbers, at the time of notification. I was told none of these.' She took up the hospital contract forms and moved out as smoothly as she could manage in her clamorously wrong shoes, saying over her shoulder, 'It's that sort of inefficiency that gives Hospital Admin its bad name. I'll complain for you to the bank locum agencies.'

She set off down the corridor, her heart sinking. What a way to begin a day. The 'Neoplastic Support Clinic', in the jargon of hospital classification, was more properly the Patient Counselling Service. It was a job shunned by many doctors, a punishment posting. She quite liked Dr Daubney. She could have done with a quiet clinic day, to think things out, make a few discreet phone calls. Her unreasonable irritation at the cancer specialist's bout of flu worsened her feeling of guilt. And that wretched Mrs Wensford would of course get her own back. Sooner or later the fat cow would engineer some default, lay it, sweetly and with utmost regret, at Clare's door instead of her own plodding ineptitude.

No illusions, she cautioned herself despondently.

53

Those were for saints, who had never slogged through the six years of medical school.

'Morning,' she said with determined brightness to the desk nurse. 'I'm Dr Burtonall, standing in for Dr Daubney. Just give me a moment to settle, please.'

'Morning, doctor.' The nurse followed her in. 'Nurse Minnie Jarndiss, second year. The X-rays are alphabetic, lab reports here . . .'

Despite Nurse Jarndiss's second-year status, she was aware of any locum doctor's usual temptation to perform a swift scan of the laboratory reports to see how time-consuming each patient was likely to be.

Clare decided to try to match the other's cheeriness, and left the lab results untouched. 'I'd like time to consult the notes between cases, please.'

'That's fine, doctor. Dr Daubney takes ten minutes, but just bell us when you're ready. I'll quell any riots.' She hesitated. 'There's one patient Dr Daubney wanted to see himself. Personal reasons. He's due in an hour.'

'A relation, or somebody in the profession?' Clare's misgivings were justified. Doctors and nurses made foul patients, and relatives were notorious complainers.

'No, Dr Burtonall. He used to teach Dr Daubney when he was young.' Nurse Jarndiss blushed at her gaffe.

'Dr Daubney's old teacher? Better blip me when he arrives.'

Clare could see that was a problem. Still, cross that bridge as and when. She took up the first folder, with its accumulation of pink, blue, and

54

yellow laboratory, radiology, and histopathology forms thickening the back inserts. Social, family, and past medical history, then the present clinical problem, and the terrible finalities of the diagnosis itself.

Ninety minutes later she had seen three patients. They had all been straightforward. A follow-up patient with colonic cancer was doing well after a two-stage operation and managing his colostomy with his wife's help. The district nurse had been sound. Then a breast-cancer patient, calmly facing irradiation therapy and cytotoxic drugs, no trace of nausea now, and without evidence of a recurrence. The last was an elderly woman with a rodent ulcer by the outer canthus of her right eye, bright as a button, making a complete recovery. Clare let the talkative lady chat a while, giving her extra moments to reassure. Something she said caught Clare's attention.

'I still go to St Benedict's, doctor, from being a girl. Not many can say that, now the school's closed! I'm sure I remember that elderly gentleman outside.'

'Do you, Mrs Lacey?'

'You can't tell who's what nowadays, can you, doctor? I remember when the infant school was where Leghorn's new store is . . .'

Mrs Lacey was ushered out. Nurse Jarndiss entered.

'The old teacher you mentioned is a reverend, Nurse Jarndiss?'

'Yes, doctor. He's retired now.'

'The biopsy reports have Dr Daubney's initials,' Clare pointed out. So he had already perused them.

Clare flicked to the first page. The notes were

55

sparse, as if the compiler had been keener to conceal than inform.

The patient came in with a diffident smile. First impressions are best, Clare remembered being taught by an opinionated surgeon, because they come before educational baggage clutters up the picture. Mr Crossley was thin, almost cachectic, with a slight stoop. No clerical collar, no black suit, nothing to suggest the clergyman. His manner was apologetic yet confident, an unusual mixture.

'How do you do? I'm Dr Burtonall. Mr Crossley, isn't it?'

'Jonas George Crossley.' He had a dry, flutey voice. 'Sixty-two, perennial cigarette smoker. I'm sorry.'

She tried to give a reassuring smile, but faded. 'Your occupation?'

'I asked Dr Daubney to fudge it, Dr Burtonall.' He suddenly smiled, an engagingly brisk grin taking over his features. 'Priest, if I were in clergy-friendly country. Here, I'm lucky if people misunderstand and think me a clerk in a bookie's betting shop.'

'Retired?'

'Yes.' He sighed, but showed no dismay. 'A seminary theologian. I retired from teaching a year since.'

'A year? But . . .'

He was abruptly less inclined to humour. 'My illness came on after the seminary closed. I wasn't invalided out. Too few recruits for the priesthood, materialistic claims on the youth of today, put it how you will.'

'Retired for non-medical reasons.' She reread the histopathology of the type of the man's lung tumour. 'Your GP—'

'He has told me the cancer is inoperable, doctor.'

Clare found it hard. The pathologist's account of the histology sections implied the most serious outcome. Cancers took many forms. This biopsy revealed columnar cells interspersed with varied spheroidal cells. In this patient's thorax there would already be soft friable masses of pinkish-grey cancerous material. The range of cell size, and the intensity with which the cells took up the histopathology stains, were ominous indicators. The disparities in nuclear sizes at high-resolution microscopy signified a poor outlook.

'Please, Dr Burtonall.' The man was pale but composed. 'I can guess what you must be feeling. Dr Daubney made quite firm predictions.'

'Thank you, Mr Crossley.' She hesitated, feeling lost. 'Am I to call you by a title?'

'"Father" would be inappropriate, seeing you are probably not of my persuasion.' He did his sudden grin, so full of inappropriate merriment.

'Can I ask where you live? The address given—'

'A boarding house. Folks on social security, commercial travellers.'

She went for frankness. 'Are there homes for retired clergymen, that sort of thing?'

'There *are* residences for retired priests.' His eyes wrinkled as if against smoke. 'I honestly can't see myself stuck in such a place, atrophying among the derelict. At Turton, my boarding house, there are occasional new faces, and I like the city.' He winced at a reminding pain. 'This is the only area I know.'

'Forgive me, Mr Crossley, but I'm unsure . . .'

He helped her out. 'Finance? I'll be funded until I need, how is it phrased, terminal care.' He opened his hands. 'I'd like an accurate prediction, doctor.'

57

'I'm sorry, but the lung tumour is a primary malignancy, meaning that it originated there. It is a type that usually advances at speed.' She had viewed the radiographs, gone over the radiologist's report. 'Given the size, position, the type of tumour cells.' She saw his unspoken question. 'Some four weeks. But occasional cases—'

'Except you don't believe that I'm such an "occasional case," Dr Burtonall.' His look was sharp. Just for an instant she glimpsed how he would look with gaunter features as the tumour disseminated and took firm hold. 'One question, please. Can I ask to be under one doctor, or is that not done? I mean, these days is it just pot luck?'

'A lot depends on the care that's needed, but, yes, you can usually get the doctor you want.'

'Thank you.' He seemed relieved. 'Theology isn't much use when it comes down to it. More than times have changed, doctor.'

'Mr Crossley, I think I should go over some practical points. I will pay a domiciliary visit, make an assessment in your home, if that's all right?'

'Certainly.'

'We shall contact your GP. I want you to drop in at the clinical-pathology laboratory, haematology division, for blood tests . . .'

*   *   *

Clare finished the clinic at noon. Near the hospital buildings a park had been improvised from industrial clearances. It wasn't much, a few nondescript acres, but the trees were established now about a docile river. With ornamental bridges between flower beds, it was a place where waiting

58

relatives could pass the time. She had left her car near the bus stop there.

It promised a bright sunny afternoon, with people moving along the riverside. A small cluster congregated to watch the swans.

A young mother had a twin in its push chair. As Clare watched, the other child tottered in its reins towards the water. There was a weir, but the mother was within a yard, so Clare, like everybody else, smiled hearing the child's excited squeals. From the corner of an eye, Clare saw a young man suddenly start forward in a smooth fast run. He sprinted with intent face, urgent eyes on the toddler. Clare was too astonished to call out. A great cob swan rose hissing from the water's edge, seeming to swell as it moved against the infant. The baby girl went into the water with a splash. It happened all in a second.

The huge bird stood, slamming its wings, the alarmed crowd retreating before its fury. The mother screamed as the push chair fell over with the child strapped inside.

An older man yelled, tried to wave the swan away with his cap. Something splashed. Clare thought, where was the little girl? The cob charged, hissing in outrage, its wings massively thudding the air. Clare was thirty yards away but could feel the wafts on her cheeks, so powerful was the force.

The running youth—no, man, twenty—hurled himself through the crowd, took a flying leap, and kicked out at the swan as he passed it. Something cracked in the old man's arm as the swan's wing caught him. He shouted, scrabbled back, hauling himself away one-handed. People were shouting, the frightened mother was hysterical, almost running on the spot, impotent.

The runner splashed into the water fully clothed, his kick having shoved the great bird off a couple of yards. Two young lads threw stones at it. A dog, barking frantically, tried unconvincing rushes but lacked courage. Clare saw the young man in the water. No heroics there, the river moving him along as he swam towards the weir, the little girl splashing half submerged. He caught her.

'Get a rope! Get a rope!' some woman was yelling.

A lad threw a stick at the male swan, which was now back in the water and beating along the surface, feet splashing, wings flapping, towards the swimmer.

The other lad took hold of his dog and urged it floundering into the water, yelling to create distraction. The young man took hold of the infant and swam obliquely downstream towards the weir away from the chasing swan. Clare realised his coolness, using the current to gain yardage by angling across.

The crowd joined the lad and the barking dog, shouting and throwing anything that came to hand to deflect the giant bird. Two ambulance men came at a run. By the time Clare reached the water, a uniformed security man was already slithering down the slope and the little girl was being brought out on the riverbank to the mother, people excitedly telling each other how it had happened, thanks mingled with reproaches, all admiring the mother's tearful exhaustion and her astonishingly thrilled child. Everyone was talking at once.

Clare, amused and relieved, went to sit on a bench as the cacophony subsided, in a way charmed by the outcome. The security man was pleased with the two lads and their noisy dog, which was still barking loudly at the swan, but did no more than take the young hero's name. With hardly a glance the drenched youth left to sit on a bench, and left it at that. The small greensward returned to normal. The little girl and her overwhelmed mother were hurried in to Casualty, while the cob swan serenely returned to patrolling the waterway, doing occasional theatening sneezes. People were still explaining, imagining fearsome outcomes a million times worse. The old man's bravery was being extolled. He was already inside being examined by the Casualty surgeon.

A doctor's fate, Clare told herself wryly, was to be indispensable one minute and superfluous the next.

She gathered up her handbag and coat. Her exit took her past the young man, still thoroughly soaked. He was sitting hunched, elbows on knees, looking dispassionately at the river. People had dispersed.

'Are you all right?' Clare asked, smiling.

'Thank you.' He didn't look.

She tried again, a little put out. 'I did tell the security man it was you and not the others who did the deed.'

'The lads were instrumental,' he said, 'but thank you.'

His detachment peeved her. Instrumental? An odd word for a pandemonium. 'You kept so calm, Mr Whitmore. Quite admirable.' She'd heard him give his name. 'The only one of us.'

'I'm not Whitmore.' He seemed shy, caught out. 'I give the names of Hollywood actors, old ones.'

Give, so therefore habitually? Was this sort of

rescue usual?

'If you wish,' she said, piqued, about to write him off. 'It doesn't alter what you did.' He didn't speak. 'Have you offended the security man?'

'Yes.'

She was taken aback. 'Yes what?'

'Yes, I offend the security man.'

His flat replies reminded her of witnesses giving prepared evidence in court. Yet he didn't seem in any way perturbed, more mildly amused.

'It was the same at the road accident, Mr Whitmore. That policeman?'

'Yes.' Unconcerned. He must have recognised her, as she him.

'Seriously? You offend them both?'

'Both would say yes. I cannot regard it in quite the same terms.'

Clare felt she ought to go, yet she persisted, irritated by his detachment. 'Quite the regular rescuer. The policeman didn't take to you one bit. Remember?'

Fishing, of course. He didn't care either way. She felt an intruder, ask questions all day and get nowhere. Yet she had a vested interest in hearing an impartial view of yesterday's accident, and wanted to prolong this, even with this wet youth who didn't even have the sense to dry himself.

Slowly he looked up, level blue eyes, brown hair a wet slicked thatch. 'I remember, of course.'

'Might I ask how you, the archetypal do-gooder, give offence so readily?'

He said evenly, 'I'm a goer.'

'A . . .?' She wondered if she had possibly misheard. What was a goer?

'Goer, street slang. Gigolo, walker, troller,

cicisbeo, jessamy. Meaning a male hired by ladies for their own purposes and use.'

That was pretty stark, she thought with wonderment. A . . . one of those people, here, in this hospital park?

'You,' she said stupidly. 'You?'

'I.'

Education, Clare thought in the warm daylight, doesn't really fit you out. Convent nuns should have prepared her. A drowning child's rescuer responds to a polite enquiry by saying blithely that he is a, what, a goer. His manner is condign; such an occupation is bound to anger propriety, it's only natural, thank you and good day.

She had a sudden absurd image, herself in the convent school, Manners and Etiquette with Sister Immaculata. *Now, girls, introduction to a goer: with a ladylike inclination of the head one extends one's hand, but only when the gentleman's hand is fully offered. Let's try that. Clare . . .?*

'The policeman and the security man recognised you.'

'Or guessed.' He nearly smiled at her concern. 'Please don't worry. The old man deserves the credit, and the lads with Rin Tin Tin.'

'Do you, ah, work alone?' she asked on impulse.

'For an agency called Pleases Agency, Inc.'

He raised his head to follow a rising kite and added, 'I like the colours on the tail.' She glanced up. A child with his granddad was flying a multicoloured kite, concentrating. 'They say the longer the kite's tail the better it flies. Is it true?'

'No. Weight is a limiting factor.' She paused, knowing she should go.

'A limiting factor.' He nodded agreement, eyes

63

on the kite.

'Are there many of you?' But where, though?

It was extraordinarily difficult to ask. She wished she'd had an hour's warning of this, to work out what to say.

'Not nearly enough.'

'I'm sorry. I didn't mean to intrude.'

'I don't mind your being intrigued.'

Which, she thought a little tartly, was hurtful. 'Intrigued', as if she was nothing more than a voyeuse, nothing else to do all day. He really was a high scorer at offending people. How on earth did he get along with those women who hired him for 'their own purposes and use'?

'I suppose your public often are.' Now she sounded combative.

'I have no public,' he said simply. Did he mean no one?

In the nick of time she held her next cutting remark in check and forced a smile, wanting to sit beside him but not knowing whether it would be right. The security man was bound to be watching from the window. Sister Immaculata hadn't done her job. Clare felt in a mess. He had begun to shiver. The sunshine was watery, a low breeze rising. Why didn't he leave?

'Hadn't you better get home and dry out?'

He gave that shyish look about the park. 'Perhaps. Thank you for your company.'

'Do you need a lift?' Against his painful politeness it was like an assault, sounding at least boorish. Quickly she amended, 'Could I offer you a lift somewhere? You will look conspicuous on a bus, Mr Whitmore.'

He made no move. 'You will look conspicuous in

my company.'

'I'll bring my car to the bridge. Five minutes?'

'I am grateful.'

'The least I can do. My motorcar is maroon.' She paused. 'Have you a name, Mr Whitmore? One I could use?'

'Yes,' he said, with apology. 'People say Bonn.'

She paused a moment for him to ask hers, but he didn't. She got her car, found him waiting at the bridge gate.

Their conversation was stilted as she drove, because she felt baffled. He said the central bus station in the main square would be fine, and there asked if 'it would be convenient' for her to drop him by the textile museum. He thanked her. She said not at all, and immediately pulled away. Ineptly, she had disclosed nothing of herself, and had learned nothing more about him.

Why had he been at the hospital? Outside, sitting waiting for a patient perhaps? She would never know.

*   *   *

That evening she scanned the newspaper. It was reported that a Mr Whitmore had assisted two local lads and their dog to rescue a child, who was pictured, from the hospital river weir. Questions were being asked in the local council about the presence of swans in the grounds of Farnworth General. Swans were known to be highly dangerous. An elderly gentleman was the 'city's real hero', and was pictured recovering in hospital from injuries sustained when he had courageously battled the vicious bird.

The twins and the mother were pictured. The hospital security services were praised.

Bonn, a goer at the agency with the lugubrious name, had been there when Leonard Mostern had been killed—no, Clare corrected, had *died* in that accident. She looked in the phone book. The agency was there. She was astonished.

That evening she described the swan incident to Clifford in general terms, but said nothing about Bonn.

*   *   *

Sleeping together was vital. It's what marriage was, is, should consist of. Other rituals were fine, even necessary, but sleeping—meaning lying, sweating, snoring, rutting, all of it—was the essence.

They made love that night. All right, Clare admitted, she was impelled by the accident's consequence, that briefcase, but so? Nothing wrong with feeling the need of a little security, which is what tonight's sex was.

She lay awake, seeing the ceiling shadows darken against the grey. Now, why had she thought *consequence*, instead of *aftermath*? The former meant a related, the latter an unrelated, event. A subconscious mistake, or a truth?

Love was odd. She was sure she loved Clifford, and he her. There was a theory that it was an invention of troubadours in twelfth-century Provence with fancy rituals written down in those oddly sexless codes. Yet magazines were emphatic enough about it: 'romantic love' flourished in 89 per cent of mankind's cultures, said researchers (and much *they* knew!). Lying there, her leg still over her

66

husband's recumbent form, Clare almost giggled. She and her friend Beth in medical school used to compose ridiculing rhymes when 'research' was cited. Most nations, tribes, cultures, throughout history—as now—distinguished between arranged marriage and love-based marriage. Similarly, there was a sharp difference between sexual intercourse for an ulterior motive—money, getting a part in a film—and sex for 'love'.

Nowadays, though, body chemistry seemed to have a say. Break it down to stages. One, encounter with sight and smell, like animals. Hadn't there been some odd experiment, when male or female pheromones were rubbed onto seats in a cinema, then people admitted to take their seats at random—and most sat on seats secretly smeared with the pheromones of the opposite gender? Secondly, after the sniff factor came phenylethylamine, the 'rush' chemical, with neurochemicals like norepinephrine and dopamine, which like amphetamines fired up elation and different excitements. This chemical response to one sexual partner lasted maybe forty months, said experts, then dwindled. Sad, really, but just as some drugs have to be given in ever larger doses to produce the same effect, so with phenylethylamine—our human chemistry factories simply get worn out producing it in response to one lover. So it fails, and with it our sexual fever. Was this why, Clare wondered, moving Clifford's hand to her breast, divorce rates soar during the third or fourth year after marriage, because our bodies get bored turning out the right chemicals? And, incidentally, wasn't something like phenylethylamine there in chocolate, promoting its randy-candy fame?

Stage three overlaps in the nick of time. Morphinelike endorphins tickle up the brain, inducing comfort and tranquillity. Oxytocin does its cuddlesome stuff, batting orgasms along to the climax. Hence satisfaction, hence peace of mind.

But competition creeps in. Maybe growing sexual confidence coincides with the chemical fade-out? Anyhow, other contestants enter the field, amorous encounters begin—and of course newcomers bring their own stimulus to rekindle the body's chemical boilers. Stage five is nothing more than resolution. Either responsibility wins out, or moral weakness chucks in the towel—the husband succumbs to his secretary's sexual enticements, or the wife scampers after some passing new male. Over and out.

Feeling suddenly alone in the gloaming, Clare decided that it was all too ornately biochemical. Sleep together, you got through the biochemical barrier. Simple as that. She pulled Clifford's somnolent weight on her, and slept.

CHAPTER SEVEN

Bunce—*money, profit, illicit or otherwise.*

They entered the hall, the entire place echoing with clangs and grunts. To Bonn it was a menagerie.

'Incongruous,' he told Rack.

Bonn's judgements disturbed Rack. There was no need for them. Bonn was like somebody seeing secret football scores in everything, to gladden or deplore. Rack couldn't understand it. Rubbish activities like pumping iron were just stupid. Finish. Bonn hadn't got the hang of life.

They stood watching. The seats were sparsely occupied, though a scattering of body builders packed the front rows, ogling those already on the stage. A good two dozen men were pumping iron; the air was thick with male sweat plus the scent of ironmongery that hung where men laboured to no purpose. Bonn stared in wonder, fellers dedicating their lives to lifting metal chunks. It was an addiction crazier than drugs or booze.

'What is it for, Rack?'

Another thing, Rack couldn't see the point of Bonn's thoughts. He should think less, sleep sounder. He'd be more cheerful. But, then, Bonn had the magic, so it was okay. Charisma, he would have thought if his mind had allowed.

'I might ask Galahad,' Bonn said, finding a seat.

And he would too, Rack marvelled. Only Bonn would demand of an obsessed mountain like Big G why the hell he behaved like a prat, shoving steel nowhere.

'Go careful, Bonn,' Rack warned. He didn't want Martina asking how come he'd let her prize goer get crushed.

Rack, Bonn's stander, was there to protect. Fall down on the job, Martina'd go into orbit. As for Grellie, well, best not to think of the effect losing Bonn'd have on that particular knife-bearing female. Luckily, Bonn could avoid setting off the fuses in people, including these great oafs thrusting, flexing, oiling, or leaning spent in glistening exhaustion.

'Bonn,' Rack said, seeing his caution got no answer. 'Everybody knows they're nerks, but don't

69

tell them, okay?'

There was an area of cork matting near the tea machine where you stocked up on kilojoules after wearing yourself out. Small tables, white-painted, chairs with fawn covers. Bonn was brought Earl Grey tea unasked. The girls were in awe, ever since Bonn tried to pay at the counter, first visit. They even put his picture up on their kitchen wall, until Martina heard and sharply banned that sort of thing. Rack reckoned it was typical birdthink, girl helpers now hating their boss but giving Bonn still greater aura.

Rack found Galahad oiling himself. The pumpers called it the machine room, as if it was filled with engines, when it had nothing but space and a coir flooring. He called to Galahad, returned to Bonn.

A smiling girl brought him a cola, ruffled his spiky hair. He paid no attention. She really wanted to ruffle Bonn's. He found Bonn eyeing him.

'How's your ma, Rack?'

Rack looked away from where a middleweight failed his snatch lift.

'Some relative's coming. She wants me to fix him up with lodgings.'

'His firm doesn't give expenses?'

'Don't know. Maybe he's milking the sheet?'

'I wonder if I can help.'

There it was again. Another bloke would have nodded, meaning fuck off.

'I can't go to Martina with this crap, Bonn.'

They watched Galahad approach, a looming alp. 'She'd understand.'

Bonn held up a restraining hand for Galahad to hang on a sec. And, unbelievably, Galahad actually

70

did pause. The girls eyed his physique as Galahad used the full-length mirrors for a quick self-appraisal. He flexed, bulging and forcing, on the ball of one foot, head back. Let anybody else put him on hold, though, he'd have gone berserk. Bonn could do that, make an insult an apology.

'Tell you what, Rack. I could ask Martina, allow your visitor some free lodging, a courtesy.'

Bonn frowned as if it was a problem, when Rack had been screaming inside for salvation. Rack told him yeah, fine, ta, relief washing over him.

By now Galahad was into a routine, the girls clapping, when Bonn raised his hand for Galahad to stop that crappy posturing and get over here. Ironers would kill for an audience, yet Galahad came like he'd got a knighthood and didn't even blink in outrage when Bonn came right out with it, Rack's heart in his mouth.

'Hello, Galahad. I assume this muscle business has a purpose?'

Rack tensed, waiting for the mighty figure to go kong at the mortal insult, but Galahad only said, 'I'm glad you asked, Bonn. Got a minute?'

'Aye, Galahad.'

'Well,' the hulk began, meek as a lamb, 'it's body image . . .'

Rack marvelled, and settled to boredom while Galahad, the goon, expounded on muscles, but meaning his own glorious physique that the whole world had a solemn duty to adore but which looked like a bag of fucking spanners.

*   *   *

'This is the corac.' Twenty minutes, and the big

71

blond was earnestly showing a ripple under his armpit Rack wouldn't have bothered with.

'Corac?' Bonn repeated, serious.

'It's a forgotten muscle left over, Darwin, you know, monkeys? The corac was huge, in caveman days. We were all birds.'

Rack almost cackled but hung in there copying Bonn's sober inertia, this moron redeveloping fucking muscles to out-fly what, some pterodactyl? If Bonn had guffawed, Galahad would have taken ridicule on the chin, yet he'd crucify Rack for an honest laugh.

From Bonn, 'You have judges? How?'

'That's it!' Galahad cried. He paced like a wrestler about to go for it. 'That's the *art*, Bonn!'

'A most serious question.' Bonn, forgetting global warming with death zapping through them ozone holes.

'Judges *judge*, Bonn!' Galahad flexed, copying Rodin's *Thinker* postered on the walls. The girls went, 'Oooh!' Galahad beamed.

'But it's unreliable, Galahad.'

For God's *sake*, Bonn, Rack urged inwardly. But never no need when it came from Bonn. Galahad shook his head ruefully.

'It's science, who's got the sharpest cuts, the max mounds.'

'Cuts?' Bonn, risking annihilation. Rack slid in his chair, casual.

'Where the muscle ends, see?' Galahad, desperate to make a convert of Bonn, who led the world. 'Flab stops it being sharp like my lats here . . .'

Rack listened to the muscle-hussle crap. A small audience of other ironers had assembled to hear their gospel propounded. Rack wondered, was he the only one who saw Galahad was a prat.

'Will you tell me more later?' Bonn asked. He rose, took Galahad a step. 'Martina's made me key. You're on my new firm.'

'Me?' Galahad was stunned. Rack watched the effect. Galahad had been single-trigger, a reserve. Only had one request for his services, and that had proved a real Balkan, no gain but mighty effort. Bonn himself had had to rescue that time. 'Me, Bonn?' Galahad's eyes filled, to Rack's disgust. 'But that time—?'

'There was no time, Galahad.' Bonn looked the big man in the eye. 'I want no votes, no backchat. Martina picked two of you.'

Rack winced. Wiser to keep shtum, but this was Bonn talking.

'Thanks, Bonn.' For instant wealth plus status.

'Meet at the Café Phrynne when I send.'

The ironer looked about to shake hands, didn't, stayed humble, in unknown territory. 'You'll have to tell me what to do, Bonn, eh? I'll give it my best.'

'Thank you for the talk about muscles. Really interesting.'

'Cheers, Galahad,' Rack said, adding silently, you boring misshapen fart, but he grinned as Galahad clasped both hands over his head like a boxer. The other ironers clustered for the galactic news, slapping his shoulder.

'That crap they talk,' Rack said as they left. 'Even with their girls in bed. Jammy bugger's never been so lucky.'

'Rack. Will a studio flat over the Phoenix Theatre do?'

'Thanks, Bonn.' Rack really meant it. He'd be

73

able to give Mama the news for her visiting creep. Jews grumbled about mothers. Give the bastards Italian mothers, they'd really know suffering. Italian mamas, you had to make Pope *and* give them a prial of grandbabbies.

Grellie was waiting for them outside, pleased about something. She wore a new cobalt-blue dress, a king's ransom. Rack knew it was for Bonn alone, but Bonn couldn't see these things, probably thinking incongruous or, yesterday's word, icono-something.

'Bonn? Some flowers came for you.' Grellie walked with them. 'You should *see* how many.'

Rack stared. This was new. 'Somebody having us on?'

This was his area. Martina's syndicate couldn't get dissed, not in this city. Respect was down to Rack's war team, ten minutes, if need be.

'No. A client, silly!' Grellie tutted Rack down, him firing off half cocked. 'From a Wirral florist. I had Libby check back. The whole place is packed out like Chelsea Flower Show. Cost a mint!'

Rack subsided, disappointed. There hadn't been a rumble for weeks.

Grellie linked Bonn's arm. 'Who sent them, Bonn? The girls are agog.'

'Nothing to tell, Grellie.'

'"A grateful client, for services beautifully rendered,"' Grellie quoted.

Bonn moved off up Coffee Alley without speaking.

'I'll make up a story, then!' Grellie called, annoyed, her idea of threat.

'Best thing you can do,' Bonn said, but Rack it was who turned and raised one warning finger.

74

Grellie tossed her head and strolled into the square, by the Royal and the Grand. 'Rack. Lancelot in thirty minutes, Café Phrynne. I'll check with Martina. The studio flat will be on the second floor, the exit stairs.'

And Bonn would take the fallout, if Martina put on her frown that could kill.

'Ta, Bonn.'

'Done nothing.'

That was Bonn's eternal reply, whatever favours he'd shown, which was truly weird for a person who was climbing fast up a whole syndicate.

*   *   *

The pity was that the Café Phrynne was in a narrow back street in the old city centre. Impossible pavements, slender shopfronts, creaking pubs, and new fast-food joints trying to belong. Fashionable in parts, grotty in patches. Bonn thought it down-at-heel without being sordid, his home patch. A Huguenot church, dedicated to the memory of some ancient king who had given the Continent's Protestants succour, stood behind railings that made nonsense of the inches of pavement. Opposite, a bookmaker's, then shops trying for the boutique image selling handbags and fashions, delicatessens, shady bookshops, and a street market of barrows strung with electric lights brilliant through the brightest day.

Phrynne was a lady of the ancient world who'd got up to no good.

'Carol? I'm here.'

'Right, Bonn.'

Carol was on the door, a slim smiley girl with long

75

black tresses. The café was genteel, its decor feminine and fetching. She was a talented interior decorator. Trellises that seemed ridiculous when carried in from the pantechnicon suddenly became exactly right when she'd done. Impossible vines took on a warming air. Grotesque wall hangings became Mediterranean. Scarey lopsided pots became submerged amphoras. It wasn't travelogue, either. It stopped short of excess. Carol was class.

Most tables were set back in alcoves. Small wall bays, as for statues, refused to become illuminated grottoes by careful-casual settings of incidental shows, haberdashery, perfumes, sewing mementoes. Each week Carol had her 'performance', as she called it, a wall showing garments—Japanese, Old English, Damascus embroidery, muted by discreet floral arrangements.

Carol was a sort of genius who kept waiters in their place, brooked no nonsense, and reported in secrecy to Martina. Bonn approved.

'Lancelot,' he said quietly to Carol, pushing through the curtain. It was never quite drawn, open just enough to invite.

He took in the ladies who were there, walked through, passing where Yoff ruled his environmentally controlled kitchen—no cooking aromas, no sounds of culinary slog.

Bonn went down the corridor's right branch. Ladies' rooms and a lounge were set apart, Carol's instinct deciding the feel. A disguised office stood at one end, Carol again earning her crust. Bonn marvelled. It felt welcoming, but homely would have repelled women entering alone for illicit solace. Excess luxury would have challenged. The balance was friendly acceptance. Carol spent a fortune on flowers, to Rack's ridicule. Bonn countered that Carol always got it right, so where was the problem? Get the flowers.

The office was Spartan. He sat. The wall opposite should have opened to the Dickensian alley, with a fire escape backing the video-rental shop next door, but didn't. It couldn't. Bonn had worked it out, never tapped the wall wondering where the missing pieces of the café were. Martina designed what she designed. He only spoke his mind when asked, the rates of return, Grellie's girls' conduct, the risk of competition from the Dutch ZeeZees in Stratford.

He waited. No clock, a radio playing, never anything raucous, the background signal that all was well. Any interruption meant aggro, Rack's Rash team urgent, Poncho and the lads if they were handy.

The trouble was Carol's replacement. Time off, Lynne and Liz coped, though neither was up to much. Carol he trusted, though lady customers found Lynne likable. Liz was too brassy, too ready to grin, out of place.

'Bonn?'

The coloured lad entered. Lancelot was the ultimate in companionability. He had everything Bonn would have said was right for the job: the wickedest grin, teeth with it, swift recognition of moods. Today's gear, a bolero, cummerbund, click heels of the dancer ready for off.

'You came through the kitchen, Lancelot.'

'Yes, Bonn.' He looked injured, sat, crossed his legs with not quite a pout. He wore gloves and a huge thumb ring with a yellow stone. He knew what Bonn meant—You didn't come through the caff dressed like that?—and showed petulance at the

77

implied rebuke. Others wouldn't need to be told. Lancelot needed watching.

'I'm made key, Lancelot. Martina says to set up a new firm. I've got Galahad so far, and she wants you in.'

'Me? Goer? On a firm?' Lancelot seemed dazed. His eyes glistened. Lancelot's spectacular tears had to be tolerated or you got nowhere.

'Galahad's at the Rum Romeo. You can celebrate.' Bonn smiled. 'In a restrained manner, please.' One of Martina's admonitions, but Lancelot was away into his own dreamery.

'Me!' he kept saying, over and over. 'Me! I made goer!'

'It's the difference between not much,' Bonn said, to cool him, 'and being a millionaire in ten years. House, motor, one side business. As long,' he added, for Lancelot's proclivities, 'as Martina rules every breath.'

'Without saying, Bonn.' Lancelot rose, flexed his arms, did a sidestep, looking down over one shoulder. Bonn guessed a tango, some formation dance?

'I'll have a key meet soon. Have you anything on tonight?'

'No.' Lancelot was instantly defensive. 'But some enquiries.' Others wouldn't have needed excuses, another worry. Lancelot posed, undisguised camp, fist on hip. 'Who's the other goer? Three plus the key, right?'

'I shall tell you later.' Bonn wasn't going to be interrogated, not even by Martina's appointee.

Lancelot's grin finally burst. 'We're rich, Bonn! Motors, mansions!'

'One of each, Lancelot.' Bonn made his warning

a shared joke. Martina forbade employees to hold more than enough, and she defined sufficiency. Millionaires couldn't be choosers, Martina's words.

'Bonn.' The other was suddenly diffident. 'I appreciate this. I really do.' He pursed his lips. 'Would you like to see me dance? The Palais Rocco. Veeree Hip's playing, y'know? Big band.'

'Is it that mogga dancing?' Bonn put on a show of interest. 'I like that.' He didn't, but it was Lancelot's speciality. 'Thank you. I'll be delighted.'

'I'm sixth on. Starts at eight.'

'Half past, then?' Four minutes or so would give Bonn a margin, after which he could respectably leave. Mogga dancing was the city's most yawnsome event. 'I look forward to it. A treat.'

'Thanks, Bonn.' Lancelot pivoted, gave an extravagant bow.

Bonn watched the door close, none too happy. The stick-and-bush trade was no place for a loose cannon, however elegantly it moved. He would say nothing to Martina. Another thing to worry about.

He should settle Rack's problem of that visiting uncle. Then time for a light meal with Grellie before wasting time seeing Lancelot dance. Rack would sulk. Bonn wondered about those flowers.

On the way out he told Carol he wanted to meet Grellie, please. Carol never jumped to conclusions like Rack. She had a sense of the long term. Maybe ten, a dozen, ladies were in the Café Phrynne having tea, two pairs and the rest singles. The lads waited graciously on, Carol never looking but seeing they never overstepped. What better place could a lady visit, tired from a day's shopping, to rest over tea, the cakes sumptuous, the café discreet, the serving lads ever willing to smile and

79

share a mild exasperation or two?

'Bonn?'

He'd hardly gone a yard when Oliver fell in, pace for pace.

'May I speak?' Oliver, a regular-army man once, betrayed his ultra-conformity by double-breasted suits, shoes gleamingly ready for inspection. He somehow went about older than he was.

Bonn didn't slow, nodded, knowing what was coming and thinking, Oliver, for heaven's sake, lighten; it would do you a power of good.

'Just wanted to say congrats.' Oliver was nervous of speaking out of turn.

'Thank you, Oliver. I'm just lucky.'

'No. Promotion due where it's earned, where it's earned.'

Some military axiom? Bonn wondered, pausing at the intersection. Oliver, incongruous among the street barrows, only needed a bowler hat and upper-lip sweat to complete the picture of the ex-officer.

'Bonn, ah, a question, right?' Oliver rocked on his heels. 'Heard you'll have three goers, what?' Only the world's Olivers still said 'what?' like that.

Bonn smiled to put the man at ease. 'I never gossip, Oliver.'

'No! Understood! Only,' he drove on, almost at attention, 'you know my success—fair only, first to agree—in that area.' He fixed Bonn with desperate eyes. 'I'd appreciate being considered for any possible position.'

'I shall take you into consideration, Oliver. Thank you.'

Bonn stepped away, escaping. Oliver tried so hard to integrate, yet stuck out like a sore thumb. His military service had ended in some minor scandal, leaving him lodged in a corner upstairs flat in Cotton Street, where he was kept by an imperious Chester lady mad on bridge, investments, and golf. Oliver's chances as a goer were nil. If Martina put Oliver's name forward, Bonn would have to refuse.

Rack came. 'Want me to tell Oliver to sod off?'

'Find Grellie, please.'

'Already here.' Rack waved to Jodie and Elise by the private porn cinema and called cheerily, 'I never said a word, Jodie!' and resumed conversationally, ignoring their catcalls, 'What you want her for?'

'Just a quiet minute.'

Rack cackled, his plan working, Grellie and Bonn pairing off.

'Hey, Bonn. A joke. A little sadomasochism never hurt anybody. Good, eh?' He roared. The market folk laughed along, shouting he was a noisy git.

'Very good,' Bonn said, unsmiling.

Bonn was enough to make a bloke give up, and that was a fact. Still, Bonn with Grellie was okay. Martina shouldn't find out, for safety.

CHAPTER EIGHT

Shufti—*a look, a quick scrutiny.*

Domiciliary visits were not within Clare's purview, but the old gentleman's place was on her way home, so it was quicker in the long run. Granny Salford used to say, tight of lip: 'If you doubt whether to do something, there's *no* doubt!' Here I am, Clare thought, still pleasing the old lady, gone these twelve years.

She smiled to herself, standing there looking from the address card in her hand to the long low building with its herbaceous border, early mixed wallflowers, and the lawns closely cut. White paint predominated, the bright-red brickwork looking new. Bedsit land, this faded suburb hoping to be mistaken for a chunk of holiday resort. Vaguely she wondered about developers, like Clifford. She might ask him, is it a kind of subtle hysteria that changes all architectural fashions in synchrony, or do they all simply get the same magazine?

Then she remembered that Clifford was behaving oddly. Something was awry. Light-hearted chitchat was out until this strange unease left her.

She saw the listed names, went in, 'J. Crossley', on the name board. Third floor. She noted the stairs, narrow and carpeted, holes with the edges worn. Somebody was cooking, one radio getting the best of its competitors along the second landing, an elderly lady trilling along in forced vibrato.

She knocked. The door surprised her by opening quickly. Crossley stood there in slippers and dressing gown. His face looked imploded from lack of teeth.

'Come in, doctor. I saw you arrive. Grand motorcar you've got.'

She entered. 'It's my one distinction. It's my husband's.'

'Must be marvellous.' He showed her to an armchair and offered her a cup of coffee. 'Go wherever you want, day or night.'

'Among the city traffic?' She wanted no comparisons, his past and her present. 'There are days I long for public transport.'

He was pleased at her acceptance of his offer, and set an electric kettle going while she looked about. He did an apologetic sleight-of-hand for a moment, and smiled with teeth miraculously restored, full-face.

His place was basically one room, with a curtained alcove that held a shelf cooker and a sink. A closed door presumably led to his bathroom. One window, old-fashioned sash type, looked out onto the front lawn and across to a housing estate. Crossley saw her looking at the distant church.

'Wrong denomination,' he joked. 'God's little trick. They'll all go to hell, and serve them right!'

She smiled along. 'Just a little milk, please, no sugar.'

'I'm glad you're willing. Since word got round, everybody's rather shunned me. Contagious, am I?'

He asked it quite seriously. She shook her head. 'No. Some neoplasms have viral elements, but that's stretching aetiology impossibly far. Your scared friends are more in awe of the words than anything.'

He went for cups. 'It's odd, doctor, but I've always thought how atrociously bad—intrusive, accusatory even—counselling is.'

'Like what?'

'Like the sort of counselling that is so fashionable these days. Get your flat burgled by some yobs, and some counsellor comes calling with a dose of solace. Divorce, they send counsellors to say it's really all right. Lose a lottery ticket, you write to your MP demanding a public enquiry, and counsellors rush to appease your grief.'

'I'm not here for that,' Clare said quickly.

'You're clearly not in that category, and I'm glad. Stay cool.' He explained with a twinkle, 'I learned to say that at the seminary. We had some day scholars, and depended on them for slang, to face the new millennium!'

'The seminary ended, then?'

'Yes.' He sighed, stood staring at the faded lavender flock wallpaper. It was horrible; stripes on magnolia, badly stained by the cooker. 'That's our final photograph, two days before dissolution.' He smiled sadly at the word.

There were two photographs on the window wall. Clare looked about from politeness. The furniture was oldish, worn and knocked. A divan bed stood along the nearside wall. A television, a small portable radio. No plants, one vase. A single shelf of books, looking homemade and put up slightly askew. She guessed there had been no bookshelf at all when Crossley had come. He had done the best he could.

'No family photographs, you see, doctor.' Crossley shrugged, bringing the coffee and sitting opposite. 'We didn't have cameras. Autobiographies always puzzle me. Where on earth did they get childhood photographs?'

He was trying to make it easy for her. Gratefully she took the opening. 'Your family is?'

'Parents long since, I'm afraid, though I'm relieved they're spared the consequences of my cigarette addiction.' He gave a wry smile. 'My sister's not well. She has a large family, but I'm merely the quaint northern uncle who's dropped from the Christmas-card list. I phone her every so own.'

'You haven't told her?'

'Not really. Nearer the time I'll perhaps drop her eldest daughter a line.' He looked anxiously at her

84

cup. 'Is that all right? I can thin it down.'

'No, it's fine, thank you.' She showed willing, but it was the worst brew ever. 'The question I raised the other day, about looking after you.'

'This is it.' He gestured at the room, his few possessions. 'I'm paid up here, so to speak, until . . . There'll come a time, I suppose.'

'Can I ask about particular friends? You say they know your diagnosis.'

'I know them only incidentally, staircase meetings, corridor conversations. There're fourteen here, not all elderly. The council warden does a daily visit. He reports to some office or other, heaven knows why. That's about it.'

'Have you read the literature we gave you?'

It was usual to give terminal patients documents covering disposal of effects, making wills, as well as guidance with symptoms as diseases progressed. Crossley nodded.

'Yes, thank you. The hospice, though?'

'I've already notified the St Helen branch hospice—'

'I know it.' He smiled, added with a mock grimace, 'From exercising my calling. I know the senior lady there quite well. Mrs Peggs. Might I be able to go there?'

Clare spoke calmly through a wash of sympathy. 'It seems likely.'

'Thank you.' He looked about, measuring sadness. 'I shan't be terribly sorry to leave here, doctor. I'm lucky to have sheltered accommodation. But after a life of communal living, this is like community without the community. Do I sound ungrateful?'

'Not at all.' She rose casually to examine the

85

photographs. It was going so smoothly because of the old gentleman's resolve, not from anything she brought to the visit. 'Is this you when you entered there?'

The larger photograph was in a silver hanging frame. It showed some two dozen young priests in black cassocks standing behind a row of seated older clergymen. All were smiling, posed on an expansive lawn before the ornate façade of a pale building. It was not quite sepia.

'I've worn well, don't you think? Pick me out.'

'Standing, third from the left.' She looked at the next photo.

'That's the final year. The world had rolled on by. I'm not at all sure that we noticed time's passing. I rather wish we had.'

The smaller photograph showed a very different scene, though it had been taken in the same spot. The pale elegant building was scruffy. The bushes, curving from the balustraded walk to the ornamental gardens, were now gone. Two modern bungalows obtruded. The row of smiling young priests was reduced to two, the older clerics with their soprano capes and birettas only five.

She looked, looked harder. The light was not good, of course. Crossley was in the centre.

'You were the big boss, then?' she asked conversationally. It gave her the chance to look closer at the two young males.

'Bursar's the word you're looking for, doctor. The one with the money, feathering his own nest. Sorry.' He looked shamefaced as she slowly rejoined him. 'You become defensive, living so unproductively when the country's struggling to earn a living, in clover while the rest suffer, all that.'

'The seminary wound down rather, from the look of it.'

'Mmmh. We had to sell off parts here, bits there. The grounds shrank. The school couldn't stand the changes. And the age of religion is ended. Our recruitment dried.'

'That last day must have been sad. Do you keep in touch?'

Bonn, that day he'd rescued the little girl in the river, had been possibly waiting for somebody attending the hospital. Like, say, his former teacher, this sick old gentleman?

'Nothing is immutable,' Crossley said, lightening the conversation. 'Especially creaking old relics! Keep in touch? Hardly. Before, one was an epicentre. After, one became a free-floating bubble. I found it impossible to be on the lookout for other bubbles. It was,' he ended gently, 'a major transition.'

'If I could arrange the St Helen by next week, would you accept?'

'So soon? Can you?'

'I'll give it a serious try.' She drew breath, wondering if she dared raise the question of the identity of the young face she had seen in the photograph, but put it aside. If the young man had witnessed Mostern's accident it would be reassuring to know his full name and home address.

'Would you mind if I had a smoke, doctor?'

'I'm leaving, Mr Crossley.' She stood, smiling. 'There'll be some documentation. I'll send you a copy tomorrow, then we can get on.'

Crossley came with her to the door. 'Thank you for your kindness.'

She didn't turn to wave. On the drive back into

the city she thought of the pathologist. She'd phoned in about the accident victim. The autopsy was a coroner case, but the pathologist wouldn't mind her calling, especially as she had been the first doctor at the scene. It might lessen her sense of uncertainty about Leonard Mostern.

It was inconceivable that Clifford could have forgotten, when she could remember. She felt an urgent new responsibility, to explore this odd feeling about Clifford, and thought of Bonn.

CHAPTER NINE

Wallet—*a person who commissions a crime for payment.*

Grellie was by the bus station, Rack cooling his heels somewhere. Bonn cut through the queues to the stand caff, where podgy drivers had tea between runs. He felt only scorn for the inspectors, in and out of their bunko booths.

'Good day, Grellie.'

She looked up, smiled. Bonn was the only person she knew who used the old fashioned 'Good day', Australians excepted.

'All's well, Bonn.'

Grellie made room for him on the bench. She was admiring a crocodile of children winding through the ornamental gardens. They carried drawing pads, satchels. Bonn smiled, remembering satchels, buckles, the leather straps furry on the inside. When he was seven a little girl pinched his new blue cap.

Bonn genuinely did like Grellie. Only twenty-three, yet she headed the girls on Martina's strings. Who headed up each section was up to Grellie, but their power was meagre. It was as Grellie wanted, loose connections everywhere. She ran the street girls really well, had a flair for it. There were sparks between Martina and her, for no known reason. Just as Rack had to know drifts among the betting-shop slicers, the ackers, collers, foggies, skid sellers, meats, the whole 'buildings', as a syndicate's operations were called in this left-handed bit of the North, so Grellie bossed the girls. She usually gave Bonn the best and the worst, knowing she pleased him thereby.

'I'm finding it hard today, Grellie.'

'Really?' She stared. Complaint was not in Bonn's vocabulary. 'I heard you've got special favours from Martina. Not everybody makes key.'

'Martina nominated two goers.' Admittedly it was a superb concession, an all-time first. 'She's letting Rack have a studio flat for some uncle.'

'I heard.' Grellie fondled a small dog that tried to barge in. It got whistled on by its impatient owner. 'Got your third?'

Bonn replayed Grellie's words. She wasn't angling to have some boyfriend taken on. Good.

'What do you think of a pickpocket?'

Which astonished her. 'A subtle monger? Will Martina wear that?'

He sighed. 'Heaven knows, Grellie. I shall soon find out.'

'Be careful.' Inconsequentially she added, 'They're going to build a giant chess game over there for the old cocks. Plastic, not too heavy.'

'Won't they get stolen?'

'No. Rack's passing the word.' She smiled at a small lad spinning on a skateboard, clapped her hands in delight when he scooted down the path between the bushes. 'I wish I could do that, don't you, Bonn?'

He waited. There was more. Grellie didn't speak like this.

'That man you saw get run over?' She made it a question. 'Salvo was a mite close when the taxi hit.' She looked away, careful now. 'You were there.'

'Salvo? He's that gofer at the Ball Boys disco?'

'More than that. He's putting in for a goer. Angler's firm.'

Angler? Bonn conjured up a dark-haired, smooth-skinned twenty-two, natty, dapper, crazed on football, who went on a bender every time United did a cup run. But which cup? Nowadays there were as many trophies as there were sponsors. Once there'd been only The Cup, when trophies deserved capitals.

Angler had been a key for a year. His firm had suffered lately, one of Angler's goers being crippled in a bar fight over at Walkden. The goer was sacked, Martina's instant judgement. Bonn knew Angler but little. Sly? Too embroiled in clubs? But he did the business, got through the clients on time.

'Salvo do something, did he?'

'He's overspending. The girls are talking. He gambles over the top in the Rowlocks.' It was a small casino, not Martina's, in itself a warning.

'Do we know why?'

Grellie became uncomfortable. 'I'm not condemning anyone, Bonn. Salvo and Marla, she's one of mine. He's jealous. You know the Ball Boys.

It's promoting homs lately.'

Slowly he understood. 'Salvo's Marla has taken up with some girl?'

'Yes. It's Lana. Where's the harm? Five of my girls have women regulars.' She smiled half a smile. 'Martina hasn't put an embargo on.'

'That's no excuse for a money angle, Grellie.'

'Tell Salvo that.' She looked at Bonn, saw he hadn't quite caught her up. His background too restrictive, though why and where were unknown. Bonn needed looking after by somebody like herself. 'He hires out.'

No good asking to whom, not even of Grellie. What Grellie meant was, Martina didn't know this.

'How far has Angler got in replacing Ferdie?' The goer who'd got knifed, then sacked.

'Look, Bonn.' Grellie drew breath, then paused as she saw one of her girls among a crowd of football supporters, yellow scarves and bonnets. She tutted angrily. 'That Irina. If I've told her once I've told her a hundred times.'

Bonn curiously watched Irina, a slight dark girl, vivaciously mingle with the boisterous soccer fans. Grellie's orders were never to take the initiative.

'The girls say Salvo's offering gate money.'

Bribe? Bonn almost blurted it out. Nobody was stupid enough to bribe a key to be taken on as a goer. Unless there was something deeper, long-term payment beyond day-to-day body work.

'To Angler?'

He was reluctant to put Grellie on the spot, so spoke softly on.

'Is this it, Grellie? Salvo asks, but gets binned. So he starts putting in the word. Angler responds. Do this, do that, maybe something really naff.' He

91

stroked a cat that came on the bench. 'I'm only surmising.'

'More or less, Bonn.'

'Angler makes Salvo a goer, and Salvo gives him a cut? Then why hasn't it happened? Rack would have heard.'

'Angler got cold feet.'

He wanted to know what the payment would have been, but his relationship with Grellie was the most fragile plant in the city, and was not to be risked.

Had Salvo helped the accident along, for money? A man that money-hungry was dangerous to all. Bonn told Grellie of the incident with the swan, said he'd given his name as Whitmore. They argued about old film stars for a few moments before Grellie faltered.

'Bonn. If ever, you know, you wanted some girl, would you come to me?' It took her four attempts to say. She'd never been this frank. 'I'm careful. I don't go mad with the punters, nothing like that.'

'Thank you, Grellie.' He rose as Rack hove jauntily into view. 'I am grateful. There might come a time.'

'Them buses'd run cheaper on waste whisky.' Noisily Rack closed in. He wore floral zigzag braces like edelweiss-toting prancer. 'Know why?'

'Carburettors,' Bonn said, to shut him up.

'You don't know a carburettor from a carrot,' Rack gave back. 'Greater piston velocity.' Rack interdigitated his hands. 'Know why?'

Bonn gave up with a look at Grellie. 'Why?'

'Pistons are like tin cans, see? The spark plug . . .' And Rack was off, gesturing, talking, inventing ignorable crap, his alternative to thought.

'Ta for the time, Bonn,' Grellie said.

They separated, Grellie to vent anger on Irina, Rack coming with Bonn.

'No more goes,' Rack told him. 'So we pick your third goer, right?'

'Yes. A pickpocket.'

'He'll be drunk. Okay, okay,' Rack said. 'Just so you're warned.'

Today was turning out all warnings, Bonn thought.

*   *   *

'Forget it?'

Salvo almost spat the words back at Oz, who was cleaning his fucking taxi, ducking round it like somebody under fire. Oz hated flecks, saw them everywhere on his old crate.

Oz sighed. Salvo would bring it down on them both, him and his crazy temper. The yard, Oz's, behind a pub, was almost derelict. The council had forgotten it—a faltering school, rotting terraces, the frittering Fox and Stork pub, rubble and rusting springs. Keeping a motor spotless was uphill effort. Now his pal—loosely, him being mental—was going to cripple some tart.

'Salvo. Women have women friends. So? They talk, hold hands.'

'She's getting shagged.' Salvo threw a spanner. It clanged on the wall.

Oz wearily went to retrieve it. 'Have you asked her?'

Salvo gaped at the innocence. 'You think she'd tell me?' He went falsetto. 'Oh, sure, Salvo. Me and that dyke Lana's at it night and fucking day.'

Oz was fed up with Salvo's macho crap. 'You've no evidence, right? Lana's her pal. See it like that.'

Salvo paused for a train on the viaduct. Then, 'I'll do her. No woman fucks me about.'

'Don't.'

But Oz's heart wasn't in words, not when his wing mirrors were spattered with fly carcasses. Priorities were priorities.

'Switch that light on, Salvo,' Oz called from under the taxi, but the idiot was already stalking out of the slanted wooden gate.

Oz couldn't believe some people. For hours Salvo'd smoked, paced, fumed about his tart Maria, who was close with some bird Lana, who worked the hotel saunas. Okay, a couple of girls shared a wank. So?

His taxi gleamed. It ought to, after the work he'd put in cleaning it free of grease and bone fragments after Salvo'd put that fat prat under the wheels. But wheels were a problem. You took bleach, washed the tyres. Then soap, then one egg to half a gallon of water to neutralise the bleach, or the fucking tyres rotted. He'd be finished by now if Salvo hadn't stopped by to talk of killing some girlfriend.

Night coming on, and still he hadn't done. That's what comes of listening to friends. Good money, and still Salvo grumbled. It was a daft world. Nothing made sense, except his lovely machine.

He knelt to his tyres. The world was unspeakable filth, and that was a fact.

94

CHAPTER TEN

Drop—*to take or pass on stolen money or goods.*

The mortuary was at the rear of the hospital. Clare called on the off chance of seeing Dr Wallace, the taciturn old pathologist.

'Always my turn for forensic. Notice that, Dr Burtonall?'

'You haven't quite as far to go, Dr Wallace.' The standard sour joke, an aged pathologist without many years left.

He laughed at that. He still liked to smoke his pipe, but had forbidden it in Pathology. He bore his abstention like a cross.

'Is this that accident?' Clare asked.

'Mostern,' Bruno the mortuary technician said. He was an elderly refugee from some forgotten European catastrophe, chunky and weathered, never took a holiday. 'Taxi, Victoria Square. Funny.'

Funny? Clare gave him a look, but knew the reputations of mortuary attendants: being crude simply to shock, stoics with elephantine memories.

'Multiple injuries. A depressed fracture, temporal artery, did it, but take your choice.' Dr Wallace pointed with a Baird Parker scalpel. 'Remember your anatomy, young Burtonall? The temporal artery—not the biggest or hardest-walled in the world—runs in this bony depression. Such are the appalling design flaws of the Almighty, that the pterion—the temple, to one from *your* inept medical school!—is paper-thin. Hold the dry bone

95

up to the light, the damned thing's quite translucent. An idiot could have designed better.'

'Haemorrhage,' Bruno said. 'His clothes no good at the pawn shop.'

'Poor man,' Clare said.

The cadaver lay on the slab. Always running water, always drenched flagged floors, and the sort of impedimenta they never showed you in feature films. Here in the real world, it was depressingly sordid, carnage and mementoes of carnage. What was it made the living more acceptable, when all the risks and tribulations were still with them? This inert mass of damaged muscle and bone, the skin mottled and pitted ugly pebble dash, had no problems now. Those were ended. It lay there, its own solution to its problem of existence.

The pathologist saw her looking.

'Skittered along the road, no distance. Take a shufti. Bad luck, really.'

He held the calvaria up, the skull cap neatly cut and dissected away to present a shallow bowl. The grooves where the blood vessels ran were distinct.

'See this side?' He squeezed his forceps, as all pathologists did for use as an improvised pointer. 'The skull splits literally like a potato crisp, slices the artery. Always does. Wish we'd a quid for every time we'd seen that, eh, Bruno?'

'Dollars. Only one side, though.'

Dr Wallace grinned to indicate Bruno's disagreement. They'd obviously had this out before Clare arrived. 'That was the bad luck.'

'Bad luck?' Clare asked. She'd come hoping for good.

'The taxi kangarooed over him again as he lay, poor chap. Fat as hell. What's his Quertelet Index?'

96

'*Guinness Book of Records*,' Bruno said impassively, earning a chuckle.

'Come on, Bruno. He's not as fat as all that.' Dr Wallace put his head on one side, judging the cadaver. 'Thirty-two?'

'The taxi hit him twice?' Clare examined the deceased's effects, briefcase, clothes, shoes, all bagged and ready to go.

'The cabbie must have panicked.'

Or not, Clare thought. Funny.

'Compression injuries to the chest. Spleen ruptured to buggery, liver also. Death certification when the coroner says,' Wallace said primly. 'What's your interest, young visitor?'

'I attended. He was already dead when I reached him.'

'He never stood a chance.' Wallace laughed. 'Were you checking up that I'd read your scribbles? Caught out again, Bruno. She'll have it all over the hospital by coffee time.'

He started sewing up the cadaver's chest, placing the brain in the pleural cavity as usual. She watched him haul the stout twine through the skin with the triangulated hage-dorn cutting needle, decided that she wanted a word with Bruno. To temporise, she asked about his request for better facilities.

'Those stingy bastards—pardon me—on the finance sub-committee. Never noticed that hospital mortuaries are always hidden in the woods, with Venereology?' He grinned. 'I heard you declined Dr Hodding's offer of a permanent post. Pity. We'd have liked you here.'

Clare blinked. Dr Hodding had sworn her to secrecy.

'You must be loaded, the fees Hodding pays.' Dr

97

Wallace looked shrewdly from her to the wall chart, pathologists on the rotas. 'Not expecting, are we?'

The Fifer was a grandfather and could say these things. 'Not yet awhile.'

'My youngest grandbab set my books afire last night,' Wallace said reminiscently. 'How the hell did she get hold of matches? Incendiarist aged two, what tomorrow?'

The phone rang. The pathologist stripped off his gloves, stamping on the phone cue to put it on hold.

'Coroner's office,' he called over his shoulder. 'Always the wrong time.'

Bruno chuckled, took over the sewing. It's their gloved hands, Clare realised, that are so repellent. Rubber gloves underneath loose canvas bloodstained gloves, once white, to prevent undue slipping while they handled the organs. They wore wellington boots and a long plastic apron. He washed the scales noisily.

'Bruno, why funny?' She couldn't bring the words out for a moment. 'The taxi made a misuse, didn't it? The driver panicked. That's how it must have happened.'

'That's what is funny.' Bruno indicated the briefcase. It was in a plastic bag tied with a kitchen twist.

Clare went to look. 'This?'

'An executive, carrying an empty briefcase? That's very funny.'

It could have been identical to the one in her house, on the hall stand.

'How come?'

'That's what Dr Wallace said.' Bruno's expression was a picture of disgust. 'Too many books. Too much learning. You doctors don't see the obvious.'

'And what is obvious?'

'Somebody stole his real one, swapped it with this new empty thing.'

She stood there. On the wall were different histopathology sheets, investigations colour-coded. The postmortem sheet was white, name and address inked in, next of kin, family history, occupation, distribution of this report to . . . *Insert Designations Here*. Wording she'd seen countless times. She read the details painstakingly, getting colder, memorising.

'Is this complete, Bruno?' she asked the old man.

He had almost finished sewing up, tilting the head back to get to the angle of the jaw.

'In America is more difficult,' he said laconically. 'They make a scoop incision, low collars, necklines for cosmetics, put on a show. Real morticians, America.'

He shot a glance at the lists.

'The BID details? Unless you know more than Dr Wallace.'

Brought In Dead. The next of kin was a brother in Barrow-in-Furness. Marital Status: single. Offspring: Zero.

'No,' she said quickly. 'Just came from interest. Bruno, why is the briefcase . . .?' She knew that she had already asked once too often.

'Brand-new, doctor.' He pivoted the cadaver's head as she'd seen rugby players on television handle a ball. 'The price tag inside.'

'So?' she said blankly.

'So somebody switched the briefcase. He was going along okay. Some hoodlum shoved him under the wheels, does a swap, leaves him the empty new one.' Bruno laughed towards the office where Dr

Wallace was visible through the glass. 'We make up stories. Sometimes they feel right.'

She raised a smile to show how amused she was at their games, keeping themselves sane in the most macabre task on earth.

'Thanks, Bruno. Please tell Dr Wallace thanks also.'

'Funny, though, eh?' Bruno said. 'My idea.'

*   *   *

She left the hospital to drive home, but found herself taking the oddest route, through Victoria Square, by the textile museum, turning left by the Granadee TV Studios with its ectopic soap-opera set. Several street girls were standing near the bus station.

It was here that she had dropped Bonn. Did his sort simply hang about? He'd implied that client ladies telephoned—what, placed an order? Bonn, a strange nickname. She might ask—if she ever ran into him again, she amended quickly.

And drove on home, thinking all the while about Leonard Mostern, deceased, of the brand-new briefcase with its price tag still inside.

Where had she met him? Among investors in a hotel. She'd just driven past that same hotel in the circling traffic. Mostern came alone, she vaguely recalled. Wives had striven to laugh and be memorable, brittle from pink gins, wearing jewellery like contestants displaying their husbands' financial attainments.

Some politician had been guest of honour, she remembered with sudden clarity, London. Clifford had joked about Trade and Industry. Under-

Secretary sounded so mediocre but, Englishwise, was frighteningly pre-eminent. One of the man's quips came to mind: 'You must come to London and see the sights, Clifford. Well, *some* of the sights, perhaps!' to roars of in-on-it laughter. Even I'd laughed along knowingly, knowing nothing, toadying, hating to be left out, proving how pathetic we all are, Clare thought at the intersection where the accident had happened, this traffic easy if you beat the rush hour.

Mostern, though, had listened, not contributed. She remembered now that twice, not once, he'd dropped his wine glass, nervous. She'd felt sorry for the man, harshly out of breath from stoutness. And of course his chair went over with a crash after dinner. Sweaty, worried about the effect he was creating.

If she could recall so much—she was trying like mad, of course—then Clifford could do the same. Wasn't that reasonable?

Home after a slick journey, Mrs Kinsale affably in action, Clifford due back in a while, Clare bided her time. She struck after supper.

*　　　*　　　*

Clifford was in a reflective mood, Clare thought. Things must have gone well in the Exchange building. They had been talking of their wedding, her folks thin on the ground, his cohorts plenteous, both sides of the church eyeing each other across the aisle. She felt happy, truculently so, and mentioned her days on Farne Island.

'Do you think back to there a lot?'

'Often.' She smiled. He looked so content this

evening. 'It's incidentals, mostly. The shop, the village hall, the sea trickling in, then suddenly engulfing the strood road to the mainland. The monastery, of course. It's a very small place.'

'You don't have pictures.'

Playing into her hands, or maybe something linked their minds.

'Like me. Teams, university. You never go to reunions.'

'I was never unioned in the first place.' She wanted to say it lightly, but it came out too sharply. Clifford raised his eyebrows. She hurried to make amends. 'Sorry. I can't recycle. The very thought of reunions chills my spine.'

'Not even a leaving party? No send-off? Woman of mystery!'

She laughed. 'Keep that image, darling! Every woman wants that!'

Clare had made instant coffee, wanting to get down to it.

'Your old acquaintance won't be attending any more,' she said, too quick a switch but knowing she had to try.

'Acquaintance?'

'Poor man. I remember he looked so hot and dishevelled.'

He had red wine after supper now instead of whisky, which was Clare, thinking cardiac. The glass paused. 'Who're we talking of exactly?'

'Mr Mostern. It was on the radio. I was at the PM.'

'Local radio?'

'Mmmh? Who knows? I can never find the same wavelength twice. Poor man.'

'Tragic.' Hesitation, then, 'You went to the

postmortem?'

Those pauses, Clare thought in despair, tracking the conversation like a spy. She felt guilty as sin. 'Well, I was there. Quite hopeless, like I said. Has he a family?' She was treacherously innocent.

'Wife and two kids, I seem to remember.'

Longer lag phase still, for a non-existent family? Clifford was chatting, true, but looking into himself somehow, his newspaper on his lap.

'Will they be provided for?' To his blank gaze she said, 'Insurance?'

'Oh, I should imagine. It was his field.'

'Did you know him well?' As he refocused she added, 'I never know if your business acquaintances are temporaries. Mind you, there's no reason I should, is there?' She smiled brightly, overdoing it.

'No.' Clifford came smoothly back on course. 'From the start, I vowed never to bore you with work. I saw myself boring you with details about properties and exchange rates, while you screamed inside.'

'A vow of secrecy.' Clare wished her words were less ominous, heard from within.

'We both did that.' His smile was easier, reassuring. She felt stupid, worrying about fragments of a puzzle that was all in her imagination. Christ's sake, she told herself irritably in Clifford's defence, accidents do happen.

'Secrecy?' She sighed, wanting to lessen the peril in this banter. 'Come to my clinics. You'll find secrecy enough. Hullabuloo, children running amok, nurses on the sulk, tortured parents, notes scattered to the four winds.' She gave him a half-serious glance. 'Would you like to?'

'Fly on the wall?' He laughed openly. The strange

mood had passed, her interrogation ended. 'Don't forget how squeamish I am! The thought of that postmortem ... ugh!' Then he said, quite out of character, 'Was it all right?'

'All right?' she asked, concealing her dismay. 'Well, yes. The man died instantly.'

'Do you do the death certificate?'

'No. It's the coroner. When he's satisfied.'

'But it will?' He caught her apprehension and smiled. 'Just thinking insurance. So there's no delay for his family, I mean.'

'Yes, as far as I know. It seems a closed case.'

He relaxed at that. She went on, 'What I've been wanting to say, darling, is maybe we could spend more time together. Mary Fenham meets her husband Tuesdays and Thursdays. Of course, it's on her way to picking up the children, but we might meet in the midday somewhere.'

'Mary doesn't work,' he cautioned. 'And she lives for shopping, hordes of her cousins in retail.'

'You're right,' she said, stung, thinking, That's it, then. Had there never really been anything amiss, except Clifford's preoccupation with work and her own misunderstanding? Now her questions were out and settled, she felt warm towards him.

'Must we go to his funeral?' she asked on impulse. 'Perhaps I should give Mrs Mostern a call?'

'Better not, Clare. I will, tomorrow, from the office.'

She knew he wouldn't, couldn't, because there was no Mrs Mostern. She could make her own phone call tomorrow, maybe speak to Bonn.

'Oh, Clare. I forgot to tell you. Mother said she'll be phoning. She wants a chat. Seems het up about something. You know what she's like.'

Clare felt relief. *That's* what was wrong. Clifford's concern about his manipulative bitch of a mother had somehow touched Clare.

Yes, she thought, I know what she's like. And what she's het up about. Imagination could safely take a rest, with the elder Mrs Burtonall on her way to fuel troubled fires. Reproaches, reproaches, every minute.

* * *

She went out in the half light, ostensibly to take a walk. There was a coin box at the corner near the three shops. She rang Pleases Agency, Inc. A woman's controlled voice answered, quiet reassuring.

Clare didn't speak, replaced the receiver, and slowly walked home.

CHAPTER ELEVEN

Ponce—*one who supplies or touts prostitutes for hire.*

Martina felt war was overdue. She explained this to Posser, her father. Mercifully, he'd had a good night.

She found him sitting by the window waiting for the four-thirty television word quiz, reading his eternal history books. His colour looked really good. She made tea. Even with Dad, she tried to disguise her lameness. He went for the biscuits.

'Dad, I've got to clog Grellie.'

'Have you, chuckie? Saw a Jowett Javelin in

Bradshawgate. Took me back.'

'Did you, Dad?' She showed interest. 'Why not buy one? Old vintage car, go round Bowton moors, if you wrap up.'

The problem wasn't old cars. It was what if something happened to her. He'd be alone, wheezing, blue as slate, coughing up phlegm, rotting in some charity home in the tender care of idlers.

Exactly, she knew, as Posser worried for her.

'There's a choice, Dad. I can scrap it out, or sack Grellie and let Jaycee or Freshie or Reenie take over.'

'Can they run the strings?'

'One hand behind their backs.'

'And keep Grellie on how?'

'Demote her to a street stringer? Possibly, at London Road station, if she'd agree to keep clear on big race days or Cup Final.'

'She never would agree.'

'I don't want to lose her, Dad. She's a clever bitch. Cause more trouble than soft Mick, if she was let loose with a grievance.'

'She's got the girls' sentiment behind her,' Posser warned.

'That wouldn't count for much if I pulled her peg out, Dad.'

Posser sometimes forgot that Martina could be hard as nails. 'I know, love.' He made room for her in the window seat. It overlooked the small triangle of green. 'But times are past for motors now.'

'Don't talk like that, Dad.' She felt the pot, replaced its cosy, needed a minute longer. 'I can't let Grellie go on as she does.'

'Go on how?' He was curious.

Martina let her annoyance show. He was too

106

quick to question.

'It's Bonn, your favourite,' so he saw her acidity. He said nothing. 'She's developed more than a passing interest in him. I can't have it.'

'Meaning what, love?'

It was at times like this Martina wished she had an elder brother. It was unfair. The agency would go to pieces if she let it.

'Meaning she's got to back down.'

'You'll forbid her to move on Bonn?'

'Dad,' she said, patient because he wasn't a well man. 'We're in a ticklish business. Grellie runs the girl houses and the stringers. We're lucky.' She held up a hand, let her make the point. 'Grellie's excellent. The girls like her. But crossing over's not allowed. It's always hell to straighten out.'

'Crossing was all right, once,' Posser said mildly. 'Never did us any harm.'

'That was then, Dad.' Martina poured the tea, no sugar for him on doctor's orders and skimmed milk, but what happened the minute her back was turned? 'Times are new. Relationships between the girls and the goers are forbidden. You, Dad,' she said with asperity, 'forbade it.'

'Maybe we should change?'

'Nowadays it isn't a simple police payoff, a kiddie scampering to the plod's back door of a night with an envelope. That was the Dark Ages, nursery tales.'

'More's the pity, love. But you'd be surprised. The city council still takes.'

He meant recent bribes, to allow a house concession at the proposed new marina. She almost smiled. They'd had a row about that.

'We're getting off the point. Grellie must be

107

heeled.'

She was determined. Posser sighed. Grellie was a lovely girl. Twenty years younger, and half a lung more, he'd have been in there.

'Which will you do, love? Throw or blow?'

'Stamp on her fingers. Just talk,' she corrected, when he grimaced.

'Can I have another biscuit?'

She recognised the bargain. 'Yes, Dad. But no more when I've left. I've got a pudding for later. Leave space for your breath, like the doctor said.'

They talked of this and that, drifting to the old days she'd never known, when people were all-round better folk. She didn't believe his remembrances. It was transparently clear to her that Grellie would have to be put in check, so why delay? The old poem she'd had to learn at convent school, what was it now, talking about being over and all that?

*   *   *   *

From the moment Grellie entered, Martina could tell that she hadn't a clue why she'd been summoned to the Rum Romeo.

She came among the casino tables with her smiling eyes everywhere, checking the girls, seeing how they worked on the clients, scoring, dropping, promoting each other. A natural, was Grellie. Born to rule stringers galore. Very valuable.

She was petite, slender, but in Martina's opinion too heavily breasted, 'pert' she supposed was the word. Martina watched her come, feeling something near hate for the bitch. Pleasantry was an art she favoured only for its ability to deceive.

108

Grellie's dress sense proved that she used every groat of her allowance from Martina, never patronising back-street shops, the markets, never in a million years. She lived in ladyland, saved little, swung spending through major shops in Edwardian mahogany-and-crystal thoroughfares, wearing guinea-an-inch, as the local saying had it.

Grellie plunked herself opposite, miming fanning herself.

'Hello, Martina. I'm exhausted!' She leaned forward. 'See that Shani? Four weeks since I took her on, horrible in yellow, Aussie working her chit?'

Since 'I' took her on? Martina didn't pick her up, but noted it in smouldering cinders.

'Mmmh. What about her?'

'I'm bringing her in full-time, off railway work.'

'Is she that good?'

'No,' Grellie surprised her by saying. 'But she's red hot at numbers.'

'It's too soon.'

Martina saw somebody pull a five-carder at a game three tables nearer the door. Two silly women applauded. Old George was banker there, unchanging of expression, with the stupidly slick girl who called herself Abba, pretty in plum velvet with her hair piled absurdly Carolean.

Grellie digested Martina's opposition. 'Well, I think she's ready.'

'I want trust, not speed.'

It was only then that Grellie understood this was no routine peck-and-check coffee. Her expression changed, but only to surprise. Wariness would have elated Martina, given her direction, for treachery meant punishment. Grellie's expression showed only honest concern. Innocence?

109

'Is anything wrong, Martina?'

'Who's your feller, Grellie?'

'Feller?' Martina got the woman's instant hooded gaze that defied intruders. 'I take what I want from punters. I need the mood. Why?'

'I've a feeling there's something on your mind.'

'Me?' Still honest, despite those leave-my-sex-alone eyes.

Martina gave her a pulse or two, a chance to offer more, then came out with it. 'It's policy, Grellie. No crossing. You know that.'

'Who's been crossing?'

Grellie still didn't see, or was cleverer than Martina thought. 'Have you?'

The girl's cheeks coloured as she realised. 'Me? See the goers? You know the answer to that, Martina. No.'

'Can I be sure?'

'Yes. Besides, who would I . . .?' Grellie watched two floorwalkers exchange signals—shoulder hitch for too slow, pocket tap for a rush of punters on the way soon—and slowly drift on. 'You think I book Bonn, don't you?'

'It had occurred to me.'

'Then let it un-occur.' Grellie's anger was deliberate. She caught somebody's eye, smiled, waved, pooh-poohing the idea of a chat just now, tapped her wrist to say maybe later. A rather plump girl taking drinks for the fantan table, where the Cantonese girl was doing well with her graceful wand and pile of white Go buttons, waved back. 'I've never hired Bonn. Nor had him spike me. In private hours I do my own life. Those are your rules, Martina.'

Their eyes held, level.

110

'Then I needn't ask Bonn.'

A vague realisation was dawning in Grellie's gaze.

'Ask him what you like.' She spoke just short of rudeness.

'All right, Grellie. I had to ask. You understand.'

'Yes, I understand.'

All this understanding, Martina thought. But as talk shifted easily to whether Grellie could staff the new moorland motel with girls of the right sort, Martina couldn't help wondering if Grellie's annoyance hadn't been just that little bit too careful coming and a mite too extreme. For a fleeting instant Grellie had looked almost venomous.

It was important, though, to show only friendliness to Grellie. They talked of the new boutique in the main arcade that Posser had insisted on buying, against advice. Martina let Grellie win that one, agreeing not to exclude the goers from the syndicate's two hair emporiums for the whilst.

But she decided to have Grellie's sidelines watched round the clock for a couple of weeks. Akker would do that well, and what harm could it do?

*   *   *

By four Clare had finished the notes, summarised the laboratory investigations—cervical smears were problematic, because histopathologists had their tumour grades instead of cast-iron standards. She coded the follow-up cases, and said goodbye to the midwives.

She decided not to phone from the hospital's

OutPatients Department. Instead, she drove a mile, stopped near a newsagent's. These days, one phone button recalled the source's phone number, so she used her own mobile phone.

'Pleases Agency, Inc, good afternoon. May I help you?'

With a start Clare realised that she was quite unprepared. She felt her heart thump, as if she was doing something illegal. It was absurd to feel so. Wasn't she making a respectable enquiry?

'Hello? Yes, please,' she said with unnatural loudness. To her anger, she heard herself almost stammering. 'Could I ask what, ah, services you provide?'

The woman was unfazed. 'Have you ever contacted this agency before?'

'No. This is my first time.' Definite, steadying her voice.

'May I ask how you came to ring?'

'I wondered if a person called Bonn worked . . . was on your staff?'

The woman's quiet voice said, 'Might I ask why you mention that name?'

'I . . . I encountered Bonn at the scene of an accident. We both went to help, and naturally exchanged a few words.'

Clare held her breath. This was the moment. She'd been as frank as she dared.

'Then that is quite in order. The service you require?'

Another pause. Why the hell hadn't she thought, gone through this in quiet rehearsal? The girl made it easy with practised matter-of-factness.

'You do not need to be explicit, ma'am. But there is a fee, and the question of exactly when.'

'Fairly soon, if possible,' Clare found herself saying, suddenly calm as you please and determined to take one thing at a time. After all, she only wanted to ask a few questions. Could it be more mundane?

'Do you have a particular venue in mind?'

'No.' Clare was alarmed. Did they send their Bonns to your home, or what? 'I'm not exactly sure what your arrangements actually are.'

'The lady can decide whereabouts—city centre, a hotel complex perhaps. We then advise you if the place of your choice is secure.'

That hadn't crossed Clare's mind. 'Secure against what?'

'We protect our lady clients scrupulously. We can suggest a venue . . .?'

'Yes, please.'

'Some location in the city centre? There are several secure and respectable venues.'

'I think that would be all right.' As a doctor, she could visit any hotel she wanted, and claim at a pinch that she'd been called there.

'Any particular time, or day?'

Her knees were trembling, Clare realised. Yet she'd negotiated the minefield, and got there.

'Today, if possible.'

'One moment, please.' After a brief silence the woman said it would be fine. 'Does madam know the Vivante Hotel? It's in—'

'Yes, yes, I know it.' Clare wanted to ask more, but the clerk was already booking things down with professional briskness.

'One hour from now, ma'am?'

'Right. I shall . . .' Shall what, exactly? Walk in and ask where a hired man was waiting? For an insane moment Clare almost asked the girl what to wear.

'Could you give me some identification, ma'am?'

'Identification?' Clare said sharply. Wasn't the woman bragging about ultra-confidentiality a moment ago?

'I mean a name or designation by which you wish to be known. A first name is adequate, if you prefer. Not necessarily your own.'

'Clare,' Clare said stupidly before she could think that through.

'Now please give me any three-digit number, for coding. We like you to remember them.'

'Oh. Three-Nine-Five,' Clare answered, her medical student number.

'Very well, Clare Three-Nine-Five. In one hour, the person you named will be waiting in room . . . a moment, please . . . four-oh-seven.'

Clare repeated the number. 'Thank you.' She waited. Was that it?

The woman's finish was smooth, quite a patter. Clare listened. 'All future service orders will require that forename and number. Please regard it as your own personal code. Pleases Agency, Inc, runs a twenty-four-hour service, and accepts cheque cards. Standing bank orders are not advised . . .'

The prattle went on. The agency desired to please. Comments on the service were welcome. The line was open except between midnight and . . .

Clare put her phone into the glove compartment, marvelling. Why had she thought it would be any different? Men must go through this when booking some girl. Or maybe they didn't have a woman's ingrained self-criticisms? Or didn't they mind the social stigmas, was that it?

One hour! She stupidly found herself hurrying when she had time to kill.

CHAPTER TWELVE

Subtle monger—*a pickpocket.*

Rack was put out. He'd been narked a lot lately.

'Don't, Bonn. Doob's a drunk. You know what shrinks say? Winos are hooked on tits. They're all orphans. You never get a wino isn't an orphan.'

'Get Grellie and the girls to help.'

'Already pinned him.' Rack didn't give Bonn a glance. This was the shortest Bonn had ever been, doubting Rack's prowess like that.

'Before Martina changes her mind.' Bonn's joke erased his brief but wounding curtness. Martina was the oracle. You got yes, or got no.

Rack calmed down. 'You got a new go in half an hour.'

'Clare Three-Nine-Five? I know.'

Two minutes later, Bonn was admiring Doob's skill in the Butty Bar. He had seen the drama evolve scores of times. Doob never came out of his pickpocket gambit with less than a full day's dossing and grub money. It was beautiful, a whole play based on the assumption of honesty in others.

The woman would soon have her handbag stolen. She was mildly surprised that the man, Doob, sat opposite when the café was only sparsely occupied. Doob always looked the part for a steal. His hair was combed, white shirt, clean nails, quick and ready grin, but a little worried. He did the whole scene—absent-mindedly taking the woman's bread, his embarrassment remarkable. It was the whole monty—blushing apology, rushing for replacement roll and butter. The woman, so soon to be robbed, ended up laughing.

Her handbag was on an adjacent seat, safe enough. She became engrossed in Doob's tale. (Bonn's favourite was Doob's sorrow at a girlfriend's cruel expellation of her aged father. Doob couldn't live with that, it was too cruel, you see. He'd chucked her yesterday because of it.) Doob had a series of lines, each with a wry smile. Women can live without a man, but a man can't live without a woman. Then the generous smile and 'I'm hopeless, really . . .'

Big on phoney, high in skill. Bonn had first seen Doob's con in this very nosh bar, and known he was in the presence of a master. He saw Rack signal outside the window. Time was passing. He couldn't be late for this new one, Clare Three-Nine-Five.

The woman was eager to talk. They always were, after one of Doob's tales, the perfidy of young females, such disrespect of parents, liking Doob's self-deprecation, captivated by the lost-without-a-woman sentie, or the parents-deserve-*some*-consideration. The woman was married, wedding ring, looked a parent. Bonn didn't recognise Doob's scarper today, the accomplice who entered and sat with his newspaper at the next table.

The scarper left after barely tasting his coffee. Maybe he was from the bookie's round Tibb Street. He'd be doing it for a fiver, less if Doob pulled the gulp, did the steal without trouble.

It was only when Doob was exchanging addresses with the woman, wanting to take her out somewhere, art gallery, theatre, whatever, that she saw her handbag was gone. Doob did the swift burn to anger—laying it on thick this afternoon, Bonn thought. Egad! There was only one explanation, the man who'd left so swiftly! Bonn watched,

116

fascinated, Doob's superb denunciation, a whole Chaplin melodrama gestures, downright fury. Finally, the dash out to recover the lady's handbag while she fretted, helpless, explained to the bored waitress who'd seen it all a hundred times, nodding yeah, you get all sorts.

The lady became agitated, checked her watch, but no less worried than Rack at the window. The woman began to suspect the worst, looking anxiously at Bonn, should she phone the police. She'd all but given up when in came Doob. He was having difficulty breathing. Who knew what battles he'd had to fight to recover the lady's handbag from the forces of evil out there?

Typical Doob, though, his final touch: no dramatics now. He simply sat, nostrils flared for air flow, and shyly met the lady's eyes. Bonn put words into their inaudible interchange.

'Is this your handbag?' (Doob, gently.)

'Yes! Oh, thank you! Was it . . . well, *hard* to get it back?'

'Oh, you know . . .' in modest disclaimer.

'I'm so grateful.' (Swift examination of the handbag's contents.) 'Everything's still here!'

'I was just lucky . . .' etc., etc.

Doob was a quiet hero, alone worthy in this terrible city. Bonn walked out, waving to the counter lass.

Moments later Doob caught him up as he made for the hotel.

'How did you leave things?' Bonn asked, curious.

'Expressions of gratitude, mutual support should we ever meet again.'

'Nothing more tangible?'

'Is there ever?' Doob smiled. 'I've given up the
117

booze, Bonn. On my life.'

Bonn said outright, 'I've made key. Lancelot, Galahad, and you.'

'Me? Definite?' He didn't take Bonn's silence as an affront, and stuttered thanks, overwhelmed. 'Ta, Bonn.'

'Rack will say when to meet. Depends what I have on.'

He made it to 407 with eight minutes spare. Bonn felt Rack's displeasure, though he was nowhere to be seen. Best stander in the world, Rack.

Bonn settled in.

*   *   *

Clare felt almost faint, waiting in the station buffet. Which made her cross. Hadn't she been trained to meet, treat people from all walks of life? Why was she behaving like a schoolgirl entering her first dance hall?

Amid the cries of parents and the beeping of the café's space-war machines, she'd gone over her reasoning. A professional lady needed to keep abreast of social changes. It's necessary for her work, to examine Bonn's particular occupation.

And to get him to find out about an accident.

Oddly, she remembered the time she had tried a cigarette. Was this the same sense of guilt? She rose and left, passed the investment offices. The hotel was not dowdy. She vaguely knew of it, but became more doubtful as she approached. But confidence was nine-tenths of everything. She walked calmly through the foyer, seeing no one she recognised.

Four minutes to go. People were in the lounge having tea. Somebody was booking in at Reception,

118

pretty flower arrangements there. Nobody was interested, she was just one more person crossing the carpet. Her heart was pounding. She felt like ice. Her first operation came to mind, the dreadful awareness that it would be *her* scalpel that did the incision. But this? A mere social enquiry, nothing like serious surgery. She closed her mind to doubt and took the lift, alighted in a bright corridor among ferns and paintings of hunting scenes.

Arrows said this way to 410 to 440, that to 409 to 400. She stood, irresolute. What if he wasn't there? She almost turned to run, the ghastly image of herself tapping at some door while hotel guests came to stare.

Anger saved her. For heaven's *sake!* A professional lady doctor has a perfect right to engage somebody for a particular line of enquiry. If she hasn't, who has? It was perfectly above-board.

The number faced her far too soon, but delays sapped courage. She knocked. The door opened, and there was Bonn. For a moment she was amazed. The system had worked.

He stepped back, nearly smiling. She hesitated, then made herself go forward.

'I'm so glad you came.' He spoke quietly. 'Thank you.'

Not at all was her reflex, but she stopped all that.

'I was wondering what if you weren't here.' Did that sound too imperious? She stood, inspecting the room. He had recognised her.

The place was pleasant. This surprised her, though she wasn't sure what she had been expecting. A sitting room with doors off—bedroom and bathroom, she supposed. Fresh flowers in a vase of admirable plainness, couch, matching

119

armchairs, coffee table, paintings of Rivington moorland scenes. The window overlooked a small triangular green with terraced houses. Bradshawgate?

A horrid thought came unbidden, what the hotel staff would have thought had she asked for directions. Was 407 reserved for this kind of encounter? Delete that 'this kind'. She was legitimate.

'There is no other view,' Bonn remarked. 'Can I offer you a drink?'

'Drink?' She advanced hesitantly. How odd. Things hadn't occurred to her. That he would be here to welcome her, engage in social niceties. Foolishly, she wondered was everything included in the price?

'There's tea, coffee, wines, spirits.' He almost managed a smile, his look she was coming to recognise. 'Except I should warn you. I'm hopeless at cocktails.'

'In a moment, then, please.'

She sat on the couch, her action a sort of statement. This was an interview after all. The ball was in her court. She must not forget that for a single instant. She could leave at any time, just up and go.

Which meant it would be quite proper to make him explain what usually went on.

He sat on the other end of the couch, a distance away. Suddenly she panicked. There was something nebulous about him that left a space in the memory where Bonn, that person whom she'd already met twice before, should have been. He had a chameleonlike quality that she found scary. Sitting here, wooden, she worried he would suddenly assume too much, move on her, expect her to start undressing for goodness' sake, be aggressively masculine, 'Right, you've got fifty minutes, get on with it . . .' Or, even more appalling, ask her what she wanted him to do to her? She cringed inwardly, thought, My *God,* this is utterly ridiculous—

'May I call you Clare?'

So the agency functioned, its communications intact. 'Yes.' Did she sound relieved?

'Bonn is hopeless.' He grimaced. 'I made it up, not realising that it means something actually quite bad in French argot.'

'It does?' She caught his anxiety. He was asking had she known. 'I didn't know.'

'It means good for nothing. Worthless.' He seemed rueful. 'Names worry me. Choosing a new one's such an opportunity. I messed it up.'

'It was a shame,' she blurted out. 'That security man, by the river.'

Bonn really smiled. She watched, intrigued in spite of herself. It began slowly, spread until it lifted his mouth. 'He thought he recognised me. The policeman.'

'Do they all? In the city?'

'Recognise me for what I am? No.'

There. It was out, in his somewhat stilted speech. He spoke like from another world.

'Something past, I suppose.' He seemed to come to some resolution, possibly abandoning one tactic for another. She warned herself not to have any illusions about him. This was a fee-for-service contract hiring, after all.

'You could have walked by,' Clare said. 'Attracted no attention.'

'Could I?' he asked gravely. 'Given a choice, yes.'

So he had no choice but to help? 'That accident was odd, wasn't it?' she said, too quickly. This was her purpose, to find out more.

'I didn't see it, only the consequences.'

'Do you—?' She got no further. Hire out for jobs other than . . .? Any expression risked insulting him. Just for one minute she'd love to be a man, clumsily uncaring.

'Do I?' He made his question create a little amusement.

'Do you hire out for additional purposes?' Almost as bad.

'Not really. There are rules.'

'Not for anything at all?' Her dismay made him weigh her up.

'You mean while,' he became careful, 'your friend watched, that sort of thing?'

'Of course not.' This was cross-purposes. Silly to feel peevish, for no reason. 'Not related to, well, what you normally do.'

Hopeless, Dr Clare Salford Burtonall, she raged inwardly, women's euphemisms at this stage. And did she know 'normally'?

'I'm sorry. Some days I'm just so slow.' He was honestly puzzled. She thought, Is he thick?

'I want something found out. Need.'

He went still. The only creature she had seen so motionless was a heron, on a canal once, a longboat holiday in Cheshire, the bird a statue reflected in the gleam of early morning. Now it was in the clear, she found it oddly difficult to go on. 'You know the city. I suppose there would be a fee?'

'I would have to see.'

'Haven't other women . . .' Just as bad. 'Have you not been asked this before?'

122

'Sometimes. But not relating to non-sexual matters.' He shook his shoulders as if freeing himself of some encumbrance. 'Once I was asked to discover whether a lady's friend had ever hired a goer.'

'Goer.' That word. 'And did you. Had she?'

'I never disclose a lady's confidence.' In gentle reprimand. 'This "something" is unrelated, I assume.'

If he can do it, why can't I? she thought. He managed to be oblique, yet precise. Was it practice?

'Unrelated to anything, as far as I know,' she said, trying. That was better. She rose, crossed to stand opposite, demonstrating her right to remain uninfluenced. The interview was over and done with.

'Very well. I shall ask general permission. Will that be enough?'

'Not really.' She felt on surer ground. 'I must know if there will be any disclosure.'

'None from me,' Bonn said courteously.

'And your . . . what are they, bosses?' Mentors? Rulers? Pimps couldn't be right. Guv'nors, perhaps?

'One person whom I would have to see. Can I be told more?'

Clare hesitated. 'I want to find something about a recent event involving one person, locally, near the square. Once you've told me what you learn, that would be the end of it.'

'The consequences would be entirely yours.'

'All of it will be my responsibility.'

'And the police, if it came to concern them, would be . . .'

'My problem, not yours.' She became firmer the

123

more she went on.

'I'll say a provisional yes, then.' He didn't rise with her, leaned his head on a hand, half sprawled in his corner of the couch. 'The accident?'

'Yes.'

She paused, and suddenly lost it. He was waiting for some explanation, but what on earth did she want to know? It was their only point of contact, except for that aggressive swan. The taxi driver was identified, after all, hadn't made a run for it. It was all in the newspapers.

'Give me a day, maybe two. Tell me how I get word.'

'I had better ring you. Can you give me a number?'

'No.' No apology, just that. Nope. He caught her surprise. 'You will have to say.'

'Then I'll call the agency.' She found her handbag, remembered in the nick of time and said rather breathlessly, her new firmness frittered by having to fulfil her part. 'I must pay. I'm sorry, but I'm not quite sure how I go about it.'

'However you decide, Clare,' he said, rising with a man's angularity.

In near anguish at her incompetence, she left money, notes she had previously counted out, on top of the small television.

He seemed not to notice, and let her out as if she had been for afternoon tea. She walked off in a daze, still aware of the risk of being seen but now relieved and almost exhilarated. Success felt warm. One thing made her really glad. Bonn had looked at her, really *at*, instead of vaguely in her direction. She had been given his complete attention throughout. She must have been really worried,

124

deep down, about being treated as if nothing more than a passing client, spoken at instead of with.

Patients must feel the same when seeing doctors. How horrid. Her relief stemmed from Bonn's concern. *Show* of concern, perhaps? No, no pretence. Back there, Bonn had been genuine.

It was odd to realise that the concealment was all his, yet she knew more of him than he did of her. She felt it ought to be the other way round. But she would soon know more about the accident than even the police. It excited her, like the acquisition of a new and potent strength.

CHAPTER THIRTEEN

Mogga dancing—*that type of ballroom competition dancing where each couple changes their dance rhythm to a different style every few bars—usually four or six—throughout a single melody.*

Possibly something in his religious past made Bonn embarrassed to watch the dancers swirling onto the floor. Cymbals crashed, lights flickered enough to set off epileptics everywhere. The MC screamed announcements in his glitzy suit, wriggling and exultant.

'Mogga dancing!' he screeched. 'It's . . . here . . . *now*!'

Except it wasn't, yet. Bonn sat at a balcony table. The Palais Rocco lived in gloaming, its splashes of light too fleeting to give eyes a chance. They flashed, rippled, dazzled, wheeled overhead, the dancers below under attack from a celestial

125

dogfight.

'You know the rules!' the compère boomed, whipping his mike's trailing wire like a lash. 'The dancers randomly draw one dance . . . *each*!'

Please don't say *eacheroo*, Boon prayed silently, please, please.

'And I do mean . . . eacheroo!' The compère laughed inanely. Unbelievably, people at the tables applauded. 'One dance only! That's *how* many?'

'One . . . *dance*!' the audience screamed. The girls twirled their skirts, their partners waving boxer fashion as if they'd floored somebody.

'You *gad* it!'

The pseudo-American accent was obligatory. Bonn was astonished by the enthusiasm. He'd only been here a couple of times before, and wondered if Martina knew of mogga dancing's mad popularity. Spectators were rushing about the dance floor to touch their favourites for luck. One group at tables near the band had bouquets ready.

'What hap-*pens* now?' the compère bawled. The mike whistled deafeningly. 'Here's the great . . . mo*ment*!'

He marched about, generating tension.

'The couples draw a dance. Old-fashioned waltz for one luck-eeeya couple. Cha-cha-cha for another. Maybe the ga*votte* for some, who knows? And so-o-o-o *on*!'

The audience fell about. Bonn squirmed. Everybody clapped and stamped.

'Our super . . .?' The MC cupped his ear, face enraptured.

'*Dooper!*'

'Orchestra, big-band sound, everybodee, is Merry Jerry Doakes! And what do our finalists do,

126

everybodee?'

'Dance-dance-dance!' The place thundered.

'With this proviso.' The MC hunched, grim, talking with hushed intensity. 'The dancers must ex-ee-cute as many dance styles as possible before the music ends!' Tumultuous approval drowned his climax. He waved a card.

'First couple, let's hear it . . . Lancelot and Guinevere!'

To roars, Lancelot and a girl Bonn didn't recognise walked with stateliness onto the dance floor. They wore matching electric-blue costumes, shimmering with sequins.

Rack slid into the next chair. 'Put-up job.'

'The MC said it was random.'

Rack grinned. 'Dance competition's rigged worse than wrestling.'

'Lancelot has drawn'—people hushed to hear—'the tango!'

Whistles, jeers, catcalls, and boos met the announcement. Lancelot grinned and waved. Guinevere pouted.

Rack whispered as the pandemonium subsided, 'The tango is Lancelot's favourite. He'll win hands down.'

Bonn didn't know if Rack was having him on.

'Straight up. You'll see.' Rack made sure nobody could overhear. 'You have a visitor. A wannabe, Salvo.'

'Is the girl one of ours?' Bonn asked. Salvo?

Rack choked back a laugh as the old 'Blue Tango' began and Lancelot and Guinevere swept into the dance.

'Leave off, Bonn. She's a pro dancing teacher. Lancelot doesn't want to be lumbered with some scrubber all left feet.'

Bonn watched Lancelot swoop, the girl draped languidly over his arm. After a few steps they snapped into a synchronised tap-dance routine, then into the English slow waltz.

'Foxtrot!' He recognised that, been taught as a lad. Now into a mad jive, quickly abandoned for the military two-step, all to the tango strain.

'He'll get another twelve in,' Rack predicted, engrossed as he counted. 'They've to finish back on the tango, six bars min. I had to clobber this bandleader.'

All round the ballroom people were already arguing. Rack rose to shout at a nearby table. They gestured back. The band was hardly audible as the racket worsened.

'Bonn?'

He stood before their table trying to look at ease.

'Salvo,' Rack said in Bonn's ear, then stalked off to bawl insults.

Bonn went through the red plush door, Salvo following.

*   *   *

From the moment Salvo saw the one they called Bonn he guessed the interview might go bad.

He saw Bonn's stander, called Rack, a short stocky bloke who was arguing, poking people in the chest—what a prat. Salvo had seen him telling some street bint how weather came. Who'd believe such a pillock?

But this Bonn. Salvo had never seen a bloke like him.

He'd tried to get to talk to Bonn outside earlier

in the day, every city prick excited about a new key man going to recruit, but suddenly Rack had appeared from nowhere and shunted Bonn aside like he was secret fucking royalty that mustn't be bothered. For a minute Salvo wondered whether to do the noisy little nerk over, but finally swallowed his pride, put the word in while Rack talked to some goojer who'd pulled a fake-pickpocket dop in a caff.

Salvo could hardly keep his eyes off Bonn. A furlong off you noticed nothing special, really spit average. Closer, he seemed a pillock, casual, at a loose end and maybe unemployed, no home to go to. Step closer, your eyes began to stare until you wanted to look away in case somebody got the wrong idea and thought you wanted a scrap.

Cool, maybe, was it? Definitely weird. Not the sort you'd scrap with, though, because he wouldn't scrap. He'd stammer sorry, be worried he'd narked you some way. But inside his fucking head he knew things. He was like somebody sad for nothing, heartbroken for fuck all. He'd be a good mate, be there when the fucking graves opened. Not fashionable, dressed real mankie, definitely no mode. But the birds looked at him, made moves told you they wanted next, any price. It was more than fucking weird, it was sort of sick. Only time he'd felt this was seeing his dying auntie.

'I'm Salvo,' he said before he was asked.

'How do, Salvo,' Bonn said.

They stood leaning on the corridor walls. A couple of dancers pushed past. He heard Rack's voice, loudly telling somebody about music and trees, fucking lunatic. The door closed with a hiss. The noise went to a distance.

Bonn looked direct, right at you, not trying to fix

you, just seeing in. Like going in somebody's house, you look about, walls, the windows, furniture. It astonished Salvo, seeing interest. That was it! Interest! He felt important, and wondered if it was some trick.

'I heard you're key, Bonn.' Like they were friends.

Bonn, still looking round in Salvo's skull, shrugged, apologetic. Applause sounded, dancers coming off. Salvo suddenly knew, but had to go on despite. People knew he was in here, asking, birds itching to spread word, bitches.

'Say where you are, Salvo, please.'

Which felt odd, because Salvo had never been asked that, yet he knew exactly what Bonn meant. Should he tell Bonn outright what he thought of birds—including his own Marla and her queer girlfriend Lana, their giggles excluding him? He'd get laughed at, and nobody laughed at Salvo.

'I handle birds okay. Before, I did labouring, driving.'

So he started telling Bonn about his girlfriends, mentioning Marla but not by name, giving Lana some stick as he went.

'And you do like older women too, Salvo,' Bonn said. Salvo had said nothing of the kind.

'I had one or two.' Salvo's face broke into a grin. 'Holiday camp, near Skegness. It paid, until a pal got me city work.'

'It proves satisfactory,' Bonn said. Weird.

'My job's part-time. Cars, helping my mate. Oz sees me right.'

'Your pal, who is married and settled down.'

Salvo, duped by this style of talk, almost agreed before he caught himself and said no, Oz was a loner, daft about his bloody engines.

Bonn said, as the music struck up for a new couple, 'Salvo. I can't take you on, but I am grateful that you considered asking.'

'Can I go on your waiting list, Bonn?'

'I keep none, Salvo.'

Salvo was sure this Bonn admired him. 'Maybe you'd put in a word with, like, Ton Atherton or Fret Dougal? They'll listen to you. I'm dead keen.'

'They do not know me. I have nothing to do with anyone, Salvo.'

Which Salvo could not believe. 'Can I get in anywhere, Bonn?'

Somehow Salvo had calmed. He'd been ready to erupt. Instead he was calmer than in a pub. This Bonn talked it like it was, for all his sadness beyond that calm. Did Bonn ever gamble? Odds to follow, if he did.

'I do not know, Salvo. I heard rumours, but gossip is only that. You know as much as I.'

'Thanks, Bonn.'

'No, Salvo. Thank you.'

*   *   *

Clare found the two policemen waiting for her in the doctor's office. It wasn't allowed, and she withdrew to chastise Sister Bristowe.

'Be with you in a moment,' she said, heartier than she felt, beckoning the senior nurse aside. The last patients had gone from Dr Fettisham's afternoon GP surgery. It had been short and straightforward, one problem of late-onset diabetes for investigation.

'Why did you let them in, please?' she asked

Sister Bristowe, cold.

'They're police, Dr Burtonall!'

'They cannot be left unsupervised where the patients' confidential notes are kept. They have no right, and well you know it!'

'They said they're investigating a death. A man's been killed—'

'Which leaves us with responsibilities for the living, sister!'

Clare wished before she'd gone a yard that she had had a better exit line. She entered her office. The two men rose.

'I've met you before, by proxy,' she said, taking her place at the desk.

'We didn't touch a thing, Dr Burtonall,' the older man said. He wore a thick overcoat, too heavy this mild weather, and looked balding, tired. His younger colleague was a natty dresser, coloured shirt, sandy hair waved. 'This is Windsor, who's no help. He wanted to rifle your belongings. I'm called Hassall. I've heard all the name jokes, and I'm past the pilfering stage.'

He'd overheard her lambasting Sister Bristowe. Which was fine.

'Mr Hassall, Mr Windsor.' She ignored their identification cards.

'You were first medical assistance on the scene of an accident in Victoria Square, Dr Burtonall. A man died, one Leonard Mostern?'

She almost smiled. Converting statements into questions by a casual inflexion was a trick every doctor learned in embryo.

'That's so. I attended the autopsy in Morbid Anatomy.'

'Was anything unusual about the incident, Dr

Burtonall?'

Odd how names intimidate, Clare thought. You see name tricks used daily on TV talk shows, interviews. *But can't you see, Mr Blenkinsop, that . . .?* Sister Immaculata's put-down all over again. Hang on—incident, not accident?

'Dr Burtonall?' Hassall was diffident, cool. Windsor was fed up, all this routine.

'Have you any specific question, Mr Hassall? I'll try to answer.'

'Right.' He waved away his assistant's notebook. 'Can you describe exactly what you saw? Brief as you like.'

'Very well. I was driving my motor—it's a maroon Humber Supersnipe. There was traffic thrombosis, so to speak. A taxi cut in front of me, then went two cars ahead. It was all very slow, you must understand, inching forward.'

'Would you say the taxi was driving recklessly?'

'We were hardly moving.' She thought a moment. 'No, I wouldn't say so. Maybe jerkier than the rest, but it was all stop-start-stop. He was trying to get through, that's all I'd say, like everybody else.'

'Did you see anybody at the scene?'

Her throat constricted. She pretended to dwell on Hassall's question.

'Many. It was the rush hour. I remember seeing a lot of pedestrians coming from the railway and thinking, Oh heck, another swarm to block the lights.'

'Did you notice any one person?'

'The taxi driver, behaving rather stupidly— though it was possibly excusable. An elderly lady kept saying it was the victim's own fault for pushing. A middle-aged man told the cabbie to reverse, and

133

finally did it himself. The policeman.'

Hassall waited patiently, all benign. Windsor was desperate to butt in.

'You don't remember anyone else?'

'In the crowd? None in particular. Can you not be more specific?'

'The answer to that's a plain old-fashioned no, Dr Burtonall.' Hassall smiled. 'The Stockholm Effect—isn't that it? Create the answers you're after?'

'Aren't there cameras, like in the shopping precinct?'

Windsor looked away, tricked to anger. Hassall heaved a veteran's sigh. He'd been a troubled parent in his time.

'The camera by Warrington exit wasn't working. Pity, really.'

'Not nicked, but broken,' Windsor cut in, blaming everyone.

'All right, Windsor.'

Hassall held out his hand. Windsor hauled him up. Clare wondered if it was an act they'd seen on TV reruns and felt clever copying.

'Is something wrong, Mr Hassall?' she asked. Suddenly she didn't want them to leave without more explanation.

'No answer to that, doctor, even for Jack the Ripper.' He smiled, edged towards the door. 'All sodding stairs, these clinics. Thanks for your time.'

'Not at all.' She stood in the corridor to watch them go, then asked Sister Bristowe, regretting her earlier asperity, 'How long were they waiting, sister?'

'Not long, Dr Burtonall. I'm sorry about—'

'Sorry. I shouldn't have snapped. What did they ask you?'

134

'Nothing, doctor.' The nurse seemed surprised. 'It was you they wanted.'

'That's done, then, thank goodness.' Briefly she told Sister Bristowe about the accident. She'd read of it in the local paper. It didn't seem odd to her.

*   *   *

The house was more of a chalet bungalow set back in a short cul-de-sac. Rack had whizzed past—'I did a one eighty, second gear, transed up to first and slided out, four seconds!'—and said it was secure enough to post Bonn through the woman's letterbox.

'Thank you, Rack,' was all Rack got, as he stopped sedately to let Bonn off within two doors. 'Fifty minutes.'

'Here, Bonn,' Rack said, all serious. 'Know why homers are always quicker than in hotels?' And when Bonn didn't reply, 'It's because the bird is scared you'll pinch things, see? Give us a yell if, eh?'

'Certainly.' The car moved off to the end of the road.

Bonn walked along the pavement, up the path. No dogs, a small Ford before the garage. Plants tied back so as not to straggle, neat pots with begonias, reds and yellows, cleverly increasing the size of the lawn.

The door opened. A man stood there, looking almost surly.

'Are you him?'

'Hello. I believe I'm expected. Is that right?'

'You don't look like one.' The man held the door for Bonn. The only way when doing a homer was to seem routine. Humour was out.

135

'We do vary. Have you any requests, Clint?'

The man had made the booking, his woman speaking once for authenticity. Bonn's use of the man's assumed name had the right effect. The man swelled with importance.

'I want to see you start.' Clint was more assured. 'And you stay while I ask her questions after. Okay?'

Bonn detected a little uncertainty. He nodded, not quite frowning.

'You're the boss, Clint. Make sure I don't overstay.'

The woman was nervous, standing by the bedroom window. Bonn guessed that she'd tried every position in the room, finally settled for something resembling the Gainsborough Lady without the ostrich-plumed hat. She wore a dressing gown. Wedding ring, heavy cosmetics, hair freshly done.

'I told her to get ready,' he said.

'Like your hair,' Bonn said to the lady. 'Where do you go?'

She said quickly, 'I've been going to Vernon's. You know, Eltham Street? They're dear, but the girls are nice and never pester you to have different.'

'It's a risk,' Bonn agreed. 'Find a hairdresser that you like.'

'That's it.' She seemed astonished that she was actually holding a conversation, and in her bedroom.

Posser said the thing was to distract them from examining you, make sure you got that out of the way straight off, because a woman looked at a man different. A woman did it piecemeal, face, contours, hair, eyes. Then and then only—Posser's

136

expression—did they take the man in, find his motives, kindnesses, his passions. A man saw the whole woman, then only later registered her breasts, her face, maybe threw in her eyes for good measure, and all only after she'd made her total impression.

'It's harder for a woman,' Bonn said. His glance checked with Clint. Such power in that name! 'Dresses, fashions changing, colours.'

'That's so true!' she cried softly, pleased. 'And we haven't got the shops—'

'That'll do,' the husband cut in. 'There isn't all that long.' He gestured to his wife, who went obediently to the bed.

She looked at her husband. He wafted a hand, and she slipped under the bedclothes. He tutted irritably, yanked the dressing gown off her, and beckoned Bonn.

'I want it orthodox, nothing unusual.'

Bonn smiled at the woman. 'Can I call you by your name?' he asked.

'Vanessa,' she said hurriedly.

'Lovely name.'

Bonn shed his jacket, and smiled the man out of the room. Clint went, with a backward look. Bonn closed the curtains, glancing casually round the room. Two cameras, on angle supports in the top corners. It was par for the course, he thought with sorrow. They could be ignored.

He started to strip, sitting on the bed and looking at her. She sat with the sheet raised to her chin, staring. Bonn wondered how long it had been for her. The children's photographs in the hall had given little clue. Wiser not to ask.

'You know, women have it made,' he said with a

137

sigh.

'How?' Her voice was defensive.

'They look so lovely, undressing. Look at us men. Bag of frogs, however we're seen. Front or rear, top or side, we look ridiculous.'

'Not always.' She hesitated, and he looked over his shoulder at her, smilingly denying it. 'Some women aren't at all pleasing. I mean, I'm . . .'

'You are beautiful,' Bonn said, stripping off the rest of his clothes. 'So it's easy for you to say.'

'I've been on a diet since—'

He rolled under the bedclothes, and put a gentle hand on her mouth.

'You, Vanessa, are a delight. Believe it. I have the evidence of my own eyes to prove it. Say what you want.'

She had tears in her eyes. 'I don't know what to do.'

'Bonn.' He smiled. 'I'm called Bonn. I'm yours, to do what you want. This is your hour.'

'What did . . . Clint say I had to do?'

'You, Vanessa,' Bonn whispered. 'I do whatever you decide.'

Her eyes were round, staring. He placed a hand on her knee, gently moved his palm to the inner side of her thigh.

'I don't know what to say, Bonn. I never do. Is that ridiculous?'

'No, Vanessa, love. There's another way. Just close your eyes. Simply let go, Vanessa.' He was looking into her eyes along the pillow. 'Slip away. Feel the coming love. Think of yourself for once.'

'I want to tell you,' she said, lips near his ear. 'There's a camera—'

'Forget them, darling. Forget everything. Shhh . . .'

138

Bonn got in and shook his head at his stander's interrogative look.

'Cameras in the bedroom. Two that I could see.'

'They'll be camcorders on auto. Any stillers?'

'I don't know, Rack.'

''Kay.' Rack drove to a phone box.

Bonn switched on the radio, retuned, listened until Rack returned.

'What's that crap?' Rack demanded, glaring at the radio. 'Listen to something proper.' Rack filled the car with a heavy-metal band. 'Know what makes this better than that old stuff you had on, Bonn?' he asked as they drove on. 'They put codes in, like trigger words in adverts—'

'Excuse me, please, Rack. Did you obtain—?'

CHAPTER FOURTEEN

Cicisbeo — *a male paid by a female for sex plus, usually, regular companionship.*

Some goes were doomed, or dangerous. This was one. Bonn felt it the minute he stepped to meet her. Open plan, Rack called this sort of encounter, never liked them.

The woman was practically purring. Bonn was being amusing, chatting, but it was hard work. She was not at all fazed by his youth, her middle years.

The Conquistador Bed and Grill had been

unfairly described as a misplaced motorway service station. Converted from a derelict cinema, it now did for salesmen, passengers seeing a halt between London and Glasgow, and visitors to the International Free Trade Hall's concerts.

He had twice asked Rack to be sure to be on time, a sign that something felt bad. Rack was talking overloudly to the sparsely populated lounge's bar staff. It had enough mirrors. He talked his theories, but watched Bonn.

'It isn't a lot to ask,' the lady told Bonn. 'It's for somebody else.'

He'd already decided that she smiled too much, preening herself.

'Not for you?'

'Why, no!' She still wasn't in the least put out.

Comfortable, other women would have described her. Sensible shoes, makeup a little overdone with wrong colours for her complexion. Hair newly permed, handbag from a weddings-and-funerals wardrobe.

'A friend?' The commonest fiction. Bonn never minded.

'Yes. Does that matter?'

The armchairs in the lounge were not quite facing. Bonn regretted offering her coffee. It was unwise to prolong this. Being hired for her friend was one thing. Being hired to create trouble was something else entirely.

'Not at all. In fact,' he introduced carefully, 'it's commoner than you might expect. It's surprising how often people want to give a person like me as a gift, to a lady friend. Or husbands pay for it, for their wives, a celebration. Nobody would think twice if it was a present of, say, a necklace, a

140

bouquet, or a new dress, so why should pleasure be looked down on?'

'Is it really? Common, I mean.'

He talked quietly into her fascination. 'It's a new tradition.'

'How, exactly?'

This was outside the lines, Martina's phrase when she was niggled, but he played it through, the woman hired him after all. If it came to nothing it wouldn't be his fault. He was simply there until the clock ticked out. Expenditure and expense, Martina's law.

'It varies,' he said in his steady hushed voice, the one that got the best results. 'I can't disclose any details of ladies who . . . you understand.'

'Oh, certainly!' she cried softly. 'I wouldn't want it any other way!'

Which raised the question, Bonn thought, why this meeting was taking place in an open hotel lounge at this time of day.

'Confidentiality is everything.' He reflected a moment, stories he could risk. 'Some ladies want to fix up a friend.' He had the words off pat. 'You can imagine. Girls at work, having a plain friend on, a cruel joke.'

'What happens?' She was still as a stoat. Sadly, he'd guessed right.

'Strangely, I always enjoy the company of such plain ladies, even if they are hoax victims.'

'Do you tell? Own up?' She meant herself, but he was not to know this.

'I obey my instincts. Sometimes I concoct stories, so the plain lady in question can extricate herself without being embarrassed.'

'Extricate herself?' She didn't like the sound of

141

that, and lost drive.

This was it. She was into something personal, destructive. He was relieved it was the Conquistador after all, Rack talking, mirrors full of eyes.

'Well, think of the emotional scars a vulnerable lady might suffer. A cruel joke, her ashamed, her friends laughing at her.'

'Joke.' She tasted the offensive word. She'd wanted an automaton, a malevolent one at that, and got Bonn.

'Or some hurtful game.' He winced, so sad. 'Maybe somebody wanting evidence for a divorce, or to do some other lady down.' Then he smiled, at his best. 'I'm to give love. As you know, I am expensive.'

'Well, of *course!*'

'If it's for some neffie purpose . . .'

'Neffie? What's that?'

'Neffie, nefarious.' He reached for her hand, disclosing terribly clandestine secrets. 'Like, suppose some lady wanted me to see her, to damage her, by getting back to the wrong person. It wouldn't be fair.'

'Aren't you paid for that?'

Here it comes, Bonn thought in despair. What street lads called luck-fuck-buck sessions were the norm out there. But in the real goer trade two out of every seven were this kind, the client wanting you to ruin some other woman.

'For love, yes. The ideal,' he said, frankly now willing her to cut her losses and abandon her sorry plan, 'is for an attractive lady to hire me for herself.'

'And this . . . this neffie thing?'

He groaned inwardly. She would make

142

complaints, vicious ones.

'It is unacceptable. To provide evidence, disrupt her life, like that.'

'But you're hired!' She came back to it. Furious any second now.

'For you,' he said. 'I would be disappointed if it was for somebody else.'

'It's my friend.' Her lips set in a rigid line. She forced herself on. 'She isn't suitable for my Eric. She's known for doing all sorts.'

Bonn started his countdown, Rack there.

'Eric and I are real friends. We met two years after I was divorced. It was *right*. Then she came along. We go to this club.'

'You hired me for her?' He made himself utterly disappointed.

'Yes,' with non-negotiable truculence. 'I've arranged to meet her here in half an hour. She's always punctual.' She was bitter even about that.

'And you want me . . .?'

'To take her out, and . . . *do* it with her.' She swelled with rage. 'I asked most particular if I could. The telephone woman said yes.'

Thank you, Miss Rose. 'Love, could I make a suggestion?' She was a one-woman wrecking crew, focused on ruination. 'I like you.' He was so apologetic, wanting no more to do with her but acting anguish at missing the chance of serving her personally. 'It's the agency makes these rules. I'm so disappointed.'

Bonn put both hands to his cheeks, the universal sign of alarm.

'When I saw you I was really pleased—'

A crash sounded, to Bonn's huge relief. Rack was throwing glasses.

143

'One,' Rack bellowed. Crash, crash. 'Two! Three!'

'Good heavens! Quickly, darling.' Bonn stood, took the woman's arm, urging her up, out, away. 'There's a disturbance!'

'Get the frigging manager!' Rack bawled. 'I've got the wrong drink! What sort of a fucking place is this?'

'This way, love.' Bonn made a real drama, darting with her down a corridor and through the restaurant. 'The police will be here.'

'*Police?*'

Bonn got her into Quaker Street, where he disengaged.

'Please look casual, darling. Phew!' He smiled, confident and helpful. 'There'll be newspaper photographers along soon. Disturbances always bring them. You don't want to be arrested with a stranger.'

'No! No! That man started throwing, breaking things!'

'Some drunk,' Bonn intoned gravely. They walked towards the shopping mall, safe on crowded pavements. 'Football supporters, who knows?' He drew her into the multiple store. They moved among shoppers, stood at the leather-goods counter, drifted on. 'There are better places, darling. The Conquistador isn't as secluded as it might be.'

'Where?' She gathered herself, conscious of the risk she had taken.

'Where you and I could meet? Not for anyone else?' He timed the hesitation. 'You see, darling, *you* deserve pleasure. I think it's silly.'

'What's silly?' she asked sharply. 'Do you mean me?'

'No, love. Wasting your best years worrying about some other woman.' He made sure nobody could overhear. 'I'll bet you always put others first.'

'That's true. I have.'

He was at least halfway.

'Naturally, I'm disappointed, because I took to you straight away. I'm sorry about that drunk. I'll tell the agency there's no charge.' He hesitated, obviously wanting to take his leave in a more intimate way. 'I just hope that you place an order. For me. For yourself.'

He pressed her hand, and they parted. She stood a moment, not quite sure what had gone on. Bonn walked away, wringing with sweat.

Outside, Rack was sitting on the pedestrian barrier by the kerb.

'It's okay. She's heading for the Tibb Street exit. Well out of that one, eh?'

'Ta, Rack.' Bonn spoke with feeling. 'She wanted me to wreck her friend. You did excellently.'

Rack barked a laugh, shaking his head. Nobody like Bonn for adding '-ly' to words that didn't need.

'Martina's barking mad, Bonn. The bill's a fortune, and it's down to you.' To Bonn's gaze he said, guffawing so much he rolled about the pavement. 'Ted the manager's dropping an invoice.'

'Didn't you explain?'

'Me?' Rack paused to help some woman fold a push chair while she put her infant into her car. 'Me?' He walked on. 'When have I had the fucking time?' He laughed so much he could hardly get words out.

'I want to speak to Tuesday and Glazie. They on duty?'

'Now? Sure. Why?'

'Tell you later. Do I have to see Martina?'

145

'Wouldn't be in your shoes, for half Grimsby.' Rack left, laughing.

Bonn went to investigate the death of the man Leonard Mostern. Two workmen were replacing the surveillance camera at the corner of Victoria Square.

*   *   *

The Weavers Hall was a palatial remnant of the city's industrial wealth. One floor held banqueting rooms, with an elite club. No more than twenty night guests, with sitting rooms overlooking the square's shopping mall. Inside, an ornate balcony ran round the great central well of the lounge. The man on the desk, Glazebrook, was a stoutish blond bloke whose appearance belied his record. He'd done time for knifing two men over some forgotten trifle.

'Glazie,' Bonn greeted him.

The receptionist, Glazie's live-in girlfriend, Harriet—'Hattie' at your peril—moved away to defend their conversation. Bonn smiled his thanks.

'Bonn. Still no chance?' Glazie's eyes gleamed in his specs.

Bonn checked the lounge, old jewel-drop chandeliers, leather armchairs. He'd asked Glazie if they really did iron the morning papers before laying them out for breakfast, been told yes. Details fascinated Bonn.

Glazie was too eager. He had heard about the promotion. Glazie's dream was to become a goer on Martina's syndicate. He did endless favours, though Bonn would never recommend him and Glazie knew it. No AC-DC goers were wanted, and that was it. Needle histories and sexual shifts were too

146

risky these permissive times. Bonn let Glazie hope. The fiction sufficed.

'Anything, Glazie.' Bonn wanted information.

'Two football managers in one-oh-nine fiddling fixtures. Remember the Midland club relegation? Same blokes.'

'Referees again, I take it.'

'That's it.' Glazie had his facts ready. 'And some Norwegians on a scam Harriet overheard. Only buying Olympic results.'

Harriet said candidly, 'Lovely bums. Skiers, I'll bet.'

'Wait until Bonn gets me into Pleases,' Glazie said waspishly. 'That'll cost you guinea a word.'

How Glazie found things out—or Harriet, for that matter—was not Bonn's business. Time to go. Nothing about Mostern.

'Thank you, then.'

Glazie, Bonn thought, was becoming a risk. He wondered whether to see Harriet on the quiet, get as much gossip from her without Glazie. But what about payment? He couldn't service Harriet by way of fee, as Martina forbade that, though once, in Glazie's absence, Harriet'd asked Bonn outright.

He had time to cut through the alleyway to the Worcester Tea Rooms. Nothing like as elegant as they once were, with their wall tapestries. Now the elite name was a jibe, for it had become a place of bevelled mirrors where live models rotated in tableaus. Bonn was embarrassed, often felt himself go red.

With a preoccupied air he walked through the lounge to the decorative trellises, and found Tuesday. She stepped into the clerker's cubbyhole.

'Hurry, Bonn. I've only a sec to change. What?'

She was a pleasant dark girl topping twenty, thin as a lath and always out of breath from being in a desperate rush. Her father was a Barbados cricketer who'd got religion. She lived in terror of his hellfire morality.

'Just time of day, Tues, no more.'

'Bonn, I'm *late*, for heaven's sake!' She caught sight of herself in a mirror among pinups over the desk clerk's locker and started a busy primp. 'News? I never know anything! There's some insider-trading thing, French, their government owning some company, who knows? One of the girls shagged one last night, really boring, talked of that Yves Thing's finance on the wobble, French Cabinet ministers moving fortunes. Musical chairs. Well?' she demanded.

'Ah . . .' Bonn, blank, wondered, Well what?

She glared, whizzed round in the confined space. 'What do you think?'

'Oh. Lovely, Tues. Anything's superb on you.'

She pouted, knowing the effect it had. 'Some cow from the SFO, her bin going three *days*. Ever heard anything so crazy?'

'Three days.' Bonn simply spoke the words and she winced.

'I forgot! For he'n's *sake*! You make me feel *bad*, Bonn! So I forgot you a goer, is it a crime?'

'Please don't worry, Tues. Serious Fraud Office are heavy.'

'I oughta told you. I heard him outright. The SFO woman, a bitch with a long voice, y'know? Sent Jefferson's black-pepper steak *back*! The ultimate mare.'

Tuesday giggled. Jefferson, her reputed cousin and the club's comi chef, was also her lover, and a man of jubilation.

'We were doing it, y'know? Jefferson has this gadget for lissnin'. Some man called Mossern wanted out, like what man wouldn't? That Antrobus mare got teeth like a fucking carn-ee-*vore*, Bonn. So Miss SFO Bitch of the Year wants a pile to let him off, him mighty scared, Section *Two*, for fuck sakes. Jefferson has me in fits, wagging his dick at the wall.'

'Thank you, Tues.' Bonn bussed her to show her delay didn't matter, he was pleased.

She darted out squealing at her lateness. Bonn considered her news; Mossern was Mostern, most likely. And a Serious Fraud Office woman called Antrobus was supposed to be trapping other people's fingers in the till, not dipping in herself.

Reassuring to know this and that, especially bits that even Rack might not learn. The ideal was a balance. Out here, gossip gave an understanding of scale, of pace, and news, tattletales, were a lifeline. Clare Three-Nine-Five wanted the news.

He adjusted his features, and drifted to keep his appointment. Hilda, did Rack say? Martina's anger about the invoice for the Conquistador's wrecked bar would have to wait. Cheap at any price.

CHAPTER FIFTEEN

Ploddite— *a policeman, especially a uniformed constable.*

It had been drummed into Clare that the need for a confidante was a weakness, a failing likely to lead to

149

revelations that should be reserved for parents. Her one friend was Dr Agnes Ferram. They had met at Breightmet General some eighteen months before.

With Agnes, it was always light-hearted arguing, a real bonus. Her friend was from a severe northern university, not some plush ghetto of idleness—Agnes's words, to needle her—and was unrelenting in her pursuit of data, numbers, statistics. They ruled her attitudes.

'There's no question,' Clare was giving Agnes back. 'Every unit in the country must recognise that atherosclerotic renovascular disease scores high among causes of acute and chronic renal failure.'

'Figures, figures.' Her friend's mantra.

Clare could do with Agnes, but the paediatrician made these incursions into adult medicine with impunity. She proved herself right every time by adopting a punitive air—*you* can't draw a quick histogram on the cuff of your white coat showing percentage incidences, so *I'm* one up, so tough luck. Clare was thankful that she hadn't been a house doctor partnered with Agnes Ferram. It would have been intolerable.

'These ACE inhibitors have been implicated in some twenty per cent of renovascular acute cases,' Clare said, risking it.

'Some. "Some"? You mean maybe?' Agnes laughed her melodious laugh. A passing nurse smiled as she herded three toddlers and their mothers to the hospital reception area.

'And fifty per cent in chronic.'

'Possibly, or not?' Agnes taunted. 'Come back full-time, Clare. You have a responsibility to medicine. Hone your bone. Abandon suburban housewifery.'

'My heart's not in it, Agnes.' But was that true? 'It's different once you're married.'

'Wrong, Clare.' Agnes could be firm about anything. They had finished their work less than an hour late, and surrendered their lunch break. 'Doctors can't exit. Leaving is for nurses and radiographers.'

'Look, Agnes. If you're going to ask—'

Agnes had the remarkable facility of making notes, checking the enormous X-ray folders, filing complex metabolism updates, while chatting. 'Once a doctor, always. Medicine never lets go.'

Clare recognised the cause of Agnes's irascibility. It was about now that her friend needed a smoke, one of her customised secret cigarettes.

'Medical problems follow you, that's for sure,' Clare said ruefully.

Agnes appraised her. 'I *thought* you were looking peaky. Is Clifford well?'

'Fine.' Clare told her about the accident. 'I had the police along. I didn't mention something I ought. I'd met the dead man once. Some function of Clifford's.'

'Why didn't you?'

'It slipped my mind, I suppose. I'm not sure.'

'See?' Agnes checked her watch. Clare wondered if Dr Ferram had some way of neutralising smoke alarms. Her temper would sour soon. Then she would eel into the ladies' room, and smoke herself into a coughing fit. 'You shouldn't let thoughts like those haunt your pathetically narrow life.'

Clifford had left the house unbelievably early this morning, long before Mrs Kinsale had arrived. It was the sort of start he only made when leaving for the city's Ring-road Airport, but he had said

151

nothing.

'You're feeling guilty, Clare.' Agnes could be too astute sometimes.

'There's nothing wrong, Agnes. The accident was at a notorious black spot.'

'You women with husbands.'

Agnes handed Clare six sets of notes. More than a year before, Agnes had co-opted Clare to help with preliminary scans of possibly cystic-fibrotic children. Clare put them away to take home. Her friend was a crusader against the stuffed owls of Admin, who, cruising to awards for long service, packed the committees of the Regional Hospital Board. Her grievance was that Clare shirked the fight against such forces of darkness.

'We ought to have the resources,' Agnes grumbled, waiting for Clare to pack the clinical details and go. 'One in twenty with the CF genes, as far as we know. About one in four hundred couples have both parents featuring it.'

'Surveys are all right, as far as they go, Agnes.' It was old ground. 'Chromosome Seven is the pig. A hundred wonks, the gene on Seven. They should fund research on the delta-F-five-oh-eight mutation, get down to where the business bit does its stuff.'

'Hire more cleverclogs?' Agnes demanded. 'That's the modern myth, invest more in "research". Research does little except raise bureaucrats to ever snootier heights. Ivory-tower research is empire building in lucrative black-magickery. Come back to medicine, where you belong.'

'Maybe I've given up the struggle.' Clare zipped the folder, got her things.

'You've no right. We need simple things. The

country has six thousand of these patients who need looking after.'

'You're right, Agnes.' Clare felt tempted. Was this what Agnes was leading to? 'Autosomal recessives get the short end of the stick. It's as if people are somehow to blame.' She went into the corridor. 'See you, Dr Ferram.'

'Fine. And,' Agnes got in, 'tell Clifford your dark secret. He could fund me a survey unit, lend me his wife to run it!'

Clare laughed and left. It wasn't the first time Dr Ferram had given that hint.

She put her files on the old Humber's passenger seat, and sat a moment watching. Should she tell Clifford, or was that making too much?

That man she had seen behind her house on the evening of the accident came to mind. She had since inspected, actually examined, the footpath that curved towards Old Seldon church. The footpath was merely that, inadequate even for a motorcycle. In parts it was troublesome to walkers, with puddles, and a small brook undercutting the path opposite the hedge.

The man had been dark of hair, no beard or moustache in that brief glimpse, wearing a fancy jacket—tall collar, the jagged cut. And the glint of a gold earring! She felt satisfaction at the small detail, as if she had come across some clues. But what was she compiling, for heaven's sake? And why?

She had work to do on the patients' notes. She would use the city library, work through them there maybe. Then she might phone Bonn's agency. It annoyed her. She would have to pay for Bonn's time merely to ask questions that were probably pointless. But if she had hired—fanciful, but just

153

suppose—a private detective, she would have had to pay, wouldn't she?

The maroon motor started first time. She drove sedately into the city, thinking of Agnes's insistence that it was high time to return to full-time.

*   *   *

It proved to be the heaviest day since Bonn had joined. It made him recollect how he'd begun.

The girl Hilda was a sudden order, Rack racing to find Bonn watching the players in the Lagoon, a sombre place where cards were played for nods and winks, settle up elsewhere before the pubs got going.

Hilda was pert, brisk, surprisingly sure of herself in a way clients were, once they became regulars. Lovely long hair—astonishingly, a natural blonde dyed jet-black. She certainly achieved a look. It made her even more lissom, conveyed a languor you had to notice.

'You've got connections, Bonn,' she said, getting dressed.

'I have connections,' he said.

'Don't be so wary, darling.' She was all smiles, having reached the ascendancy in their forty-minute relationship. What was she, eighteen, nineteen? 'I'm good in the sack. You can testify, right? I'm educated. Get me a chance with a good working house, I'll prove my worth. Give better return than any of the slags round here. You can do it. You know the way in.'

He dressed. True, she was skilled and strove to please, with just enough sexual deviance to excite further, and had come with him laughing when he'd

154

hurled them together off the edge of sanity. Fine. But she used in-words—'houses' for brothels, 'return'—suggesting she knew trade. She'd probably once been a prostitute. Martina said once meant always.

'You don't live near, Hilda.'

'No. But I hope to.' She drew a stocking over her hand in casual inspection. Stockings, not tights. She looked at him unsmiling. 'There'd be a slice, Bonn, permanent as you like, if you'd fix it.'

'Slice' meaning an illicit backhander. This dark-dyed girl was a veteran.

'I know what syndicates do, Bonn. They take your money, money that should be yours by rights.'

This would go down brilliantly with Martina. Bonn was enveloped by sadness, at what this would lead to.

'Say where and when.' She didn't answer immediately, so she also knew the risks. He cleared his throat. 'Where can you be reached?' He added to allay suspicion, 'I can't promise, Hilda. They might, they might not. There's always plenty of girls on hope.'

'The First Drop, Affetside, room eight-six. I'll wait two days, okay?' She posed, showing off. 'You can visit me, if you like.'

'Thanks, Hilda. But they'll have contacted you by then.'

She found her shoes, four-inch heels, laughing. 'You sound like a teacher.'

'Wish I was,' he said in apology, thinking, God help you when they come knocking, Hilda. And may God forgive me.

He kissed her forehead, bringing a surprised cackle out of her. Then he went to phone. Rack intercepted him, told him of an urgent take. Hurrying to the Vivante Hotel, Rack trying to interrupt, Bonn told him about Hilda.

*   *   *

By seven that evening Bonn was ready for a rest in the Volunteer, where he appeared to read the sports news, races at Doncaster, football scandals, while watching the rain fall on the central gardens as the night drew in and the traffic shone. He liked the old Volunteer tavern, with its amber lights and dark alcoves. He saw Rack, told him of his misgivings about a second client, Nicolette, said something queer was going on. Rack said he'd let Martina know.

The Nicolette lady had sounded Italian, or maybe French? Nicolette had also been an expert lover, capable and demanding, needing a second time before she lay back replete and ready to talk. She was correct in manner, yet oddly posed more threat. He had been warned about these risks by Posser: 'Some clients who aren't really clients. They are exploiters, journalists exposing the trade, revealing all to bored readers. Others are simply trawling for information to sell to rival syndicates, the police, forces of righteousness keen to eliminate city sin.'

Two oddities in one day? One was chance, but two?

Women never ceased to surprise. When he was first made a goer, his second take was an older woman who insisted on mouth contact only, kneeling to him, leaping away in alarm when he'd reach for her breasts, and only resuming her busy fellating when he was supine. He'd been firmly

156

repulsed as she'd worked harder, squirming to a climax, concentrating on her remote passion. Only when he had spilled did she rest, lying there, untouched, purring.

She had paid by credit card, a platinum gleam from several in her expensive handbag. Wealthy, brisk as any younger woman, checking the time and saying things like, My God I'm late, all that. Parting, she had kissed him, told him she really loved his company, and departed with a gay wave. He wondered what she had gained from the encounter, why she'd even bothered to go to such expense.

The TV news came on in the saloon bar, some boxer fined, a racing driver fiddling his weight for better octanes, the usual. A man came between him and the screen, just as Bonn caught sight of Rack's face by the frosted-glass door.

'You the one they call Bonn?'

'Yes.' The crowd in the Volunteer magically thinned. 'Can I help?'

The man flashed some authority. 'Windsor. You can call me sir. Bring your drink.'

Bonn went with him to the iron table, sat in the attitude of one under interrogation. He wanted the others to know. He left his mineral water.

'Leonard Mostern. You were first on the scene. Tell me about it.'

Bonn narrated the bald details. 'I wasn't first. I didn't see what happened. A lady screamed. I saw a man tell the taxi driver to back his cab off. The cabbie was sick. The man himself reversed the cab off the dead man. There was nothing I could do.'

'Then?'

Bonn knew the technique, made a demand however vague, then criticise the answer. It got

157

people flustered, the old courtroom trick. In a way, Bonn almost enjoyed these encounters. A religious training in mediaeval rhetoric did wonders for the composure.

'Then a policeman came,' Bonn continued, 'and said piss off. A lady doctor came. The station slope was crowded.'

'Your job?' Windsor's sandy eyes looked dry, slightly inflamed, with a hating opacity. 'Be precise.'

'I am an observer for an agency.' Bonn had the party line ready. 'Precision Counts and Counting, Ltd. I survey pedestrians. Proportions of female to male shoppers, numbers of motors going through Victoria Square. Last week it was old-car registrations.'

'Who uses the information you collect?' Windsor asked.

'You'll have to ask the bureau. I just get told where and what hours.'

'Where's your information now?'

'Back there.' Bonn went to fetch the folder that had mercifully appeared underneath his newspaper. He handed it to the plod. 'Should have been in an hour ago, but I wanted to hear about the championship.'

Windsor's sandy eyes scanned the folder. He handed it back.

'What's it about?' Bonn didn't need to act to appear intrigued. 'There must've been a hundred witnesses.'

Windsor leaned forward. 'Mind your own fucking business. Precision Counts means cunts unlimited. We'll have you. I mean that.'

Bonn did a surprised stare as the man left. Rack came in after a few minutes, when the bar had

158

returned to normal.

'Thank you for the file, Rack. Glad you were on hand.'

'Martina would have killed me if I hadn't been. She wants you.'

They left together and made the Shot Pot with only minor distractions. Rack told Bonn he had a go booked for the next afternoon, Clare Three-Nine-Five, plus the councillor's wife from the Wirral. Bonn asked Rack to be by when he'd seen Martina. He had too much to think about for the minute.

The pool hall was in uproar when they arrived, the home team losing badly to Oldham. Already a couple of fights were being settled by the ponchos over wrong bets.

'Is there a right bet?' Osmund said. 'Go through, son.'

Martina was waiting in her tilted office. She was as angry as he'd ever seen her.

'Forget Hilda Two-One-Four,' she ordered without preamble. 'What about Nicolette Nine-Two-Five?'

Bonn summarised the encounter with Nicolette, sexy, post-coital talker, asking about the trade.

'To which you replied?' Martina demanded.

'Nothing to write home about. I think she's investigating us.'

'Like your Hilda? Rack said you thought Hilda Two-One-Four was wrong. How wrong, and why? A partnership?'

'Hilda is a prostitute, maybe a loater, or a stringer. She's accomplished.'

'Sussing for?'

Bonn's ideas had formed on the way over. 'Big money, new in town.'

'Nicolette was also a working girl?'

'Doubt it. She's high time, posh resorts, foreign money, not like us.'

Martina bit her lip. 'Have you any further thoughts, Bonn?'

'Very well.' He hesitated. 'Please don't have Hilda injured, Martina. A warning will be enough. Promise?'

She agreed. 'I promise. Is all well otherwise?'

'Police asked me about that accident. Hundreds of witnesses.'

She watched him go, waited a burning minute, then buzzed Osmund and told him she wanted Akker. The Burnley lad came in smiling, a pale thin form. He appeared a lazaroidal fourteen, but was twice that age. Martina told him of Hilda.

'Make it look a chance thing, Akker. Do not—repeat not—be seen.'

Akker licked his bloodless lips. 'How far do I go?'

'Something moderate, just so she'll limp.' She spoke with great calm. 'No traces, nothing to investigate. I have enough trouble.'

'Can I take Tooth?' Akker's mate, the Jamaican snooker player.

'No. Tooth can alibi you. And don't touch her—you know what I mean.'

'Hilda, room eighty-six, First Drop, Affetside. No traces, on my own.'

Martina saw the door close. Which, she thought, leaves only Nicolette.

*   *   *

The Worcester Tea Rooms consisted of two separate parts, a lounge of Edwardian tranquillity

160

where meals and teas were served to the city's affluent elite, and a kitchen filled with flame and unholy din. Bonn found Jefferson there, exuberant as ever, to suss out Clare Three-Nine-Five's mystery.

'Antrobus?' Bonn repeated the name while Jefferson almost reeled into the fish chef. 'Are you sure?'

'Am I sure? Tuesday couldn't stop giggling. I shut Tues up with my spe-shull giggle stoppa!' Jefferson slapped his thigh. 'Funny voice, that lady.'

Bonn was actually scared among the kitchen's clashing trolleys, the heat, the clang of ovens, the mass of cooks. He'd seen chefs actually clobber helpers. He had asked Jefferson to slide out into the alley. The commis chef had stared, then been convulsed when he'd realised.

'Man, *we* is normal here! It's the fuckin' *world* that's crazy!'

So they stayed in the mad carnage while Bonn asked about Mostern.

'Him and that Antrobus woman? Jeez, Bonn, she talk like a fuckin' graveyard. Bass voice like my dad, she.'

'Made you laugh, though.'

'She talkin' Section Two, that Mostern prick. They shagged, but it came to paper and money.' Jefferson paused to yell abuse across the kitchen. Jefferson laughed to his mate, watch this hero here, scared of a fucking *roast*. Bonn was desperate to get out of the place.

'Tuesday got scared—worse'n you, man! Told me to stop listenin' at the wall. That Mostern's mate come with his wife. Posh doctor, she. Your luck's in. He's inna the lounge.' Jefferson mimed taking tea,

161

very grand.

He pretended to glide on spread wings, out of the kitchen. Bonn came on the chef peering from portholed doors.

'That he, younger honk. Dunno the name.'

Bonn looked through, memorising Clifford Burtonall. 'Thanks, Jefferson.' He made to go. The chef held him.

'See the far corner, Bonn? That Antrobus, man.'

Bonn inspected the large-boned severe woman dining alone. So that was the SFO lady. 'Thank you, Jefferson. I'm indebted.'

'Hey, Bonn. You make key?' And Jefferson struck. 'Look, man. I know you, never ask no favours, right?'

Well, maybe. A door went as they made the kitchen. Jefferson saw something wrong, leapt through screaming abuse at a lass about to decant some unspeakable fluid. The girl staggered away into the steam.

Jefferson resumed conversationally, 'My friend, a Kingston 'laat, you seed him, Gyearbourn? Plays blower, Goon Hoppa, them studios?'

'Tall trumpeter.'

'That's Gyearbourn.' The chef had to keep pushing Bonn out of the way of waiters.

'You need Askey and his paper team for Mostern. Gyearbourn wants *in*. Y'know? Give him a tryout. He's my fren.'

'No tryouts, Jefferson. But I'll see him, he finds me.'

'Thanks, man. Let him down light. Mention me, the good mouth.'

Bonn spent a few minutes recovering from Jefferson's kitchen. Then he caught Disco, the

162

suavely quiet dong domo at the reception counter, and went through the club registers, noting times, dates, who. He reached the pavement in Victoria Square, where the team of bikers were talking revs. Askey was on pavement singing.

'Askey.'

The diminutive man resembled the long-dead comedian, large head on a frail body, black hair with a calf-lick, spectacles big enough for the night sky.

'Yes, Bonn.' Askey bounced to his feet, quivering to carry messages.

Bonn tilted his head, walk along. Askey fell in. 'Things are bad, Bonn. I need dosh.'

Askey lived with a frail elder sister in Pendleton. He only went home once a week, to see she was all right and neighbours were still doing her shopping.

'That accident was terrible luck, Askey.'

Askey snorted with derision. 'Police couldn't tell the frigging time, Bonn. Salvo did the shuff with the case.'

'I hadn't heard that. They said a taxi.'

'Ponce, he is, double switcher. Has this bird Marla, quite nice.'

The little messenger eyed Bonn, eyes bottled in those great specs. Bonn believed Askey only wore them for effect. But what effect exactly?

'You need more messages, Askey, I think.'

Askey had never seen Bonn nod before, and watched the grave process with admiration, at once a promise and a reward. He felt rescued.

'Ta, Bonn. I'll get agate. Oz did the wheels, heavily built feller, uses a girl in Waterloo Street, on Grellie's string.'

'Thank you, Askey, for your assistance.'

163

The messenger grinned, years falling off him. He could only be twenty-eight, behaved a tired fifty. Bonn was saddened, the world too worn by anxieties. Askey should have a parcel of children, a wife, hobbies.

'I'll send a slider into the Ball Boys, where Salvo's lass goes. Pell's the best. He won't charge, get word in an hour.'

'Do I know Pell?' Clare Three-Nine-Five's task was more complicated. Too many asking the same thing made the wrong noise.

'He's given up night walks.' Pell, Bonn remembered now, the cat burglar, a slider who could enter anywhere without trace. 'Just alters tom—jewellery and such—in his brother's workshop.'

'Fine, Askey. Soon, please. I'll see that you're used more. One thing.' They stood at the corner by the Volunteer. The traffic was crowding the lights and damming back pedestrians. 'If it turns out to be the real mother—the genuine truth—you give me it all, and point Salvo out, please.'

Bonn wanted no mistakes.

'How is your sister?'

'Still got her bad legs. It's the stairs, see.'

Bonn said to pass on his regards, and watched Askey eel off towards the Triple Racer, where the bikers and the skateboard messengers hung out, cramming the pavement with their gadgetry, motorcycles, stacks of leather boxes.

'Bonn?'

He found himself looking almost vertically up at Gyearbourn, trumpet man of the Goon Hopper. It felt coming on to rain.

'Jefferson told me you'll listen a sec, you making

164

key and all.'

'Would you care for a cuppa, Gyearbourn? Out of the rain.'

'Bonn, man. Why you so fuckin' po-*lite*? It get a man down, y'know? Done wanna tell yo business, but you'll get no takers, that polite.'

'Thank you, Gyearbourn. I shall heed your advice.'

'Jeez, Bonn. You never say fuck off, once in a while?'

'No, Gyearbourn.' They went for tea, chatting.

CHAPTER SIXTEEN

String—*an organised group of prostitutes, esp. female.*

The name Wigan Pier was perpetuated buffoonery, for Wigan was miles from the sea, and even in industry's heyday was served by a network of canals. Except now the joke was on the jokers, for Wigan Pier had become, in a witty tour de force, exhibitions, restaurants, a centre of unmatched excellence. It was also the fashionable place to dine out.

Clare had chosen it as a neutral place to meet Clifford. Not without guilt, the sense of betraying a surely innocent husband. Unfair, she scolded. 'Neutral' suggested a treaty between warring factions, not a meeting of loving spouses.

Clifford seemed in high spirits. They chatted, watching the school parties, children among the museum sets, and all the young actors and actresses

165

cavorting in eighteenth-century costume, hearing the laughter, the muted chug of engines. The sun did its stuff, shone on Clare's lunch table as she chose her moment. Salmon, a curry with rice, vegetables just undercooked, thank God, white wine diluted to extinction by soda, and the weather unseasonably warmish, a loving, loved husband.

'The police came to see me, Clifford.' She didn't give him time.

'The police? That child in social care?'

She had mentioned having to go into the Wirral, a little girl with a drug-addict mother.

'No. The accident, that Leonard Mostern, insurance or something?'

'Mmmh? Yes, I remember.'

Too studied, her mind shrieked. How many fatal accidents did she mention in one week, for heaven's sake? She smiled the waitress to refill his glass.

'Some policeman called Hassall and a callow tempest called Windsor trying to show off in a rather shop-soiled way. They asked who was there. Can you imagine?' Her trill of disbelief fell short of a laugh. 'The London express was in. People were pouring out!'

'What were they looking for?' he asked.

Would an innocent husband ask exactly that? She was being unfair. After all Mostern was Clifford's business acquaintance.

'Heaven alone knows!' She smiled at two children in linked push chairs, probably twins. Their older sister, maybe six or seven, pushed them vigorously, the father vigilant between them and the canal, the mother telling him a tale of scandalous prices. 'You'd think they'd have better things to do.'

'Than ask about what? Who?'

166

Which gave her the chance to defuse the conversation. 'Don't you start!' she said, with proper exasperation. 'Bad enough having them! Their constable had told them about some young man.' For the first time, she described the irate man who'd angrily urged the taxi driver to back the cab off Mostern, then did it himself.

'Did they say what they were looking for?'

'No.' Her smile was now concealment. 'And I didn't want to keep them from their social club, or wherever it is police go.'

Clifford chuckled at that. 'It's a pity they bothered you.'

'Isn't it.' Clare felt a kind of grief, but made herself say it outright. 'Is there something wrong, darling? You looked so worried when I mentioned it.'

'What's this "it"?'

Reasonable, first define your terms. She thought a moment, conscious of breaking new ground.

'Leonard Mostern's death.' He didn't answer. 'I thought you looked shocked.' Still nothing back. 'Was he close? I remember him. He doesn't have a family, no next-of-kin. The police,' she invented quietly, 'said so, I think.' A get-out clause, in case he challenged her on it later.

He nodded, eyes on the opposite bank, a festive fairground mood to the whole Pier concourse. The sun chose that instant to go in.

'I didn't know him well, Clare, just business. Some days I see dozens.'

'Have the police been to see you?'

He stared at her in alarm. 'No! Did they mention me?'

'Certainly not.' If only she hadn't made the

negative so defiant, failed to think this out. Was she an accomplice now? It felt like it.

'Darling.' Her hand went to his. To anyone watching, it might have been a tender anniversary moment. 'Is there anything I can do? I've read of people absconding with office records. There was that investment bank, wasn't there? Is it like that?'

'No. It's caused ripples in other companies, nothing serious.'

'Thank goodness! I was starting to worry.'

'It'll blow over. After a person's gone, it's a dickens of a job unravelling their data. Reports start flying about. They can go on for ever.'

'If there's anything I can do, darling, you will say?'

He smiled at that, really smiled. 'Do you think I wouldn't come screaming?' he said. 'My one and always ally!'

They drank to that, then Clare told him about Agnes Ferram's insistence that she return to medicine full-time.

'I'm not sure I want to,' she confessed.

Clifford looked askance. 'Would there be advantages to you at all?'

'You don't like the idea.' She was pleased. 'I've had part-time offers.' Deliberately she became coquettish, joking her way out of that mistrustful feeling, making up to him.

'One benefit is that you aren't embroiled in the city's innards,' he said. 'It's a relief. Everybody I talk to all day long is in finance, analysing subplots.'

'Then I'll not go back full-time, darling. Every doctor I work with knows what's best for me—except me!'

They toasted their resolve. Clare hadn't yet

broached the question of the briefcase, or of the man who she might —*might*— have seen among the pedestrians in that freeze-frame instant memory at the scene of the accident, but who, she tried not to remember, she had seen over her garden hedge.

But she had done the loyal thing, talked it over with her handsome husband the way a loving wife should. Now she could tie up those loose ends with a clear conscience.

*   *   *

Martina was in her worst possible mood when Bonn arrived at the control office. Bonn disliked the name for its pretension, sounding like Bomber Command Operations when it was only elderly ladies on a switchboard over the Pilot Ship Casino. Martina was checking a recorded voice. Miss Rose was in floods of tears. She'd been a headmistress, and did not wilt easily.

'It's a Dorie, with a false number. She gave Seven-Seven-One.'

All double digits were out. It was a foray, God knew where from. Newspapers, drunken office jokers, who knew? After Hilda and Nicolette, this was one too many. Bonn listened to the voice.

'It's that broadcaster, Verity Hopeness,' he said. 'Relinquish it to me.'

'Relinquish?' Martina snapped. 'What is this, Certificate English? To? For? Why?'

'I shall solve any problems that might arise.'

Martina thought, I need Rack here. Bonn talked like a fairground guess-your-weight machine. He took the cassette, hesitated.

'A lady client wants to hire me for a job, Martina.

169

Nothing sexual.'

'What else can you do?' She was aware of her rudeness.

Bonn seemed not to notice. 'It's to find out about some accident. Clare Three-Nine-Five. One hiring so far, just to ask.'

Martina stared. Unusual, but not unknown, that a client wanted only talk.

'Very well. Don't become a private detective service, though.'

'Thank you. And I have appointed Doob for my third goer.'

As he turned to leave she said, rage thickening her throat, 'I wouldn't have let Rack hurt this Verity. I want you to know that.'

He nodded, waved to Miss Rose. Martina slammed the door after him and sharply told Miss Rose to make up her lost time at the end of her shift. Bonn must have got wind of her orders to Akker about that Hilda.

Time she spoke with Dad about her future. It was overdue.

CHAPTER SEVENTEEN

Straightener—*an illegal disciplining, by financial or physical punishment, of one who transgresses.*

Akker waited in the dark. Moorside blackness was rotten stuff, miles from anywhere. Only ten o'clock, and so remote he was sick from isolation.

He was impatient. His mates told him that impatience buggered things up. But what was a

170

bloke to do? Do the girl, then scarper.

This Hilda bird was shagging her way through a whole run of blokes. Three so far, trolled up from the saloon bar. He'd sussed her game. She allowed herself fifteen minutes after each fuck before clipping down to the taproom to hook a new shag, ten minutes flat. Clockwork. Why didn't Martina hire her for Grellie's strings? That wasn't his problem.

The bedrooms at the First Drop were arranged along a balcony, wooden steps outside. Cars came and went, the car park lit by two burning torches. Doors slammed, women shrieked, blokes laughed. Music sounded, a right hubbub. A posh restaurant glowed with golden light. Akker waited.

The bloke emerged, about time, called something back. Christ, he looked tired, staggered down the steps. For a moment Akker was tempted. This Hilda must be rattling good to drain a man like that in, what, twenty minutes top whack. But Martina had to be reckoned with.

He let the bloke vanish into the bar, then walked up the steps and along the dark balcony. He knocked. Nobody followed. No answer.

Akker knew she was in there. He did the lock— old heavyweight, the sort a babby could do with a buttonhook—and slipped inside. He stood blinded by the light. She was in the bathroom, running water, something clacking into the sink. He looked for a weapon, to his disgust found nothing.

The bathroom door was closed, not locked. For a second he paused, then shoved the door, and there she was sitting on the loo. Akker thought her surprisingly young. She gazed at him in astonishment, the pair of them frozen.

171

No good hanging about. She was drawing breath to speak, scream for somebody, so he leaned forward and fisted her head to keep her quiet, then raised her left leg and stamped down on her kneecap.

He had to do it twice before he heard the proper snap, after which it was safe to let it flop. She cried out, even though she should have been unconscious, because he'd given her a hefty thump.

Her arm he pulled out, straightened and broke it with a thrust downwards over the side of the bath. Its sound was sharper, better.

A moment later he was in her bedroom. Birds had so many clothes, beyond fucking belief. Jesus, but it was tempting. Who'd know, if he nicked a few quid?

Except computers checked banknotes, bankers too idle to read the fucking things, lazy gits. He'd used household gloves. And Rack, Martina's chief stander, was a fucking animal. He ended up not taking a penny, a fucking saint, which was a pig.

He switched off the lights and left as Hilda started to whine away in there. Untouched! He wasn't seen. Martina'd be pleased.

An hour later he was in the Shot Pot, challenging Toothie to a game, being noticed, there half the night anybody asked. But they wouldn't.

*   *   *

'Mr Burtonall? How do. Hassall, rhymes with tassle.'

Hassall entered Clifford's office acting weary. Windsor introduced himself formally. Clifford was easy, willing, had Beatrice in with her pencil and pad.

'Just that Mostern accident, Mr Burtonall. Needn't detain you long. He was an associate of yours?'

Tautology, Clifford's mind scored. 'Detain'? He wasn't being detained, but delayed. 'Long' meant these police defined *how* long, for their own purposes. Which purposes, exactly?

'Yes. We need an insurance broker now and then.'

'Always Mostern, was it, this brokerage?'

Brokerage, not broker? This Hassall had some terms off pat.

'We make several compete, to get the best value.' He shrugged, forced into disclosing the ruthlessness of commerce. 'We shop around. If some pal can't give us better rates we let him go. That's business.'

'Pal?' Windsor barked while the older man sighed and glanced apologetically at Beatrice, scribbling away. 'Mostern was a "pal" of yours?'

'No. Just knew him.' Clifford expressed surprise at being taken up on this. 'Beatrice, how many brokers do we use?'

The girls in the outer office kept glancing, thrilled by the police visit.

'Seventeen, Mr Burtonall, fourteen different firms, six in the city.'

Clifford spread his hands. 'Mostern was one of many.'

'Who had been here just before his accident,' Hassall said casually. 'Had a new briefcase, nowt in. Did he take anything.'

'Don't think so, Mr Hassall. Beatrice?'

'No, sir. The canal-marina contracts were to be couriered to Mr Mostern the day following. We

173

heard of the accident, and instead contacted'—she flipped pages—'a Mr Rohan, of Bettany and Barclay's. Who,' she added in prim disapproval, 'has yet to appear.'

'Did he have his briefcase with him?' Windsor demanded.

Clifford thought. 'I can't remember. Do you, Beatrice?'

'Yes, Mr Burtonall. He took it in with him.'

'New, old?' Hassall got in before Windsor did one of his shouts.

'His usual, I think,' Beatrice said. 'Brown, a bit frayed, heavy.'

The rest was all repetitious and inconsequential. Clifford showed them out after more of Hassall's platitudes. He mentioned about his wife, Clare, at the accident. Hassall told Clifford about the video camcorder's failure, a pity.

Clifford thanked Beatrice and told her, as casually as he could, to file her notes of the meeting. He faffed about the office for a while, gave the police time to clear off, then drove to the sports ground.

*   *   *

Clifford met Goldoni hours before kickoff. They walked among straggles of fans to stand beneath the awning of a food stall. Goldoni accepted a cola and a rock cake with distaste. He hated the cold damp weather, the pokey little flat found for him by some young lout of a relative. He hated this weak man.

'I take it your action was necessary?'

'Yes.' Clifford mouthed the word because a tannoy suddenly started up, blaring news of the

174

coming evening match. Girls were among the drifts of spectators, scarves, hats, red-and-white favours. Boisterous fans charged past, arms linked.

'So defensive?' Goldoni asked. 'Clifford, if your action was essential then you did the right thing.'

'He was grassing. I had to get the documents back. It's down as an accident.'

Goldoni sighed. It was the same old carousel. 'A miracle of organisation, Clifford.' He detected the instant sharpness in Burtonall's glance. Weak, but no fool, so patronise at your peril. 'You have earned my thanks.' He let the other find his ease, the doom of weak men. 'You met your friends?'

'It's set. Half of a per cent's needed by tomorrow.'

Goldoni pursed his lips. 'Formidably more than we agreed. Such a bribe!'

'Can it be done, Gianni?'

So weak, this example of a declining race. Goldoni looked round for somewhere to throw the inedible cake. What digestions! Had they truly once ruled the world?

'I've given commitments.'

A coach arrived, spilling cheering fans. They looked so forlorn in the wide macadam spaces.

'Then I had better guarantee the transaction!'

'You will?' The weak man's eyes shone with gratitude. 'Thank you.'

Goldoni timed his remark. 'A private angle, Clifford. I want a personal investment. The city has a small syndicate, a casino here, snooker hall there, girl strings, an escort service. Not much.'

Clifford's lips were dry. 'A private one, Gianni?'

Men without balls even think sterile, Goldoni thought with contempt.

'You and I will finance a buy-out. I will be your sleeping partner.'

Clifford dithered. 'What if they won't sell?'

Goldoni smiled. 'They will. You will see to it. I shall give you details in the car. Shall we go? You know what will do the killing, Clifford?' he asked mischievously as they left among the thickening crowd.

'Killing?' Clifford thought he had misheard, but it was only his visitor amusing himself.

'It's your catering. International chefs have voted your cuisine to be Europe's most interesting, yet you serve crap. Is this civilisation?'

Clifford did not answer the jibe. He had to find Salvo, check that nothing was about to jeopardise Goldoni's new sideline.

CHAPTER EIGHTEEN

Slider—*a cat burglar, who burgles without trace.*

Bonn had asked for the end room of the longest corridor in the Vivante Hotel. Rack said where the hell was a stander to wait? You could see into the next *county*, the stairwells noisy as a race crowd, people up and down in streams. Bonn typically said nothing, assumed it would all be as he said.

The councillor's wife from the Wirral arrived pretending outrage. Bonn knew it was nothing of the kind, silently helped her off with her coat. Pouting was never angry, he knew, oil and water. It merely invited attention for the lady who'd complained volubly to the control office. Martina

176

ordered this go, so it was unavoidable.

Exactly how absolute *was* unavoidable, when a troublesome client had insisted on having Bonn this evening or she'd sue, bring the world tumbling about Martina's ears? Hysterical overstatement, true, but Martina had said, quote, the cow's threats had to be taken into account so Bonn must get the syndicate out of the scrape, unquote. The scrape that he, Bonn, had got them into, thank you.

Rack brought the 'unavoidable' message. Which was all very well for Rack, that cosmic black hole of non-information. Bonn was here in pole position, confronting this woman's vengeance. She was an attractive fortyish.

'You were angry,' she said, her eyes enlivened as she accepted the sherry she'd brusquely demanded.

So far neither was even sparring. Bonn guessed that sex would come slowly. He knew to go with her, not dictate.

'Angry.'

Considering the word. He'd somehow learned, osmosis his teacher, that women liked repetition. They saw it as a kind of confirmation. And they liked opinions firm, nothing conjectural. Appetites were, after all, their stock in trade. Babes, men, hungers were the stuff of life, what they coped with by joy, rewards, duties.

'I can tell,' she told him, quite jaunty.

'All right, then.' He injected a smattering of truculent don't care.

'Say it.' Her eyes watched, bright.

'Very well.' Agree, agree. He said, all reluctance, 'Yes, I was angry.'

'Were you punished?' When he nodded. 'How?'

She bade him sit beside her. He made sure the

length of the sofa was between them. She budged closer, turning to inspect, full of curiosity.

The silence became a cue. She was within reach, staring into his eyes, devouring his expression.

This was new to him. He'd had a client once, Dorsetshire or somewhere, who'd quite blithely come in and stripped, lain down naked, brisk as you please, told him to beat her. Startled, he had obeyed, delivered several smacks, gentle and somewhat trusting, wanting her to say that would do. She'd been disgruntled, risen after his gentle blows, wanted nothing else, and left in disgust without paying. She too had complained to Martina, drawn comparisons between 'the gigolo'—using the taboo term openly—and a 'worthwhile' service in Birmingham where they 'knew how to'. Bonn was sent to discuss the Dorsetshire lady with Posser, who'd put him straight. Bonn used Posser's advice now.

'Punish me? I'm not allowed to say.' Look away, assume inner torture.

'Did it hurt?'

The councillor's wife—was she really such?—was thrilled. Bonn said nothing. If the client said she was a councillor's wife, then she was.

So, 'Yes, it hurt.'

'Bad?' She accused, 'You don't want to talk about it, do you?'

'I can't.' Nostrils flared, pent-up anger simmering in there.

'I did it. I *caused* it, Bonn.' She was excited, provoking.

He turned and fixed her, cold. Her jacket had slipped from her shoulders. Her blouse was buttoned. He had to control his quickening breath

178

to keep himself steady. She was exhilarated.

Only two ways to go. The crux, in Posser's words. Transmute into action, or shunt swiftly into different emotions. Social chitchat had a million alternates, but here? Here it was act or leave the arena. And guess right.

She edged closer. 'I had bruises, Bonn, from last time. You made them.'

'I was careful.'

'I told you what to do with me. Then blamed you.'

'That was bad,' Bonn said.

'I sent you the flowers. Did you guess it was me?'

He recognised taunt in her huskiness. She seemed to melt before his eyes, almost sprawling onto him. He resisted the urge to clear off. But what then, blue murder, and more complaints? Act or leave the arena, but guess right.

'You had no right.'

'I know, Bonn. But I had to.'

'It got me into more trouble, all those bouquets.'

'I meant to, Bonn.' A hint of yearning in there? 'I did wrong.'

Sadness moved him. But there was no time for that.

A month earlier, a woman from Strasbourg had wanted to take him into the Lake District, and had been astonished to be told it wasn't on. She'd been furious, she had the money, proved it in three currencies for heaven's sake, *she* had hired *him* and he'd better not forget it.

The average lady, he thought, looking at the Wirral wife, kept to the one hour, two at the outside. Posser said they planned orthodox sex by the clock. That, and having a hair do, which necessarily stuck at one hour or, perm time, ninety

179

minutes. Women thought the hour was defined by the Almighty, another Posser dictum, instead of a candle cut by Alfred the Great any old how.

'Why have you gone quiet, Bonn?' she asked. Her mouth trembled.

'It simply isn't good enough,' Bonn said, tight. He clicked his fingers once. Her eyes darted down.

'What are you going to do?'

'I won't put up with it.' Posser advised contradiction, in the right place.

Her hand fumbled at her blouse. She glanced as if looking for a way out. Bonn remembered the first time, her casual demand for hurt, and took strength from it.

'No. I can't stay. I'm meeting somebody.'

In that instant Bonn decided to act, not leave the arena.

'There's no escape, not for a bad girl like you.'

'My husband will be here soon.'

He ignored that. 'Do you really think there's any excuse for being bad?'

She tried to laugh, scale things down. 'Good heavens!' she cried softly. 'Sin? What I did can hardly—'

'Stop it. I haven't said you can speak.' He reached for her blouse, took hold of the flimsy material, and savagely ripped it downwards. 'Get stripped.'

Frantically she started to obey, shoes off with that quick effortless grace women did, the hurried problem with the skirt waist.

'Do I have to get my toy?' she asked, anxious.

Toy? 'No.' He cuffed her so she almost fell over, righted herself. 'Last time was only playing. I have to give you what you deserve.'

'Bonn, darling, I think I'd—'

180

Never change an act, Posser's law. She almost undressed, Bonn quite still.

'What do I have to do?'

She went into the bedroom, pulled the bedclothes away, sat upright looking in terror that was nearly pretence.

Bonn moved slowly after, undid his jacket, then fed his belt out to its full length. The buckle clinked mutedly. She groaned, her tongue wetting her lips.

'I told you to stay silent.'

'You didn't! You didn't say anything about—'

He lashed the bed with his belt, making her squeal. 'Don't argue. You'll wish you'd never told those lies.'

She was weeping. 'It's my fault. I know, I know.'

He hurled his clothes away, flung the bedclothes off her, shoved her onto her face, kicking her legs straight and deliberately pausing after each swing of his arm. He used the belt's free end, hitting her gently in spite of her hoarse exhortations and keeping the buckle in his palm.

She wept, groaned, laughed once aloud even, her moans rising after each blow. When she was whealed and red he straddled her hot frame and gently entered her, letting the act take over.

Almost instantaneously she started to move with him, reaching back to pull him deeper.

Later, as she left, embracing him at the door while she made him promise to reserve time for her in exactly a week's time, he reflected that Posser was correct. Guess right was the rule for all life's choices.

*   *   *

181

Dr Ferram had left a message for Clare when she reached the small surgery at Westhoughton, please to ring urgently.

Agnes was even more peremptory than usual. 'Clare? Get over here and sign on the dotted line. You've got a plum position itching for you to fill it. No. Something you could do standing on your head.'

'Look, Agnes. I have the GP's surgery here.'

'Cardiac, male, preventative care of. Interested, or do I go and eat humble pie with people I loathe?'

Clare said, troubled, 'I've not answered any offers—'

'But I have, dear,' Agnes told her sweetly. 'I forged your name. I have their lies—and mine, incidentally—right here in my hand.'

'Agnes, what on earth have you done?'

'I've told them you will commence work at Farnworth General in two days.'

'You have no right—'

'See you in the staff canteen, my dear. Where the soup is a foul sea of *Klebsiella*, though of relatively low pathogenicity—'

Clare disconnected, and belled the first patient. She was in no mood to show compassion towards an elderly post-hysterectomy lady, but forced herself to postpone her annoyance at her friend's presumption.

She let the nurse bring the patient in, and started scanning the notes, concentrating. The problem of that desirable cardiac post could wait until afterwards, when she would find reasons for refusal, Dr Ferram or no Dr Ferram.

*   *   *

Bonn reached the Vallance Carvery after getting Askey's message from Grellie and found Pell the slider, ex-burglar, now mender of stolen jewellery in his brother's workshop. Bonn hardly knew the man, found him difficult to assess as they found a place to sit. He felt worn out.

So far today he'd had two clients, both pleasant, one a little worried, but those were often easiest. The second was irritated at learning he would not be able to spend time on a cruise. She vowed to ring the control lady. 'I'll get round that little problem, darling,' she'd told him, bright with confidence. 'I always do!' Next time would be her fourth time with Bonn.

'Pell,' he told the ex-burglar, 'pass word I've asked Osmund to use Askey for snooker messages.'

'Ta, Bonn. He'll be pleased.'

Pell had the shakes, a heavy drinker and his usefulness short-lived. Also he was old, hands becoming transparent. Somebody Pell's age craving drink didn't need chitchat. Bonn cut to the point.

'Askey said Salvo did the accident.'

'Aye. Oz did the wheels. Taxi. Oz has a woman, in Sale, down in Cheshire. He does Grellie's girls in Waterloo Street betwixt.'

Which relieved Bonn, one woman less to worry about. 'Salvo, then.'

'The Triple Racer lads, the paper team, all saw it. Oz wheeled Mostern down. Salvo shuffed the briefcase. He'd already slit the camera.'

'The briefcase?'

Pell winced. 'Look, Bonn. I'm out of the game. Too old.'

'Don't worry. I won't ask you to burgle anywhere,

Pell.'

'It went to the wallet. Called Burtonall, somewhere out on the A666, wife a quack. Salvo and Oz done him straighteners before, one that St Helens canal job.'

Mostern was wheeled, his briefcase was nicked and taken to the man who'd funded the killing. Burtonall, husband of a doctor. Clare. A straightener could be an inexplicable fall under a train, a crushed hand, or a quiet word.

'Detail, please.'

'None, Bonn.' Pell was crestfallen. 'Salvo's girl Marla's seeing Lana, an eachway lass. Salvo's playing hell at Marla getting dyked on the sly. He's an idle sod,' Pell said with distaste. 'Earns round the halls, fiddles deliveries. A knit man.'

A small-time thief, from the joke saying: knit one, purl one, drop one.

'But troublesome, Bonn.' Bonn sent a waitress to Molly on the desk for a pencil and paper. 'Salvo shacks up in her flat, Marla's.'

'You've done well, Pell.' Bonn thanked the girl for the notepaper, wrote, handed it over. 'This is a promissory note to Osmund. At the Romeo, ask for Fay. She will pay you. Please thank Askey.'

'Ta, son.'

For a long time Bonn sat there. He accepted a drink from Molly, made a deferential apology when a woman tried to converse.

He finally rose, thanked Molly with a glance, and left. Molly looked after him. She didn't like the thought of Bonn being in that horrible syndicate business, even if it did mean him getting made key and everything. He was the sort that life ought not to go wrong for, but life wasn't fair and she had the

184

grief to prove it.

CHAPTER NINETEEN

Walker—*a male paid to escort a female regularly to social functions, whether or not he provides her with sexual services.*

Clare spoke with Dr Porritt of the Farnworth General's cardiac unit as he was going over the electrocardiographs from Male Out-Patients. Clare was admitted into the aquarium gloaming of green and fluorescence. A registrar greeted her, resumed his goggles before the radiograph.

'No criticism, Burtonall,' Paul Porritt warned. 'We're old-fashioned.'

'I've not said a word, doctor.' Clare perched on a stool, careful lest the roller ferrules carried her violently aside, the newcomer's mistake.

'She'd better bloody not, eh, Ashcroft?'

'Advisable, Dr Porritt,' Ashcroft said, concentrating on the P-A and left lateral X-rays of a patient with cardiomegaly and expansion of the aortic knuckle. Clare's eyes were drawn to the translucent areas of the radiograph.

'See?' Paul Porritt complained. 'All I get is diplomacy. I want serious sloggers who'll work for pennies, not smart alecs who can't utter an opinion. They say, "There is a school of thought . . ." I want yes or no.'

'We were too indoctrinated, Paul,' Clare said equably. 'They aren't.'

Ashcroft cheerfully gave her the thumbs-up sign

185

behind Dr Porritt's back.

'I saw that, Dr Ashcroft,' his senior said. 'Consider yourself sacked.'

'Yippee. Can I go?'

She had known Paul Porritt at medical school. Even then he had been a semi-joker, though the most industrious student. His interest lay in the technological aspects of medicine as long as they could be proved to set morbidity tumbling, get people to their feet all the faster. Research purists opposed him at finance meetings, on the grounds that fundamental research at molecular level was true progress. Understanding, the boffins claimed, was everything. Porritt's view was, let the molecules take care of themselves, just shut up and prevent or cure, get on with it.

'He needs you, Dr Ashcroft. He only pretends he doesn't.'

'Know what I do need, Clare?' Dr Porritt showed her a strip of an ECG as Ashcroft sniggered with deliberate loudness. 'Take a look. I need you to come and do a heart-fitness survey, that's what I need.'

Clare held the strip obliquely to the green glimmer, straining to see. She went through the PQRST sequence, judging the intervals, the heights and troughs of the trace's pitch.

'No cardiac infarct—'

Porritt took the strip. 'Nine traces, Clare. *Nine!* For a case who's well on the way to jumping in the next Olympics. Know why?'

'No.'

'Because the patient was a hospital bloody administrator, that's why. Can you imagine? Fit as a flea, so some bloody registrar puts on a show of

186

concern. Spends a fortune of my unit's money doing it, too!'

Clare said laconically, 'You once did the same, to impress a junior nurse.' Dr Ashcroft whooped with glee, laughed outright.

'That was different!' Dr Porritt said huffily. 'Times—and research funds—were a world away.' He grinned unexpectedly. 'She was gorgeous.'

'I'm in no position to judge, doctor. Why me?'

'Needing you, Clare? Because you speak up for yourself. Gumption. At least, you used to have.'

'Have you—?'

'Been talking to Agnes Ferram? Of course. She says you're desperate for a proper full-time job.'

'She's lying, Paul.' She paused. 'What *is* the post, exactly?'

'Surveying a block of male patients in general practices, double-ICGTM. It'll have all the mumbo-jumbo, quality-controlled, cohorts levelled and ranked, codes done, lab support, industrial links.' IICGTM stood for If I Can Get The Money, every hospital doctor's wry joke.

'How many?'

'One doctor, namely you, plus technicians, choose two nurses. It's a WICGTM survey, doctor.'

'When,' Clare said. 'No date?'

The cardiologist sighed. 'I'll come clean. I used your name on the fund form. Hope I got your qualifications and dates right, incidentally. Deal?'

Ashcroft stopped checking the radiographs, lifted his goggles, and looked across. Clare shook her head, feeling sad at having to refuse.

'Paul. I'm happy as I am, but thanks.'

They both resumed work as she left. 'Hey, Burtonall,' Dr Porritt called, 'I guessed your age at fifty. How close'd I get?'

Clare heard a nurse stifle a laugh in the outer office, and found herself smiling as she cut through Casualty. She was right to refuse. Four sessions a week was enough, whatever friends might say.

*　　　*　　　*

The three goers were waiting for Bonn. Pencey the Ghana display stroker was showing off fancy cue work, running the white along the cush, then dropping the pink, top right pocket, in an actual game. Tonto, Toothie's Guadeloupe cousin, was disbelievingly screaming fresh odds against any of this, and losing time. The crowd was engrossed. Osmund was disgusted.

'Know the trouble with Pencey, Bonn?' Rack was close to despair. 'Can't do it in championships, see?' He glared at Galahad and Lancelot as they followed to one of the alcoves where Rack could get a beer. Doob was already waiting, spick-and-span, edgily on parade. The other two were contemplating themselves in mirrors.

'Thank you, everybody,' Bonn began. 'You all know each other. Martina's rule is, you each get your own stander. You never—that's never—do a go without your stander. Rack, please.'

Rack was delighted. He caught Bonn's glance, no theories.

'Sooner or later your stander'll not turn up,' he said round the table. 'You think, Oh well, sod it, I'll do it anyway. So you go ahead, the hotel room's booked, all safe, okay? No! Because that's the one time she'll panic, scream rape, fire. Worst is, there's no records when that happens, see? Martina lives by

188

Posser's book, and Posser's law is, all screamers get ditched straight off.'

'Doesn't the hotel work for us?' Lancelot asked.

'No.' Rack was enjoying himself. He should have brought a cigar, maybe got cufflinks, say 'City desk!' Like on the pictures. 'The hotels do nothing for you, me, Bonn even. You go without your stander, you're done for.'

'The other problems, Rack.'

'Coming to that, Bonn,' Rack said grandly. 'The lady's bloke might follow her. Your stander protects you and her, see? Stander does his job, you never know there's been a disturbance, and she's in the clear. It's up to her what tale she fobs him off with when she gets home. Hotels get things wrong— double-book rooms, mistake floors, we seen everything.'

'Who do the standers report to?' Galahad asked.

Rack leant, arms on the table. 'Mind your own fucking business.'

'Thank you, Rack. Very succinct.' Bonn regained their attention. 'I'm setting up rules, beginning today.'

'Martina is rules.' Lancelot shuffled in his chair, looking at Galahad.

'Martina's rules stand. I want a couple more.'

'Does Martina know?' Lancelot, pushing it, Rack slowly turning to stare.

Bonn kept it cool. 'It's up to me. No question. If you object, say now, and depart.'

They considered depart. Rack had never heard Bonn so blunt. The three new goers watched him and each other.

'First rule.' Bonn spoke with slow precision. 'Fret Dougal's firm, I hear, sometimes take clients on

189

with no stander. Rack's boss stander. Disobey Rack, you disobey me.'

Lancelot said, wanting Galahad's backing, 'It's not just Fret's goers.'

'Not on my firm, Lancelot. This rule is without exception.' He let it sink in. 'No scruffs, heavy drinkers, pals taking your stander's place, because it's the Two Thousand Guineas.'

Doob asked nervously, 'Can we get good standers?'

'Rack can,' Bonn said. 'The city's got plenty working the ladies' clubs, reception desks. They want in, and to serve their apprenticeship.'

They digested this in silence. Galahad swigged his fluid. Bonn gave them time.

'Next rule: no homers unless your stander's within earshot.'

'When homers are so easy?' Lancelot was now frankly rebellious.

'Are they,' Bonn said with inflexion.

'Well, yes.' Lancelot shot defiance around the table. 'You simply get the address, meet the mark. It's usually a husband, who takes you to his missus. You shag her, whatever. Collect, and off out of it.' He did his dancer's imperious so-what, which worked so well with ballroom judges. 'She won't cut and run because she's seen some friend in the foyer. Homers are easy peasy.'

It was too pat for just hearsay. Lancelot would be trouble. Bonn suppressed his irritation. Did Martina know? What was Rack doing? Lancelot really was doing amateur homers ... A dancing career cost.

'Thank you for pointing it out, Lancelot,' Bonn said kindly, to Rack's wonderment. 'Yet such a lady, who loses courage, is good money. Invariably she becomes angry at herself and regrets her defection for denying herself a treat that she's paid for, after all.'

'Hey,' Rack said, thrilled at psychology. 'That's true! Remember—?'

'Well done, Rack,' Bonn cut in. 'I want us all to understand this. No talking about ladies, even among ourselves. Not with the standers, not even in your sleep.' He smiled, shy. 'Especially not then!'

'I'm talking about homers.' Lancelot stuck sullenly to it, his argument filled with grudges. 'They're a cinch. There's only the husband to consider.'

'A gander job,' Galahad said, pleased to contribute. 'I did three in a month once, shags with the husband looking.'

'They are acceptable.' Bonn could sense Rack stirring, wanting to lash out, bawl at the goers that they were on Bonn's firm for fuck's sake and do as they were frigging well told or piss off back to the street. 'I am pleased you're enthusiastic, but my rule is, no homer unless the stander is on hand, on watch.'

'How do we fix that?' Galahad wanted to know. 'Where does he wait?'

'Hangs on the rafters?' Lancelot suggested, sarcastic, a dancer's twirl at the ceiling.

Rack lost his rap. 'Watch it, cloggie.'

'Thank you.' Bonn defused it. 'It is your stander's problem, not the goer's. If your stander's in doubt—like the house is in a tree-lined avenue a mile long—then send your stander to ask Rack.'

Rack looked sideways at Bonn, wondering if there was a barb in there because he'd once sent

Scal along as sub, when Bonn had had that difficult Wirral masochist woman who sent forests of fucking flowers, silly cow.

'Please agree.' Bonn smiled at them. 'All or none.'

'You mean it's agree or the firm's finished?'

'Yes, Lancelot. I won't continue as key. My way, we shall succeed and survive intact. Disagree, we part, no hard feelings.'

Bonn showed no amusement as Lancelot came to heel.

'I know. But I want absolute safety. You read the papers. The wife talks, persuades, ultimates. Then it's ructions. Your stander saves skin.'

'Sometimes it's the husband,' Doob put in. 'He brings in some extra bird, or a pal. I've heard that.'

'The stander copes.' Bonn had to be firm. 'Maybe he's the driver, which is Rack's favourite method, has a cup of tea in the kitchen while the goer does his job. There are scores of different ways of going about it.'

'Third parties, though, Bonn.' Doob had been brewing this anxiety.

'No third parties,' Bonn answered. 'No threesomes.'

'Why not?' Which took Bonn by surprise. 'A feller wants his wife while she has you. Sharing.'

'I've done a couple of them,' Galahad said, morose. 'It puts you off.'

Bonn said, thinking it out, 'The Soho. I won't have it.'

'Are there *more* rules, Bonn?' Lancelot asked, foot tapping.

'Girls for your own use. You have one. Change her, that's allowed, but stick to one.'

'That's a bit much.' Lancelot again.

'One,' Bonn explained patiently, 'will understand that you have to work, will see it as that and nothing more. A decent goer has his own girl on the side.' He caught Rack's hooded glance meaning Grellie, but did not rise. 'It's what we goers are for, to make love, please a client. A girlfriend accepts that. It's you bringing in the bread.'

'Then where's the problem?'

Rack had had enough and pointed a finger to shut the dancer up. Bonn shook his head, but it was coming that close.

'The problem is two girls on the sly.' Bonn smiled, how patient he could be. 'Your girl will see a second non-paying girlfriend as a bitch cutting in on her man. Then it's knives out, and people getting split.'

Lancelot asked silkily, 'You mean me?'

'Yes.' Bonn took his time adding, 'And you, Galahad. And you, Doob.'

'When does the firm start?'

'Now.' Bonn stood, waved to Beth, beckoned Rack with a tilt of his head, and they left, Rack whooping at Pencey, who played a spectacular bounce shot over a black and three reds as they passed. Bonn called his admiration. Rack snorted.

He said dolefully, 'Pencey can't hack competitions. Here, Bonn.' Rack became surreptitious. 'What *do* blokes do while you shag their missus?'

'Watch television, the pub, wait outside.' Bonn shrugged. 'It's life, Rack. Who's on the Worcester?'

'Now? Jefferson, and Tuesday. Know why girls like being on show in them glass cases? They're poor when they're little. It turns their minds—'

193

'Mmmh,' Bonn said.

Rack was thinking, He's fancying Tuesday, maybe wants her on the side? He really ought to be shagging Grellie, who'd give her teeth. He decided he would have to work, pair Grellie off with Bonn once and for all. Should he ask Martina about it? Maybe not. Mention Bonn, sometimes Martina hit the frigging roof. He'd not worked out why.

*   *   *

The room reminded Bonn of his former place. That was the reason he had chosen it when first he'd taken up the life. Here, he cooked beans, oven chips, vegetarian pasties, made tea with skimmed milk. Profligacy a milestone down some half-forgotten lane. With it had gone greed, and with that ambition.

He switched on the lights, one each side of the boarded-in fireplace. Here, he had just the traffic, the coloured patterns made after midnight on his ceiling, and the racket of Grellie's girls bickering with crude raucousness before the passion in motorcars, doorways, alcoves, on church steps.

It was one room, Spartan clean, with a curtained alcove over a sink hiding a miniature electric stove, minuscule refrigerator. No pictures, because of what? No photographs, because who? A sliding door let onto a boxed-in landing, six by four. Miniature bath, a toilet, no handbasin.

He brewed tea in his one mug, stoneware—never visitors here—and eked out the milk. Less left in the bottle than he'd thought. He would have to go down to the all-nighter near the Triple Racer. He never minded these discovered tasks. Each confirmed his status as free, and alone. He might consider change, but it would be spontaneous, abstract. His room was, well, an intellectual problem.

With his mug of tea, he went to the window and saw Bradshawgate, the grassy triangle that petered out into tilted paving stones. He saw Posser on the bench. He liked Posser. The old man looked ill.

For a second he imagined Posser's eyes glancing his way, and drew the curtains as a politeness. The past was there, the city's enormous churning vitality somehow enshrined in that vestige.

He shelled his jacket, his shirt, singlet, trousers, underpants, his socks, and lay naked on the divan bed. He was tempted to switch the television on but news seemed made up, coined by redundant sixth-formers, to be marked for 'originality and dynamism' once handed in.

How much longer would he be here? He paid a pittance for rent, nothing for electricity, water rates. It was a haven, a monastic cell, given as a gift almost as from God. His mind drifted.

*   *   *

The seminary was closing, due to be sold, and the furnishings were already gone. Three brothers, none yet ordained, were leaving for the sister seminary in Tuscany, where the Order had been founded. The nineteen remaining priests were dispersed. Last week, each had received the Letter of Submission, made his peace with the novice brothers, and gone. The Rector, and the lay Brother Francis with the starched collar and pinstriped suit, were the only ones remaining.

195

It was not exactly a tearful diaspora. The seminary had existed since 1898, when emancipation reached its, what, third generation among the reformers of the sinful island. 'Let us pray for England', was the Sunday admonition, the country doomed by Reformation, with the blissful *for Thine is the Kingdom* pointedly omitted.

Bonn had felt singular, among those brothers who had convinced themselves that they should leave the Order for a life outside among the laity. It was escape to perdition. Bonn had been adjured to go to Tuscany, for a life among the religious devout. Bonn closed his mind, and left the other two brothers to it. One went to the Midlands, the other to Tenby, to search his soul.

There had been occasional defections before, individuals who suddenly decided to leave. Bonn had no real friends among the four who had left like this during his time at the seminary. As they had said their goodbyes they had seemed merely tired. Bonn still worried about them.

He himself had reached the city, also tired out, after saying his own goodbyes when his time came. Father Crossley had been kind, asked if he had the fare, joked about The Great Wen with its Protestant sinfulness. Bonn had pretended to be amused, and that had been that.

In the city he had gone into a hotel, trying freedom, eager to experiment.

He had sat in the hotel lounge at four in the afternoon. His idea was to sleep on the London train, rouse in tomorrow's dawn, and embark into life. A waitress asked him if he wanted tea. He said yes, too ashamed not to conform. He instantly started worrying about money. Tea, scones, crumpets, marmalade, all were brought.

He felt obscure, a distance from the foyer, where people talked in idleness so complete that he found it offensive. Had they no jobs, no families?

The mood changed quickly. Pouring his tea and daring himself to look at the folded bill laid beside his saucer, he felt on display, as if he was a prison escaper. Then a smiling lady seated herself opposite.

'Could I share?' She beckoned a waitress, who provided an extra cup with a strange look at Bonn. 'I *know* I'm early, but it's since I've had the new car. The *traffic*! I'm not *terrified* exactly, you know what I mean.'

She laughed, shaking out her hair. Pleasant, smiley, thirtyish, expensive clothes. He was disturbed to see that she wore a gold ring and a large diamond, ring finger. Married. And speaking without introduction to a stranger. And asking the stranger to share his tea. Was this how the outside world behaved? He had heard of liberated normality.

'Well,' she said, amused, imperious. 'Aren't you going to pour?'

He reddened. 'Certainly.' He shook, managed to serve her tea, offered her cake, cut it with feeble inaccuracy.

She watched, even more amused.

'Your first time?' Was she laughing at him?

'Here, yes.' His smile cracked and he felt absurdly shy.

'That means yes,' she said. 'I'm Chelsea Five-Four-Eight.'

He realised he was expected to say something, hesitated, wanting a clue. Hers was an odd name.

197

Nickname, some club membership, perhaps?

'Do you mean my name?' he offered nervously. 'They call me Bonn.'

But who were 'they'? Nobody had called him that since his childhood. He'd been astonished to learn that it was spelled with a double n. He did not know who decided these things, spellings, etiquette in hotels where ladies commandeered the food of strangers.

'I thought Hame.' She was surprised.

'No,' he said in weak apology. Who was Hame? 'Bonn.'

'I rang for four o'clock, Bonn.' Chelsea glanced meaningfully at the lounge clock, ten minutes to. 'Barely time.'

Did she know the times of trains too? Bonn's train was at quarter past.

'Thank you,' he said politely for her reminder. He struggled to find conversation. 'Er, did you have far to come?'

She was immensely amused. 'Bonn, darling!' she exclaimed softly. 'You needn't be so ... *scared*. Heavens! I won't *eat* you!'

Which caused her even more inner laughter. He felt made fun of, and coloured. He wondered how you made the excuse to leave. The mental reservation, which neo-Thomistic theologians now called an outright deception, was sometimes justified. But in this baffling encounter?

'Though,' she ended coyly, 'who knows what chance might force me to do?' Her smile faded, became speculative. 'You really *are* concerned, aren't you? Maybe they should give you some preliminary training. I mean, it's rather a responsibility.'

198

He was shocked at her recognition. She must have identified him as a seminarian leaving for the outside world. He felt obliged to offer a defence.

'An acceptable one, however,' he began, thinking of other seminarians.

'Chelsea,' she sang in a chant.

So names were quite proper. 'Chelsea,' he repeated obediently. 'I believe we must enact spirituality, honestly see it as a prime duty. It's the basis of all love. Do you not think so?' He took her stare as agreement, or at least understanding, and went gravely on, 'There is no more solemn duty than love of that kind.'

'There isn't?' she asked as if mesmerised.

He lowered his gaze, wondering if he had gone too far, mentioning spiritual implications of duty on so short an acquaintance. 'I believe that we complicate our inner life unnecessarily.'

'You do?' she was saying, staring, when they were interrupted.

'Chelsea Five-Four-Eight? I'm Hame.'

A youth stood by their table. Chelsea looked up, her face suddenly pale. She glanced from him to Bonn. The young man glared at Bonn.

Chelsea appraised the newcomer, then Bonn as if seeing him anew. Her colour slowly returned and she smiled. Without looking away from Bonn, she addressed the newcomer.

'Go up and wait, Hame.'

Hame turned on his heel and strode off through the lounge. Chelsea inspected Bonn, cool and analytic.

'It seems I jumped to conclusions, Bonn.' She took in the tea table with frank amusement. 'And leeched onto your private tea party.'

'I'm sorry.' Bonn was worried about the effect his presence had on the lady's friend. 'Should I try to explain to, er, Hame, perhaps ameliorate—?'

'Darling, don't ameliorate.' She was now vastly amused, and reluctant to go. Bonn wondered if the language had altered during his seminary sojourn. 'I must say I am rather disappointed.' She extended her hand. He shook it awkwardly. Her fingers pressed his.

'Er, thank you.' His face reddened, felt uncomfortably hot.

'Please.' She opened her handbag, gave him a card. 'My home address. Do call, please. I would like to continue our conversation.'

'How kind.'

'And here.' She dropped a note on the table. 'Let me pay.'

'Certainly not.' This encounter had got out of hand. He was lost.

She leant forward and kissed his cheek. He was overwhelmed with perfume, a sense of closeness, the touch of her mouth. He almost leapt away, but stayed. She went, smiling, almost swaggering, to the lifts.

He sat staring at the money, not sure what had happened or why. The world out here had mutated out of all recognition. He had never been in a hotel before, which worsened his confusion.

An elderly man, wheezing with some chest complaint but respectably dressed, approached and stood nearby.

'Good day,' he said politely. 'Might I ask if I could take this seat?'

'Please do,' Bonn said warily. Now what?

Bonn almost wanted to breathe for him, so hard

200

was it for the old man. His eyes were rheumy with age and effort.

'Please indulge an old man who has greater experience of life than yourself.' It took a minute to get the words out. Bonn nodded, responding to the other's weary smile.

'Is there anything I can get you?' Bonn asked.

'Thank you, no.' The old man composed himself, came to the edge of his chair in preparation. 'I was at the next table. I couldn't help overhearing.'

Bonn said he was not offended.

'The misunderstanding was the result of the lady's assumption that you were her escort, her personal escort.'

'Escort?' Bonn thought a moment, wanting to point out to the old gentleman that the lady had followed Hame, her 'escort', into the hotel lifts, and not been escorted at all. 'That can't be so. The lady failed to recognise him. And I don't think I ought to be discussing a lady in her absence.'

The sick old man wheezed into a pause for a moment, then politely extended his hand. 'I wonder if I might introduce myself, Bonn? Posser.'

Bonn rose. They shook hands formally. 'How do you do?'

'Do you have time for me to explain a few vital matters, Bonn?'

'Ten minutes only, Posser.' Bonn found himself warming to the other.

'There are, Bonn,' Posser began, 'a few truths in current society. One is this: There are only three sorts of people. Earners, thieves, and spongers.'

Posser waved Bonn's interruption down. 'Please. Nine more minutes. Another truth is that a woman craves to be a nun *and* a prostitute—life's extremes.

201

Why? Because she wants to know the difference!'

Embarrassed, Bonn interrupted. 'Sir, I'm not sure—'

The older man abandoned it as futile, and said bluntly, 'I need you to come and work for me. You may enter at any stage, Bonn. Either be a field worker—we call them goers—or an administrator. Frankly, a job.'

'A job,' Bonn repeated. 'Goer?'

'A slang term, I'm afraid,' Posser said. 'Some individuals appear to be naturals, Bonn. Shall I go on?'

CHAPTER TWENTY

Cackler—*one who participates in a con trick, by speech alone.*

Some places in this city Salvo hated. One was the Ball Boys. It was 'Our City's Finest Disco', it said in lights with two bulbs missing. Its paint was chipped, the boards were weathered, one of the five broad windows was cracked, and another taped over like cladding on a seaside stall. It stood in a side street. Once the alleys had echoed to the rattle of clogs, mill folk hurrying against mill hooters. Now the terraced cottages were gutted and inhabited by cardboard-city mumpers burrowing to make some corner secure. The top end, near traffic lights in Victoria Square, shed patchy coloured light onto the pavement. The bar's entrance was a foyer transplanted from a defunct Salford cinema. It dazzled with swivelling bulbs.

'Ponces,' Salvo said, fuming even before he saw Marla.

They were all ponces, in designer jackets. They looked crap. He could take on any dozen.

Tonight Marla was wearing her red. He'd watched her dress. Going out to see her mother, she'd said. Red, with the frothed hem proving her legs were smashing, her claim. Lana was the bugbear. If he found her with Marla, that would prove it. Lana the dyke, Marla the feather. Lana was a vicious cow. They said she'd stabbed a bloke once, everything bad round Lana.

He stood by the entrance, glowering. All very well for Oz—fucking name *that* was—to say leave off, it's normal. Not with his bird it wasn't.

A queers' bar, studs-and-buds mockery. Blokes arrived giggling like tarts, red hankies hanging from their gob-jobbers' pockets, silver alchemical jewellery for mash-and-bashers. It made Salvo ill, his tart one of these queers.

He couldn't wait any longer. He'd seen Lana in here. It was her place. He shoved in through the press, got stalled by a bruiser who made him pay entrance. A whole note, for this? Inside, the place was hot as hell, air thick with enough scent to gag you. All sorts were bounding to the deafening music, some snogging. Two girls embraced, whispering. A DJ was giving it the falsetto.

No sign of Marla. That made him angrier. Somebody spoke to him. He pushed the ponce aside, plenty of elbow, and blundered to the side tables. Went through the gloaming, came to a great red curtain, realised he'd gone all the way round the dark turmoil. Maybe she was in the loos?

He stood by until the women emerging were the

ones he'd seen go in, then gave up. Six dykes sat guffawing at the bar, competing loudly for one feathery mincer who Salvo pinned as a trans, their lookout, not his.

The bar staff tried chatting him up. He snarled them away, hauled himself through the bobbing dancers, ripped aside the entrance curtain. Three bouncers grabbed him and slammed him against the admissions counter. One forced his head back against the paybox amid excited squeals.

'What're you up to, feller?' one bruiser asked.

Salvo croaked. 'Looking for my bird.'

'Here?' the bouncer said, incredulous, looking about to prove Salvo's mistake.

People screeched, the joke repeated by the foyer crowd.

'Get him out,' the head bouncer said. 'Don't come back.'

Salvo was thrown onto the pavement. He intended to wait opposite, but saw one of the bouncers coming after him and walked away towards the square.

He was almost blind with fury. His face was bleeding, his eye feeling tight. Marla. Would she cheat him with a dyke? He'd been cunning, sussed the bitch out. Some women did cheat.

But would Marla?

Inside, Marla emerged from the loo with Lana. She was white-faced, and spoke to one of the bouncers.

'Jesus, Marla.' The bruiser was solid cuboidal. He was the one who had held Salvo's face in one crushing hand. 'Could have started a fucking war.'

Lana said, 'That Salvo's off his fucking head. A psycho.'

204

'I can handle him. But let us know in future.' He looked sumo-fat, beringed, balding, but was respected for ferocity. 'Lie doggo a night or two, okay? Pacify the mad bugger.'

Lana objected. 'Marla's better off with me, Postie. I can take care of her.'

'Lots say that, Lana.' Postie shrugged, went back to the paybox.

Lana coaxed Marla back to the dance floor, to the cheers of friends. Marla felt better as her sense of security returned. It was pleasant, without that frantic anxiety she always got with Salvo. With Lana she felt in control, could withhold or give, submit, or award pleasure.

The music came on, an eighties rehash. Marla forgot Salvo.

*   *   *

'I'm sorry about this, Evadne,' Clare told her mother-in-law, leading her into the hospital cafeteria. 'Will here do?'

'Don't mind one bit, dear!' Evadne gushed. Her long-suffering husband, Arthur, trailed behind, trying to guess the specialisms from the various uniforms. 'We can rough it, can't we, Arthur?'

'Let me get coffee for you both.' Clare found them a table. 'Unless you would like something...?'

'Allow me.' Arthur went off to join the queue.

To Clare, her mother-in-law looked only half dressed without numerous packages from expensive shopping expeditions. Evadne always seemed too elegant. She whispered, 'I mean, eating in this sort of place is, well, rather macabre, don't you think?'

205

'Not really.' Clare got the point, and deliberately showed surprise in retaliation.

'With those diseases so *close*, I mean to *say*.'

'Don't worry. You're quite safe.'

'But are *you*, dear?' Evadne Burtonall leaned back, gazing with distaste at the table's laminated surface. 'Time's getting on. Clifford is so eager to start a family. There are better uses for your time.'

Clare kept control. 'When did he say that?'

'A mother knows her own son's mind.'

'And what does my husband's mind say?'

'He desperately wants to be getting on with raising a family, Clare.' Evadne leant away from a couple of radiographers passing in their white dresses. They carried trays holding plates of pasta.

'We've never discussed it, Evadne.' Clare thought, One day we'll meet and not fight. But one day is none day.

Evadne patted Clare's hand. 'But isn't it *uppermost*, dear?' She waved away Clare's reply. 'Time waits for no man. Or woman!'

Her mother-in-law drained Clare. It had been like this from the start. Arthur wasn't so bad, but was completely swamped. He'd been defeated years ago, lost the battles and the war in one go.

'Evadne, we'll make our own way, thank you. It's up to Clifford and me—'

'Coffees!' Arthur arrived with three cups. His wife looked at hers with ill-concealed distaste. 'I was talking to a most interesting man in the queue—'

Evadne wiped her palms together as if ridding herself of a noisome contaminant. 'Did you check the cups were clean?'

'Of course, of course.'

Clare thought, The man sounds positively

206

humbled. 'We'll let you know when we decide anything, Evadne.'

'Mind if I interrupt, Dr Burtonall?' Dr Porritt stood beside the table, smiling. 'Sorry,' he said to her in-laws, 'but I've only a minute. About the offer, Clare?'

'Still thinking, Paul,' she answered. 'I'll reply very soon.'

'Drop in.' The cardiologist pursed his lips. 'The whole thing's set up, everything a cardio survey needs.'

'Good. Perhaps I shall.'

'The subvention might come through any day. I'd want a flying start.'

'I really do appreciate it, Paul.'

'It's the room by the old surgery. Sister Gascoine has the key.'

'Ta, Paul.' Clare prayed that he would leave.

'The night staff know the key's in Sister Gascoine's office.'

Evadne took the offensive the instant he went.

'Offer, my dear?' she cooed. 'Offer of what?'

'Oh, some enterprise or other.'

Arthur began to look uncomfortable as his wife pressed on.

'It didn't sound at all casual, Clare. It was more like the offer of a job. Might it interfere with family plans?'

'It's a scheme Dr Porritt wants to set up,' Clare said, exasperated. 'It isn't even off the ground yet. Nothing's fixed. They haven't even the money to start.'

'Any day,' her mother-in-law quoted in reprimand. 'And fully equipped. He as good as said so.'

'What if it is, Evadne?' Arthur said, in sympathy with Clare.

'Don't carp, Arthur!' Heads turned at adjacent tables. 'I'm being perfectly reasonable. Some things are best said!'

'Look, Evadne,' Clare tried, anything for peace. 'Perhaps it was a mistake for me to invite you here. Come for tea next Sunday. How about that?'

'Fine!' her father-in-law said heartily. 'We'll be there. Make some parkin, we'll never leave!'

'I see we've outstayed our welcome,' Evadne said frostily, rising. 'You have your new unit to inspect—and your new contract.'

'No, Evadne,' Clare said. 'Please finish your coffee.'

'Another time, Clare.' Evadne swept out, Arthur following, turning to mouth a miserable apology.

CHAPTER TWENTY-ONE

To blam—*to injure, to attack, a person.*

The rage was like being ill. A year back, Salvo had been under the doctor for flu, but he'd felt like death, three whole days. Take everything lying down, she the ball breaker, you were a laughing stock. Rather be shot at than laughed at. Salvo recalled Marla's lies—see you at the Domino or the Shot Pot eightish—but never the Ball Boys, where she'd really be with that Lana. It was vital to stand your ground. Bonn telling him thank you, Salvo was great. A bloke like that, paid to dick birds one after another, polite, hinting—hadn't he?—that one day

208

Salvo would make it. Gelt plus grumble meant heaven.

He'd lost Marla near the Waterloo Street junction, the old mill in Oberon Street, where the shops began. She'd changed direction twice, but all the time doglegging to the Ball Boys. He headed for Marla's flat. He'd wait there.

Climbing the stairs, he felt proud. Oz would be impressed, hearing how Bonn himself had talked to him. Better than Angler, better than Faulkner from Horwich, better even than the tall Commer from Liverpool, everybody's front runner until Bonn came.

He paused on the landing. Not much noise, but what was it?

A muttering telly next door along. A babby wailing. A bloke shouted up the next stairwell, something about his bike, Christ's sake, this hour, night already out there with half the fucking bulbs missing from lads laying throw-stone bets. He deserved better, folk stacked like fucking sardines.

Somebody inside? The crack near the hinges showed nothing, which it would if there was a light on. Somebody hurting? He looked about.

The landing showed droppings from the flying years: dust, paint flakes, ceiling plaster heaped like snow drifts smoothing out corners, fragments from imploded light bulbs. He stood listening, the shitty life he lived. Bonn's firm would have been his way out. The noise couldn't be in the flat. Marla was out. He'd followed the bitch, hadn't he? So who the fuck was inside, that keening noise? It wasn't the babby. The little bugger had finally shtummed.

Why had they asked that moron Lancelot, the mogga dancer? And that prat Galahad? Everybody

209

knew muscle hustlers were poofters. Bonn wasn't to blame, poor bugger, syndicate keeping tabs on him.

He turned the key, the door chain not on, went in.

The notes had changed to breathless grunting, chugging. Except it wasn't pain, as he'd imagined out on the crappy landing.

No sense closing the door now he was in. His one good burglary—a solicitor's office after hours—he'd been helped by an experienced mate who'd done time, so everybody knew he was good. The old tea-leaf told Salvo, never shut the door behind you. Good advice he heeded now.

He moved quietly down the narrow corridor. Bathroom, kitchen, the broad room for bedroom and living. There he'd watched racing from Haydock this afternoon, losing a few quid, Marla nagging and slamming things.

The bed was down from its wall position, as he'd left it, except now the bed held Marla and Lana, with Marla, whore that she was, making all the chugging any tart had a right to, her legs spread like Marble Arch and Lana's head working like a fucking excavator between. He could see in the light from the windows, the whore not even the decency to pull the curtain.

In the strange orange light he saw Marla reach for her dyke's hand, Lana grunting and Marla's head thrown back, the cow, like she wanted to lose it over the headboard.

He stared, rage swelling. The most insulting thing was Lana hadn't even bothered to un-fucking-dress, just down to the waist for tit work before really getting down to doing it to Marla.

So how many times had Lana dyked his Marla

and made a right prat of him? Maybe ten times a day, then everybody at the Ball Boys sharing what a good fucking joke it was?

Which meant the syndicate must already have word about him not being able to keep a bird, not even from a dyke as rough as Lana. It was this dyke who'd burked his chances of goer, picking rich.

A bubbling fury filling his throat. He took his time, silent on the stained carpet. Lana, to start with. He stared down at them. This one-sex act in the weird neon light was loathsome. At school, the roughest area, he'd been punished by one of the schoolmasters—and who the fuck called them *that* now their glory days were done and they had to do what they were fucking well told? He had this saying, the cunt, chanting while he lashed out, 'You have the arrogance of ignorance', like fucking Holy Writ. Salvo never did know what it meant, some insult.

He was curious in spite to see how she managed it, where the tongue went, how fast, the other hand slowly doing what, flicking ahead of Marla's whimpers or, in time, details.

Stupid, he cursed himself, standing silently there. Time they paid up. His fury filled him and he moved on them then, ready steady. One of Lana's shoes had come off and was on the bed, spiky heel a mile long, glitter down the back.

For a moment, his knees touching the bed, he stood looking down onto the features of his Marla. Her mouth was agape, her protruding tongue lashing one corner of her mouth to the other like she was taunting, going carnie over some street bint who sold her arse for a quid. He'd never seen Marla this far over. For him, she just lay there like a fucking plank. Habit, she'd given him. She'd conned him.

Habit, for him. But this Lana bitch got the real thing, this bitch slavering and chewing, grazing in his field.

Lana's shoe was in his hand. He prodded Marla's face with it. For a moment she didn't understand, opened her eyes to smile, maybe ask Lana what now. It would have been funny, given him a laugh, as the bitch started thinking, coming to, horror in there, caught redhanded, redcunted, under her slobbering dyke.

For just an instant he wondered whether to do an Oz, let them get on with it, who cared. But then what? They'd giggle, decide it was Lana's turn, his Marla doing the gob work while they gave the whole city a laugh, him not having the nerve to raise a finger. Not this time.

'Surprise,' he said, causing Lana to squeal and jerk back, head lifting, mouth dripping. The arrogance of ignorance? For a fleeting instant he felt the fury of justified disgust and lashed out.

*   *   *

In the office Clifford had little to do. So he told himself. He shifted files, got letters written, Dictaphone stuff that could wait anyway. The girls were gone, that Mona, calling irritatingly cheerful reminders, do this, don't forget that, before six o'clock. He'd faffed about. In the morning there'd be gales of laughter. 'He'll forget his head next!' and suchlike whimsies.

There didn't seem any road round his problem. Hassall and Windsor were moving slowly through

212

Mostern's acquaintances. He had to do something. Some *thing*. Inactivity was out. Goldoni had seen that straight away.

The police were nearing, plod by sombre plod. The question was, were they moving randomly, or did they have a list for the killing of Leonard Mostern?

Every deal had weak links. The woman Jane Antrobus had been well paid. He'd seen to that himself, the master of currency. She'd been grateful. He'd seen the light in her eyes more than once, the rapture of gratified greed-lust, the money paid over. It was Jane Antrobus who had told him the statistics: the Serious Fraud Office's conviction rate was 71 per cent. 'It sounds impressive,' the large-boned woman had told Clifford when he'd met her for a drink with Mostern, RIP. 'But the number of *alleged* frauds that are *dropped* is in the thousands!'

And, later, after a few drinks, 'The SFO wants a crime of fraud, when our legal system has no such thing.' Gales of laughter, then she and her sweaty boyfriend Leonard had retired to her bedroom to discuss how much to take Clifford Burtonall's development scam for.

Clifford sat in his great black swivel chair, genuine Dakka leather, as the office lights faded in and the city darkened. The picture window gave him a view of the city's centre, Victoria Square. God, he'd developed a good tenth of it even in the few years since he'd started. He couldn't lose it now.

Odd, yet interesting, how a deal tied your hands. This new deal, in every way routine, forced Clifford into taking steps he'd never imagined.

Once before, he'd had to correct somebody who

213

had become uncooperative, a supplier in St Helens. That had been easy, some ugly canal business he really didn't want to remember. The supplier's girl had been sanctioned—he carefully thought of it in those terms.

They say about generals that they are serene once the order's gone out and the battle joined, men sent to their deaths in thousands. It had been that tense, a nail-biter. But Clifford felt absolved, sitting watching the night city. He was not—repeat not—to blame for the outcome. Salvo had exceeded his orders. The idea was simply a smash-and-grab business, that time of day. Clifford had certainly said nothing about killing. The briefcase had to be rescued, that was all.

He pondered, then took a decision. He tried the contact numbers with no success. But he had an address for Salvo. He had time. If Salvo was alone, he could instruct him should there be any police interest. If Salvo wasn't alone, Clifford could do a wrong address, off the cuff.

Morally or legally, he couldn't be blamed. Mostern's death was a misunderstanding. Jane Antrobus was still in the hotel, because he'd checked. She hadn't called. Maybe she was so shocked by the news of Mostern's death that she was stunned. The SFO didn't have a leg to stand on.

Except Salvo. Wise to visit, simply check that everything was still safe and quiet. It wouldn't take more than an hour. Clifford left some office lights burning and locked up. He decided to walk through the square. His car, and the lights in his window, would prove he was still hard at it on the top floor.

CHAPTER TWENTY-TWO

Mother—*a truthful warning to friends in perpetration of a crime.*

The woman had been more pleasant than Bonn felt he had a right to expect. She was importunate, wouldn't take no for an answer. He felt fond. This was her sixth time with him. She told him stories of her children's antics, while she dressed to go. She insisted on his remaining on the bed. It was, she'd told him, something she'd once seen in a film, the heroine leaving her lover as she flitted back to propriety.

'The things children write at school!' She knew Bonn liked to watch her.

'What things?' Bonn lay on the pillows, smiling, arms behind his head the way she'd described the cinema's hero lover.

'Honestly!' She drew on her stockings, pointing her toes. 'I'm ashamed! The teachers must have a really good laugh! Children! You have to be careful.'

Bonn sensed that she was leading up to a vital question. She came slowly to the bed.

'Bonn?' She sank slowly, the bed tilting him. 'You know so much about me.'

'I wouldn't say that, Yasmine.' He added, 'You're a woman of mystery.'

She didn't smile. 'That's the point, Bonn.' She took his hand. 'If I wanted to invite you ... well, out, could you come?'

'Come where?' He was startled, a different request.

'I don't know, a drive in the country. Just us, I mean.'

'It would depend, Yasmine. They allow a visit to a home, as long as it won't complicate the lady's life.' He pressed on. 'And they don't mind if a lady wants to go away somewhere for a night, but they lay down strict conditions, what and where.'

'So many rules, Bonn, darling,' she exclaimed petulantly.

'Without rules, Yasmine, there'd be no me.' He raised himself on one elbow, but she pushed him back and pressed her head to the pillow next to his.

'What would they allow?'

'A cottage in the Peaks, say. But not gambling in some casino. Too many witnesses.'

'Not to a dance, then?' she asked wistfully. 'It would be wonderful, just the two of us. My husband'd rather be off drinking with his pals.'

'I wish I could, Yasmine. Honestly.' He stroked her.

Martina had called a meeting of all the keys. Rack would already be champing at the bit in the corridor, hoping to hear the door go.

'Shall I ask?' That was always a good ploy, its implications of something decided.

'Please, darling.' She pressed her mouth on his, lingering, inhaling his breath as she loved to do when nearing a climax.

'I promise, Yasmine.'

He would keep his promise, and ask permission. Of course it would be hopeless. Martina would refuse, wondering why he'd even bothered to ask. Yasmine's attitude was no longer that of the client. It was the beginning of friendship, and therefore dangerous. Were their positions reversed—he the

216

hirer, she a prostitute—then it might be tolerated. But this way, the risk was never far from the surface. Plain fornication must not become a tryst.

'You won't forget, darling?'

'Never in a million years, Yasmine,' he said.

* * *

The Bar Owl was a floor in a converted mill that was sectioned for small enterprises. The second floor was the size of a tennis court, with carpets higgledy-piggledy and a central black-lead stove. Huge paintings, a job lot from a redundant art school, blotted the whitewashed walls between great rectangular windows. This was Martina's meeting room. Posser only rarely attended, but he was here. Martina would be the last to leave, keeping her lameness to herself.

She sat, her dad beside her on a straight chair for his breath, as the keys arrived. It didn't escape Bonn's notice that Martina's early presence effectively prevented idle chitchat among the keys.

All the keys' appointments had been deflected to preserve the hour. Grellie entered last, shaking rain from her coat, grimacing apologies and mouthing embarrassment.

'Names, please,' Martina kept to Posser's custom, since they saw so little of each other.

Bonn spoke first, as the newest. 'Bonn.'

'Fret Dougal.' The lanky Accrington key was rumoured to be some vague relative of Posser's. Nobody was sure.

The others stated their names: Ton Atherton, Zen, Angler, Faulkner from Horwich, Canter, Suntan, and Commer the Liverpudlian beside

Bonn. They were disposed in a circle, Martina and Posser completing the ring. The old man's wheezing was audible, worse than Bonn remembered.

'Some have clients later,' Martina began, 'so get this over with.'

'Lads.' Posser sat forward, hands pressing down on his knees. 'There's a development. I want you to hear it from me first, before rumours fly.'

He inhaled, sat back a moment, glancing at them all in turn.

'There's interest in the syndicate. I mean money. We've been asked to sell out.' The sudden stir caused Martina to shoot them a warning look, them interrupting her father. 'I've more or less refused, so far. I want Martina to carry the syndicate on.'

He would have wiped his forehead free of sweat but couldn't spare a hand.

'There's no question of hiving off parts—the caffs, snooker halls, the girls, the goers as one lot, bingo corners, whatever. I've explored that.'

'And?' Canter asked, who had five goers on his firm, the largest, since he dealt with towns within a dozen miles of the city. He alone had a special phone inlet, and a part-time woman to handle calls.

'They are serious, Canter.' Posser halted to breathe noisily, and nodded to Martina to take it up.

'This approach was made some two months ago,' she said. 'The offer came through one man who knows the city, or seems to. He's anonymous. It's all public-phone communication direct to Posser. We have been given definite proof that they have the money.' She invited questions.

'How did they know of us?' Canter again, most concerned of them all.

218

'We don't know. Some informant among the teams, the stringers even? He might have sent in dipsticks—that's standard practice. It certainly wasn't an advert in *Exchange and Mart*.'

Nobody laughed. Grellie spoke up with diffidence.

'What now, then? If we've turned it down.' She got no reply. 'I mean, isn't that the end of it, us going on as we are?' She looked about hopefully. 'There's no reason for this meeting, if we've said no. Right, Posser?'

Mistake, Bonn scored. She ought to have addressed Martina.

'The problem is,' Martina answered, 'we don't know who these people are. Europe is money shore to shore, and it's spilling over here. Continentals find their old exploits aren't as profitable as they used to be, and move into other areas.'

Posser, recovered, put in. 'Europe is hack-worthy. Subsidies invite scams. Heavy money wants a home.'

Bonn thought of Rack's friendly uncle who needed a quiet place to stay unnoticed. But Rack was trustworthy. The doubt was unwholesome.

'You mean they might force us?' Suntan, the one key who insisted on two standers, asked the question for them all.

'That's our worry. You know my feelings. I won't be party to a scrap.'

Suntan had been done for knifing a drinker in Leeds, and thought mayhem a part of normal life. He had taken five years to make key. Rumour said he was negotiating to move to the Midlands, for reasons unknown.

'If a rumble finishes it, where's the harm?'

219

'The harm is sides, Suntan,' Posser was fond of Suntan. Bonn wondered if he saw himself as he had been in youth, violent and enjoying the danger. 'People take sides. Somebody—I don't mean here—will take sides against us. That will be remembered. Words like "traitor" and "betrayal" never go away.'

'Not if we suss who they are, Posser.'

'Assuming we get it right, you mean?' Posser rasped, raising a finger so nobody would use the space to interrupt. He breathed harshly into speech. 'The odds are enormous. Nothing's easier to hide than Continental money.'

'Posser, please.' Bonn's interruption caused a silence. Heads turned. 'Do we know its origin?'

'No, Bonn,' Martina answered for her father. 'We checked as far as we could. In trades and out, they're solid.'

'Martina. What now?' Grellie asked. 'Will something more happen we won't know about?' She looked startled. 'Sorry, Posser, Martina. I didn't mean—'

'Don't worry, Grellie,' Posser said. 'If they have cannon, that will be it.'

'The minute we have details, you'll all be told, Grellie,' Martina said.

'Until then we carry on as before?' Bonn did a pantomime, hands in supplication, the others smiling at his joke, him so newly promoted.

'Please,' Posser said.

Martina looked her disapproval. It should have been a command. Bonn knew that he was witnessing the end of Posser's era.

Martina said quietly. 'If you please.' A command after all.

As they left, two women from one of the hotels nearby came out of the service lift wheeling a covered tea trolley. It seemed to be laid for two, no more. Angler started to make some joke to Suntan, but the mood was not on any of them and they went out into the drizzle without speaking.

'All right, Bonn?' Rack was at the corner. He knew it was serious news, all the keys and Grellie in one street.

'Rack, would you suss out Salvo? You know, that contender.'

'Right. See you where?'

'The mogga dancing.' Bonn paused, cars whizzing by, drizzle hazing lights and haloes round every face. 'Rather quickly, please.'

CHAPTER TWENTY-THREE

Plant—*one who will testify for money, if necessary committing perjury.*

The door was shut, but Rack hadn't walked five streets to be baulked. He went through hardly breaking step, grinning. Old Pell would pull his leg unmercifully: 'You *what*? Used a comb and wire to dub through an effing prewar wood *door*?' And the lads in the Spinners Arms would make wanking gestures while he told them made-ups about special reinforced locks with them flanges.

He'd been lucky, seen Salvo come out, hurry off towards the square. That meant the place was empty. Was Bonn thinking of stuff nicked from Martina, something like that? No harm to have a

221

quick shufti. And the way Salvo had gone, like a frightened ferret.

Rack went silently down a corridor and in the room where Salvo—

Where two girls were, who looked dead.

Except one, Marla maybe, if there'd been enough light, moaned and raised a hand. The other girl, skirt up around her waist and bruises black on her white thighs like mottled ink. Brown bloodstains on walls, spatters, a few streaks made by hands desperate for something, shit on legs and bed, puddles of piss. He thought, or maybe said, 'What the fuck?'

'Rack,' the battered thing that might be Marla said.

'Yih?' He stood, not knowing what to do.

Marla, if that slow-motion creature with the blood-matted hair and teeth hanging—teeth *hanging*, fuck's sake?—on her chin like ivory saliva and eyes that bulged in blue-black mounds, Marla lay against the wall side, one leg twisted like legs couldn't be. Her legs were soiled, her clothes ripped and everywhere, her arm was swollen, her shoulder somehow heaped up one side of her neck.

Somebody had lashed her, stripes on her face, if it was still face there. A tuft of hair, surely hers, was stuck on her left tit like for some mad effect. Her shoe, a high heel, was stabbed into her neck, the stiletto heel pronged into the skin, russet blood congealing round it, shelved on display, except it wasn't a shelf but her neck.

Lana, if that lifeless thing was Lana, was cleaner, lying with her head wrong, turned to the window. The curtains were the sort you could tell daylight through, except it was night, orange neon.

Somebody had wiped blooded hands, rucked the drapes up like a lavvy towel.

'I'll get help, Marla.'

She recognised him, with her jaw sprawling out of her face, the chin pointing to her other shoulder, away from the shoe stabbed into her neck. Jesus, he thought, said, not knowing, Jesus. He felt sick, kept cool.

'Don't move, Marla.' How long had he been standing there?

'Lana,' Marla managed to get out: '*An*-a.'

'Lana's,' he said, licking his lips for the lie, 'Lana's okay. Lie still,' he added in wild inventiveness, 'both of you, okay?' This needed Bonn.

'Lana?' he babbled. 'Lie still. Don't move. And don't,' he burbled in a burst of genius, 'don't either of you talk, okay?'

He looked about the room. No phone, but then he thought how stupid that would have been, dashed out across the concrete space with its twisted basketball circle, and rang Martina. She came on straight away sounding tired, but woke up when he gave it her.

'Call an ambulance,' she said, precise. 'Any sign?'

'Of Salvo?' he asked straight out, wondering why she tutted in annoyance. 'Nar. He's left enough traces even for the Old Bill. I saw him.'

'Do it. Then ring back.'

'Okay, Martina.' He obeyed, telling the address to some dim cow at the ambulance station in Wythenshaw, for fuck's sake, like who'd believe city ambulances had to come from fucking Mars? For good measure he rang again, demanding where the fuck's the ambulance, saying he'd rung an hour since. He told them there was a fight, two blokes injured, and there was also a fire, so get the fucking brigade out. Cursing the spluttering bitch made him better. Okay, less worse.

He got Martina, running out of money quick.

'How many phone boxes are there?' Martina was mad at him. Why?

'Four. I'm in one.' He'd only done what he'd been told.

'You've got your phone card. Switch.'

He changed to a card phone, two along, mercifully unvandalised. 'Hello?'

'Stop there.' No preliminary chat. 'Watch.'

'Shouldn't I go up to Marla? Bonn sent me—'

'*Silence!*.' Him a kid in school, her the bullying teacher. 'Watch.'

Rack felt narked. He was about to explain, Bonn's orders, suss Salvo, all that, and gets shut up.

'Watch what for? I reckon Lana's been snuffed—'

'For anything you see, anyone you recognise.'

So like a fool he stayed at a silent phone while his card clicked its cost away. The odd person came and went, nothing out of the ordinary, an estate like this, the odd bloke running, bawling riots upstairs hardly noticed. One or two cars drove through the road loop, lights cutting night. Young lads shouted footer abuse to each other, scuffling, City versus United, one lot doomed to relegation. No ambulance.

Then into the light, quite close, walked this bloke. Smart suit, wristwatch gleaming. He'd never been here before. Rack could tell. He checked the numbers by the lifts, went up when he found Salvo and Marla's number. Rack got excited. He told Martina this. It was half past seven.

224

'He's on the balcony. Jesus! Silly cunt's *switched the light on!*'

He saw the man enter, light casting his shadow back. Rack had had the sense to wipe the doors. Then the man came hurrying out, was sick on the balcony, looked about, frightened, pausing like a kid playing hide-and-seek, left at a fast walk, too fast for honesty in rough housing estates.

The ambulance came, its crew standing doing sweet sod all while they sussed out hoax calls, the flats up there safe or not. One ambulancer pointed to the door ajar. Other folk opening doors now, the blue light jampot to fucking flies.

Rack told Martina he was off out of it. Police wahwahs sounded nearer. He struggled to yank the receiver, failed, so wiped and shattered it. He did the same to the previous phone, let them sort it out.

He slid into the dark, and was gone, side alleys by the old closed canal. He had an idea, ran for the distance, emerged into respectable lights near Victoria Square, and saw the bloke, same one, walking quickly past the Vivante. He followed, saw him go into an office block by the museum for old frocks. Rack stood outside at a bus stop, looking up. Window, fifth floor? He crossed over, checked the name. He could hardly read, funny scrolly writing.

Martina hated phones, so he went to tell her face to face. She looked knackered, lines on her face he'd never noticed. Outside, Osmund was doing his patience, some Leigh lads—third in the league table, their tails up—doing trick shots, making a racket.

'Tell it to me in order, Rack. As it happened.'

He wondered why Martina was narked. Then it hit him.

'Hey, Martina! You didn't want names talked, right?'

He got a tut-tut. Obviously didn't want to admit that he'd done brilliant, been fast and smart. He detailed his destruction of the phones, his care.

'The scene?' she demanded, really pissed off.

Rack was astounded. She wasn't like this. He still hadn't heard about the big meeting. He should be out in the street ballocking the girls for gossip. And he hadn't yet told Bonn all about Salvo, when it was Bonn sent him.

'No point me watching them cart Marla and Lana out.'

He could have said what would happen anyway: estate kids getting clobbered for fiddling with the ambulance wheels, police trying for statements, nobody seen fuck all. It was always the same.

He told Martina all about the city gent. She became headache-alert then, made him go over and over it. Then the bit he'd dreaded.

'Why were you there, Rack?'

Bright cow, Martina, he thought grudgingly. It was time she moved on Bonn. For an instant he wondered if this was the right time to say how about you and Bonn, really tactful, bring it up like, Hey, Martina, whyn't you shag Bonn? Graceful, the way birds wanted, cheer her up. Except birds wouldn't recognise tact if it slapped them in the face.

Second thought, if he got her under Bonn would he be doing Bonn a favour? A bird gets too close she starts on your teeth, nails, comb your hair every fucking minute. Maybe first thoughts were best, Grellie for Bonn? He felt really bad at the thought of hurting Bonn's feelings. Though it wouldn't matter, because Bonn's teeth and nails would be

226

clean. Hundred to one, Bonn's teeth would dazzle. He'd look.

He ended his account, Bonn ordering him to suss Salvo. Martina was all headache-attention, eyes wrinkled like in smoke.

'Thank you, Rack. You did really well. Ring a plant.' He copped the name Martina gave.

'Am I to tell Bonn?'

'Yes.' But a pause, all was not well. Women fucking wore you out.

Rack went outside to ring the plant girl. He was gleed up, because he liked this one in Wythenshaw. Martina had seven or eight of these plant lasses, just alibi dills really, never did sex or gambling, bints on nothing but money. They gave evidence to the Old Bill to order. You worked out your tale like a menu, this ingredient, that cake mix. This was some married lass he'd used once before after some greyhound racing at Burnden Park frittered and the plod went berserk. Her husband saw no harm, and Martina paid case by case. Plant women were cheap, no retainer except a lousy Christmas bonus, did as they were told.

He was sick in the lavvy at the bus station, spewed his ring up but proud. He'd tell the lads. They'd bet on Marla, say 13 to 8. It was her neck and jaw that made him puke. He'd lay twenty on her making it.

Bonn came by as Rack was talking with Grellie's studio stringers by the bikers' stand. From his look, Bonn had already heard.

'Wotcher, Bonn,' Rack said, buoyed up with triumph, the two girls listening. 'I got that thing you wanted.'

'Thank you, Rack. It is good of you to have taken

the trouble.'

'Not at all,' Rack said grandly, eyeing the girl he fancied, Liz from Pendlebury, diamond in her nose making Rack wonder did it hurt. *Not at all!* just like Bonn sometimes said it. He caught the admiration in Liz's eyes, speaking to Bonn like an equal.

'When you're ready, please,' Bonn said, moving on.

'I'll be there, Bonn.' Rack strolled after, no hurry, seeing Grellie cross quickly to intercept Bonn by where two street buskers danced, mouth organ and ricks clacking away. Life was back to normal, at fucking last.

CHAPTER TWENTY-FOUR

Honcho—*one who enforces order at a place of entertainment.*

It was always going to be difficult. Bonn waited nearly an hour for Clare Three-Nine-Five. Rack was on stand somewhere, doubtless incubating theories about lateness. Bonn'd made fresh coffee twice, binned both. Mistake to watch TV, sloppiness was in the eye of the beholder. No, probably Clare Three-Nine-Five had become scared of what he might have discovered about the dead man, rationalising that she'd misunderstood, forget she'd ever doubted it.

He was halfway out of the door when he heard footfalls. She came at a breathless trot. He suddenly thought her pretty.

'I'm so sorry.' Careful to omit his name. Good.

He re-entered the room, closed the door. She grimaced at her watch. 'Does this mean you have to go?'

'I'm so sorry, but yes.'

She shook out her hair. 'I had to see an elderly gentleman. He was leaving his home today, for terminal care.'

'I must report in on the hour.'

'Can you not extend?' She had hoped the hint of Father Crossley would make a difference. 'He had old photographs of his seminary. What hell, to leave such tranquillity.'

'I wish I could stay, Clare.'

'Did you find anything out about what I asked?'

'Yes. It would take time to tell.'

'And you're going to somebody else?' It came out unexpectedly bitter.

'No. But I must clear my next hour.'

'Checking in, like a child?' More bitter still. She was astonished at her inexplicable anger. I'm scared of what he has to say, she guessed. He was already opening the door and stepping past. 'Wait. Please. It was your old priest made me late, for heaven's sake.'

'You will excuse me.' He left the room key in the lock. She held his arm.

'After, then? The evening's early.' Listen to me pleading, she blazed at herself, like a woman ditched by a lover. She felt obscene. 'Can I phone and book you?'

Fright. That was it. Not anger.

He waited while she phoned the Pleases Agency, Inc. Foolish, giving her code, Clare Three-Nine-Five, while Bonn was within reach.

'I've been delayed,' she explained. 'I need

229

another hour. I mean,' she said, colouring, 'to speak.' Pause. 'No, it must be tonight.'

'I'm afraid Bonn is heavily booked this evening, Clare.' Miss Rose's soothing voice asked her to hold. Then another female voice, firmer and less restful, came on.

'Is it a mere conversation, Clare, or something more?' it asked frankly.

'What I said. To speak.' Clare felt her anger return. 'It will not take all that long.' She could have finished by now.

'Meet Bonn at the mogga dancing fifty minutes from now. You may remain at his table for half an hour.'

'Thank you.' Clare failed to suppress her relief. The woman would now sense her desperation. 'What dancing, please?'

'Bonn is there with you,' the voice stated, cold, 'and will explain. You will be billed as for a whole hour. Thank you.'

Clare heard the phone purr. She looked at Bonn. 'Mogga dancing?'

*   *   *

It was shameful, to feel defenceless entering a dance hall. Clare found herself hesitating. Everybody seemed young, knowing the way.

It was garish. She had imagined something sedate, a scent of lavender, uniformed gentlemen holding doors. Instead, here was a wide recess of mirrors, coloured lights racing round posters, youths and girls blocking your path, everybody screaming with laughter.

Great cream letters flashed *MOGGA DANCING*

on and off. Inside it was as Bonn had told her, no real throng of spectators. No embarrassing box office. She walked with assumed calm through the foyer.

There was the wide staircase with scarlet hand-ropes, crazily ornate. A young couple argued on the stairs about some dance, voices raised. Clare walked past the bored bouncer, taking her time, clearly used to being here.

Music sounded, a jerky melody with a thumping beat, far too loud. She came on a wide balcony overlooking the dance floor. Most tables were unoccupied. A corner bar served coffee, cakes. The spectators were mostly women.

Clare walked to a table midway down the balcony. Three couples were already on the dance floor, wearing everyday clothes, performing a varying routine with different degrees of slickness. Astonishingly, they changed their dance every few bars, no pattern evident. She sat to watch.

'Your coffee, missus.'

She looked up. Bonn was placing cups from a tray. She said awkwardly, 'Thank you,' wondering. Half an hour. Had it already started?

He sat, gave his attention to the dancers. 'See that couple?' He pointed. 'We're sticking up for those. The others stand no chance.'

She eyed the pair. 'We are? Why?'

'They will win.' He added, 'Unless the judges are wrongly bribed.'

'Bribed?' She thought she'd misheard. 'All bribery's wrong.'

'It happens. But it's fair.'

She thought, *He's shy here.*

'Am I all right sitting here?' It seemed important

231

to be in charge with him. She was paying through the nose, for heaven's sake. She tried to erase that crudity, but still felt aggrieved. 'I mean, you have so many rules.'

'Then don't obey.' His eyes were on the dancers. 'You can leave.'

For a second it seemed a taunt, but he was too serious. She looked away. He brought bad news, and was inviting her not to hear.

She put her elbows on the balcony edge, looking down with him. The dancers she was supporting were by far the best. The male was fantastically supple. His partner was a showy girl, hair tightly got up, wearing a skirt that went anywhere. Their shoes were the only formal items.

'Because they need to practise in their actual performance shoes.' Bonn divined her thought. 'You never see mogga dancers without.'

'Do you do this?' she asked, biding her time.

'No. I would be embarrassed, though I am a fair dancer.'

'Fair,' she heard herself say and thought, God, I'm starting to speak like him, saying instead of asking. 'Are they your friends?'

He didn't hesitate. 'No. I know them. They are the best, are they not.'

There he went again. It could irritate. If ever a woman got close enough she'd have every right to tell him so. Except that would be hard to do.

'Is this all there are?'

'Two hundred started out. Sixteen reach the regional finals.'

Clare laughed, as did other spectators, as Bonn's couple broke into a tap dance, then changed smoothly into the palais glide. She recognised it.

'They're dancing wrong. How can they score it?'

'Dance ability, slickness of change, degrees of dance difference, partnership conformity, transition, harmony, audience captivation, flair, musical distance, overall impression. Those ten. I believe there is an eleventh.'

'You do.' She shook herself, said sharply, 'You do?'

His gaze returned, disconcerting her. 'Fix on one couple, Clare.'

She did as he said, picking a hardworking pair. 'Yes?'

'At whom do you look? Ask yourself.'

'The girl.'

'So does everyone. The girl is flamboyant, the male stereotyped.'

'That is your eleventh test?' she asked.

'Yes. Style turnout.' He spoke solemnly, wanting to be correct.

'I'd no idea this went on. What does mogga mean?'

'Mixed.'

Bonn clapped casually as the dance ended. Clare thought, His pedantry is a kind of extended care. The couples walked off the dance floor. Conversations began among the spectators. One pair argued, angrily showing each other how their steps ought to have gone.

Clare looked about. Nobody she recognised. It was all as casual as Bonn had promised. Below, several new dance couples were coming on, one doing a soft-shoe shuffle as a joke. So light-hearted.

'Sorry?' she asked.

Bonn had said something quietly that made her stare. He tilted his chair back to be shielded from

233

the staircase entrance.

'Your fears are justified, Clare. He was killed. A designed accident.'

His news, he was telling her his news. She spoke in sudden fury.

'I told you—'

He held up a hand, wait for the music. Killed, though. He'd said killed. His expression was one of unutterable sorrow, beyond mere sadness. An old Beatles number began, orchestrated almost out of all recognition.

'I am sorry, Clare.' It was as if he wanted to take her hand. 'Mostern was killed, for his briefcase. It was replaced by an empty one by the two men who killed him.'

She tried to swallow, feeling sick. 'What are you saying?'

'I do not know who the wallet was, but he received the briefcase—'

'Wallet?' Her heart drained, cold but not shivering.

'Wallet is the person who pays for a killing.'

Received the briefcase after the killing took place, Clare repeated silently.

'Who did it?' Where had Clifford been during Mostern's accident? That afternoon he had been at home.

'One drove the taxi, the other pushed Mostern. Unfortunately, there is a further complication, evident today.'

'For . . .?' She faltered, had almost said Clifford.

'A girl, two girls, have been . . . hurt. Today. A man from the Burtonall office might have visited the scene.'

'What scene?' Too shrill. It was his mentioning

234

her name. He gestured her to be quieter.

'The flat is where one of the men lives. Who perpetrated the killing of Leonard Mostern. You do see?'

'I do see,' she said, savagely mocking his manner. Anger at Bonn almost blinded her. Ancient emperors slew bad-news messengers.

'One of the two men was mentioned in the newspapers after Mostern was killed.' He let it sink in. 'Today's crime, the two girls, will be in the papers soon. A man went to the scene, but didn't call Emergency. He went to the Burtonall office. It's by the TV studios.'

'Everybody is identifiable, then.' She was outraged by Bonn and his horrid, detestable information, his sadness.

'The Serious Fraud Office were about to Section Two an associate of Mostern.'

'An associate,' she sneered. The music was intolerable, the dancers' rigmarole absurdly frivolous. She had no idea what Section Two was.

'Clifford Burtonall,' he said. 'Same dining club as Mostern. If *I* know, the police will.'

'I see,' she said dully. How often had she, telling a patient the grimmest news of all—some fatal cancer, some heart-rending birth defect of a newborn—heard the same meaningless reply. *I see*.

'The SFO lady is Antrobus.' Bonn clapped mechanically at some remarkable dance change. 'She maybe guaranteed Mostern immunity from prosecution if he handed over documents. I have no more information.'

'Give it me all!'

'Shhhhh.' Bonn whistled through his fingers, applauding.

The dancers snapped from a samba to a Viennese waltz, did a mock sand dance, a *paso doble*. She forced herself to watch the rhythm. She could only wonder why they were dancing, when she was in hell. Clifford Burtonall. Bonn actually said the name just like that. She shook.

'Please,' she said. 'All you know. Clifford Burtonall ordered Mostern killed, to stop him helping this Fraud woman?'

'It's almost certain, Clare.'

'*Don't call me Clare*!' she hissed, suddenly furious with him, his life, his repellent status, the things he'd brought to tell.

'I apologise.'

Someone began calling out, as in mockery. 'One-two-three, one-two-three!' A row started, abuse, noise of a scuffle, running feet. People on the balcony craned. The music came to a ragged halt.

It was as if her mind was suddenly ill and unable to cope. She had no idea how long it was, but the broil below had died down and new dancers were taking the floor, the music different and now twice as loud.

'No, Bonn. I apologise. Thank you.'

'Your handbag is under your seat.' It was his dismissal. She—*she*—dismissed, by him?

She found it, appalled at her misery. In a moment she would leave and be alone with his news. She didn't want to be alone.

'Please. Is there somewhere we could go, just to rest?'

'That is proscribed.' He made to rise, decided to let her go. 'All appointments have to be made the same way.'

'I see.' *I see* again, when she didn't see anything.

236

'Could I possibly ring you? I don't actually know where you live.'

'Not really.'

'You must live somewhere, for God's sake.'

He checked they were not being watched, overheard. Was his entire life so secret?

'The Café Phrynne. I might be there about this time, the next two days. It is quite in order to be alone there. It is secure.'

She repeated the name. 'What do I do if I'm there and I see you?' Quite pathetic, talking in guarded circles.

'Just say good afternoon. Or here, at the finals.'

'Thank you.' She spoke in a dreadful monotone. 'Goodbye.'

'Goodbye, Clare.'

Feeling foolish coming in, feeling foolish leaving. She walked out, knowing she must look pale as death. He had used her name when she'd blurted out that he was not to. It had been like a blessing, a forgiveness. More stupid still, she was walking away from her one ally. She found her vision blurring at his compassion, stopped in the ladies' toilets.

The mirror showed her face. Jesus, an advert for poison. How ugly, hearing Bonn say, 'Clifford Burtonall' straight out.

She went out into the street as the next tune ended. Ripples of applause followed her through the velvet curtains. The garish lights split her head. Really, she was in no fit state to drive. The wise thing would be to rest in the Humber awhile, close her eyes. Soon, she would focus them on her husband, Clifford, whose very name now sounded so alien. One might say new, and utterly unknown.

CHAPTER TWENTY-FIVE

Plod—*the police.*

On days you didn't want day calls, the phone issued messages like an evil oracle. Switch the thing off, it nurtured malice, splurging out terse bleats the girls would bring in. All right for them, Clifford thought. Come in, do your nails, chat, type some Dictaphone, lunch, home.

He played the message again. It lodged on his heart like a stone.

'Mr Burtonall? Windsor. We met. I'd like a word.'

Silence. Then somebody wanting currency for overnight transition in Tokyo, tied to the Hang Seng, if you please, having the unmitigated gall to demand a review of commission. Any other time, he'd have flown into a rage at the insolence. Now he listened, then closed the office.

He had the Ford today, Clare the Supersnipe. Efficiency, not style. No 'please', no 'thank you', punctuating Windsor's Napoleonic assertions. You were to conform.

Clifford felt that his hands were too large as he drove, as if the ghastly experience at the flat had changed his size. He'd touched the door. Had he touched the wall, blundering out, making himself walk, not run? He'd rested a hand by the door. Had he worn gloves? They were in his jacket pocket. No good now.

Who had seen him? He had vomited in the office loos, sweated pints, still felt sodden. Those two girls,

238

Jesus. He'd switched the light on as he'd gone in. He remembered letting out a screech. Or had he uttered a sound? He now thought not. And nobody had come out as he'd fled that terrible place. A handful of lads had been kicking a ball in a concrete area lit by two dim bulbs. Had they looked his way? He'd heard them calling pass the ball, useless, dribble, street cries heard everywhere. No 'Wotcher running fer, mister?' Nothing to implicate.

But had he touched anything, recoiling? Did fingerprints smear?

Why was Windsor ringing? The timing device was off, that useless cow Val in the outer office forgetting. He was latish getting home. Mrs Kinsale had gone, her notes everywhere for Clare. He was relieved to be alone.

The answer device was on. They were ex-directory.

'Hello, Clifford.' His mother, who always avoided Clare's name. 'I have some information about schools you both might like to see. I'll drop it over. *So* many changes!' A light planned laugh, ending with a goodbye of reassuring brightness. He couldn't even remember sitting with Clare in the conservatory for almost an hour.

And, 'Mr Burtonall. Windsor. Ring this number when you get in.'

Had Clare given Windsor this number? Clifford stood in the hall, worrying. He hadn't turned on the lights, as if that would erase memory.

He went to the front door. He'd left the key in the lock, dark out there now. The trip lights were on upstairs. Clare's caution and the housekeeper's careful checking.

How had he switched on the lights at that flat?

239

Felt round the doorway, then moved the switch with fingers? He put the hall light on, starting to hope because he'd simply moved the back of his hand on the projecting switch. Had he done the same at Salvo's place? He repeated the trial. Maybe he'd left no fingerprints at all?

Fingerprints were from fingers. Could they take them from, say, a knuckle? He switched the light off, repeated his home-coming, only it didn't work this time, his reflex somehow lost by concentration.

He was sweating badly. He needed to bath, rest, brew up, have a drink.

Then the inner-city project. He went over it, frantic. It had started as a simple development, make a routine slice on the side, the usual dipping and swarming, squeeze this, relax that. He felt enormous waves of self-pity. It was all so unfair. It was *routine*, for God's sake.

Then Mostern got to that bitch Antrobus. On the sly, earn his own immunity while ruining others. Clifford felt contempt for the dead man. Once a fool, always a fool.

The whole thing had been compounded by hiring Salvo. The money he'd paid Salvo was untraceable. No holes there. But he'd wanted a blam-and-lam job, not a massacre. Was Windsor ringing *about the two women*?

'Clifford? What are you doing?'

He almost leapt in fright. Clare was in the hall. He hadn't even heard her motor arrive. She looked unusually pale, but what didn't look strange now? He felt so weary. His greeting seemed robotic, at a great distance.

'Sorry.' He forced himself to invent, 'I thought the light was on the blink.'

'And is it?' She kissed him, waited. 'Broken?'

'Er, no, no.'

She took off her coat, put her handbag down. It was return home by numbers. He suddenly thought, What does she know? She went past him into the kitchen, putting the lights on as she went. He heard the kettle start its low hum, crockery, the oven click.

'I'm just wondering,' he said to the space she'd left in the hall.

'About Leonard Mostern?'

This was ridiculous. What could she possibly know? She'd been to a couple of functions, Mostern simply one of scores in some hotel club months back. Anger shook him. Was he being threatened by his wife? Christ, he had nothing to do with any deaths. He, Clifford Burtonall, provided full employment to hundreds, and he was being treated like somebody with everything to hide. It was repellent.

Those two dead women were nothing to do with him. Who knew what the lower classes got up to in their seedy stack-shacks? He was clean. Let the police ask what they wished. He'd been elsewhere when Mostern had died, so tough. And tonight he'd made a simple mistake over some address, that was all. He wouldn't stand for it. He strode into the kitchen. Clare was standing there as if she expected him to come.

His tremor was gone. He confronted her, cool, taking the reins.

'Why mention Mostern?'

'Isn't he the crux in the whole thing?'

For a fleeting instant she seemed as determined as he, but he'd found a new resolve. He'd been pushed around and wasn't going to take it.

241

'"Whole thing" sounds so all-embracing. What do you mean?' He smiled, glancing aside before capping the remark, one of his tricks that showed his witty grasp of subjects. It stood him in good stead in board meetings.

'His accident.' Clare had as much difficulty saying it as Clifford had thinking it.

'What are you implying? Nothing sinister, I hope?'

Clare laid aside the oven glove. The kettle did its faraway whistle. She absently clicked it off. Fingers, he observed.

'I wonder if it isn't. Sinister, I mean.'

She put that in because he was waiting, eyebrows raised, for clarification. Doubt took her. Easy to accuse, and heaven knows she'd almost worried herself into a stroke planning what to say, but until this moment she hadn't doubted Bonn. His account had damned, she'd believed it and hadn't wanted to. Now that she had to get the accusation out, anxiety immobilised her. She blushed like a child.

He poured the water, slapped the electric kettle back on its stand. Nothing wrong there. Perhaps it was in her?

'Out with it, Clare. Something's on your mind.'

He found Mrs Kinsale's tray, checked the cups, milk, spoons. Calmly he crossed into the living room, elbowing the light switch as he went. Clare followed. She needed sleep, see what had gone away when she woke.

'Is it because you were at the accident, and realised you couldn't do anything?' His expression was sympathy and rue mixed. 'I understand how that must feel, all your expertise no use and some poor man—'

242

'Killed,' she put in dully. She sat. 'Clifford. That briefcase. Who delivered it? What for? It came the evening Mr Mostern died.'

'I explained that. Some courier—'

'Who, Clifford?' Her voice caught like a finger on a thorn. 'Salvo?'

He stared. She watched his face go pale. He started to say something she didn't quite catch.

'Salvo?' he got out finally. 'How did you hear that name?'

'I've heard it. That should be enough.'

She felt tears come, blinked them away in anger. His response proved she was betrayed. The killing was nothing really to do with whatever schemes he was involved in. It was between herself and her husband.

'From Hassall, Windsor?' He said the names, then realised.

'No. If I've heard the name, then so have others.'

'How—?'

'Never mind how!' she shouted, then composed herself. She wanted to punish his idiocy, sacrificing everything in her marriage for some stupid scheme. 'It's what's happened that's the problem. You . . .' She halted, impotent. She didn't know any word. She found one. 'You were the instigator. You paid for somebody to see that Mostern was . . .' She ran out of euphemisms '. . . executed. In order to prevent his meeting the Fraud lady.'

Clifford sank into his armchair, staring at her aghast, his wife suddenly a complete stranger.

'I can't believe . . .'

'You're hearing this?' Clare listened as the phone rang in the hall, heard Windsor's message. 'How much do the police know, Clifford?'

243

His lips moved. They'd become rimmed in purple. 'I don't know.'

'And the Serious Fraud Office lady?'

'She has nothing to justify an investigation now.'

'Now?' Clare almost yelled at him, calmed with a struggle. 'Now Mostern is dead? Is that it?'

'I don't know. Honestly, Clare.' He was almost tearful, his hands spread in appeal. She'd never seen him break down. 'If I could put the clock back, I would. Honest to God, I never meant it to happen. It was an accident. I didn't mean them to go so far.'

'Is that police message about the two women?'

He began to cry at that, tears that Clare should have shed for herself streaming down his face. 'You've not been to the police?'

She was astonished. Her emotion, she realised, was contempt, nothing less, at the man who'd been her husband all this time. As if she would betray him, as he had betrayed her. He saw her expression harden, and tried to make amends.

'They've not been at you, putting ideas into your head?'

'No. I worked it out all on my little own.'

'How? Why, darling?'

She ignored the endearment, not caring what showed. 'I knew there was something wrong the day of the accident. I saw a man by the hedge. Thieves don't bring—they take. Couriers don't creep—they roar up to the front door.'

He visibly tired. 'Had you met Mostern without telling me?'

'At your stupid investment dinners.' She was furious at his suspicion. 'You went to the girls' flat. Hadn't you better explain?'

'Jesus.' He covered his face and wept, his

244

shoulders shaking. 'I'm not involved, Clare. You must believe me. It's God's truth. I just went to find the man.'

He wiped his face, sniffed, and sat staring at the carpet. 'I found two women. In bed. I think they were dead. They'd been beaten. I thought one tried to say something, but I ran.'

'You *ran*?' It corroborated Bonn's account. 'You didn't phone for help?'

'How could I?' he complained. 'They'd have asked why I was there.' His eyes rounded in horror. 'Maybe accused *me*.'

'So you left them.' Clare inspected him clinically, a species beyond her understanding. 'Didn't phone anonymously.'

'I couldn't think, darling. I was bewildered, scared. Jesus, I'd have been taken into custody. Me! *Arrested*!'

The words seemed to scare him even more. He went over his account, why he'd decided to visit the flat, why he had to know what the police had asked the man Salvo.

'Who'd done it?' Bonn had told her one was dead, the other maybe.

'Honest to God, darling, I give you my word. I don't know.' She watched his self-pity grow, overcome him, tears again.

'You'd never seen them before?' She was allowed to sound callous.

'Never! Honestly!' He made a helpless gesture. 'When you came home I was trying to remember if I touched anything.' He looked up soulfully. 'I switched the light on.'

'Then ran,' she said, deliberately scoring penalty points.

245

'I was careful once I got downstairs.' He was pathetically eager to prove his common sense.

'They saw.' Clare met his shocked look. 'You were seen walking to your office. You went in using your key.'

'You . . .?' Points of red appeared on his cheeks. 'You've been having me followed?' He stood, outraged. 'Of all the—'

'No!' She was a deal angrier than he could ever be, with the facts she possessed. 'I wouldn't *do* such a thing. As you didn't tell me about your involvement in Mostern's death, I think I had the right to make my own enquiries.' She raised her voice. 'I think I was justified. Don't you?'

'Who is he?' Suspicions flitted across his face.

'Male, yes,' Clare said, furious at his implications. '"Another man", no.' He had confessed to his marriage-long deception, yet had the gall to reproach a blameless wife.

'A private detective?' He was blustering.

'Nothing like that. It was a fluke more than anything.'

Hope showed. His words became almost wistful. 'You mean there isn't a trace?'

'No. It's as far as it will go.'

'But how—?'

'Leave it, Clifford, *leave* it!'

'It's medical confidentiality, isn't it?' he begged, clutching at a straw. 'Doctor—patient obligation not to reveal a patient's details?'

'Something like that.' Let him have his bit of solace.

'You're sure, darling?' His eyes shone with relief. He saw her impatience and quickly appeased her. 'Thank you, darling. You're marvellous—'

246

'What now, Clifford?' She moved away.

'Well, I simply . . .' He remembered the police calls and faltered. 'I suppose I'll have to speak to Windsor.' He drew breath to ask, but Clare shook her head quickly.

'I won't make your call, Clifford.'

'Please, Clare.' He showed her his trembling hands. 'What could I say? I'll have to phone soon, or they'll come here. Bloody police read whatever they like into everything you say. Please?'

'No, Clifford. I might inadvertently get it wrong, too.' And implicate Bonn, his agency, people she didn't even know. 'Do it yourself.'

'Clare. Please don't be heartless—'

She blazed up. 'Heartless? After what you've put me through?'

'I'll do it, I'll do it!' He composed himself, then gave Clare a nod as if he'd decided to do his wife an immense favour. 'I'll ring Windsor now, darling.'

Clare didn't answer. He went out to the hall phone. She heard him dial, and at last she began to think.

*   *   *

That Bonn'd been so apologetic at first had seemed almost insulting. Now it seemed merely sadness. He would have spared her if he could. She felt ashamed, the way she'd spoken to him. Out in the hall, Clifford lifted the receiver. She heard the clicks. He would walk about as usual, a pace or two, pause, then return, his handsome head tilted. Telling the police what he knew of Mostern, possibly what he also knew of the two women in a flat he had no honest reason to visit.

She had been used. Was this self-loathing always the same, a wife realising a husband's contemptuous betrayal? Her marriage, once so sound and forever, was a cloak for Clifford's deceit frauds. What had he been doing, all this time? Worse, how many other crimes was he involved in? She felt giddy. One death, maybe three. More?

How piteous to have wondered as she had, about the morality of asking Bonn to find out. She'd accused herself of treachery, infidelity even. How often had patients come to her with similar questions?

There had been a couple only last week. The wife had contracted a venereal illness from an incidental lover—some casual holiday affair. Mercifully, it was easily cured. But the contact tracers—health auxiliaries responsible for finding other sexual contacts—had wanted the husband to report for examination. The wife had flatly refused to admit her address, her name, the identity of her casual coital partners, and had left in outrage.

'But they may still be at risk,' Clare had explained—reasonably, she thought.

'It's *my* business, doctor,' the wife had stormed. 'Nobody else's. It'd be admitting everything.' Later she had fumed, 'Think of the effect on my husband. It'd mean I'd let him down.'

The argument had gone on. Confidentiality forbade a doctor to simply send out the contact tracers to find the sexual partners of index patients—those who first came with an infectious illness. Unless they could be persuaded, there was simply no way of finding out other people who were at risk. Patients with more conscience persuaded their lovers to come to the clinics, all under codes.

248

Clare had been pleased to find prostitutes accepting health assessments every three months as a matter of course.

Why was she thinking this? She heard Clifford's voice in the hallway.

'No, I was with my wife.' A casual laugh then. 'Yes, certainly.'

But that was only one side of infidelity. If the husband was unfaithful—how she hated the pompous word, with its pejorative overtones!—then was the wife free from marital constraint? To be so juvenile as to retaliate? Betrayal meant dissolution, didn't it? If a firm reneged on a contract, then wasn't the contract void? Or at least unpinned?

Clifford had treated her as someone who didn't need to be told anything. She made herself listen.

'Certainly, Mr Windsor. I'm sure she has!' How calm Clifford sounded, mmmhing along, good on the phone. 'Though what records the National Health Service keeps these days heaven knows!'

Records? Of what?

'No. I'll dig it out.' Pause. 'I'm sure my wife can!'

And a laugh, mild and unaffected, nothing all that important.

'Clifford?' Clare called, worried. She went to the door.

Far from being at ease, Clifford looked in a state of exhaustion. He was actually shaking, the receiver trembling at his ear. He was a man at the end of his tether. He replaced the handset. She wanted to go to him, but stayed herself.

He turned an anguished face to her.

'Clare, darling. You'll have to help me.'

'Help how?' But she already knew, from the little she had heard.

249

'I've said that you were giving me a medical examination.'

She stared. 'Me? Examine you? It's never done, not in families!'

'I said you did, that you have records, tests and all that. The times.' They remained standing apart, like fencers before a bout.

'But I haven't!' Was this all in one day?

He met her gaze with desperation. 'You must, Clare. We've no choice.'

'How? *It's impossible!* You mean, for an alibi?'

'Darling.' He moved but she instinctively stepped back. He nodded as if it constituted a new agreement. 'There's no other way. It seems there's been some business involving two young women at one of those high-rise blocks of flats. Windsor wants to know my movements.'

'What did you say? Tell me exactly.' It was unreal.

'I said I was with you at a clinic, being examined. Anxieties about my ticker.' He tried a smile, wan and tired. 'I confided in you, old girl.' He never called her *old girl*. Why now? 'You took me along to some cardiac place you're involved with, ran the rule over me. Heart, all that.'

'You said that? You're out of your mind! It simply can't be done. Dates, times are incorporated in the electrocardiograph, the ECG. It's the same with the serological tests, the lab reports, everything.'

His face set. 'You have to, darling. We've no other way. Please don't forget that I love you in all this.'

We now? She flapped her hands as if to deflect sentiment. 'Do you know what you're suggesting? I haven't a surgery of my own. I can't simply walk into

250

some hospital or surgery and say, Excuse me, but I need to establish an alibi for my husband!'

'You're an accessory, Clare. You're in this with me.' He spoke with a new quiet firmness, suddenly belligerent.

'An accessory?' She didn't follow.

He seemed to grow, and spoke as if they both agreed on a solution.

'You and I are in this together, darling.' No tears now. 'Let me remind you that you were—what did you imply, suspicious?—*before* the two women were attacked. You could have gone to the police. You didn't, did you?'

'That has nothing to do—'

'With the case?' he said for her. 'I'm afraid it has, darling. You see, Windsor says they are linking this new event with Mostern's demise. You told the police about the accident, but said nothing that could have helped them further, did you?' He had her. 'An accessory before the fact, darling, and an accessory after.' His smile was one she had never seen before.

She said warily, 'Meaning what, exactly?'

'You are both, darling. Exactly as I am—unless you give me an alibi. Clear me, you clear yourself.'

'It's against all medical—'

'Rules, darling?' His confidence returned. 'Bend them. Not too much. Just enough.'

'It's out of the question.'

'It's what we must do. You can teach me the symptoms, then create the alibi. After all, I didn't murder those girls, so really you're helping to prove the truth.'

He drew a breath. 'I suggest we have a drink. Then we can provide the police with the evidence

251

they need. All right?'

*   *   *

That night Clare sat alone after Clifford had gone up. She drank a little wine, that emblem of tolerance, to 'think things through' as Agnes would say.

Wasn't it that Clifford was simply afraid—why else would he have spoken as he did? All men were children, unable to face problems, wanting the woman to provide solutions. And he was right, of course, in that the cardiologists insisted on the maximum number of males of Clifford's age for the cardiac survey. Heavens above, under any other circumstances she might have enrolled Clifford without another thought, so why make such a fuss?

She remembered his look at their first dance. She still laughingly teased him, calling it his 'desperate visage'. Surely she was reading far too much into what was, after all, a natural anxiety? You can think too much about an event, make it into something it never was in the first place. Why, a year previously a hospital vehicle had accidentally knocked down and injured a visiting father outside Casualty. Every single person on the staff had felt personally guilty for days afterwards.

But if she was going to include Clifford, it had to be soon, tomorrow. And was it wrong to simply do Clifford's preliminary tests and write them up? What would it matter? Somebody had to be the first. She rinsed the glass. Tomorrow, actually taking him to the hospital, her doubts might well recur, but for now she felt calmer, back in control, reasonably sure what to do.

252

CHAPTER TWENTY-SIX

Cran—_a place where money, especially a bribe, may be left for collection._

They parked outside Farnworth General. The hospital lights were on; the huge car park was full of visitors' cars. Clare yanked the handbrake on. Beside her Clifford's face shone in the gloaming.

'You know what to do?' she asked. She felt leaden, weighed down by what she was about to create, a false record for a false patient. Who was, she reminded herself bitterly, a false husband.

'Yes.'

'Tell me again.'

He crinkled a piece of paper. She had drawn directions on it for him. He held it against the light. Nearby, an anxious family noisily alighted, predicting misery for some elderly relative in the surgical division. Clifford waited until they had gone.

'I wait five minutes. I go to the second-floor corridor, bearing right. It's fifty yards. I will see ECG signs, blue on white, by the stairs. I descend one flight.'

'And if a nurse comes out of the wards?'

'I pretend I'm lost, turn back, and repeat my arrival.'

'Right. Go on.'

She couldn't disguise her contempt. It was mostly aimed at herself for succumbing the way she had. She could simply walk away, let him stew. But she hadn't. Instead, she was perpetrating a crime to conceal his *other* crimes. It could have her struck off the Register, eradicate her life's ambitions. And she was abetting a criminal. Why? Because of an archaic ritual, that betrayal called marriage.

She took a perverse glee in thinking of Evadne. I should give the bitch a ring and say something like, 'Oh, Evadne, glad to catch you. This marvellous son of yours. How should I handle this?' And give the details straight out, the killing he'd arranged, his association with two murdered girls.

'. . . the door marked Cardiac Surveillance, which will be ajar. I check I'm not seen from the ward, and go in. You will be—'

'Waiting.' Clare finished. 'And after?'

'I wait. You will go into the ward, to prove you're around.'

'I,' she added, sleek, 'have no need for concealment. You'll give me one minute exactly, then go to the visitors' canteen, have a coffee. Don't be surreptitious. Then come for me, asking everybody the way.'

No cars arriving for the moment, an opportunity. Clare made to get out. Clifford put a hand on her arm.

'Darling. Thank you.'

'Not at all.' She wanted to punish him for stealing her world.

'One thing, darling.' He sounded nervous. 'Will it hurt?'

'Hurt?' She almost laughed aloud at the incongruity. 'Christ, I betray everything I've sworn, and you're worried about a needle?'

She shook him off and walked away, tears of anger in her eyes.

It went well. Sister Gascoine was not on duty. Night staff were arriving, making it easy for Clare to go to the cardiac section ostensibly to 'have another look' at the new surveillance unit, take the key from the wall, and leave the nurses to their reporting.

The room was about thirty feet square. Two alcoves, desks, couches, chairs, screens for radiography, the 'rollers', as cardiac registrars called the arteriography monitors for viewing the radio-opaque dyes inserted into arteries. It wasn't much, but it was enough.

She hung her coat, drew the blinds over the frosted glass of the doors, quickly switched all the lights on. If anyone intruded, she would have to blag it, think up some tale on the spur.

Her alcove was at the far end. The men would enter for blood pressure, height, weight, body-mass indices, body-fat measurements, and morphology assessments. Then blood samples would be taken for peripheral blood cholesterols and the high- and low-density lipoprotein factors. The laboratories did those, despite the dot-spot tests. Freezers and refrigerators already hummed, with wire baskets for shipment to haematology. Further along, the ECG, with the gels and pads by the last couch, plastic covers in place. Everything was ready to use, just as when Dr Porritt had shown her round and said innocently, 'Get a few volunteers in and give it a go. The clerk might be sober enough.' And he'd added with a disarming grin, 'Once you're back, young Burtonall, you'll never escape.'

So it was the cardiologist's idea, this caricature.

255

She found the sterile syringes, pulled clear the sequestrated ampoules, the needles, and, before breaking the covering seal on the three syringes she would need, freed each piston action—she'd been caught too often to omit this. She labelled the containers which would hold the blood, giving Clifford his full name, age, and carefully putting the time he'd told her. It was the exact moment he'd been at the flat. It was the time he'd told Windsor that he was with Clare, being examined for cardiac symptoms.

Behind her the door went and Clifford slipped in. For a moment it almost stopped her heart. She beckoned him over quickly, told him to strip to the waist.

Working swiftly, she placed a rubber catheter—the best trouble-free improvised tourniquet—round his upper arm and broke the syringe seals. The small white haematology tray was down to its bare essentials of cotton wool, antiseptic, ampoules. The Hazard Sharps containers for waste needles and syringes were ready, their two seals properly ripped.

'Keep your arm straight, please,' she intoned.

She cleaned Clifford's skin, and capped the syringe with the needle.

'A prick now. Stay still.' She drove the needle into his antecubital fossa, picking up the vein cleanly and aspirating blood, checking the marks along the piston.

She pulled the tourniquet, as usual letting it fall anywhere, and pressed a dry sterile swab to the puncture wound.

'Press with the fingers of your other hand.'

How many thousand times had she said that, she wondered, distributing the blood. And how wrong to be doing this. She disposed of the syringe and needle in the Hazard containers, and placed the blood in the refrigerator. They were now circumstantial evidence that she had examined Clifford earlier. If everything went right.

Even before the puncture wound had sealed, she had Clifford on the ECG, setting the terminal lead pads on his body. The machine signalled its auto-dating facility. Carefully she clicked the time to zero, then advanced the timer to read Clifford's alibi time. Time, place, date.

She took readings, switching the leads to make the tracings in the usual order. She became aware of Clifford's gaze.

'I've never seen you so rapt like this before, darling.'

Her mind screamed. *Don't call me darling.*

'I'm just taking traces of what your heart is doing,' she said. 'We have names for each of the flicks and patterns on the trace-out.'

'Am I all right?'

'So far,' she said cryptically, talking to give normality to this double betrayal. 'We do them in order. Chest discomfort makes a doctor hunt Lead Four. The electrical changes can stay there longer than other wiggles, and go earliest, especially in the Q-wave bit. Some clues are especially good, like the T wave suddenly inverting.'

'Do all doctors do this?' He was still watching.

'It's like knowing a language.' His stare disconcerted her, and she babbled on. 'I check ECGs in a set order, or I'd miss one. X-rays, the same thing, you stick to your own pattern.'

'Like the police.'

'The T wave is my favourite,' Clare said, to shut

him up. 'Once the ECG goes back to normal—it can, even after a heart attack—the T wave in only one lead can stay inverted. Doctors call it the registrar's friend.'

'I've never heard you talk like this before, darling.'

'I've never done this before, under quite these circumstances.'

She dismantled the leads, and changed back the auto-dater.

'Get up. For completeness I'll do the Quertelet Index, body-fat measurements, and BP, enter records with earlier times. I'll start a new record book.'

'You will enter seven-thirty?' he said, alarmed.

'Don't worry, Clifford,' Clare said evenly. 'I'm learning to lie superbly well.'

'Thank you, darling.'

'Don't call me that,' she said evenly. 'On the scales, please.'

*   *   *

Ten minutes later, Clifford came to find her as planned, and they left together. Some hurrying nurse might vaguely recall that, yes, she'd seen Dr Burtonall waiting for her husband, but that would be it.

The times and date of Clifford's blood samples that Clare had clipped into the cardiac ward's haematology baskets would be replicated in the laboratory's records. She would phone in, and make sure the false times were correctly reproduced in the lab's computer printouts.

After that, there was little more she could do to

protect her husband. It wasn't foolproof, but it was the best a lying, treacherous doctor could do.

She drove home in angry silence. On the way, she made a new resolution. This time, it was for herself, not for Clifford, not for her marriage.

That night, she only half slept, and awoke with her bitterness still there, the anger renewing itself and circling. She told Clifford she would call in at the hospital, make certain his blood samples had been processed.

By nine o'clock she'd given Mrs Kinsale her day's instructions, and stopped the old Humber on the A666 before half past. She called the agency number on her car phone. Subterfuge be damned. They answered on the first ring. Clare quickly identified herself.

'I want Bonn,' she told the voice. No diffidence now.

'Very well, Clare Three-Nine-Five. What time would suit you best? Please give a choice of three—'

'Today,' Clare almost snapped. 'This afternoon, two o'clock?'

'That is in order, Clare. Venue?'

'The same as before?'

'Vivante Hotel, suite number four-two-six. Repeat, please.'

'Four-two-six.' Clare wrote it down. 'Vivante. Am I limited to one hour?'

'No, Clare. But an extra hour is chargeable, with—'

'Then until four o'clock, with a possible extension afterwards.'

'Your order is placed. Thank you for calling the agency. We assure you—'

'Thank you,' Clare interrupted. She was nervous, but it was no longer pure anger. Betrayal was in the air. It entitled her at least to sit with Bonn, talk over the problem, maybe just watch the afternoon TV film with someone gentle, and sad enough to listen.

Who knew the pathways of city evil, where her husband walked.

CHAPTER TWENTY-SEVEN

Carnie—*grave physical injury, a wanton brawl.*

Lancelot caught Bonn as Rack passed him three bookings. One double, Clare Three-Nine-Five, plus a homer, which old Posser still called a 'dommy'.

'Dommy? In her home?' A new home client was unusual.

'It's checked,' Rack assured Bonn. 'She's maybe an upper from somewhere else, finding her feet.' Bonn didn't ask the obvious. Rack said, 'The address changed hands last week.'

'Fine. That other new one, tell Galahad to do it. Lancelot does the next.' Bonn looked up through the car window. 'Yes, Lancelot?'

'Listen, Bonn.' Lancelot danced when agitated, as now, springing from foot to foot beside the car. 'Can I postpone my goes today?'

'Are you ill?' Lancelot was a picture of agitated health.

'Bonn, man, it's my partner. Stupid cow wants four leps revised.'

Bonn looked at Rack. Leps?

'Changes from one dance style to the next. Tango
260

to moonlight saunter. Know why they lose? Wrong heels—'

'Thank you, Rack.' Enough. 'No, Lancelot. Ladies first.'

'Bonn!' Lancelot wailed, dancing as he whimpered. Passing people smiled. One raised clenched hands, wishing him luck. Lancelot beamed, returned woefully to plead. 'Christ's sake, Bonn. I've never got this far. And a second lady's booked me twice running. She's getting—'

'What she pays for, Lancelot,' Bonn said, still pleasant.

Rack in the driving seat made Fangio noises, vroom vroom.

'But Galahad closes them down,' Lancelot cried.

'Lancelot. Dancing second, clients first.'

They pulled away, Rack doing his crash start. Bonn nudged Rack—slower, please—then told him to find Galahad. Rack yelped with glee, did a lunatic 180 and screeched wrong down a one-way. Bonn said nothing. At the Rum Romeo he alighted, said thanks and he would make his own way to the General Hospital. Rack was hurt.

'I'd get you there fastest, Bonn. Honest.'

'Tell Galahad the front coffee bar, if you would.'

The muscle man came instantly, nervous, Bonn let Rack bring the problem up, just sat to watch.

'Galahad. You closing the clients down?' Rack asked straight out.

'Closing down?' Galahad looked hunted.

'Telling them you're too booked up when you're not.'

Rack leant forward, threatening. He did this very well, Bonn could see. The stander gave the counter lass a glance, don't interrupt.

261

'Who told you that?' Galahad's indignation was too weak.

'Why, Galahad?' Rack loved violence. He slowly lifted the table edge, and slowly let it down. The simplest threat.

Galahad gave a cough to get his voice going.

'Look, Bonn,' he said, but to Rack. 'I have to look my best, see?'

Rack didn't even glance at Bonn. He'd been given the job. 'Galahad. You gone against Bonn's rules. You could've said your piece then, butcher di'n't.'

Bonn listened curiously to Rack's changing speech. His Cockney reversion came out in aggro. Deliberately?

'I might make the championships, Bonn.' Still pleading to Rack.

'Diggin' yer grave, Galahad.' Rack opened his palms. Bonn thought, *Oremus*, let us pray, before the Consecration. 'How many yer closed?'

'Two.' Mesmerised, what could he get away with.

'It's six, innit?'

'Well, yes. But two were repeaters, honest.'

'Galahad.' Rack sat back, sighing. 'Six ern two int four, yer stoopid cunt. It's eight, geddit?'

'Why?' Galahad bleated, sensing the verdict and no way out. The counter girls had vanished, and the customers.

'Is yer stander in on it, or just you?'

'No. Me.'

Rack nodded to the air, telling Bonn he would check that.

'I believe yer, farzands wun't.' Rack said, 'Eight, Bonn.'

'Galahad.' Bonn touched the body builder's arm

262

sympathetically. 'You are suspended. It grieves me. You are fined a year's earnings. And please withdraw from the championships.'

Even Rack gasped at such punishment. Galahad stood, stunned.

'Where'll I get that much money, Bonn?'

Bonn spoke quietly and with compassion. 'I might reinstate you, in time. When that comes, repay the whole sum plus half as much again interest monthly, by working it off. There will be no physical hurt.'

Rack stirred. Punishment should be done proper, fists, bludgeoning, make people understand. He'd tell Bonn his theory of straighteners.

'Thanks, Bonn.' Galahad was hangdog, in tears. 'I'm sorry.'

As they started to leave, Bonn paused. 'I am so disappointed.'

The body builder recoiled as if struck. Bonn walked out, Rack following.

'Bonn. You oughter let some carnie in,' he urged, even if Bonn would never go back on a sentence. 'Coupla kicks straightens a bloke out. Think the girls'd get up if Grellie didn't have one tanked now and again? Jesus, walloping them two Aincoats saved Grellie more trouble than—'

'No, Rack.' Bonn paused at the entrance. It was coming on to rain. 'Find if Lancelot is also closing down. And check that Doob isn't still subtle mongering.'

Rack guffawed. 'Any more?'

'Yes,' Bonn stilled him by saying. 'Check Grellie too, please.'

Rack sobered. He looked at Bonn. Cold had come over him all of a sudden. For the first time he sensed that something was badly wrong.

Rack wanted to cheer him. 'Hey, Bonn,' he asked, brightening. 'You talk to Grellie about using her regular?'

'I suppose she is at the hospital.'

'Grellie? Yeah, she's taking some of the girls.'

Bonn relented. 'Get me there, Rack, please.'

Rack dashed for the motor before Bonn changed his mind.

*   *   *

The General was hectic. Bonn found it daunting. Trolleys clashed, thumping doors' rubber edges. Children howled, patients blundered. Rack was annoyed that Bonn said not to come in, the plod might see him and make the connection with Marla's flat. Rack started a theory, but Bonn looked him to silence and walked in.

He asked at the enquiry desk after Marla, her real name, Marlene Patricia Lancaster, off by heart. The clerk was slow, but told him Marla's ward, A-17, intensive care. He talked the lady into letting him use the internal phone. The ward sister told him nothing.

That was it. He wandered through the corridors to suss the layout, locating the lifts, wards. He wanted to ask after Lana, but Lana had too many names and the clerk might become suspicious.

A policeman was having coffee with a nurse in the anteroom of A-17. Glass panels allowed a partial view, but the patients were screened.

He followed the main drift. Most people left through the Out-Patients concourse. Doctors were being called. It was an hour before he decided

264

enough was enough, and gave up. Too much risk to find Lana, alive or dead.

Halting to let a nurse pass as he turned to leave, he heard an announcement over the intercom, a doctor wanted in Cardiology Surveillance, please . . .

Burtonall. Dr Burtonall, on extension six-one-four-six soonest.

Easy from there to visit the Reception. The hospital's internal phone list was cross-referenced, department and alphabetical. Ten minutes, he'd located the number. He invoked her smooth face, her air of being unsurprisable, capable of strong decisions. And her sudden stillness at his mention of Burtonall's name, the photograph that could have been her among club members by Glazie's desk. Make way for the doctor, at the accident.

'Bonn?'

His heart leapt, then he recognised Grellie by the fountain in the open area, seated on a bench. He joined her.

'I didn't see Marla, but I phoned. You?'

'She might be blind.' Grellie had been weeping. 'I said I was her sister. She's not recovered consciousness yet.'

'Dictaphones everywhere, I suppose.'

'There's a WPC in.' Grellie eyed him. 'You asked too?'

'Of course,' he said evenly. 'I'm as anxious as the rest. Lana?'

'Lana's . . .' Grellie sniffed, blotted her face, watched some children enter with their father, her eyes following the anxious little family. 'Bonn? Don't let me speak out of turn, but y'know? Like I asked?'

'Have a woman for my own.' Bonn nodded, the

265

subject grave.

'I'm in your queue. I feel it's time I went steady. I know there's your job and everything. I don't want to find you've got some girl.' She tried to smile. 'I know I look a mess. And it's unfair, what with Marla and your goers . . . y'know?'

It was as far as Grellie could go. Making it plainer might push him away. You couldn't tell with someone like Bonn.

'Thank you, Grellie. I'm finding my way still.'

'Is it my work?'

He looked at her. 'No. I shall woo someone soon.'

Woo, she thought, almost laughing at the archaic word. Considering what they did, for God's sake, 'woo' was deranged. She'd done poetry at school, *Idylls of the King*, old talk, trysts, mysterie. Was that Bonn's charm, that he could step back centuries, behaving proper in this city of knee-trembler shags in back streets?

'May I invite you for supper one evening? Nothing, well, y'know?'

Listen to myself, she thought distractedly. *May I invite* . . . Like she wasn't the whip for Martina's street stringers, working girls all, and like he wasn't key goer shagging the arse off any woman with gelt enough. Chivalry.

'Thank you, Grellie,' he replied, smiling as a child trotted round the fountain edge tracking a goldfish. 'I'm honoured.'

'Ta, wack,' she said, slang restoring sanity. She was rewarded by a brilliant smile that became more grin than she'd ever seen any man show, not silly wide, but of dazzling intensity. 'Tell me a time, luv.'

'I shall.' He rose to go, paused, and said, 'I like

you, Grellie.'

'What?' she said, startled. He moved off. 'Thank you,' she said foolishly after him. Her eyes started filling, but she instantly put a stop to that nonsense.

Rack was chatting up two girls in the car park, a risk Bonn didn't like to see. The girls said hello to Bonn, who said hello back and got in the car.

'Lana's dead, God rest her,' Bonn said, the minute they pulled away.

'Thought so.'

Rack started on how rain should be used for electric power in hospitals, save the kingdom a fortune. Bonn's mind was on Clare Three-Nine-Five.

CHAPTER TWENTY-EIGHT

Wadge—*an amount of money.*

At the last minute she volunteered to help at the Well Baby Clinic, from disguised motives. She had never felt so drained since her house jobs, when days and nights merged into a six-month blur, landmarked by tricks—like keeping the time and date you last ate written on your white coat sleeve so you didn't faint from hunger all over the place. Worn out, you had crazy suspicions that you'd missed some diagnosis, forgotten this new patient, that old case, or some patient you'd discharged last week... The mad total-time kaleidoscopic year that followed doctoral qualification.

Motive, she thought, making sure of her car keys. Self-correction, possibly, chastising herself for what she was about to do. Yet what *was* she going to do exactly? Meet a younger man—okay, think it outright, a *hired* male. So? Firms hired hostesses, didn't they? And men hired women, when need arose. She had hired Bonn, to investigate her husband. With, she angrily reminded herself, good reason.

But that hidden motive might be preventative.

She shuffled the clinical-pathology forms into one lot, handed them to Nurse Bushey, whose impatience clearly announced that such tardiness never happened in old Dr Rochford's day. Clare made herself be maddeningly casual, then hurtled from the hospital without using a changing room to see that she was decently turned out. Still, she was presentable. And she only intended to talk to the man, for goodness' sake, not ravish him the moment he stepped through the door.

That thought disturbed her as she drove from the car park. The instant *he* stepped through the door—wasn't that the wrong way round? *She* was going to make an entrance into *his* domain.

The traffic was flooding up from the south, of course, just when she was in a hurry. The M6, the car radio said, had lane closures today, single-lane stretches throttling the flow. She drummed her fingers on the wheel. Her motor seemed slower than usual.

Half her irritation was that she still smelled faintly of hospital, some disinfectant which clung to your clothes and hair. You could get rid of it by leaving your blouse on a warm radiator for an hour. Her spares were in her clothes case, which she carried for catastrophes. She never took that into surgeries, in case her fresh clothes took up the

268

disagreeable scent.

The approach to Victoria Square from the north was choked, hopeless, and thank you, God. She should have gone past the cathedral, but it was too late once you'd locked into the flow. She could have used the mobile phone, but Bonn had cautioned her. Home enthusiasts logged in and tapped messages, for psycho reasons.

Twenty minutes late, after all her rush.

*   *   *

It was as well, because it gave her less time for nerves. Bonn was unperturbed. He took her coat.

'I would have waited,' he said. 'Would you like a drink?'

You would have waited because you had to, she thought, oddly irritable. The aroma of coffee was about. Be perverse. 'Tea, please.'

'It's ready.'

He moved away, immediately reappeared with a tray. She felt annoyed. He must have made both. Then she warned herself. She was here in a new way.

'You have a new jacket,' she surprised herself by saying.

He sat across from her by the window. A suite, not merely one bedroom. Was this a clue to some change in her status? His jacket hung on an upright chair by a bureau, flowers in the vase. She liked that, but why was it reassuring? And his every gesture could be part of a plan. She hated the idea.

She didn't know what she was doing here. He poured the tea with routine questions about sugar, milk in first or last. Normality was needed.

269

'Have you been busy?' she asked, then could have kicked herself.

He paused to think, awkward as any man with crockery. *Checking what he's allowed to tell me?* she wondered. A 'client', as she now was, might be a risk.

He was unabashed, conversational. 'Yes. I have this difficulty. A stander.'

'Stander?' It sounded like furniture.

'Guardian, of the client and the goer. One who minds you, me.'

'Stander.' She savoured the word. 'A guardian . . .' Another mistake, in view of his background, from her visit to the priest's flat.

'Angel?' He smiled. 'Not quite. Standers are really rather vicious.'

A thought struck her. She asked uneasily, 'Do standers see the client?'

'Not normally. I mean, mine won't have seen your arrival.'

'But he's nearby?'

'Within call.' Bonn frowned, guiding the teacup to her. She thought, It's saucers that worry men. Why? 'Please don't be put off. He is totally committed to protecting our meeting. Nobody can intrude, invade, follow.'

'Yet you're having trouble?'

'With an applicant.' Bonn was full of apology. 'I have to reject so many.'

'You make it sound so normal.' Clare reproved herself. She wasn't doing very well, implying that he and his were utterly bizarre.

'It's our life. We have to keep it apart.'

So don't ask, is what he meant. 'You rejected him?'

270

'Sadly.' Bonn had Glazie in mind. 'He isn't alley-wise. Avenue-wise, yes.'

Clare couldn't help judging. Here was this ex-seminarian, with an august reputation, in a scandalous trade. She'd seen how spectators at the mogga dancing looked at him, as if he were somehow honourable. It was unnerving, the wrong way round.

His gear was less than trendy. She'd noticed this before, but not in the same detail. He wouldn't stand out in a crowd, yet once you were with him his reticence dwindled until you became struck by a sense of immediacy. Aura, was it? Impact, in Hollywoodspeak? No dangling medallions, no platinum wrist bands or startling watches, his chest hair not fungating with fashionable manliness. No buckles to be seen, no glints of power.

'Do you go to one place for your clothes?'

Or does somebody pick them for you? But did not ask. So far she'd identified at least two different voices over the phone. Those females, perhaps? Did he go to some fashion house with arty girls arguing how far to go when cladding him for a stint? From seminarian to goer. She had a mad image, him taking the Offertory collection from clients. 'Client' was offensive. She refused to think of herself like that.

'I have no dress sense.' He guessed her thoughts, offhand.

'Do you have, well, a code of dress?'

That stopped him in mid-reach. Instead he sat beside her.

'Not that I know.'

'Haven't you asked? I mean, you've not been a . . . doing this for long.'

271

'I'll see if I can find out.' Closing that conversation. 'The dancer won.'

'Dancer? Your friend?' That strange dancing, from style to style to a constant melody.

Bonn was at ease. He slid to the carpet with that awkwardness of the male, several quick successive changes. 'The bribe worked. He sacked his girl, though.'

'Is he also a . . .?'

'I make terrible coffee.' It was a reminiscence. 'I tasted some Camp coffee, as a little lad. I was quite ill. I'm on tenterhooks, in case you ask for it.'

She was almost amused, but held herself in check. A gambit, was it? She decided to risk it. 'How much of you is tactics, Bonn?'

'The same as everybody else, I suppose.'

Clare digested that. 'You never ask questions, Bonn.' He raised his head to look up at her. She went on. 'Not even about Clifford Burtonall. He's my husband.'

He didn't even nod. 'There's no reason I should. Questions are pretend.'

'They can't be, or why ask?' He said nothing. 'Pretend for whom?'

'For what.' He seemed not to want to meet her eyes. 'I don't think much of motives. Motives are pointless. All those murder mysteries, pretending that a motive provides the solution and justice follows. Motives are the pretence in questions.'

'For the women you meet? Is that what you mean?'

'For the game.'

That shocked her. She sipped his atrocious tea. 'Game' sounded hateful, not even 'trade'. She wanted to go, have no more of this charade. He'd

272

served her purpose, found out horrid facts about her criminal husband.

'Game? The women you meet are a game?'

She'd astonished him. 'Certainly not. To me it's special.'

There was a limit to what she could ask. 'Whose game, Bonn?'

'Theirs, of course.' He rolled over and lay there, a hand propping up his chin. 'Women play question games. It's their compulsion. What if, what happens when, how do you, endless. It's almost an ailment. I don't mind.' He spoke flatly, obliged to endure. 'It's what they do.'

'It's interest,' Clare said, defensive. If he felt so strongly about it, he ought at least to be upset. His clients deserved it. 'Women are interested in such things.'

'Interest is wrong. I wish it was only that.'

Clare argued, 'Women are interested in your life, how you see them. It *is* fascinating. You must see that, especially after your earlier . . .' Career?

He answered to cover her gaffe, 'No. The question game is one gigantic risk. Their questions, but my risk. And the questions merge into one.'

'And what is women's one question?'

'Are the other women better, lovelier, sexier. They don't ask it outright, just proxy, skate round the rim hoping you'll shout the answer from the middle of the cracking ice, save them having to skate out where the ice is perilous.'

'That's offensive! It's chauvinist!'

'No. It is merely sad, and innocent.'

It was also absurd. She was so tired of his bloody calm. He should have bawled. '*You're* calling *me* chauvinist?' because after all she'd hired him. This

273

visit was a disaster. She should never have come. What on earth was she thinking of, childishly wanting to get back at Clifford? She was ashamed for having used Bonn.

She asked in expiation, 'How long will you keep on with it?'

'The life.' He considered that. A fluke, but still a hit. He said eventually, 'I feel a constancy that is new. I never felt like this.' He gave her his apology look. 'Even finding out what you asked was quite proper.'

'It feels the opposite, to me. Chagrin.'

'Don't.' He reached and took her hand, examined the nails, palmar creases. 'It might have been worse.'

His angers felt warm, hers cold. She began to feel nervous. Clifford, the two girls, financial roguery, were so awful that she hadn't thought beyond the facts. 'Worse how?'

'Two deaths. He might have been involved somehow in both.'

She gazed down blankly. 'Both?'

'One girl's died.' He saw her stricken look. 'The other might give evidence. The police will want Salvo.'

'And Clifford?' She said bitterly, letting the cloak drop, 'My husband could have been more honest with me.'

'Let me.' He subjected her other hand to the same intense gaze.

'Are you a fortune-teller?' Her laugh was unconvincing.

'The police might not link Mostern and Lana— the girl who died—with Salvo. If he was the one who killed Lana and blinded Marla—'

274

'Blind?' She was instantly contrite. 'I sound like I'm hoping.'

'They don't know yet if Marla actually saw Lana killed . . .' Bonn halted. He still held her hand.

'They'll arrest him for murder?' Clare decided not to withdraw. If it was some tactic, she thought tiredly, then so what? It was a comfort, and she'd missed comfort lately. 'Salvo might tell the police about Clifford.'

He touched her face with his fingertips. The gesture surprised her.

'No. He has to stick to his story.'

'Are you sure?'

'Can I look?' he asked. And slowly turned her face so he could see her in profile. He gazed so long that she felt her colour begin to heighten. 'Somebody in prison has to obey once they take the wadge.'

'Wadge?' Her cheeks were prickling, her mouth feeling paraesthesia. She didn't move away.

'The money a villain gets for work. That—'

'—that Clifford paid Salvo?'

'Yes. Break the code, Salvo would be lucky to survive a week.'

'What would happen?' Listen to me, she thought, aghast, discussing the next murder with a man I've hired.

'He'd be found hanged in his cell. The verdict would be suicide.'

Does Clifford know this? she wanted to know. And does he care, that the deaths might not be finished even now? Her rage returned.

'This is unusual for me,' she said quietly. She meant that she was usually the one who inspected, diagnosed.

'I know. Except you are bonny.' He spoke as if wondering how that came to be.

'I haven't been called that for a long time.'

He looked at her as if curious and pleased with what he saw. She almost expected him to begin the inept lover litany, how she'd previously met all the wrong men, Bonn earning his fee. Instead he let her go.

He was closer now. She realised she was staring at him in something like astonishment. His eyes were blue, she saw, filled with an emotion she could not quite identify. His finger touched her lips.

She felt her throat tighten. She wanted him not to go, to explain if these gestures were a ritual that he'd been trained to perform for, on, a client.

'I wonder if it's time,' he said, almost not to her.

For a moment his meaning was unclear. 'I was wondering,' she began, but his finger pressed gently on her mouth. Not cinnamon, she thought, not quite coriander. But, then, did she still stink of hospital?

'We have the chance, Clare.' He removed his hand before she could notice. 'Here,' he said gravely, 'you are unknown. Safe. The world will neither know nor care. It is a kind of beauty, to possess a new part of life.'

He isn't trying to persuade, she thought, not quite put out. She felt becalmed. Nobody would ever know.

'It is my purpose,' he said softly, absently, 'to offer you time unknown to anyone else. I shall never remember. The memory will only ever be yours.'

'It's just . . .' She halted. *What* was it 'just'?

He stood slowly, and raised her without effort.

'I'm not at all sure whether I meant to . . .'

'Meant to be unknown? Nobody knows you here. If you decide, I shall be secret and invisible too.'

He walked with her. They entered the bedroom. It was simply furnished, bright from a bedside lamp, the sheets turned down. Flowers, freesias this time, so few as to be almost symbolic.

Without a word he sat on the edge of the bed, drawing her round to stand close. Frowning with concentration, he started to undo her jacket, taking so long that she had to help him. He caught the garment as it slid off her shoulders. Then her blouse, not pulling it from her skirt but simply undoing the button nearest his hands.

His clear wonderment was not simulated, as the blouse came free. He lifted his shoulder for her hand to rest there while she stepped from the pool of her skirt, bright amazement on his face. As the last garment went she was smiling at his transparent delight. Still sitting, he conducted her in an arc. Three paces, and she sank to the bed's fresh cool sheets.

The feel of his body against hers was a novelty, his impatience startling. It was then that she knew herself to be his accomplice. She was astonished, then gratified, when the sensation was there exactly as she'd imagined. It was as if a deep excitement had been waiting to be released. He usurped her body with her treacherous consent. The moment he entered her she felt brilliant, defiant, triumphantly serving somebody right, giving them their own back—all the childish phrases.

Gratification swamped her as he still held her before the slow movements began. That was the most astonishing thing, her body chasing his faster movements. This was effortless. She'd earned this, she almost cried out, and she made a sulky defiant decision to leap the barrier of taboo. Bought joy was her joy, her act of buying proof that she owned and deserved it.

For a moment she let him wait, lifting to ease his steady rummage in her. This too was an amazement, that he accepted her gift, pleasing himself. It was important, she told herself, breathing harder, but for later, not now.

Bonn steadied a moment, already sweating. She heard herself groan with pleasure as her hands roamed on his chest, feeling the dampness. It was tentative at first, her hand on his flank, down the slight recess of his waist. She sniffed, the doctor in her smiling inwardly at the thought of pheromones at work. Then she inhaled greedily, glad of his scent, cupping him with a grunt of ecstasy. He lifted himself to look down questioningly, relaxed at her smile, and resumed work more purposefully. She didn't mind *work* now one bit.

Somehow she'd gone through a different barrier. With Clifford, it was slow finger play first, then a gradual coupling. Good, usually, but this was different because of Bonn's otherness, removed from the ordinary. She heard herself yelping as she dragged behind to prolong the delay between his ploughing and her reception, feeling a relish that became startlingly new as they worked. The barrier was in herself, had been there like a wall. With a growl of pleasure as her concentration began to weaken under his moves, she thought, I am now able to say, with a terrible crudity, I *want*.

Perverse, she groaned and gasped, 'Wait, wait!'

He stilled, matching her groan and came to rest

278

with a slight shudder. Obeyed. She realised she was ruining her moment, yet gaining by testing her right. That was the newness. She had procured him for this, exchanging her woman's mere presence for authority over this shoving male. He was not currying favour, persuading, paying court. None of that. He was here, for her whim. Copulating on her demand, the terms hers. She could tell him to withdraw, come now fast, or take his time. She could be serviced like a motor, used, abused, treated, or mistreated.

It was freedom, she thought, gazing up at him with astonishment, a breaking of chains.

She kept him motionless, looking down at her, by a swift shake of her head on the pillow and a tightening of her clasp about his waist. Sweat was running on them. She was almost furious at herself for tormenting this way. He tensed in query as she moaned aloud, as she clung to the terrible, baffling thought of freedom. Love was something aside. This was coupling, hers. She beckoned him with a lift of her chin, and when he lowered bit his shoulder savagely, thrilled. This inner dawn absolved. This domination was her absolution. It would not be wrong. There were no more boundaries. She registered the amazing notion, strained not to let it go.

Drenched, she sank back, tasting her own salty sweat, feeling a vast relief as he began to stir her. She pushed a hand beneath him and tugged, her rogue fingers maddeningly urging him to speed.

A keening rose in her throat. For a moment she struggled to contain it, then gave vent and rushed with him as they beat together and dissolved.

*   *   *

Clare dreamed. Her dream was nothing to do with the man dozing beside her, his chest expanding, deflating, his arm heavier by the minute, her leg still cast over him. She wondered whether to move it, a weight, but caught herself. No, because I close that particular door, Bonn, bear me. Only then can you go free—until next time, when I come and take possession of you again.

She was replete. This almost made her laugh, satiety an achievement.

She felt justified, as was her right. The princesses of old donned masks and simply announced to all and sundry that they were incognito. They could then go visit lovers, theatres, anywhere, while the world politely ignored them. A token mask put recognition out of the question. How civilised, how perfect!

But love? Love nudged her mind.

Anthropologists from New Orleans, or was it Nevada, proved 'romantic love' in over 88 per cent of the world's cultures they investigated. Dreamily, she recalled a furious argument among medical physiologists over this finding. Was love poetry a mere biological stimulus, then? On the other hand, divorces peak at the fourth marital year. Anthropologists had a field-day over this, claiming it coincided with the time when a primitive tribal three-year-old child could start foraging for itself, with luck, as it wandered with its parents, who were in search of other mates.

Love, though? She stroked his body. She had the right to.

Bravely she let her dream glide into doctoral

mode. The excitement of love is not—she forced the thought—something generated chemically in the brain by phenylethylamine, with maybe a slow dribble of the neurochemicals norepinephrine and dopamine to buzz you to reach orgiastic thrills with their amphetaminelike whirr. That accounts, though purely chemically, for the elation and, well, the passion of love's coupling. Her sluggish, purring, satiated body joined the argument by thinking of the love act's sheer sexual rut. The lovingness, maybe? Maybe, not to put too fine a point on it, that was the fuck quantile?

Well, okay, her dreamy mind conceded. But chemistry left out the cosiness of love, something she had never truly met before, which was really odd. The comfort should be something discovered at home, with a husband, not newly come across in bed with a hireling. Neurochemically speaking, you could call it the thirty-month kick, because it's then that the body becomes tolerant of its glandular drugs squirted in under a particular male's stimulus. As if one male was no longer enough. Like drug tolerance? The dose of heroin that relieves the intractable pain of metastatic cancer, and the appalling cough of bronchogenic carcinoma, no longer has the same effect day after day. You have to increase the dose, then double it, then raise it to erstwhile lethal quantities to give the poor patient any relief at all. So could *person* tolerance exist? It was offensive, in a world where true love 'should be' for life.

Maybe neurochemicals, weakening smartish after marital monogamy sets in, knew better?

There is a gratification seeing pairs together, hand in hand or, she almost giggled, genitalia with genitalia. Her mind delved into its memory bag and slyly brought out a memory of an elderly couple who for forty years had experienced marital difficulties—the wife's ailments worsened by the husband's countless betrayals. When, seeing them together, she had asked in detail about their perseverance, the man had expressed astonishment: 'But we're married!' The woman too had been quite indignant. 'Good heavens! The very idea!' Clare remembered having a hard time mollifying them.

Was that love longevity, then? Or was it simply a preference for endorphins, those other chemicals—so like morphine derivatives—that warmed and cocooned your mind so it believed itself 'safe' near the loved one? Rubbish magazines talked about 'cuddle chemicals', like the pituitary gland's special oxytocin secretion, but slang nicknames only meant that doctors too wanted everything reduced to a glib catchphrase that pretends to be an explanation.

She found that she had rolled into Bonn's awakening embrace.

'Yes?' she asked.

'It's close to time, Clare.'

Stretching in annoyance, she grunted, collapsed, huddled closer.

'What a pest. Are you sure?'

His voice changed. She could tell that he smiled. 'Afraid so.'

A thought struck her. 'I asked for an extension. What if I wanted the rest of the evening?' Surely things had changed?

'I would like to.' Maybe it was more complicated now. 'I couldn't. I'm sorry.'

Was he really? More complex still.

'Could you as an option?' She could have

phrased that better than a clinical interrogator. Treacherous endorphins to blame? She was tempted to ask, indignant, how other women got extensions.

'No, Clare. It's time.'

She was still swaddled down, he half reclining. She moved her head to lie on his belly, freeing her face for air. Her watch was still on her wrist, quite incongruous. And look at the time.

They dressed without speaking. She felt no compunction leaving the money. He held the door for her. She did not look back.

*   *   *

Her old Humber was no longer sanctuary, as it so often seemed. Now it was a nuisance. Bonn was back there. She thought of a hundred questions she might have cleverly introduced, penetrating his apologetic defence.

Frankly, she'd had time for a bath, and she could have changed. But her fresh clothes were untouched, and she'd kept his sweat on her. To *wear*. He'd sweated cobs, as locals said. She'd never known a man like him. Wet through, they'd been, the pair of them. The bed must be soaked, she thought with guilt. Once he'd got going, working with that mindlessness she'd puzzled at, rivulets ran from his body onto hers. Like a meniscus in a tube, she thought impiously, that hugged the capillary glass. She settled down for the run into the Wirral and home.

Grandma had called it the man-smell. It lurked in Grampa's own sideboard drawer—which, once daringly opened, contained only old medals, three surprisingly fine old silk scarves, lone gloves, a masonic charity badge, and faded football programmes that, astonishingly, showed Grampa triumphant—moustache, long baggy knicks, folded arms, slicked black hair. The scent was thick, alien, definite. A dark pungent tree-smell. Not 'smell' either. Aroma, more like.

She'd wanted Bonn's aroma. The pity was that it faded. Did pheromones leave so soon? It might be worth looking up, some ill-remembered biochemisty.

'Perfume?' she corrected aloud. 'A smell is a smell is aroma.'

An overtaking driver looked askance, intrigued, seeing her talking away. Clare was embarrassed, pretended to be singing along with the mute radio. What the hell, she thought, 30 per cent of shoppers talked to themselves, said social surveys. Much they knew.

She had pulled something off today, a remarkable achievement. She would have time for a bath, that unwonted riddance, before Clifford came home.

Her behaviour was truly innocent. What she'd done was no more than a pastime. Other women must be doing it by the million, like having your hair done, changing an uncomfortable bra. That was it. She mustn't think of Bonn as world-shattering.

And what, she told herself, a tart anger starting as she pulled onto the Wirral motorway, if that was a lie? It was her lie, nobody else's. Everyone harboured lies. Now she too had one all her own.

She could cope, Clifford, police, and all.

284

CHAPTER TWENTY-NINE

Stringer—*one prostitute (especially female) of a group.*

Next day there was a rumble at the Ball Boys. Rack had to drag out two of Grellie's girls. They'd started it, Rack told Bonn.

'It's the disco's air, see?' Rack waxed as they walked among the street crowds, police sirens all wahwahing. 'You breathe in what other people've breathed out, you start shoving people—'

Bonn had had enough. 'Please find Doob.'

'Doob? At the Triple Racer.' Rack added disgustedly, as they angled through the traffic near where Mostern had been downed, 'Our two tarts squabbled over Drummer. He pays for a shag in scag.'

At the Triple Racer, Bonn stood under the awning listening to the couriers' tales of wheelies, donkers, and slidders, incomprehensible talk of how they did a needle and saved forty-eight seconds on a run to the Corn Exchange.

'Doob.' Bonn kept his voice civil. The new goer was pleased to be seen talking with his key. 'Please say how much you drink now.'

'Soda water, Bonn. No spirits, no beer, no wine. Honest.'

'When did you last do a dip?'

The traffic roared and chugged, a car horn parping. Traffic lights had failed on the station slope. A policeman was on point duty.

'You saw me, I think. I've done nowt since.' Bonn waited. 'Honest.'

'Very well, Doob, I want you to dip something from a lady's handbag.'

The pickpocket looked from Bonn to Rack. 'You *want* me to do a tarpaulin? You threatened—'

'I do not threaten, Doob. It will be cleared with Martina.'

'No comeback?' Doob pursed his lips. 'Say when, Bonn.'

They parted, Bonn and Rack heading for the snooker hall. Grellie waved and crossed to meet them in the bus-park gardens.

'Those two girls, Rack. Do they use scag themselves?'

'That's the trouble, Bonn. Grellie decides that, and Martina.'

'Rack, please,' Bonn asked. It had been worrying him. 'What is a needle?'

Rack was proud. 'Needle's when you drive up a one-way street the wrong direction, see? Saves you hours. Bikers like doing it. They run a book, who does most needles in a week. Know why? Petrol's like blood, see . . .'

*   *   *

'There's some connection, sir.' Windsor wouldn't give up. He alone of the police loved the coffee, drank it black, some said a dozen plastic cups a day.

'Any word?'

'Somebody local gave him the mother.'

Hassall sighed, shook his head. 'I'm always tired these days. I like short cuts—when I don't land up to my knees in muck. Who warned Salvo off?'

'I don't know yet, but I'm convinced.'

Hassall had a coughing fit, eventually came to

wiping his rheumy eyes.

'My age, you never get shut of flu. Lingers. Doctors, bloody useless.' He lolled at his desk. 'Salvo? How come it's all Salvo?'

'He's the tart's bloke. Lived at the flat.' Windsor ticked points off, the way Hassall hated. 'Seen nearby. Aggro over Marla. The camera when Mostern—'

'Don't count,' Hassall said heavily. 'I tried that inhaler stuff from Boots. You shove it up a nostril, squirt. I sneezed my bloody head off for two days. Cost a fortune. The camera was put out.'

'The other one showed Salvo descending the railway—'

'You're not in court,' Hassall interrupted rudely. 'Sorry. Think what some clever-dick barrister'd make of *that*. "So, Mr Windsor, you pick out a random subject from several hundreds, and make unfounded accusations . . ." Salvo—what's his real name anyway?—must help us with enquiries. Find him.'

'Sir.'

Windsor left the office. Hassall gazed after him. Soon, Windsor would be in the canteen mouthing off about pedantic old bastards who should get the fuck out of it. Play crown-green bowls. Hassall was the wrong side of forty. He hated age. Age was what younger officers forced you to. It wasn't fair.

*   *   *

Grellie, Bonn, Rack stood before Martina's bare desk.

'Lana is dead. It means problems for us.'

'We're not to blame,' Grellie said quickly.

287

'Nobody says you are, Grellie.'

Martina was cool, still in there thinking possibilities.

Grellie rushed on, worried, 'I mean, Martina, we're not responsible for bits on the side. Marla liked Lana. So what? It happens both sides of the fan.'

'You're jumping to conclusions.' Martina hadn't yet asked Rack for new details, which Bonn thought odd. Some warning in there. 'The police are already busy-busy. It's rotten luck for Marla, Lana. Some punter battered them. Stick to the tale when the plod come. We have no idea. Understand?'

'Yes, Martina.'

'We're never mentioned,' Martina ground quietly on. 'You all go, "What syndicate? What's it mean?" over and over.'

'The girls're up in arms, Martina.'

'Keep them quiet, Grellie. They can murmur only among themselves.'

'Can we visit Marla?'

Martina thought for a moment. 'Yes. But go through the motions.'

'Right.' Grellie asked, uncomfortable, 'I want cover. A feller.'

'She means Bonn,' Rack crashed in cheerfully. 'She doesn't want the Bill reckoning her one of Lana's lez pals. Don't blame you, Grell.'

Grellie coloured, stung. 'I'll be a friend calling at Marla's.'

'No.' Martina thought a moment. 'Too chancy. Let the plod find their own clues. Posser's going to Cardiac OutPatients. *Don't* go with Bonn.'

Grellie didn't dare make the challenge directly, but it had to be said. 'The girls'll be upset nobody

288

from my side's visited Marla.'

'All right.' Martina made a show of being talked round. 'You go too.'

'See?' Rack brightened, Grellie and Bonn paired off at last, some good coming out of this shambles. 'It's like I told you, Martina—'

Both women interrupted him together, Grellie quickly giving way.

'Go separately, Grellie, not as a couple. Take up a collection for Marla. I'll quadruple the sum raised.'

Martina asked Bonn to stay back as the other two left.

'It's all one, Bonn,' she said after a while. She told him Rack's story. 'The man—Burtonall, is it?—called not long after Salvo left Marla and Lana. I want to know all you've learned. Is it this Clare Three-Nine-Five?'

'Yes. She's a doctor, married to Burtonall. He's grafting some inner-city development.' He hesitated. 'I can't see why it's gone through the roof.'

'This Goldoni. You asked me for a studio flat near the theatre.'

'Rack's relative? I remember.'

'He's a money man. Friend of Burtonall. They're funding our takeover.' She judged the effect her words had on Bonn.

Bonn looked at the wall behind Martina's head, returned. 'I didn't know.'

Martina seemed satisfied by his reaction. 'I don't know where Goldoni gets his information. Does this Clare know anything more?'

'No. I blew her mind.' Bonn's slang tasted awkward.

'Goldoni's able to fund our takeover with, by, Burtonall. Who is simply doing both—peeling the city councillors, and partnering Goldoni's wedge.'

'Martina,' Bonn started up, not wanting to ask outright.

'Goldoni uses renters from the Ball Boys,' she said impatiently. 'That's all.'

Bonn blinked. She watched him for signs of perfidy. He sighed, went over what he had learned from Jefferson, Tuesday, Glazie.

'Nicolette,' he remembered. 'I reported doubts about her.'

'She's Goldoni's. She susses out businesses.'

Anyone else would have instantly jumped in, professed honesty, that they'd disclosed nothing. Not Bonn. He simply waited, his honesty beyond question.

Bonn mentioned all his other sources, Askey the diminutive messenger, the Triple Racer lads, Rack, Grellie. She listened attentively, pushing her hair away from her face.

'This Clare Three-Nine-Five. What hinges on her?'

'Nothing that I can see.' He dwelt on the problem. 'She pays cash. I think she'll be back. Her husband, after all.'

'She's punishing him by hiring you?' Martina really wanted to know.

'I surmise so.'

'Then surmise what further steps we take about La Burtonall.' Immediately Martina wished she'd avoided sarcasm. 'Do we follow her? If so, why? Do we sanction this husband? If so, why?'

'Sanction how?'

She wanted to pace, show body language to make
290

herself more assertive. Lameness was the ultimate insult to a woman. 'There's only one sanction here, Bonn.' She barked a harsh laugh. 'He could be simply removed.'

'Remove?' He could accept evils done, but not evils planned.

She said with vulgar bluntness, 'It would pacify the girls. They see themselves in the mortuary, or blinded like Marla. Can you blame them?'

Bonn gathered arguments. 'Do nothing, Martina. Let the police sort it out. Salvo is the link—we know that, they can't prove it. Burtonall too—we know that, but the police can't prove that either.'

'Where is Salvo?'

'No idea.' He considered. 'He'll have to keep going. Somebody will have to be . . . reproved.'

Martina was relieved he'd spoken out. It showed his allegiance, which she'd never doubted anyway. 'Grellie's girls would mutiny otherwise. It'd take them a year, then our whole thing'd go to pieces.' They gave each other the chance to speak, then Martina asked, 'Clare Three-Nine-Five will book you again?'

'She said so. She behaved so.' Fair to Martina, he told her that he'd mentioned the Café Phrynne, that they might meet at the mogga dancing. 'Somewhere open.'

'So.' Martina felt cold. If there was something between Bonn and this Clare, she of the don't-suffer-fools voice, then Clare could pick her own way through the minefield without the syndicate's help. 'She does pay?'

'Of course. A client, after all.' He knew what she was asking.

'See Marla without Grellie. Invent some story,

you used to go out with her once, like that. Suss out what you can.'

'Very well.'

'And, Bonn?' He raised his eyebrows in query. 'Come to Posser's this evening, maybe eightish.'

Even that command couldn't faze him. 'Thank you. I shall be there.'

She passed word to Osmund that she would leave immediately.

*　　　*　　　*

Thinking what had happened, Clare relived without shame her new vehemence. The feeling of complicity did it. She'd been assertive, shoving Bonn with her heels, moving him round for herself without considering him in the slightest.

She thought of her abandon. His movements had been softer than she'd wanted, so she had drawn him close, harder, for a more rasping sensation, to achieve on her own terms. As their bodies beat to her pace, his mouth at first evaded hers, why she didn't know, but she remembered grabbing his face with her fingers brutally curved into his cheeks, talons almost, and forced her mouth to his. She even cried out coarse instructions, flailing so he had to strain to keep hold.

The noise, moans, her crudities might have been angelic voices for all she cared.

And afterwards, she'd been as replete as she had ever been, feeling astonishingly light-headed and stunningly refreshed. She had taken possession, for the first time had ruled.

That day, renewed, she drove to the hospital and found the cardiologists. She told Dr Porritt that she

292

would accept his survey, and begin almost immediately. She visited the small surveillance unit and checked again that Clifford's results were through. The laboratory reports were on the printout, timed and dated as she'd written.

Nothing could go wrong. She left, went round to Clifford's office, and gave him the news. They made routine politenesses. Clifford took her to a small café.

'It's plain sailing,' Clare told him quietly.

'My results okay, were they?'

'Fine.' She tried a laugh, unconvincing. 'I ought to charge you.'

'Thank goodness, darling.'

The endearment did nothing to put the clock back. 'What now?' she asked. Last night they had slept together, but turned away.

'That Windsor came.' He pulled a face. 'I proved I was with you. He implied that he'd check up.'

'And?'

The café was unbearably noisy. Actors were in, one demonstrating how he'd faced down some director, to approving roars from friends.

'That's it. The news said some bloke is being sought, to help with enquiries.'

'What will you do?'

Clifford asked, 'What will *I* do? Not us any longer?'

She was ice of a sudden. 'You did everything without telling me. Why consult me now?' Yesterday she would have been all worried sick. Now she saw the gulf between them.

'I'll have to think, darling. It depends if they catch him.'

'How direct is your connection with Salvo?'

'There's no evidence. He can say what he likes. I'll deny it. It's that simple.'

'Clifford.' She almost relented. He was putting such a brave face on it. 'If you decide to, well, do anything else, you will tell me, won't you?'

'Promise, darling.' He put his hand on hers, and looked into her eyes. 'This has made us more married than ever.'

CHAPTER THIRTY

Homer—*the hiring of a goer for coitus or other sexual purposes by a woman in her own home.*

Drizzle came on, nothing like the north's usual heavy stuff. Salvo hated it. A bloke couldn't wear the right clothes in this. Darkness turned into a shambolic slutchy seep. He told the tart this. She said it would clear. She wasn't much good, did sex like having a kip, groused that he'd left a ring round the bath. So?

'The next water'll wash it off. It's what water's for, for fuck's sake.'

Even that pissed her off.

'Don't swear,' she said, like she was some saint, selling her arse in Vaughan Street. 'It'll stop when the tide turns. Rain always does.'

Fucking tides, Salvo thought. The fucking sea meant Liverpool.

Not knowing what to do maddened you as much as anything. He'd gone to Oz's, but the taxi was gone. He'd asked at Oz's local, but he'd not been in. Oz's terraced house was locked, no life. Twice he'd been back, until some old hag next door started watching from her steps. He'd picked up this ammy tart to get a place to rest until he could find Oz, decide.

Her room was over a barber's in Moorgate Street, where the buses started back to the square. Grellie's stringers hated ammies, casual tarts who'd shag for a drink, charge what they thought they could get away with. Her name was Robina.

Grellie's stringers were pros and proud of it, working girls. Salvo'd often heard them blamming any ammy who peddled their patches, fought them tooth and nail on the pavements, kicking and squealing. Twice he'd asked to be a ponce, used to keep Grellie's streets ammy-clean, but that bastard Rack had his own mob. Closed shop, was unfair to blokes with ambition.

Robina was bottle-pale, twitchy, a user. He'd found her on the working men's club car park, two good comedians on that night so dense crowds, raucous noise when he'd passed. No car was the swine, because wheels were everything. He'd gone to suss the motors, but there was a hawkeyed bouncer on lurk who just belly-laughed in the semi-dark when Salvo tried a car handle. It was enough warning, the lurk sure of himself even with groups of noisy drinkers six, eight, a dozen strong arriving. So no fucking wheels. Salvo knew better than try nicking one from the streets this hour of the night. The street thieves were all on frannies, the bought-and-paid-for right to steal parked motors.

Salvo had even tried to get in on that four months back, got told to piss off. A little black Salford nerk, thin as a whippet and a cough like a Mersey horn, got took on with hardly a blink. It wasn't fair, when

295

Salvo could do anything he turned his mind to. He watched Robina.

The slut was humming, doing her face in a mirror you could hardly see through. One bulb lit the room, a flex trailing in under the door, typical whore's trick of bleeding electric from the landing. Salvo hated flies. One thing about Marla, she kept flies out of the flat, spent more on fucking sprays than on rent. He'd remember the pong of her sprays for ever—red containers, three to a window sill.

He didn't want to be with this Robina cunt. He'd only shagged to get his feet under her table. She said they'd go out, get a pizza, a drink before the pubs closed, like he was some fucking football hooligan.

'Got a phone?' He stared at the ceiling.

'You'll be lucky.' She didn't even look, just anybody on her bed.

'Got telly?'

'I use my mate's.' She did that thing they did, folding their lips in before seeing what she looked like after all that expensive beauty care.

'Where is it?' He wanted news.

'Upstairs, but she does club turns till gone midnight.'

'Turns?'

'A singer. We go halves.' Now she looked. 'It's got to pay well, or it's not worth it.'

'Can you get into her place?'

'No. We don't lend keys. You might get a psycho.'

He almost laughed at her. He'd done Mostern, thought that didn't count because Oz'd helped. He'd done Lana on his own, so she counted.

He'd a few quid left. He'd best leave the city,

296

softer down south.

'I'll go for a pizza.' He got up.

That stopped her checking how gorgeous she was, drawing on her eyebrows. Marla did that.

'What's your game?'

'I'll bring one in.' He got his jacket. 'Not be a sec.'

She stood with quick anger. 'I'm coming—'

He clouted her down. The mirror fell forward, cracked on the floor, a piece cutting her leg. He'd had enough, everybody giving him lip.

Her handbag was hanging on the door. He got her few measly notes.

'Where's your fucking money?' he bawled at her. The dizzy cunt hadn't the sense to answer. The insolence of ignorance. He kicked her. Enough to piss anybody off, the run of bad luck he was having.

He started ransacking the room, pulled drawers out, yanking the pictures off the wall, yelling, 'Where? Fucking *where*?' throwing her chair at the stupid bint.

Somebody shouted, too far off to worry about, maybe upstairs. He hauled the rug up, then had a brilliant idea and looked in the microwave. A fold of notes. He crowed, waved them in the silly fucker's face, yelling.

'Think you were clever?'

She'd been trying to crawl to the door. He booted her back, rage taking over so he couldn't speak, just had to do things, make her realise you didn't use people. Get away with anything because you're a tart's all right most times, but you can do it once too fucking often.

He kicked the paraffin stove over, emptied the spare tin, half full, over her fucking useless bed, and

297

got her cigarette lighter from her handbag. A gas lighter, thank Christ, first bit of luck. Fires burned off dabs, he'd heard, never a fingerprint that survived burning.

Its flame he clicked tall, said to her from the doorway, 'Robina, one fucking word, I'll be back.'

She said nothing, lying there still, so she'd learned some fucking sense. Salvo almost laughed out loud. The silly cunt would soon move fast enough.

He opened the door, stepped onto the dingy landing with its trailing flex, chucked the lighter into the room, and ran.

* * *

Martina herself opened the door to Bonn. For a moment neither of them spoke, then Martina moved aside and held the door.

'Thank you for being so prompt, Bonn.'

'And you for your kind invitation.'

He went inside, stood awkwardly in the hallway not knowing quite what to expect. The scent of cooking. He hadn't known whether to have something to eat coming through the square, or whether to trust to luck. If she offered a drink and he refused, it might give offence. Drink gave him a blinding headache on an empty stomach. If she didn't, he would have to last out manfully and get some fish and chips on the way home. But even there he'd have to be careful, because Martina knew everything before dawn. She would know that he'd left her home famished. Which, he agonised, preceding her down the hall when she gestured him to go ahead, might make her think that he'd been presumptuous in assuming that he'd been invited to dinner. Had his acknowledgement of her welcome itself been an arrogance, that word 'invitation'?

The table was set for three. He tried not to notice, and went to greet Posser.

The old man was sitting upright on a straight-backed wooden chair. He waved Bonn to an armchair opposite. His exhalations were prolonged squeaks, an old leather bag at a fire that would no longer draw.

'Sorry for the racket, Bonn,' Posser breathed. 'Put up with me, eh?'

'Glad to, Posser.'

'Would you care for a drink, Bonn?' Martina limped to a drinks cabinet. 'We have sherry, wine, something short if you'd rather.'

'I,' Posser puffed. They paused. Bonn had learned from a priest who'd stuttered the art of waiting for faulty speakers. The trick was not to feel anguish, or you ruined their attempt. Sit there not worrying, just waiting—above all, no help—and they made it. Especially don't interrupt. Their struggle had a right to a silence.

'Had a liking for whisky, once,' Posser completed in a rush. 'Until my daughter here forced me to drink red wine for my health.' It took a minute or so to say.

'Red wine is better for you, Posser.'

'Don't you start, Bonn. I get enough from Martina.'

'Thank you,' Bonn told Martina. 'Have you lemonade, please?'

'There'll be wine with supper.'

Bonn saw Martina had guessed his anxiety, and felt his face redden. Now he didn't know whether to pretend astonishment that he was to stay for a meal, or to protest he'd decided against having any alcohol.

'If I had the wind.' Posser made them wait, then managed, 'I'd ask what the hell's going on. Youth, against us wrinklies?'

'It's salmon,' Martina said, amiably cuffing her father. 'Red wine, no spirits. I've told you.'

'Listen to her.' Posser sat forward, his eyes closing as his daughter went to make a din in the kitchen. 'You don't know the pleasure, Bonn.'

'What pleasure exactly?'

'Of sitting like this.' Posser now leant with his elbows on his knees, shoulders slumped, head a little projected. He could only maintain the posture for a short while, after which he had to sit up once more. 'I used to see the old men sit like that on our steps, after they'd got home from the mills. I used to envy them.'

'When you were little, you lived round here?' Bonn knew the answer.

'Aye. I love it. A vestige, though, of a once-great city.'

'A return can cause pain.'

'Don't tell me,' Posser managed to say eventually, starting to sweat. Bonn had the idea that Posser had just got up. The evening would be hard going for the old man. 'Everything changes.'

'I wouldn't say that, Posser.'

'It changed for you, Bonn.' Posser grinned, false teeth brilliantly white. 'I can see you now, that woman in the hotel lounge, baffled as a kid at a console. And her thinking, how sweet, a novice! Truer than she knew, eh, lad?'

Bonn was embarrassed at the memory. 'I was

300

nonplussed.'

Posser beckoned Bonn. He glanced towards the kitchen door. 'I told Martina to give us a minute.' She couldn't have failed to hear his loud rasping voice. Bonn wondered how much of all this was put on. 'Different from a seminary, eh? Sussed you from the start.'

'I know,' Bonn said candidly.

'Eh?'

'Two days after we met, I went to say goodbye to my fellow tutee. He was leaving for the English College in Rome. He told me somebody had made enquiries. Answered your description.'

'Good, good.' Posser must have told Martina this, so why the charade? 'About Salvo. What do you reckon, we have him topped?'

Bonn looked into the fire. The seminary had had only electric bars, draughts, and a simulated gas-log in the rector's study. Posser beckoned Martina, who was closing the kitchen door behind her.

'I've told Dad what we discussed, Bonn, Grellie et al.' She served the drinks. Posser pulled a face. Martina grimaced comically back, their game.

'The reasons,' Bonn said. He realised with alarm that he wasn't at all appalled. He wondered if he'd passed the point where morality called a halt, his near-crime existence an imprimatur on immorality. Or was his life simply totally new, and he'd cast off old yokes?

'Salvo's a hand grenade rolling about the city, Bonn. Anybody can pull his pin and, kaboom, we'll all go up.'

'Is Salvo anything to do with us?' Bonn phrased it carefully.

'No. You turned him down. A pub conversation.'

301

Posser did his best to shrug, propping his thorax stiffly on his arms, the trick of chesty old cotton workers. 'But this Burtonall lady, our client, you asking around.' Posser closed his eyes, raised a forbidding hand as if Bonn had striven to interrupt. 'Fair. We allowed it. You reported in, all aboveboard.'

'Dad?' Martina gave him a glass of water. Posser obediently sipped.

'But your questions—Glazie, Jefferson, Tuesday, Askey, Uncle Tom Cobbley—are untraceable, even if the plod tried hard.'

'And the Burtonalls,' Martina added, sitting near her father.

'The subject of my questions was Mostern's accidental death.' Bonn felt forced into having to make a case for their having given agreement.

'That hasn't gone away,' Posser reminded him. 'The plod were asking round the Triple Racer, the Shot Pot, the casinos. And the Ball Boys.'

'They know we own those, in one guise or another, Bonn,' Martina said.

'Why Salvo, though?'

'Because he *leads* to us. He mayn't implicate us in Mostern, in Lana or Marla, but he's common ground.'

Bonn tasted his drink. 'Is there something else, Posser?'

'What else exactly?' Martina demanded.

Posser gave her a rueful glance, as if he'd been outwitted, drew a bubbly breath, and answered.

'The Italian chap. He gets info about us from Salvo, and possibly from Rack. He susses us out by dipsticks—Nicolette—plus tourist blokes he ships in for Grellie's lasses. He must have quite a dossier.

302

About buildings that I got freehold or leased for a song when you couldn't give inner-city streets away. And about franchises I quartered and sold on, renovations at government or council expense. He must know almost everything about us. We're only a dozen limited companies, after all.'

'So he's the one?'

Posser said heavily, 'He knows there's only me and Martina, and such street loyalty as we've got.'

Resistance was out of the question, Bonn could see. It was either sell out or lose out.

'Clare Burtonall makes it all one and the same.'

'Two minutes.' Martina limped to the kitchen, calling over her shoulder, 'I'm listening.'

'Goldoni's money's to buy us out. How does he know we're here, that we're unprotected? By sussing, by informers—Salvo's one, Rack's possibly an innocent other.' Posser beckoned Bonn for help to stand, puffed his way to the table. 'And why is Goldoni here in the first place? To back Clifford Burtonall, who owns city aldermen in time-honoured fashion.'

'He must be astute.'

'Businessmen are.' Posser lowered himself into a chair, leant on the table with relief, and gestured Bonn to take a place. 'Opportunity here, he wants a hack.'

'Totally.' Martina brought in the first course, mushrooms, tomatoes, black olives, pine nuts, and hot bread rolls.

They watched Martina serve. She spun it out, her woman's trick.

'Posser,' Bonn asked finally. 'I assume there's nothing other than what I know.'

'You're right, son. Nothing.'

303

'Then the question becomes, where can Salvo go.' Bonn spoke with certainty. 'He'll need help, money, a car.'

'Go? To Burtonall.' Martina looked about the table, checking. 'Please start.'

'Thank you.' Bonn passed the hot rolls. 'He'll have to go tonight.'

'That's what I thought,' Posser said. 'Martina, love. Who's handy?'

'Akker, two or three others.'

'God, this is hot,' Posser complained. 'It's microwaves. Before they came in, we have everything decently cold as a frog.'

'Manners, Dad.'

'Sorry, sorry.'

They had red wine; supreme of salmon, which Bonn had never had before; and a summer pudding that he hated because it was basically bread and butter. It had been Brother Anthony's gruesome special at the seminary. He told Martina it was the best meal he had ever had. She wanted to ask about his origins. He'd never had salmon cooked like that, never had that starter. He dared himself to ask what the vegetables were but his nerve failed.

After, they sat before the fireplace talking. Bonn said little. Posser said nothing would be done until the morning, by which time they would have reports in about Salvo, when they would decide. Meanwhile, the girls were up in arms over Lana and Marla, wanting action on Salvo, all saying he'd done it. Grellie had her hands full stopping them from making anonymous calls to the police.

When Martina went to make coffee, Posser knelt to poke the fire. Bonn knelt beside him, hefting the coal scuttle near, using the fire tiger. Posser

304

checked the distance to the kitchen, the faint clash of crockery.

'Bonn. I want to know what you feel about Martina.'

'I admire her.'

'Don't flannel me, son.' Posser smiled, determined. 'As you see, I'm a picture of health.' He sighed, rested on his heels. 'This thing's brought it to a head, rather. Made me think of time running out.'

'What then, Posser?'

'I knew it might come to this.' Posser sounded so sad. 'The best daughter a man could wish for. But look now. All the money in the world, nobody to trust. Her injury, scampering about after street carts when she was little, was my fault.'

'Come to this,' Bonn repeated.

'This.' Posser looked round, indicating his place. 'Martina. The others are good lads—as long as I'm here. After that, I'm not so sure.'

'I'll do what I can, Posser.'

'Move in here, son.' Posser's eyes held Bonn. 'I need an answer.'

'Into your home?'

'It's not sacrosanct, Bonn. It's a house. The dosshouse you live in's a right fleapit. Bare as a prison cell. Others'd have their own place out on the Wirral, moorland grandeur, if there's still any about.'

'Move away?' Bonn was shocked. 'I need a city, Posser.'

'Like me!' Posser was pleased. 'Will you move in?'

'Martina might say . . .'

'I'd ask her, if you'll come. Then I'd say you'd

305

asked.'

'That would seem as if I . . .'

'Wanted to be near Martina? Aye, son. That's my idea.'

'I would be afraid that she would want me to leave.'

'I'm too old for strategies, Bonn, like getting you two paired off. Unless you've taken against her for some reason.'

'No. I told you, Posser. I like her.'

'Then why haven't you asked before? Supper here or there.' Posser was aggrieved. 'Why not?'

Bonn stared at the flames, rising gracefully. He knew a trick to make it draw, but that was wasteful where he came from.

'I'm scared of Martina,' he said at last. 'I didn't know. Now I'm sure.'

Posser stared towards the kitchen door. Martina reappeared with a tray of coffee. Bonn helped Posser back to his upright chair. They talked of holidays, Bonn especially interested in how you went about arranging one, what you asked the travel agencies, when you paid, their reliability. Posser already knew Bonn had never had a holiday.

Bonn was shown out at eleven o'clock. He bussed Martina, Lancashire fashion, as he left. She returned to sit facing her father.

'What did he say, Dad?' she asked.

'First get Askey on the blower, love. Tell him to come here.'

'You're sending for Akker?'

'Maybe,' Posser said. 'Time something got done.'

CHAPTER THIRTY-ONE

Dip-and-scratch—*to pickpocket for effect alone, without profit.*

The problem was non-existent. Clare felt calm about everything. She returned fairly late, and heard his car on the gravel drive.

Clifford was safe. His blood samples were recorded for all time, the ECG, weight, body-mass indices, her notes all showed that Clifford was a subject in the cardiology health survey of males twenty-five to fifty. His first examination had taken place exactly when those girls were attacked.

She had had an interesting and amusing time working out survey protocols with three cardiology registrars. They had given her a surveillance nurse who'd just finished her S.R.N. and was eager to start. Things couldn't be better. Some plainclothesman—not Windsor, thank heavens—came to check, strictly against confidentiality, but Clare said it wouldn't matter. Things couldn't be better.

Virtually almost nearly they couldn't, because the girl Lana was a BID, Brought In Dead, because Marla's injuries were permanent. And because Clifford seemed even more disturbed that evening.

Clare had had a meal at the General Hospital. One of the registrars wanted serial ascorbic-acid levels as a spinoff, and she opposed letting that take over her survey. She had temporised, she'd have a word with Dr Porritt. Clifford had had a meal.

'The police were round today,' she said. She'd changed, had a bath, got into a dressing gown. 'I proved what had to be proved.'

'Thanks, darling.'

He was watching a TV gardening programme that would normally have had him taking notes, getting the odd book out to check soil acidity. Tonight, nothing. The worry had worn him out, but Clare cautioned herself against sympathy. What guarantee did she have that he hadn't done worse?

'Is that it?' she asked. 'When I've risked everything to save you?'

'I'm eternally grateful, Clare. You'll never know how much.'

'It's all over, then?' She so wanted it to be.

'Yes.' He saw she was waiting, and flicked the remote control. The screen blanked. 'If Salvo surfaces—'

'He can't say anything. It's obvious.'

'Is it, Clare?' He stared across. She was suddenly uncomfortable. 'How come you're so sure?'

'His confederates wouldn't let him say anything. They have ways.'

'Ways of what?'

'Of forcing him to stay silent.'

He was quiet, assessing her. 'Who've you been talking to?'

'I overheard two patients on about it,' she said weakly. It had sounded so convincing when Bonn had said it. Under interrogation from her husband, it seemed terribly weak.

'Who were these two patients?'

'How do I know?' she said, distressed. She'd only been trying to reassure him, and suddenly she'd become the enemy. 'Some person who works on the streets.'

'Person? One, not two now? Who is he? And what does he do "on the streets"? Barrows? Street vendor? Messenger?'

'Yes, one of those, probably.'

'What else did he tell you?'

A suspicion stirred, that Clifford knew more than he was letting on. She might have been seen going into the hotel, emerging later with spring in her step. Maybe some friend quick to gossip had . . . No. Bonn's words. Absolute security.

'I asked the patient,' she invented stoically. 'He said Salvo would stay mute about the wallet.'

'Wallet, the one who pays for a crime? How did you know it was called that?'

'He told me.' A lie is a compound fracture of truth. One lie is never enough.

'What a knowledgeable chap, Clare,' he said. 'You doctors, such funds of information walking right into your surgeries day in, day out.'

'I simply said I'd overheard him talking. We discussed the murder, the girl in the hospital. It's a conversational highlight.'

Clifford judged her. 'I don't suppose you went to see how she was getting on?'

'Marla? Of course not. No reason I should, is there?'

'Only to tell me if she'll see again, spot me in some line-up.'

'What possible explanation could I give the trauma surgeons? Or the police? They're in regular attendance, I heard.'

'More overhearing? You're a mine of information.'

'Why are you so preoccupied? You're in the clear,' she put in bitterly. 'Who would accept the evidence of a girl who has had three major operations after massive traumatic injury?'

'I had a phone call,' he said bluntly. 'Salvo, at the office. Bloody fool.'

'Salvo? The man who came here?'

Clifford paused as he leant away to take her in. For the first time Clare realised that she too was a witness. She had seen Salvo leave the garden that evening.

'What did he want?' She wasn't afraid. 'I suppose money?'

'Blackmail?' He barked an unrecognisable laugh. 'Him? He hasn't the brains. He wouldn't last a minute.'

A threat, another traffic accident, for Salvo himself this time?

'He wants a car, some funds to get him out of the city.'

'He's still here?' Therefore vulnerable, Bonn had implied.

Listen to me, she thought wildly, just *listen*, talking over how a murderer, Clifford's hired killer, can escape from justice. She'd be offering to drive him next.

'He won't ring here?' she asked, scared. 'He won't come?'

'No.' Clifford had recovered. 'I told him the police were watching.'

'Are they?' Her hand crept to her throat. Involuntarily she glanced at the windows, curtained against the dark.

'Of course not.' He was a little unsure of that, repeated it. 'I can see that he gets money to travel. After that, it's up to him.'

'Can you?'

'Don't be stupid.' His smile chilled her with its narrowness. 'Money's what I do, remember.'

310

He'd never spoken to her like that, terse and damning. She coloured at the insult. Well, she had her new confidence.

He listened as the hall clock chimed the quarter hour, got up, giving her his new smile.

'I'll do some computer work. If anyone rings, I'm in the bath, okay?'

'Very well.' She thought, Where have we gone?

'Wish me luck, darling.'

'Good luck,' she said, withholding her irony, and watched him go.

Without even having to think, but watching her husband's study door, Clare telephoned the agency, and booked Bonn for the following afternoon, for no other reason than to test how she felt about what had gone before. The alternative was to visit the Café Phrynne. There was no guarantee that he'd be there.

She read the local news. The day after tomorrow, the northern counties' mogga-dance championships. He would be there. Hadn't he said something about supporting that dancer? She could meet him there accidentally.

Was it too soon to see him again? She simply wanted to. All right, she mentally challenged imaginary gossips, it might seem odd for a practising doctor to have a goer as a friend, but so? Stupid to feel unjustified irritation, at other clients Bonn might see, be seeing, in the meantime.

Edgy, she poured herself a glass of sherry, and switched on the television. Some girl had been rescued from a burning flat, an overturned paraffin heater the cause. A passing couple had seen a man run out, and called the fire brigade. Two darts players returning from a club match had somehow

311

got the girl out. A hospital spokesman said she would survive.

The man was being sought by police. He answered the following description ... Clare paid attention, and wondered if Clifford had seen the news earlier.

Only from force of habit, she told herself, she checked the door locks, the window catches. Caution did no harm. She would watch television in bed until Clifford came upstairs.

*   *   *

Bonn met Doob by the gigantic budgerigar cage and the huge glass waterfall clock. The shopping mall was the noisiest place in the city, infants and shoppers, with the inevitable rim of elderly men by the fountain. Rack hung about. He'd given Doob a clean bill of honesty.

'How have you done, Doob?' Bonn asked.

'Not bad, Bonn.' The goer was nervous. 'Three clients, and a homer. Another tonight.'

'Did the homer go all right?' Bonn smiled apology. 'I'm always concerned.'

'It was fine.' Doob was eager to explain. 'Her feller said—'

'Thank you, Doob. No details, please.'

'Is it enough, then?' Doob was anxious and wanted to know. 'I heard Lancelot's been notching them up at a rate of—'

'Shhhh,' Bonn consoled. 'I am pleased.'

Doob coloured, embarrassed by the praise. 'Ta, Bonn.'

'Which brings me to my problem, Doob.' Bonn made space for a young mother to walk her toddler

312

round the rim of the fountain. It squealed with delight. 'Do the dip-and-scratch, Doob,' Bonn said, making sure he moved his head often as he spoke. Directional microphones were not unknown.

Doob asked, staring, 'Me and whose army?'

'You, Doob. With me as the cackler.'

'*You* help me to do a dipper? Who's the mark? It's a bird, right?' Doob looked ready to laugh in case this was some hidden joke, except Bonn wouldn't joke.

'Yes.' Bonn held a woman's shopping while she loaded an infant into a push chair and did the straps. 'I'll be at her table in the dining room. Don't be showy.'

'What's she got, then?' Doob was still unsure. 'Coat pockets? Handbag? Purse? I hate doing a job for one bleeding credit card.'

'Language, please. I don't know what she carries.'

'What happens after, Bonn? I don't like the sound of this.'

'We shall discover in God's good time, Doob.' Bonn turned away, saying over his shoulder, 'And neither do I. Good luck.'

'Ta, Bonn.' Doob felt he'd received a knighthood, doing a special with Bonn. It was a pity he couldn't brag. He went for a coffee in the Butty Bar. He wanted a real drink, but Bonn would know, and that would be the end of it.

*   *   *

Martina cleared the money with something like ill grace, the nearest Bonn had ever seen to a sulk. She insisted on speaking to Posser. There was an extra, smaller wadge for the desk records, but that would

313

be arranged by others, Posser said, when he had the whole story.

The woman Jane Antrobus entered the restaurant a little after seven o'clock, as Glazie had said. Guests were on their way out to the theatres at that hour. From behind the red velvet curtains Bonn observed her thick-set figure seat herself, lay her handbag on an adjacent chair, and consult the menu. Bonn saw Doob come from the foyer, and started his inner clock ticking. On the count of twelve he entered briskly.

Doob was just among the tables. Three waiters were quietly about their business, none with the Fraud Office woman. Bonn had tipped Glazie off, saw the receptionist stroll in.

The woman was on the point of summoning a waiter when Doob reached her. He stumbled, almost fell, but righted himself. Her handbag fell.

Bonn, pausing to read the large engraved menu between a double bank of flowers, couldn't help but admire Doob's dexterity. Elevation to the rank of goer had certainly done Doob a power of good. From a slipshod youth with frayed elbows, he had now become neat, his clothes fashionable, making him look younger. He exuded confidence. It could have been a young executive who straightened up, apologising profusely as he handed the lady her handbag back.

Bonn's count had reached nineteen, which was about right, when he reached the table. Doob was ostensibly making for the lounge bar just visible through the partition that separated the private dining suites from the main restaurant. For a moment Bonn hesitated, glanced down at the Antrobus woman.

314

The SFO researcher was disconcerted. 'Yes?'

Bonn, standing there: 'Excuse me a moment, madam.'

He strode after Doob, who was having to pause to speak to one of the waiters because Bonn, inexperienced, had miscalculated somewhat and took too long.

'You, sir.' Bonn went for decibels, for the few diners already seated. 'Can I have a word?'

Doob made to go. The waiter vanished on Glazie's signal.

Bonn placed himself between the exit and Doob, then spoke to the pickpocket in a meaningless jabber. He pointed to Jane Antrobus, stabbed a finger at Doob, who shook his head, mutter mutter. Doob was excellent, pantomiming a giveaway outrage at such a false accusation.

Hand held out as if for the cane, Bonn stood in tableau. Doob shamefacedly extracted a small purse, placed it on Bonn's hand. Bonn beckoned him, and together they returned to the SFO woman's table.

'Lady,' Bonn said, frowning, 'I regret to say that you have been dipped. I saw it all. This man is already known to me.'

'My purse!' she exclaimed in horror, frantically grabbing her handbag.

'Please, Inspector,' Doob said, collapsing into a whining scrounger. 'Don't take this any further. It's a mistake—'

'Quiet, Cullingson,' Bonn ordered. 'Ma'am. Is anything else missing?'

The researcher delved, shook her head. 'Are you a policeman?'

Glazie approached. 'Excuse me, Inspector. Can I

315

be of assistance?'

'I need you.' Bonn shot an eagle-eyed look round the restaurant. Everybody was staring. 'Make a list of all the waiters, waitresses, and clerical staff on duty at the time of the incident.' He did his best at a glacial smile. 'Note down time, place, date.'

'Yes, sir.' Glazie retreated.

'Please, lady.' Doob pleaded. 'I didn't mean anything. An irresistible impulse. Hand on my heart, I'll never do it again—'

Bonn grasped his arm. 'Shut it, Cullingson. You're caught redhanded. This time it'll be in every newspaper in the country. You'll get sent down—'

'Inspector.' Jane Antrobus's face had paled. 'Let it go.' She checked her purse, tried to look reassured. 'This poor man. I'm willing to overlook it.'

'You are?' Bonn told Doob to stay put, and lowered himself into a chair. 'Ma'am. He was apprehended in execution of an obvious theft in a hotel restaurant. I'm sure the management want maximum publicity—'

'No!' She gathered herself. 'No. Please. That would be too embarrassing. I'm a professional lady, with heavy commitments.'

It was getting easier as the process went on. You tended to lose yourself in the arguments, whether you believed in them or not. Doob had told him that. Confidence tricks were an assumption of truth, any old truth. 'Please proffer charges against this man. He is a regular pickpocket. He does untold harm. You have a golden opportunity to put him through a rigorous process of trial. It would be a deterrent.' He shrugged, sad that triumph was to be taken away. 'However, if you refuse—'

316

'Inspector.' Her relief was painfully evident. 'The incident is closed.'

'Bless you, lady.' Doob came round, took her hand, bent low, and kissed it, smiling into her eyes. 'Thank you for what you've done for me.'

She was nonplussed, took back her hand. 'Yes, of course.'

'Better leave, Cullingson.' Bonn looked at Doob. 'Palms up.'

Doob stood, showed his empty hands. 'Can I go, Inspector?'

'Yes. Get gone.' A failure in accent, tone, syntax, everything to do with speech, Bonn scathed himself critically. He gave her a serious frown. 'A narrow squeak, er, Mrs . . .?'

'Antrobus, Jane Antrobus.' She kept her handbag on her lap.

'Are you here on business, Jane, if I may?'

'No. I have a night or two before travelling to London.' She was looking. 'Aren't you young for a police inspector?'

'Youngest in the division,' Bonn said, on thin ice. He waved Glazie over, and told him to abandon the lists.

Which left them alone. The conversational hum returned to the restaurant, the event was over and done with.

'Might I . . .?' Bonn hesitated. 'Would you allow me to share your table? I came in for supper—off duty! Of course, if you wish to dine alone—'

'No. Please.' She had to brave it out.

'You're sure?' Bonn smiled, on home ground. 'Providing you will allow me to be the host. Fair's fair.'

He smiled, reached across the table, and touched

317

her hand.

*   *   *

At nine, Bonn reached the Triple Racer. Askey was already there.

'Done, Bonn. Everything like you said.'

'Thank you, Askey. How is that sister of yours?'

'I'm hoping to take her to Blackpool, a trip out.'

Bonn pondered. 'That's a good idea, Askey. Perhaps we might run to a car, with a driver. There are orthopaedic vehicles now, aren't there, take wheelchairs.'

'That'd be great, Bonn. But I don't know . . .'

'Leave it a moment. The photographs?'

'Camcorded the lot, Bonn. And stills.' Askey blinked, peering. The bikers were all talking noisily. 'I've got somebody who says he can edit, but you said to be careful with this one.'

'Thank you, Askey. I'll have a Granadee Studios girl edit it. She's unattached, and wants to come in with us. Rack?'

Rack left the crowd of bikers.

'Rack, please.' Bonn shook Askey's hand in thanks. 'We've had excellent service tonight. Please arrange a car trip to Blackpool for a sick lady.'

'Only Blackpool?' Rack glared at Askey. 'Not the Continent?'

'She hates being away for long,' Askey apologised. 'Thanks, Bonn.'

Rack went with Bonn, beckoning to Grellie. 'Know why they all like Blackpool, Bonn?' he started up. 'It's ozone. You breathe it, you're an addict.'

'That is interesting, but Grellie—'

318

'Grellie wants you to okay what the girls have raised for Marla. And wants you for supper.'

Bonn thought, another meal? He listened to Rack's ozone theory.

CHAPTER THIRTY-TWO

Crisper—*a person burned to death, as in an accident.*

Oz counted army service one of life's blessings. He even approved of the porridge he'd done in the Glasshouse, military prison, and the endless jankers, bastard sergeants.

He lay beneath the vehicle fixing the string, almost laughing.

One thing, the Army had room for anyone. Off your trolley or a bookish saint, mardy or macho, barmy or bright, the Army took you in. And it taught you. With Oz, it had been cars, tanks, anything with an engine, and the tricks that came with every set of pistons. Like this, the phosphorus-in-water that Hairy-Arse, the warrant officer who'd done unmentionable things in the Balkans, and everywhere else for that matter, called the rope trick.

Any job was gommon, common sense. Try telling Salvo that, silly bleeder, Oz thought ruefully, testing the string—more silk than cord, actually, for strength. The lunatic sod was a psycho. Four years, maybe a six-and-ten, in some boozy regiment would straighten him out, sure as God made trees. Stop the useless wanker dreaming he was 'really somebody'. The lads wouldn't tolerate a shirker. Do the job, keep the platoon out of trouble with Hairy-Arse, make sure that if any three-tonner failed in a night column it wasn't your engines, thank Christ.

This motor was one of ninety parked at the City Vehicle Saloon Auction Co, Ltd, an area of semi-dereliction beyond the football ground. Boisterous pubs, a bingo hall, high-rise blocks watching TV soaps instead of getting on with something decent, a rotting mill, and a canal's fetid turning-pool. Their security was crap, Oz thought in disgust, working on. Odd, because the majority of security blokes were from the PFI, poor fucking infantry. No pride in their engines or their jobs. Way of the fucking world.

He rolled out from under, lay there not moving for a full minute. That was how long a thicko with a truncheon and flash-light could hang on, wait to see if that noise was anything, before walking back to his ale and the telly match thinking, Thank fuck, no knacker's yard tonight. Tomorrow, if questioned by some narked Filth, he'd say he'd thought it was maybe kids, out with his standard lie that he'd searched everywhere and found sod all.

Minute up. Oz knelt, groped for the plastic bag. Still squishy, no leaks. In the water the waxy stick. A squat candle of pure phosphorus. Oz always thought it marvellous that water, that extinguisher of fires, should stifle phosphorus. He'd tested it, cut a fragment—under water, of course—in his back yard. No sooner did he lift it out of the water on the point of his knife than the bloody stuff flashed into flame and oblivion. The warmth of your hand could start the fucker.

To make sure, he'd got a safety fire-lighter.

320

Chemical reactions were best, Oz always thought. There was a place for electric, but how often did you hear of things going wrong with electricity? Loose connection here, some damp there, even a fucking cockroach shorting a circuit, clanged alarms one end of the county to the other. No, good old chemicals burned themselves into nothing, no traces for nasty sods with their nasty sample bottles. Mind you, Middle East these days, soon there'd be no room for real bomb expertise. They got a jar of 3-acetone, and that was it, blow up the frigging skyline, and theirselves too like as not.

The fire-lighters were elementary campers' strips. Remove from pack, tear apart, place beneath the fuel, and there's your campfire.

Oz sat, going through his checklist. Phosphorus in its bag of water. String, emerging through the waterproof seal that he'd made with the iron over a double fold. A tug on the string would tear the phosphorus stick free of its water bag. Air would ignite it. But phosphorus itself wouldn't bang. It was more of your flash and smoulder, not enough for a motor like this, that he'd chosen for Salvo's getaway.

The string would also rip apart the two strips of the campers' lighter. Flames enough there, though too tiny to be any use to anybody except a girl guide. Useful second support, the regimental Hairy-Arse used to call such devices. He would bawl in your earhole, 'Dozy fuckers like you who forget one may then rely on the other doyouunner-stannnn you 'orrible man . . .'

Oz'd prepared it all in his yard. One string for both, lay them close together, the freed phosphorus doing its stuff by erupting into fire and the camper's

321

strip ripping into a fast flame. One plus one equalled Gawd Almighty.

The nylon-silk string, which he'd filthed in Indian ink, he tied to the plastic bag's cord. He crawled to the high wire-mesh fence and tied its other end to a concrete upright. No sense in standing up to walk the short distance, careful the game. Assume everybody was watching you, not United and some unpronounceable foreign team on telly.

The motor was a mundane Ford, easy to get into, its registration five years old ALL FULLY SERVICED AND READY TO DRIVE! the neon sign said. If the fucking motor let him down, Oz swore, there'd be fucking ructions, welshing on a promise.

He rose slowly—fast moves spelt crime. He crouched by the driver's side, and from his pocket took half a tennis ball. With a grunt he shoved it flat over the lock. Holding it in place, he slowly let it return to its hemispherical shape. It sucked air in. The car door clicked open. A rubber kitchen-sink plunger would do it, but was harder to explain to marauding Old Bill.

Quickly Oz dived in, clicked the interior light off, and sat still. No shouts, no alarm. He went to retrieve the half tennis ball. Four cursing minutes before he happened on it. He put it away, careful, careful.

There *was* another quick way, simply smash half a brick against the front bumper. If the car was fitted with air bags, all the doors would instantly spring open as the air bag exploded. Except that was hellish noisy. Fine if you were nicking the motor from outside a football ground, but no good here, the car lit up like fucking Christmas with its lights on and its alarm wailing.

If he'd not brought his half tennis ball, he'd have used a tyre lever on the window, quiet and quick. But how do you explain a tyre iron? Drop it, it makes a clang. Half a tennis ball's almost as bad, seeing everybody knew the trick, but at least you could drop it through a hole in your pocket while you were being all innocent.

Beneath the passenger seat was the ideal place to bomb a motor. Mistake to put it beneath the driver's. You wanted a sideways blast, rather than beneath, in a confined space. He placed the phosporus bag against the seat-support bars, and trailed the cord out. It led to the fence. Move the car, and you'd get a nasty phosphorus burn. He'd got the smoulder. Now for the rest.

Must be getting on for eleven o'clock. He took a silicone spray from his pocket, and sprayed his fingertips carefully, wafting his hands to dry them. Artificial skin drowned fingerprints. He pulled on leather gloves from his pocket, still more caution, and made his way to the line of three petrol pumps. He avoided using the small flashlight he'd brought, seeing by the city's sky glow. He could hear the TV commentators, see the faint reflection of the telly's luminescence from the office. That was security, he thought. He wouldn't pay them in tap washers.

He passed the pile of gallon tins at a crouch. Their filled petrol containers were the ones on the ground, never stacked like empties. He knelt by the last one, tapped it. Full. He hefted it, and returned to the car.

Over the next ten minutes he decanted the petrol into a large freezer bag, thin plastic but with a seal that would be, in a certain immortal phrase, useful secondary support. He chuckled. There would be a brief smell of petrol, but with luck Salvo would be too worked up to bother.

The bulging container of petrol had now to be carefully stroked with kitchen wipes to minimise smell. He sealed the used tissues inside a smaller freezer bag, then placed the petrol bomb inside a larger bag. More than satisfactory. His whole kit was a small plastic bag of water, four freezer bags, gloves, and a ball of string. The tennis-ball half could go into any litter bin. Silicone spray was necessary, but what could you do?

He tied a length of nylon-silk cord tightly round the petrol bomb, hourglass style, and placed it under the seat, trailing the free end to tie to the same concrete post.

Oz did a dummy run, creeping up on the car, opening the driver's door, crawling in, sitting there in the darkness, going through the motions of hot-wiring the starter. Hundred per cent certain.

Anybody moved this car a single yard, it was good night, Vienna.

*　　　*　　　*

Salvo was waiting for Oz outside the station. The city was still busy, the last trains being announced and some pop concert crowd surging.

'I thought you weren't coming, Oz.'

'Don't be daft.'

'You get the wheels?'

'Remember this registration number, okay? It's a Ford.'

It took a dozen repetitions to drive it into Salvo's thick head. Oz felt contempt. He could remember

324

cars from being a lad.

'I were you, Salvo, I'd wait until morning. Then just pretend like you're looking for something to buy, get in, and drive away. No need to hot-wire the crate, see?'

'I'm good at hot-wiring, Oz, done it a million times.'

Oz said dubiously, 'You know what you're doing.'

'That's fucking right. How'll I get there?' asked the know-all.

'City Vehicle Saloon Auction Company, Limited,' Oz said quietly. 'The twenty-eight goes right by. It's two miles, walk it in half an hour. The car's hundred yards from the end of the fence. Just run it at the gates, they're only wire and one padlock. By the time they've switched their telly off you'll be in Brum.'

'Ta, Oz. You're a mate.'

'I've tanked it up. Don't stop on the motorway.'

Salvo was uneasy. 'Give us a lift there, mate?'

'Can't risk it, Salvo. They connect us, they'd pin Mostern on you. You know the Filth.'

'I need some bunce, Oz. I got some from a bint I had to crisp.'

'I heard,' Oz said bitterly, thinking, Jesus H. Christ. 'You're more famous than a fucking Derby winner. Shake hands.' Oz still had his gloves on. He shook hands, hissed in fury when Salvo started to count the money he'd been slipped. 'Put it away, silly cunt.'

'Thanks, Oz.'

'Cheers, mate. See you in three years maybe, eh?'

Salvo grinned. Three years was the par time. After that the Filth forgot.

Alibi time. Oz went for a pint in the Volunteer,

made a couple of stupid bets, argued noisily round the dartboards so he'd get ballocked and remembered, generally made his presence known. He needed a drink, though, having seen Salvo go by in a taxi. Un-fucking-believable, the ignorance. A spell in the PFI would sort the bugger out.

He made sure he lost at darts in style, missing double top four successive darts, everybody calling him a right prat. He rather enjoyed being the centre of attention, ought to treat himself to a pint more often.

*   *   *

The car park was in darkness. Oz had said wait until morning, but that wasn't Salvo's way. He'd hung about the city too long.

He walked along the pavement. Hundred yards. He needn't check the gate, if Oz said it was easy to drive through. Nobody about. He climbed over, walked to the Ford. He'd memorised the number, felt the registration plate, proudly got it right.

The car door was unlocked. He felt almost tearful, Oz a real pal, maybe the only one he had left now. Even the interior light was out. Good old Oz.

Salvo climbed in. Smell of petrol, but, then, Oz had said he'd tanked it up. He closed the door, pulling it silently with the handle down.

For a moment he sat there, uneasy. He'd seen it on the pictures. Wiring. Ignition. Turn the key and kaboom, the CIA killing the hero and his tart. He turned the wheel a little. Nothing. He jiggled the wires from the dashboard. Nothing.

He did the hot-wire, stripping with his thumbnail. The motor started like a dream. No bang. Old Oz coming through, fucking security blokes doing sod all.

With tears of gratitude for Oz's help, he moved off.

For one instant he felt bewildered at the sudden engulfing stench of petrol. Something splashed wetly on his leg. A spark showed the dashboard. He looked down. He heard a fizz, getting louder. His eyes smarted.

Puzzled, he said, 'Here, wait a sec,' but it was too late. He had time to say, 'Oz?'

The car gave a muted whoomph as fire filled its interior, still rolling forward, then blew apart in a ball of flame, pieces skittering across the concrete among the parked cars, starting five more cars burning. Then the security men came running.

CHAPTER THIRTY-THREE

Cushy, cushty—*good, profitable, easy (Romany).*

It would be raining, Clifford thought with distaste, coming from the telephone-company offices. Get one thing right, two things go wrong. And he'd no umbrella. He seemed to hesitate, then waved down a passing taxi.

Oz was the cabbie. He slid back the safety glass. 'In a hurry, mate?'

'Traffic's bad as ever, I see. You know the Vivante Hotel?'

'Be there in a sec.' Oz laughed. 'Well, minute or two

maybe.'

'You sound cheerful.'

'Won a bet, first since I were a nipper.'

'Lucky, then.'

They spoke of bets. Clifford said once you were behind in any gambling game simply give up and cut out. Oz told him no.

'Look at me, guv,' he said, taking a side street. 'Loser for donkey's years, and now I get a run. Bit here, bit there. Suddenly it's a fortune. Cushty.'

'What'll you do with it? Rub out all your deficits?'

'What do they say in romance stories? One fell swoop!' Oz chuckled. 'All right to drop you at Asda? You can cut through, stay in the dry.'

'All right. But I'll take it out of your tip, me walking half a mile.'

'Twenty yards!'

In good humour, Clifford pushed a note through the aperture, asked for change. Oz grumbled, and Clifford relented, fumblingly repaid it.

'I'll jog the whole distance in future, save a fortune.'

Five minutes later Clifford was in the Vivante lounge ordering afternoon tea. He waited until the waitress had served before he opened his leather folder.

He examined the recorded calls, the numbers he'd queried at the telecommunications offices marked. One especially troubled him. Last evening, and there it was again. Pleases Agency, Inc. Clare must have made it as soon as he'd logged on his computer. He'd actually dialled the number from the public phone. No secret of it. The address was close to the city centre, above a casino and a courier service.

He replayed the call in his mind.

'Can I enquire what services your agency provides?' he'd asked.

'Your name, sir, please?'

'I just want to know the nature of your services.'

'Can I ask the name of the client who recommended us?' The woman's voice went singsong, the typical close-down.

He'd tried the high horse. 'Is there any reason that you can't provide me with this information?'

'We operate on strictly personal recommendation, sir. Thank you for calling!' the bitch intoned cheerily, and it was click-burr.

Hadn't there been that chap from Hull, moved into the city with a motor-insurance scheme? Burgess, wife called Lisa. They'd had a row over, of all things, the colour of their new car. Lisa had got sloshed, slung abuse at Ben Burgess, and jeered that she hired somebody to dick her. That was Ben's phrase, outraged, waving his arms when he'd dropped by Clifford's office to tell the tale.

He'd said it was right here in the city centre. Lisa, sobering with remorse, said she'd invented the whole thing. They'd separated, though, Lisa back to Norwich, the house divided, civilised.

Oz had delivered the goods. Salvo was eliminated. The billboards were already shrieking of some thief who'd started a fire trying to steal a motor. He'd catch the radio news later. First he'd make a detour by way of Ben Burgess's tacky business.

*   *   *

'Then what?' Hassall asked. The two policemen were having a drink in their social club. 'I hate these places.'

Windsor already knew that.

'Nothing I could see. That taxi was the one that—'

'—topped Mostern, aye. But did anything go down?'

Windsor wondered what he could say to mollify the other's disgust. 'There was some jiggery-pokery, change being argued over. I couldn't see for sure.' He grasped the nettle. 'I didn't camcord it.'

'No matter,' Hassall said, adding morosely, 'They'd not allow it in evidence. And somebody slipping a wadge could be doing anything. Do you really think Burtonall paid him?'

'As I sit here,' Windsor said, in total grief.

'My younger day, I'd have cuffed this Oz's licence, got some dip artist to nick the wadge.'

'Honest?' Windsor said, curious. 'What would you've done with it?'

'The lads had this fund, back then, for retirements.' Hassall pulled a rueful face. 'No good now, every groat triple-checked. Only investment advisers can grease gelt.'

'That's what I mean,' Windsor said. It would rankle for life. All very well for an old bloke like Hassall to chuck in the sponge. 'Burtonall's one of them.'

'He's got alibis as long as your arm,' Hassall said. 'If it isn't laboratory results it's cardiac traces. Any word from the bars, that snooker place?'

'Blank.' Windsor waited for his senior to make a decision, and asked belligerently, 'Is that it, then?'

'Unless that crisper turns out not to be that Salvo

330

twat.'

'It'll be Salvo,' Windsor predicted. 'Oz did him, on Burtonall's say-so.'

Hassall did feel a certain sympathy.

'I were like you, once. Just do what you can. Don't get warped.'

In twenty more years, Windsor thought, taking a hefty swig of his ale. But until then I'll cheat, lie, and sooner or later get the bastards.

Hassall beckoned the barman. 'And stop thinking like that,' quite as if he'd read Windsor's thoughts. 'I might as well talk to the wall.'

*   *   *

Akker didn't threaten Jane Antrobus until he was carrying her bags to the train. She had not spoken a word since he'd explained. Lowering her two suitcases onto the platform, he spoke into her ear. He knew he had dog's breath, but he wasn't here to charm.

'Look. You keep that bit of gelt, okay?'

She moved her head aside but Akker persisted.

'Those photos. That video of you receiving money. You and Mostern, sworn statements of hotel operative saying how you fixed not to prosecute. It's ready to go. Understand?' He shouted when she didn't respond, 'Understand? You gotter say yes.'

'Yes,' she said.

'Then fucking well nod, for Christ's sake.'

She nodded, said 'Yes' again.

'I've to say something.' Akker's brow puckered. 'Worse than learning fucking poems at school.' He composed himself, intoned loudly, 'Silence and

331

inertia are in your very best interests in respect of the city's services.' He beamed. 'Did it! Understand, did you?'

'Yes.'

'Right. On you go.'

He watched the train depart, ten whole minutes later, to make sure she didn't get off. That Bonn. There was such a thing as being too fucking careful, in his opinion, but he'd seen her off exactly as instructed.

CHAPTER THIRTY-FOUR

Dommy—*older term for the hiring of a goer for sex, by a woman in her own place or home.*

The start of the cardiology unit's surveillance was not a conspicuous success. The cardiologist said as much after Clare had spent all day coping with a meagre number of male volunteers at the hospital.

'Ten is pathetic, Clare.' He was plunged into gloom.

'I'm as disappointed, Paul.' Clare went for it. 'Ten, plus Clifford.'

'Your husband?' Dr Porritt asked.

'Yes.' Clare shuffled the files. 'I used him to time the process. To see,' she added wryly, making a joke, 'how I'd cope with the hordes.'

'Let's review what we did, then.'

They left the anteroom and discarded their coats. The canteen was crowded, some union meeting among ancillary staff. Clare avoided the cardiologist's eye, knowing his feelings on the issue.

332

For years Dr Porritt had wanted all porters made redundant, and thought the ambulance service inefficient. They sat facing.

'I've decided on three sessions a week. At this rate, we'll have enough after a couple of centuries.'

'Women are best patients.' It was another of the cardiologist's moans. 'They're more responsible. Bloody men shun medical help. Can't come, mustn't be seen ailing. Less practical. Women face things.'

Clare wondered how this applied to Clifford's criminal life.

'A few quid spent on posters isn't advertising, Clare.' He was bitter. 'I killed my bloody self screwing the money for this out of the health authority.'

'Look. This is only day one. Let's not go under. How about we change tactics?' She went for enthusiasm, cheer him up. 'I take the surveillance unit into the factories. Remember the old chest X-ray mobiles?'

'No,' the cardiologist ruled. 'I'm against that. It smacks of desperation. Men won't come forward with all their workmates pulling their leg. Softly, softly, catchee monkey.'

'How?'

Paul appraised her. 'Repeat your advertising campaign, such as it is.' He smiled. 'But start with the women. Advertise in the supermarkets. Use the stores' announcers. Ask the managers' cooperation. You know the sort of thing: "Ladies, when did your husband last go for a free routine medical check . . .?" Persuade them to bring their fathers, brothers, live-ins.'

'That doesn't give us a cross-section. It picks out

333

the married.'

'Then adapt the announcements. Get notices up in garages, tannoys in factories. Phone the motorway service stations, railways, anywhere.'

'And then?' Clare ought to have thought of these.

'The GPs. They're the ones with the lists. There's something else. I know somebody at Granadee Studios.'

'The TV place? My husband's office is just round the corner.'

'Says they'll cooperate.' Dr Porritt weighed her up before speaking. 'He'll let you have a slot.'

'Me? Go on television?' Clare felt her cheeks warm.

'If you're willing.' He nodded encouragingly. 'The old times are gone, when doctors didn't announce their names in public. Now every TV screen's bulging, doctors doing everything from lonely-heart sobbers to physical jerks. We're in a scrap to get the populace fitter, make a go of health.'

'I don't like the sound of that TV thing, Paul.' Clare wanted anonymity.

'Isn't it our duty, Clare?'

'*You* do the broadcast, then.'

'I'm not doing the survey,' he said with maddening logic. 'You are. We've *got* to get the city's males in, or the survey goes down the chute.'

'I'll think about it, Paul.'

'Quickly, please.' They parted amicably, making disparaging comments about people who didn't read health posters.

*   *   *

They met in the Vivante Hotel, late that afternoon, in a plain room with two picture windows overlooking the station approach.

This time they talked with a casual ease, without reason to maintain a show of purpose. Though Clare found her voice shaking a little as she undressed, not looking his way as he took his clothes off in time with her, their understanding enough to carry her through.

She was surprised by her own sense of ease. It was comfortable, she realised with astonishment, yet how could this be? His occupation, her need for some sort of consolation, and *this* was the outcome? She knew she might smile if she thought of double meanings. But for now, making a reasonably neat pile of her clothes on the bedside chair, it seemed perfectly in order to be feeling the cool sheets of the clean bed, realising the inevitability of it as his weight tilted her and he lay beside her.

Almost unaffected by the emotional distance she had travelled, she wondered if Bonn would now be frank if she asked about other women. Did they respond like she was doing? Did they too have enormous difficulties explaining to themselves what on earth they thought they were doing, paying for a hired man?

One question she dearly wanted answered was whether she too was 'a client'. They had come together—one of those double-meaning phrases she must learn to avoid—had *met*—for a different purpose. Surely those other women didn't have as much excuse, with sexual appetite their ulterior motive until they, like her, reached this level? Surely this degree of intimacy was impossible with each one?

His arm reached over and he found her breast, the palm warm on her skin. She turned, smiling at his ready acceptance, the assumptions of trust and rights, and reached for him. This too was startling. She didn't feel at all odd, making her understanding so plain. She heard his grunt with a new relish. God, but just holding him in one hand like she was, unmoving, was almost enough.

Client? Not for this. She felt his fingers touch her mouth.

'I love mouths.'

'Everybody's?' she said, immediately wanted to erase it. 'Sorry, Bonn.'

'No,' he answered unexpectedly. 'Some mouths are beautiful. They are the ones that make me love all mouths.'

'How much is tact, and how much what you mean?'

'I mean all of it.' He placed his mouth on hers.

'Women are puzzled, men liking breasts so.'

He drew back to see her better, the way he did. 'Women are the puzzlement. Can't see the obvious.'

That made her laugh. She tapped his face in reproach. 'Know what I want? Ask about you, the seminary—that *was* you in the old priest's photograph.' She shushed him when he made to speak 'Don't worry. I won't.'

For a while he was silent. 'Why not?'

'Because I believe too many women do. Ask you, I mean.'

'So?'

'So imagine me lying here, maybe while you ran the bath for us afterwards, me throwing out casual questions. I'd never know, would I? I mean, would your replies be your usual evasions? Or be a careful

336

gush of platitudes? I simply wouldn't know.'

'That makes it . . .'

'No, Bonn, don't think badly.' She slid her free hand behind his head and kept it there. 'If I were to ask, we'd become different. We'd become the unknown, replying to the unknowing. Could there be a greater recipe for disaster?'

'Which of us would be the unknown, Clare?'

She'd read that Lana was to be buried the following day, the coroner having released the body. That, and the cardiac scheme's dodgy start, made her think of other unknowns.

Last time had been pure revenge on Clifford, she acknowledged. There was no earthly reason to hire Bonn a second time. Infidelity was whole of itself, like honesty. Betrayal—'cheating', in modern American parlance—was a one-off, Shakespeare's dram of bile, which spoiled the goodness in the rest. One infidelity broke all the thin ice of marriage.

'I'm pleased, Clare. You wanted me for yourself.'

Real, was that, or reflex? How often did he say exactly the same? Dozens? Only occasionally?

'You see, Bonn, there's danger.' Just listen to yourself, she thought. Asking for reassurance now, a little amateur psychotherapy?

'Danger.'

'Yes.' She felt his hand grazing on her thighs. 'If you became a person with a background, parents, your first dreams, then I would be polarised. It's the way of all human pairs, when they learn about each other.'

'Danger,' he said, testing her word.

'That attitude cries out to be developed, and made into loving. The danger is that of growing closer.'

'There is a way round, Clare.'

'Yes, Bonn. Your way.' She had to be brave to go on. 'To stay at a distance. The process worries me. Does it become a mere carnal activity, grinding out repletion like a product?'

'Yes.' He said it with a trace of sadness that moved her, until she cautioned herself. It might be his trademark, to lace confession with sorrow. 'It does become like that, in some women. They keep score, mark their mind cards, keep record of methods, levels reached.'

'What does it mean? That they've learned to use it?'

'Not it, Clare. To use me.' His sadness lingered. 'Very rarely, one woman will arrive, an absolute beginner, baffled as some new girl at the mogga dancing, not knowing what on earth is going on, wondering what she's doing. She is so overcome by the realisation of her new power that she flings herself headlong into clienthood. Maybe she'll spend a fortune, jumping from one goer to another. We call them trippers. It's fine, but it's the road to addiction. It has no turning, no place to sit and wonder how far she's travelled, why she's travelling at all.'

'What happens? Do they eventually give up?'

'It's as if they see only possession.' He tilted his palm and showed her the rising nipple.

It was as Clare had guessed. 'How on earth do they cope?'

'One or two want possession to be total, permanent union the only way.' He shrugged. She could have sworn he was sincere, but, then, he was a magician at his trade. 'If they aren't rich, some eventually see the light and hire occasionally. If they're wealthy, it's harder.'

'Harder?' she cried softly.

'Of course. They can't buy me completely. They can't understand.'

'Can't? When they're so rich?' She considered this. By now his hands were moving on her, pressing, kneading, but not hard enough. They could hire, these rich clients—she forced herself to think the words distinctly—yet not buy?

'That isn't hard enough, Bonn,' she said aloud. 'Touch me harder.'

From there, all thoughts ceased.

*　　　*　　　*

The envy of others, she knew as she lay exhausted under this stranger, she could do without. Let them live in ignorance. She needn't tell anyone, or give cause for speculation among colleagues. Scandal was only women's stimulus. They wanted notoriety, risk, to be thrilled by treading close to disaster, their fear an extra fillip.

She could do without the envy of others.

Her reason? This made her feel younger. It renewed her, the way Clifford's sexual attentions no longer could, after his criminal betrayals. The carnality was the catalyst. And it was not romantic 'love'—yet who could make that claim, come to think of it?

This Bonn. Unknowable, she had decided by the ferocity of their act—she was sure to have bruises, her own doing, her own asking. She could have selected others, but had chosen this unknown. The incident with the swan she laid aside, a chance meeting like on a bus going anywhere.

339

Shifting under his sleeping weight to breathe better, she postponed one problem. Whether to go on. Once you reached the end of a theorem, that was it. You needn't keep on proving the damned thing. Leave it. Stop picking. *Quod erat demonstrandum*, therefore, QED. She completed the logic to her satisfaction, found it without fault. Shelve decision time.

She stroked his sweat-damp head, placed his hand over her face, breathed in as if the scent of him was addictive. Her problem of Bonn was solved. She was in control. Logic was her guide, and thoughts of possession were too dangerous. She wished he was even heavier.

They slept, one crushing the other on demand.

CHAPTER THIRTY-FIVE

Suss—*to investigate.*

Windsor had wanted the funeral cased, but Hassall only gave him a long look. In spite of that, Windsor was sure to clock the congregation, learning their descriptions like a school poem. Hassall stood in the choir loft getting deafened by the nearby organ some old dear was playing.

'Kist o' pipes, we called organs in the old days, young man,' the crone said, jubilation written all over her. Her mistakes came thick and fast.

Hassall smiled, but sombrely. He was not here for chatter.

Down below he could see most of the congregation. At funerals, everybody sits in singular

340

discomfort. Was it the pews? Or the knowledge that here they were, in out of the rain, relieved it wasn't them, knowing they'd go out to a cup of tea and wake cake *alive*, the guilt syndrome?

The Victoria Square girls were in. He could see them, four rows in their idea of finery. Lads, one row only. Bonn joined them. They'd left a space for him. He alone did not genuflect. Odd, that, because everybody follows the party line in church, does the decent thing.

Hassall couldn't see the last three pews, the ones near the church porch, and decorum forbade craning. He was resigned to glimpsing reflections in the brass furnishings. Hopeless. Maybe he ought to have acceded to Windsor's bleatings, record all attenders? He was sick of the sergeant's toxic harangues. Tim'd go far, but today enough was enough. Give in on that, he'd want the Army called out next time some kid used a pea shooter. Christ knows what they do in police college nowadays. Sociology, fuck all else. Sorry, God, he said inwardly, but I'm worn out.

People coughed, shuffled feet, whispered advice about the prayer books. Some thumbed theirs, found hymn numbers. A book fell, causing heads to lift. Some at the front turned to find something, but in reality sussing out who'd come, who hadn't who ought to have.

Windsor would be out in the rain counting, muttering car numbers into the recorder he'd cunningly concealed from Hassall, all that. He'd seen on some film or other, moving with the times, CIA procedures, cops and robbers. Pity was, nobody in the police guessed any more. Statistics and legal loopholes, preparation of evidence,

341

procedures for those detained, the PACE Act. It would be a laugh, if it wasn't so barmy. Loony definitions of what a crime actually was, how many your patch head counts were—police stats throttled the guess.

He mostly blamed America. Not for advising youngsters how to behave moronic through U.S. videos and films—all fucking cartoons anyway nowadays—but because of their Vietnam. Body counts—real or made up—became success criteria. Such an odd war, that. You used massive power, then moaned how hard life was. Except maybe that *wasn't* their trouble. Maybe their only crime was having a worldwide audience. You could make out a good case.

The congregation stirred, rose. Hassall stood. The organist lady glanced approvingly at him. He held his hat, remained with head bowed until the priest cleared his throat and began the service. He sat to look through the oak fenestrations of the choir-loft rail.

He hadn't seen the old priest before. A frail elderly man, having difficulty speaking. Cold coming? Getting over a chest infection? His voice, low and gravelly, seemed to take the old cleric by surprise.

They sang Number 197 from *Hymns Ancient and Modern*.

Hassall was always sorely embarrassed singing, having been made to warble tunelessly at school. He'd never recovered. His trick now was to sing bass, as far down as his voice could go without entering some silent zone. Bass voices got away with murder—he silently apologised to the girl in her coffin, which stood on high trestles before the altar.

342

The hymn trailed to a close behind the squeaking organ.

'Within Thy house for ever,' Hassall boomed gravely, and sat.

The homily was not long. The old clergyman's voice kept giving out. Hassall smiled at the old organist. She had a mirror rigged up next to her music light, to see the goings-on at the altar.

'Father Crossley,' she said in a whisper, as if he'd doubted.

'Is it?' Hassall had been Methodist. This folderol was beyond him, statues and vestments.

She said, eyes glinting, 'He's poorly. They're surprised he's alive. They asked for him specially.'

They who? Curiosity stirred in Hassall. It would do no harm to ask, while the old man gasped on, trying to project. Funerals revealed that churches had been built too big. Congregations had shrunk.

'Who did?'

'Friends.' She mouthed, thrilled with news of disaster, 'Cancer. They brought his own doctor. She's here, but I've not seen her.' She looked into the mirror with forlorn hope. 'I'll be on my voluntaries when the coffin leaves.'

'Is he so poorly, then?' Hassall stared down with renewed interest at the old priest. He was making heavy weather of it.

'His seminary's closed. He's in care.' She spoke with awe, somebody sinking that low.

'Poor man,' Hassall said. 'Poor man.'

Who'd come to conduct the funeral service, in a strange parish, in a strange denomination, to bury a whore he presumably did not know. How come?

'Who wanted Father Crossley, then?' he asked the old lass.

343

But that went too far. She made a show of checking her music, adjusting the light.

'Who?' he persisted. 'Was it her parents?'

Words were a risk in church, but reticence was too difficult. She gave in as the priest's eulogy drew feebly to a close.

'Some ladies she worked with, I heard.' She flexed her fingers.

'How very kind. Father Crossley, that poorly.'

There was a moment for silent prayer. Hassall heard some of the girls crying.

The priest announced the departure hymn. Hassall noticed that he had to check the hymn number, painstakingly read out 205, words by Charles Wesley. A newcomer, really, the old guy, to the hymnal. Everybody knew 'Love divine, all loves excelling,' or did they? Battling away, fish out of water, a game old bloke. It raised questions, not like why was he here, but who *did* bring him?

To the lady organist's disapproval, Hassall tiptoed down the wooden stairs. He was in the church porch as the coffin was carried out. And he waited in his car when the flowers were taken into the hearse.

Dr Burtonall was among the last to leave. Windsor, the prat, was skulking among the tombstones like some Apache.

The car window misted up. Hassall turned the key in the ignition like he ought to have done straight off for ventilation, and peered through the windscreen. Bonn emerged. Everybody dithered between motors at funerals. Not like weddings, where a headachy best man has the power of God Almighty and makes everybody toe the line.

The rain grew heavier as people straggled out.

344

Cars pulled away. Another vicar appeared in the church porch as the girls ran huddled under umbrellas and shrieking in that rainy voice. Windsor lurked. A fucking Restoration comedy, Hassall thought in exasperation.

Dr Burtonall left the church, shepherding the elderly priest under her umbrella, leaving the resident vicar. Bonn was there, with Rack. Hassall knew of both. Rack was a maniac, Bonn a quiet bastard from nowhere. Last, Posser himself, wheezing his head off, accompanied by a lass Hassall guessed was Posser's daughter, bonny but lame.

Engines started up. The hearse was followed off by the column. Then the really interesting thing happened. A definite tableau formed by the lych gate. Bonn faced the old priest, who was now having to lean heavily on Dr Burtonall's arm, and the two definitely hesitated. Rack was revving his motor like for a Brands Hatch start. The girl and her father also paused. In that instant, Hassall almost shouted *Collusion!* It was there, sudden and shared.

Answer one question, raise a dozen more.

They took three motors. Dr Burtonall's Humber Supersnipe, dwarfing everything but the church tower, with the old priest Crossley. Then Posser with his daughter, in a midnight-blue Bentley driven by some smarmy long-haired get. Then Rack and Bonn in an ordinary Ford. Hassall watched them leave, presumably to follow the hearse to the crematorium.

Gone. He had an address for Bonn. Dr Clare Burtonall? Coincidences were never mere coincidences, in Hassall's experience. They were always planned somethings. Happenstance always

345

got help.

Windsor charged up, opened his door.

'Sir? I reckon—'

'Hush, please.' Hassall sat thinking, all the rain in heaven falling in on him through the door Windsor kindly held open like that so his flu would recur. 'Right, Mr Windsor. What?'

'We follow them to the crem. Some others—'

'Got an address for that Bonn?'

'No, sir.' Windsor looked after the vehicles. 'You want it?'

'No, ta. You get on. I've an errand to run.'

He saw Windsor leave on squealing tyres. Hassall let things calm down, the birds start singing as the rain eased. Then he went back inside the church, to have a word with the incumbent.

CHAPTER THIRTY-SIX

To blag—*to invent on the spur of the moment.*

How often lately had Mrs Kinsale already left when she reached home? Clare was too fatigued to care, flung off her clothes and almost, not quite, had a hot shower. Instead, she filled the bath and soaked herself. Clifford had left a message to say he would have something to eat on the way home, not to bother much this evening. Only when she heard the door go did she stir herself.

Clifford was downstairs, going through the day's post when she entered the living room. Odd that he didn't have the television on. He was fanatical about news. They greeted each other warily. For safety's sake, Clare started telling him about Dr Porritt.

'The surveillance has to get more takers,' she told him, getting going.

'Can't you just tell the doctors to send people in?'

'Men are always reluctant. Dr Porritt wants me to broadcast.'

'On television? Where?'

'The city studios, near you. He knows somebody.'

'Would that be wise?' Clifford laid his letters aside. He'd poured himself a drink. 'There are reasons it ought to be somebody else.'

'What makes you say that?' she asked, suddenly aware of something being quite wrong. He often assumed this air of abstraction, but usually with a glimmer of humour. Tonight he seemed ready for battle. Her throat constricted.

'You had a high old time the other evening, Clare.'

This was it. He had found something, from a guilty husband to a combatant.

'High old time?' She gave him the chance to intervene, but he won by waiting her out. 'A cardiac survey isn't that.'

'Your reproaches would have pleased a nun.'

'I don't remember reproaching you, Clifford.'

'But you did. Loud and clear. I'm the evil bastard—not in those words—who'd caused the death of another person. Your doubts would have hanged somebody less fortunate.'

'Doubts?' She didn't go on. It was true. She still harboured uncertainties, especially about the two girls. 'Can you blame me?'

He said simply, 'I wanted support, loyalty. Did you match up?'

'Yes!' she cried out. 'Who gave you an alibi?'

347

'You did, Clare.' He sounded cold. 'But at what cost?'

'Let *me* tell *you*, Clifford.' She was beside herself at the unfair accusation. 'I went to that Lana girl's funeral today! To take care of an old priest. He happened to be one of my patients, and was too ill to go without medical cover. How do you think that made me feel?'

'Clever.'

'What?' She stared. 'Did you say clever?'

'Yes, Clare.' He looked as if balancing her motives. 'Clever. Who is he?'

'He?' She'd risen to upbraid Clifford, but sank into her armchair. 'Who?'

'You've made several phone calls to an agency. Rather a sordid business, Clare. Essentially, it hires out sexual solace to bored housewives.'

She made a hopeless attempt to look scandalised. 'Have you taken leave of your senses?'

'No. Come to them, I think.' He examined his empty glass and quite casually went to refill it. 'I checked.'

'And?'

'You've been in regular contact. The Pleases Agency, Inc, is operated by a syndicate with extensive possessions—cafés, casino places, a disco or two, snooker halls.'

Did it have all those? she found herself wondering. 'So? I contact various places—'

'Because you're a doctor?' Shaking his head, he went to sit on the arm of the couch. His easy manner was disconcerting. 'Saving lives all over the place? No, Clare, I think not. You're an upper, that's what you are.'

'A what? Upper?'

'A woman who hires a goer for sexual pleasure in some hotel.'

'It's not—' she burst out angrily, then halted.

'It's "not like that", Clare?' He didn't quite smile. 'It's been going on some time, from the telephone accounts. By comparison, my faults hardly invite your reproaches.'

'I gave you an alibi when you badly needed one.'

'For which I'm grateful.' He was positively enjoying the confrontation. She realised she hardly knew him now. 'Aren't you going to explain at least some of your actions, enough to let me invent some alibi for you, should need arise?'

'I hired one of the—one,' she said, desperately working out how much to reveal, what she might still get away with. 'I was worried about Mostern's accident. He was at the scene. The police were rude to him.'

'And at the time you didn't know why?'

'Yes. I'd no idea. I'd never heard of them, not really.'

'I'll believe you.' He maddened her. 'So you hunted him down, got out your purse, and . . .?'

'I encountered him by chance outside the General Hospital. He helped a child out of the river. We spoke.' She faced him and his insufferable attitude. 'He was just the person to find out about Mostern's accident. The briefcase, you see, and the cock-and-bull story you fobbed me off with. I'd seen that Salvo clear as day.'

'Ah, yes,' he said ruefully. 'Bad news, that. Very careless.'

'More than that, Clifford. It was murderous.'

'And did you? Find out all about me, Salvo, the rest?'

'What is the rest?'

'You tell me, darling.'

She said defiantly, 'Yes, I found out some. I heard that you were seen leaving the flat where Salvo stays. It suggests that he's your regular thug. Have you had people . . . hurt before, Clifford?'

'Go on, Clare. Most of this—'

'—I've given you an alibi for? Yes,' she said bitterly, 'so I have.'

'Which makes me wonder why, Clare darling, you're still hiring this prick.' He showed polite expectancy, teatime gossip. 'What *are* your reasons? Still raking over the accident? We've both agreed the death was a mistake, made by somebody I'd only hired to retrieve some documents.'

'No.' She was on the defensive, nothing to say.

'Then you are behaving in what I can only call an un-professional manner. Am I right?'

'Whether I say yes or no, you'll assume it's yes,' she said, infuriated at his supercilious manner.

'On quite good evidence, darling. Your bank withdrawals would show two or three little holes. Correct?'

'I had to pay him for the information,' she said stubbornly, near defeat.

The doorbell rang. He started towards the curtains, then thought better of it. He went into the hall. Clare heard Hassall's voice cursing the rain, shoes stamped, a coat being shaken.

The came in together, Hassall frozen and bleary.

'Sorry, Dr Burtonall. Just a passing visit. This weather!'

'Welcome, Mr Hassall. Would you like a drink, something warm perhaps?'

'No, thank you. I'm too old-fashioned for all that

caper.' He sat when bidden, exhaling like a much older man, his sly mannerism to deceive. Doubts were everywhere. 'Just been to a funeral today. Very sad.'

'You too?' She smiled in sympathy. 'I was just telling my husband that I was at the funeral of that murdered girl. I was with one of my patients, the priest who did the service.'

'Old Crossley? I know him,' Hassall lied affably. 'Nice old chap. In a hospice.' When Clare said nothing, he grunted. 'Ah. No doctor-patient disclosures.' He gave Clifford a wry glance. 'You didn't go, Mr Burtonall?'

'Me?' Clifford went smoothly on, 'No. I only just heard about it as you arrived. My wife and I,' he said, smiling towards Clare, 'practically lead separate lives these days. Rushing everywhere.'

'Very moving,' Hassall said. 'The girls she worked with, the goers—those are hired males, the equivalent of female prostitutes. Ladies,' he explained as if for Clare's benefit, 'need more secrecy for their goings-on than men. I often wonder how far they'd go, compromising their lives.'

'I felt sorry for her. Have you any idea who the perpetrator was?'

'Perp? One of our words, that, Dr Burtonall! "Suspect" is more usual, from the laity. There was a bloke. Salvo.' Hassall looked enquiringly at Clare. 'Did you say something, Dr Burtonall?'

'No.' Clare went to pour a drink. 'Sure you wouldn't like one?'

'No, ta. This Salvo was Marla's boyfriend. She consorted with Lana. It's supposed that Salvo found them together and did the deed. He went to nick a

351

motor, hot-wired the car. Something went wrong, petrol exploded. We've identified the remains. Very messy.'

'This Salvo was the killer?'

'We believe Marla will finger him.'

'Poor girl.' Clare carried her sherry to her armchair. It would nauseate her if she drank any. 'I hope she recovers, Mr Hassall.'

'Isn't this where you say, "What were you doing on the night of the crime"?'

'What crime is that, Mr Burtonall?'

'The explosion. This Salvo's death?'

'I didn't say it was night, Mr Burtonall. But, yes, go through the motions. Just so's I can put down "Questioned suspects" on my clock sheet.'

'When was it, Mr Hassall?' Clare cut in easily before Clifford could speak.

'We may not be able to say precisely, but as a rule we have a fair idea, what with listed phone calls, and coded work data.'

'You started your survey. I remember that. I was here, and so was my husband. Weren't you, Clifford? I remember you were on the phone half the night. The cost! I'm sure they're not all necessary.'

'I was.' Clifford made himself sound regretful. 'I had a number of outstanding transatlantic calls to make, and got through them before ...'

'Before, sir?' Hassall prompted.

Clifford stayed cool. 'Before they started calling back. It's always much easier to make the call armed with data than cope with an incoming call that catches you on the hop. They say in America: "It's your dime." '

'Clever folk, you investors,' Hassall said, rising.

352

'Don't you want us to sign your time sheet, Mr Hassall?'

'Not necessary, Dr Burtonall. Like me to sign yours?'

They made light humour of that as far as the door. Hassall left, looking up at the rain, ambling through the downpour to his car. Clare led the way back to the living room. She rounded on Clifford.

'Who'd you phone that night?'

He shrugged. 'You can't think I had anything to do with it, darling. If I had,' he said with dignity, 'don't you think Hassall would have asked outright? Look, Clare. You can't go blaming every crime on me because of that one accident. I never really knew this Salvo. I'd never even met him.' He displayed weariness. 'I'm tired. I swear I had nothing to do with Salvo, other than asking him to retrieve those documents. Naturally I wanted them back. Just as naturally I contacted an expert in that sort of thing.'

'Who just then decided to kill the poor man? Is that it?'

'No. Who accidentally caused Mostern to tumble over.' Clifford was indignant, far more emotional than Clare. 'God knows what the idiot was going to do—sell them to some rival, industrial espionage, who knows?'

'Why not tell Hassall?' Clare had been close to blurting it out.

'Because that would set him on me. I'd become his eternal suspect, Clare—like I've become yours. I'd be involved in court cases. You know how those things drag on.' He looked slyly at her with triumph in his eyes. 'Anyway, I have a sound alibi for both incidents, haven't I? Thanks to you.'

'Thanks to me,' she said bitterly.

'You're the only one who could finger me to Hassall.'

'What does that mean?'

'It means that I'm safe, darling. As are you. I keep quiet about your activities, whatever they are, and you remain a perfectly respectable doctor.'

'I see.' She saw him for the first time. Had she trusted him completely, she would never have asked Bonn to make the discoveries that he had. 'Are you proposing some sort of pact?'

'No, darling. Stating the obvious. We're inextricably linked. What's the cant phrase? Joined at the hip.'

He smiled, looking exactly as on the day they had met. Clare went to pour her drink away, and switched on the television. The news headline was that Marla had died of circulatory collapse that afternoon.

Clifford heaved a huge sigh. 'It's always bad news, isn't it, darling?' He spoke with ill-concealed triumph. 'I wonder if that was the reason that Hassall came round, one last despairing lunge?'

'God rest her,' Clare said, tears in her eyes.

'One thing, darling.' Clifford casually picked up a newspaper. 'I'm bidding for control of the Pleases Agency, Inc. Did your little friend tell you?'

'You're . . .?' She stared at him.

'Tomorrow, with any luck.' He winked at her, enjoying himself. 'We're sort of partners.'

Clare felt a stupefying loathing. Now she really was trapped. She would not even have Bonn to help her carry the burden.

CHAPTER THIRTY-SEVEN

Mogga dancing—*that type of ballroom competition dancing where each couple changes their dance rhythm to a different style every few bars, usually four to six, throughout a single melody.*

The place was sparse now. His few belongings were gone. Had he chosen so Spartan a room because it had the appearance of some Trappist cell? Possibly, but speculations required no answer. He was sad to leave the room, but it would be impossible to stay, the way things were.

He locked the door, left the key on old Mrs Corrigan's hall tray on the way out, and got a taxi by the drill hall.

*   *   *

Bonn talked with Rack fifteen minutes before he walked across to the building that held the Burtonall Investments office.

'What does it concern, Mr Fairbanks?' the receptionist asked.

'Mr Burtonall's personal investments. I have only ten minutes.'

Bonn went and stood by the fronded palms. He was taken through almost immediately.

Clifford Burtonall rose, extending his hand. Bonn evaded it.

'Would you please eliminate the recording, Mr Burtonall?'

'Recording?' Clifford gave a hearty laugh. 'I must say, Mr Fairbanks, you are certainly direct!'

Bonn waited in silence, then mouthed the word

355

'murder'. Clifford stilled, went through to the outer office for a moment, returned with a midget Dictaphone. He placed it on his desk. Bonn looked at it.

'No, Clifford.' Bonn stood. 'Goodbye. Take the consequences.'

Bonn was by the lift doors when Burtonall caught him up.

'I didn't come up the Mersey on a bicycle, Clifford.' Bonn wasn't exactly sure what the saying meant, but he'd often heard it used and the occasion seemed right. 'You have three cassette pods on the go. Showing me one is simply juvenile.'

'Look. I don't know who you are, but quite honestly—'

The lift came, crashed open. Bonn entered, pressed the button. The doors closed just after the investor darted in, flustered. He tried to persuade Bonn to return to the office, but Bonn said nothing, walked out into the street. He crossed over to the bus stop. Nobody else was waiting.

'Only,' Clifford was urging, 'it's regarded as normal business practice—'

'The murders, Clifford,' Bonn interrupted. 'Evidence has come to light linking you with the deaths of Mostern, and possibly with Lana and Marla. A witness saw you leave the flat, connecting you to Salvo.'

'Evidence?' Clifford went white. He was suddenly aware of Rebecca and Monica looking down from the office windows.

'Concealment will require your cooperation. You will forthwith abort the takeover of the Pleases Agency, Inc.'

'Wait.' A minibus was disembarking visitors to

356

the Granadee Studios.

'No, Clifford. Tell Goldoni there are other groups in the city worthy of investment. He will go along.'

'Goldoni?' Clifford gaped, staring at Bonn. 'Who are you?'

'Nobody you will ever see again.'

Clifford saw the bus coming. He suddenly guessed, Clare's abrupt streetwise understanding.

'My wife. Are you a patient? Or from that agency?'

'Goldoni will comply, when you explain. The consequences will be at least as grave for him.' Bonn felt filled with lies. 'You may purchase any other business you wish. Goldoni's pleasures with rough renters can continue. And your bribes of the city aldermen.'

The bus slowed as it approached.

'What *is* this?' Burtonall was frantic to delay Bonn's departure.

'A threat, Clifford, nothing more.'

The bus left, Bonn on it and Burtonall staring after.

As he entered the main office, Rebecca and Monica were waiting. 'Who was that, Mr Burtonall?' Rebecca asked. 'Is he an investor? I ought to get his details.'

'Mmmmh?' Their expressions confirmed his guess. He went into his office.

*   *   *

Bonn dropped off to see Glazie and procured a blank card and an envelope. At the reception desk he wrote, 'You are invited to the finals of the Mogga

Dancing. See press for details.' He numbered the card 395. She would know it was from him, the code number proof enough. He addressed the envelope to Dr C. S. Burtonall, at the hospital, and put it in the post. She would get it in the morning, and realise that he wished her to continue. Why, could be left for the future.

*   *   *

It felt odd, alighting in Bradshawgate. He paid the driver off and knocked.

Martina herself came to answer. She must have been waiting in the hallway, for Bonn hadn't heard her approach. There was no carpet, just a short rug thing down the linoleum. More light than there was at his digs, though.

'I bought two bulbs for Mrs Corrigan when I first went there,' he said, in case Martina had caught his glance and thought he was making comparisons. Martina's agency owned the digs he'd vacated. 'To light her stairwell.'

'Did she put them in? Or sell them?'

'I think she kept them for herself.'

'I heard that she's like that.'

'Maybe I'm maligning her.'

'Or not. Please go through.'

Bonn went ahead, measuring his pace to hers. Posser smiled a welcome.

'Thank you for letting me come,' Bonn said. He felt it important to go pedantically through formalities. 'I feel a refugee.'

'Don't, son.' Posser indicated a chair. 'It's all axed.'

'Oh dear.' Bonn's frown made a joke of it.

358

'Nothing to be scared of. Martina makes the rules. I manage.'

'Which, from a picture of rude health,' Martina capped.

Bonn laughed, then felt he had to say he was sorry. Posser, amused, would have none of it.

'Look, Bonn. Make this easy as we can, eh? Martina is glad you are here. I'm vastly relieved. We can cope with whatever happens.' He gestured, the city all around. 'I won't mince matters. I have hopes, now you've finally made the move—'

'Dad,' Martina said through clenched teeth.

'All right, love. Bonn understands. A father's got a natural worry. You're here now, Bonn, and can take part of the strain. It's only fair.'

'I'm not sure—'

'That's enough!' Martina cried in genuine anger. 'I'm not a liability to be talked about as if I'm not even here!' She composed herself, saw Bonn steel himself. 'Bonn. I'm glad the house has more company. Dad's not well, and his age. I'm relieved there's somebody here.' She made herself add, 'You.'

They waited, Bonn glad he wasn't being asked anything, Posser irritably wanting to speak but unwilling to irritate Martina further.

'In fact,' she continued, primly clasping her knees, daring her father to interrupt, 'I'm the one who suggested you.'

Bonn wondered if she was telling it as it was.

'Please note that your staying here means nothing more than convenience,' she went on. 'We have no doubts, Dad and I, that you are the right person.'

'Thank you, Martina.'

'None of us should read more into it than that,' she ended. 'It's a suitable arrangement. Are we agreed?'

'Yes.'

'For heaven's sake, Martina,' Posser said, losing patience. 'You'll be driving the lad away. Get the hooch out.'

She made no move. 'I suggest that each evening we keep one hour aside to review the day's activities, Bonn. Are you in agreement?'

'Yes. But what if I'm booked to—?'

'That can take second place to our nightly review,' she said.

'We never said anything about that, love,' Posser put in, puzzled.

'Client priority,' Bonn said, also worried.

'You have three goers, Bonn,' Martina said. 'They can manage. We must cross that bridge when we come to it.'

'What if—?' Posser started, but his daughter was there ahead of him.

'There's nothing against your taking on a fourth goer,' she said, smooth.

'There's the problem of other firms, Martina.'

'Yes, Bonn,' she said, smiling, 'but they will do as they are told.'

'It's a small problem,' Posser conceded, but with a doubtful look at Bonn.

'Your suitcase,' Martina said, closing the subject. 'Is that all you have?'

'Yes,' Bonn said. 'I'm sorry.'

It disconcerted her. She had told Osmund to have a van on stand-by. 'I hadn't realised. Perhaps tomorrow I ought to get you fitted out.' She glanced about. 'And I wonder if that armchair is really right, stuck there. Look. Perhaps we ought to settle you in.'

'When it's convenient,' Bonn said awkwardly. Pedantry had done little.

'Now is as good a time. Would you come?' She rose and went ahead. 'The small bathroom is yours. I'm afraid there isn't anywhere for you to do any secret cooking, if that's what you're into. You'll have to use the main kitchen. I'll show you it. Would you want your own phone?'

'No, thank you.'

'If you change your mind, just say.'

She stood formally at the top of the staircase.

'I'm very pleased that you have come to us, Bonn.' She avoided his eyes.

'As I am to be here.'

They stood in silence.

'Your room is to your right. What evening drink do you like?'

'Wine, if that's all right.'

'Very well.' She stood aside to let him pass, about to start down. 'We'll wait for you, and celebrate your arrival. We must learn about each other.'

'Of course.'

'If anything isn't quite to your liking here, please say.' She was a little breathless, but that must have been the stairs.

'You're very kind, Martina.'

She went down. Bonn opened the door of his room and switched on the light. He halted in astonishment.

The room was an exact replica of the one he'd just vacated. The only difference was its cleanliness, that and the door leading to the bathroom. The window, the one chair—could it be the very same

361

one? How on earth? The bed was similar, single, narrow, except it was spotless.

He placed his suitcase on the carpet, and that too was similar to the threadbare one he had left behind, but new. It was a statement of conviction and an assurance all in one. It was his cell.

It was just right, and enough. He smiled, and said inwardly, 'Thank you, Martina.' He could go on as before. Perhaps all life was simply a kind of mogga dancing, one episode changing to another yet to one constant tune. It was a pretty metaphor. He would see Clare as and when, but be with Martina. That would be. For now, Grellie would have to wait, very much as he himself would have to see where feelings took him, now that his vows were utterly laid to rest. First thing tomorrow, he decided, he would visit old Father Crossley in his new hospice bed, and make a last farewell while the frail old theologian still had his faculties.

He switched off the light and, assured now, went downstairs to celebrate his coming to them. He lived here now.

*   *   *

Outside the small terraced house where Bonn had once lived, Hassall sat in his motor waiting for Windsor to come roaring up with some barmy ideas.

Bonn couldn't have been gone long. The room was empty, the key in the hall. Mrs Corrigan had no idea. The loyal old bitch would make sure of that.

He had two choices. Go to Posser's, try it on—except Posser was wily. They'd crossed swords once or twice. The sick old prat had lawyers like dogs had fleas. Or he could wait things out, see what the

362

world spun for the city tomorrow.

The point was, what could he ask? Whether or not they had any suspicions? If they knew this or that? He could write their answers now: Heavens, Mr Hassall, no, we don't know a thing about a thing. The Burtonalls were different. He wouldn't be in her shoes for all the tea in China. Good luck to her, if she got a shag or two on the side. As long as she did nothing worse. Always hard for a wife, when her husband was into crime and justifying it every step of the way.

Very well, Hassall thought. Live your lives. Keep on. I'm here, and I'll have you, soon as there's enough evidence. Maybe not for the crimes done, but for the ones that are to come. I'm here.

And, face it, shagging was no crime, so good luck.

If that's the worst you do, the world wouldn't be in such a bloody mess.

He saw Windsor's lights approaching, and just couldn't face all that frigging enthusiasm. He fired his engine, and drove home.

The LARGE PRINT HOME LIBRARY

If you have enjoyed this Large Print book and would like to build up your own collection of Large Print books and have them delivered direct to your door, please contact The Large Print Home Library.

The Large Print Home Library offers you a full service:

☆ **Created to support your local library**

☆ **Delivery direct to your door**

☆ **Easy-to-read type & attractively bound**

☆ **The very best authors**

☆ **Special low prices**

For further details either call Customer Services on 01225 443400 or write to us at:

The Large Print Home Library
FREEPOST (BA 1686/1)
Bath BA2 3SZ